July 12, 1945:

General Groves smiled at Captain Finn. "Beginning at 0700 of the 16th, you'll be in San Francisco. You'll stand guard over a billion dollars' worth of uranium 235, the guts of the only atomic bomb that will be left in the world. Until you deliver it to Colonel Paul Tibbets on an island called Tinian, you will be the most important man in the world."

"Why me?"

"You're a survivor, Captain Finn. You're as fast and nasty as those rattlers you grew up with. You'll get the job done no matter who you have to kill. Is that clear enough for you?"

July 12, 1945:

Radio transmission to Tokyo from the Japanese spy known as Kestrel:

Many rumors of new, very powerful American weapon.

Russian spy Masarek plans to steal it after it is shipped to California.

I will follow and steal it from him.

A. E. MAXWELL

STEAL THE SUN

TOR

A TOM DOHERTY ASSOCIATES BOOK

Copyright © 1981 by Ann and Evan Maxwell

A Tor Book

Published by Tom Doherty Associates, 8-10 W. 36th St., New York City, NY 10018

First printing, September 1983

ISBN: 0-523-48077-6

Printed in the United States of America

Distributed by Pinnacle Books, 1430 Broadway, New York, NY 10018

STEAL THE SUN

10 July 1945
Washington, D.C.

144 Hours Before Trinity

(Synopsis of a Top Secret briefing paper from the Office of Strategic Services.)

Route to: President Harry S Truman
Secretary of War Harry L. Stimson
Joint Chief of Staff Admiral William D. Leahy
Major General Leslie Groves

The Russians control eastern Germany without recourse to American or British desires or mandates. Furthermore, *Russia has no intention of withdrawing from Germany at any time in the future.* Other East European countries (e.g. Latvia, Lithuania, Estonia, etc.) are now and will remain under Russia's direct control. Eastern Europe has become Western Russia.

With Eastern Europe conquered, Russia is transferring arms and men to the southeastern frontier, preparing for a massive sweep through China and then on to an invasion of Japan in violation of the Russo-Japanese neutrality agreement. *Intelligence reports leave absolutely no doubt that Russia can and will conquer China, invade Japan, and demand at least a division of Japan along the lines of Germany.* As in Germany, Russia has no intention of withdrawing her forces from occupied territories at any time in the future. For Russia, World War II has become a war of conquest.

The United States is faced with three choices:

1. Defeat the Japanese before Russia can invade China.
2. Accept the fact that the U.S. will win a war and lose a world.
3. Declare war on Russia.

Option 3 is beyond the purview of this paper. Option 2 requires no action. Option 1 requires that the Japanese be forced to surrender before Russian troops are committed to China. *The OSS estimates that Russia will invade China as soon as 13 August 1945 and no later than 13 October 1945.*

Tokyo
133 Hours Before Trinity

(Excerpt of cable to Naotake Sato, Japanese Ambassador to the U.S.S.R. Decoded.)

HIS MAJESTY IS EXTREMELY ANXIOUS TO END THE WAR AS SOON AS POSSIBLE . . . (BUT) IF THE U.S. AND GREAT BRITAIN INSIST ON UNCONDITIONAL SURRENDER, JAPAN MUST FIGHT TO THE LAST. ONLY THEN WILL OUR HONOR BE VINDICATED

AND OUR NATIONAL EXISTENCE ASSURED. . . THE EMPEROR THEREFORE WANTS TO NEGOTIATE FOR A QUICK END TO THE WAR USING THE GOOD OFFICES OF THE RUSSIAN GOVERNMENT TO APPROACH THE UNITED STATES. FOREIGN MINISTER SHIGENORI TOGO

Moscow
109 Hours Before Trinity

(Excerpt of cable to Foreign Minister Shigenori Togo. Decoded.)

. . . A PEACE SETTLEMENT BY NEGOTIATION WILL NOT BE SUPPORTED OR ADVANCED BY THE SOVIET UNION. IF JAPAN TRULY WANTS TO END THE WAR, WE HAVE NO CHOICE BUT TO ACCEPT UNCONDITIONAL SURRENDER OR SOMETHING VERY LIKE IT. AMBASSADOR NAOTAKE SATO

Second General Army Headquarters
Hiroshima, Island of Kyushu
120 Hours Before Trinity

(Excerpt from Field Marshal Shunroku Hata's private diary.)

The night is still. May tranquility gather around me as it does around the lotus bud.

The Emperor has given to me the task of saving Japan from the ignominy of utter defeat. In the great, climactic battle to come, may I be worthy of my Emperor's trust.

I do not believe Japan can defeat America.

I do not believe American can defeat Japan.

Therein lies our honor, and an honorable future for our children. The American invasion will begin on Kyushu . . . and on Kyushu it will end. We will be as drops of water, clinging to the invaders until they drown. Many of my people will die, for my people know that *it is better to die than to seek ignominious safety*.

Although we lack arms and ammunition, we do not lack courage and honor. I have ordered that every person in Hiroshima, man and child and woman alike, be taught how to make and use gasoline bombs.

A little thing . . . glass and gasoline against tanks and airplanes. But drops of water are also little.

Negotiated peace is not defeat!

Juarez
108 Hours Before Trinity

The sounds and smells of the district called La Mariscal welled up around Finn as he crossed the Paso del Norte Bridge connecting El Paso, Texas, to Juarez, Mexico. He moved quickly, using the deceptive stride of a man accustomed to walking. Anyone following him would soon become flushed, sweaty and obvious among the lazy throngs of people circulating through Juarez's late-afternoon heat.

Finn paused in the shadow of an old building. As he lit a cigaret, he checked the street he had just walked down. No one stopped suddenly to admire a dusty store window. No one seemed too hot or too breathless. No one seemed to notice him or to avoid noticing him.

Even so, Finn leaned against the building, his pale hazel eyes watching the crowds. Deeply tanned, wearing jeans and a white shirt, a western hat pulled down over his dark hair, Finn looked unremarkable for the time and place. Only his watchfulness set him apart from the Mexicans strolling along the street.

Finn waited. To all appearances he was a man enjoying the daily miracle of sunset, when the desert's scorching July air was transformed into wine. And Finn did enjoy the moment, despite his searching glances. He loved the desert borderlands, the sand and endless sky, people wrapped in heat and secrets, smugglers and spies, corruptors and innocents, thieves and assassins and fools all pasted together in an uneasy collage that sometimes came unstuck violently, without warning. He loved those moments too, when staying alive was a puzzle that had to be solved instant by instant.

With a last look at his back trail, Finn flipped his cigaret into the street and walked on. He passed bars and greasy cafés. The walkway was lined by whores, but they ignored him after a single glance. Their calculated come-ons were reserved for crewcut innocents from the Army and Air Force bases on the American side of the river.

Many of the prostitutes were after information as much as pesos. In Juarez, information was the only currency that was not devalued at the moment of exchange. Finn knew which whores sold information because he was in the business of buying it. So were many other people in Juarez. Like Switzerland, Mexico had discovered that neutrality was a negotiable asset.

The Third Reich had been present in Mexico since Hitler's ascendency. When war consumed Europe, Mexico City—like Lisbon, Marrakech and Istanbul—had become a magnet attracting the iron detritus of political change.

Mexico City became home to a volatile mixture of Germans, Russians, Japanese, Chinese, Koreans, Turks, Greeks, British, French and many others whose only loyalty was to violent ideologies of the left or right.

From the beginning of World War II, Nazis had moved freely throughout Mexico, celebrating their host country's "neutrality" by setting up spy posts along the border. Towns like Juarez, San Luis del Rio Colorado, Mexicali and Tijuana became secure staging areas for sabotage and infiltration in the secret Army, Navy and Air Force bases that stretched from Texas to California.

The Japanese were ahead of the Germans, having been in Mexico for nearly a century. Unlike the Germans, however, the Japanese had difficulty infiltrating their nationals into the U.S.; after Pearl Harbor, a Japanese face was an invitation to mayhem. The Emperor had to be content with a pervasive information-cum-spy network that centered around the import-export businesses owned by overseas Japanese. The network was greatly enhanced by the Nisei and Isei who fled American internment, preferring instead the social internment of Mexico's Oriental ghettos.

The war had split Finn's life almost as neatly as it had the lives of the Japanese. Desert born and raised, the son of a Customs patrolman, Finn had been recruited by the Office of Strategic Services before the war began. He was among the first overseas agents fielded by the United States. For more than a year he had fought a secret war in the jungles of Burma, tracking and testing the Japanese, learning their language and their secrets. Then came Pearl Harbor. His fluency in the Mexican language and culture made him more valuable to the U.S. in the desert than in the jungle. He returned to the borderlands of northern Mexico, organizing and overseeing a network of American agents whose job was to limit the damage caused by Mexico's rampant neutrality.

The first three years of Finn's assignment had been spent paring down the German network. As the Third Reich weakened, both in Europe and in Mexico, the number of Russian spies grew; neither the British nor the Americans nor even the Japanese made comparable gains. As the war in Europe wound down, the international community of spies gradually shifted its center from Mexico City to Juarez, a border town only three hours south of the top secret American installation called Los Alamos.

The focus of Finn's assignment had changed in the past year. He had been told that there was a secret that could reshape man's future, that the secret was in Los Alamos, and that it was his job to make certain that the secret stayed there.

He had not been told what the secret was.

He had resented the new assignment. He had resented turning over his carefully built Mexico City network to a stranger. He had resented being himself turned over to an arrogant desk general named Groves, a man who had sent Finn to Okinawa to write reports on the American invasion that any man with two eyes and a pen could have written. But most of all, Finn resented knowing less about what he guarded than the Russian spies knew.

Finn crossed the dusty street in midblock and bought a tamale from one of the pushcarts that creaked along the streets of La Mariscal. He ate the tamale without flinching from its peppery heat. As he ate, he watched his back trail. No one ducked or turned away from his glance. No one reversed direction. His caution was its own and only reward.

He crossed the street once more, heading toward a ramshackle building whose only decoration was a sly parrot painted on a sign over the door. The building had once been a series of small, interconnected stores. They had burned, leaving behind little more than a waist-high maze of thick adobe walls. Some of the walls had been razed, some had been left, and the whole had been roofed over like a huge barn. The result was the Green Parrot, center-piece of Juarez's thriving underworld, an international circus of beggars and bankers, thieves and peons and spies.

Without looking into the smoky interior, Finn walked past the cantina's front entrance, down a piss-stained alley and through a small side door into the building. Inside, the Green Parrot was more like a battlefield than a business. One skirmish line formed at the bar which took up a block-long wall. There, bar girls fought for the right to take drinks to favored patrons. Both ends of the huge room, as well as the wall opposite the bar, were chopped up into separate adobe-fenced enclaves where pimps, pick-pockets and whores engaged in single combat with their chosen prey. Smoke twisted above the charcoal fiefdoms of warlord-cooks whose food was so spicy it would devastate an unprepared enemy.

In one area of the cantina, the battle was focused like light through a curved lens. A crowd of shouting, sweat-ing, shoving men gathered around a shallow pit. Two Yaqui Indians crouched there, coarse hair bound back by scarlet bandanas. Each man hissed and grunted ritually, arousing the fighting cock he held in his scarred hands.

One man stood apart, overseeing the crowd, the cocks, and the collecting of bets. If the chaotic battles of the Green Parrot had a generalissimo, it was Refugio Reyes y Rincon. He was big, muscular, and had thick, oddly grace-ful eyebrows. Beneath a veneer of smiling indulgence, his power bulged as surely as muscle beneath fat. At his signal, the handlers redoubled their efforts over the birds.

The two cocks ignored the yelling crowd, the hisses and grip of their handlers. The cocks were fixed on one another, trading glares with obsidian eyes, flaring their gaudy feather ruffs. Their steel-tipped spurs promised death.

The handlers hoisted the cocks up high, further enraging the birds. The crowd howled. Bets were made in many languages and laid in many currencies in the instants before the cocks were released. No one noticed as Finn moved through the fringes of the crowd. No one but the cook looked up when Finn sat at an empty table near a charcoal grill.

The square Indio woman bent over her grill, poked a sizzling chunk of meat, and settled back again on her heels. Her black eyes were hooded and blank. She stared beyond Finn, where bettors seethed around the deadly cocks. After a time she turned back to her cooking.

Finn relaxed and tipped his chair until it leaned against the wall. If he had been followed, the cook would have signaled him. He was free to concentrate on one of his many enemies, the broad-shouldered Mexican who ran the cockfight as ruthlessly as he ran his network of whores, thieves and smugglers.

It was not Rufugio's ordinary criminal pursuits that interested Finn, however; it was the man's extensive connections with Mexico's Oriental communities—particularly the Japanese. In peacetime, Refugio and Takagura Omi had run the most successful smuggling operation in northern Mexico, using Takagura's high Japanese connections to import legal and illegal goods, and Rufugio's low Mexican connections to distribute the goods from Culiacan to San Francisco.

War had changed the nature of the smuggling trade. Information, not opium, brought the highest prices. If a secret could be bought, Refugio had it to sell.

The handlers lowered the birds, then raised them high again. The sounds of the crowd overwhelmed the cocks' screeches.

"Begin!" shouted Refugio.

Scarred hands threw the birds high. They slashed at each other with spurs of steel.

Partially screened by a low adobe wall that divided him from the mainstream of the cantina's activities, Finn searched the tables for a new face, a man called Masarek, who was an assassin sent by the Russian NKVD. Finn had been especially wary of the Russians since the night he had followed a team of NKVD saboteurs from Juarez to a point just below Los Alamos. When there could be no doubt of their destination, Finn struck. He hid their bodies beneath a thin blanket of sand and left as quietly as he had come. By dawn he was back in Juarez, waiting for the replacements that the Russians were sure to send.

In time, Masarek had appeared.

Finn's own network of whores, informants and spies had told him that Masarek had been seen with Refugio, heading north of the American border. Apparently their attempt on Los Alamos had been fruitless, for they had returned very quickly. The same informant had told Finn that this evening, Refugio was to meet with a newly arrived, very important foreigner in the Green Parrot. As Masarek was the only important foreigner to arrive recently in Juarez, Finn assumed that he was the one who would meet Refugio tonight. He assumed, but he was not certain. He would not be certain until he saw Masarek here, tonight.

None of the people Finn saw matched his description of Masarek. Mexicans, Europeans and Orientals occupied the cantina's rough tables. Among them circulated Refugio's whores, including his favorite, Rubia. She was limber, blond, and perhaps fourteen. Despite her dyed hair, Rubia was unusally pretty. She moved from table to table, dispensing drinks and sexual invitation with equal ease.

The crowd around the cockfight humped up suddenly and roared like a breaking wave. Finn knew without looking that one cock had been wounded. The birds varied from fight to fight, but the crowd's bay at first blood was always the same. The fight itself promised to be special, though; one of the birds was Refugio's favorite, a scarred survivor of many battles.

People screamed prayers and imprecations in most of the civilized languages of man. Bets flew among the feathers as the cocks ripped each other with bloody spurs. Sweating, Refugio waved a fistful of money, boasting and betting on the red cock's prowess. The crowd heaved and re-formed, blocking Finn's view of Refugio.

The Indio woman's hiss slid between the shrill sounds of the cantina. Without looking at her, Finn glanced to his right. Several American servicemen were wandering toward him, obviously looking for a table.

"Mind if we sit with you?" asked one of the men.

"Yes," said Finn.

"Friendly type, huh."

"No."

"Are you an American?" demanded the man.

"Sometimes," said Finn, completing the recognition sequence.

With a sound of disgust, the man herded his friends back into the cantina's mainstream. They wedged themselves along the bar and prepared to wait for a vacant table.

Finn did not look at them again. His mind was ticking off seconds with the precision of a stopwatch. When the count reached three hundred, he finished his beer, tipped the cook generously, and prepared to leave the Green Parrot as inconspicuously as he had arrived.

As he stood up, the crowd around the pit shrieked and moaned. The cockfight was approaching its climax. The birds leaped and raked over each other, steel spurs ripping out feathers and blood. He watched, realizing that the red cock had finally met his equal. The fighters were well matched. Too well matched. Like the German army at Stalingrad and the U.S. Marines on Japanese-held islands, the only winner was death.

The screams changed in pitch. One cock was down, disemboweled, its black-and-white feathers sprayed with blood. The red cock began to crow triumphantly, then reeled sideways as its blood pumped out of a slashed artery. Both cocks thrashed about in the dusty pit while Refugio yelled for his favorite to stand up and be proven the winner.

Both cocks died, steel spurs raking the dust. Vicious arguments started over which cock had died first.

Refugio shouldered into the pit, swearing at the bettors and handlers alike. At his command, the Yaquis held the cocks aloft for his inspection. Guts slid down dusty arms, trailing ribbons of blood. He prodded the big red bird while men shouted at him, shrill as roosters. The crowded fragmented into fist- and knife-fights.

As Finn watched, three men clubbed their way to Refugio's side. He did not need his bodyguards to restore order, though. His own fists and boots were enough. Men went down around him, and stayed down. Soon there was no one left fighting. He shouted over the angry bettors, pointing out that the spotted cock had gone down first and stayed down until it died. Men yelled back, saying that Refugio's red cock had died first. Refugio began reciting the superior points of the red cock.

Finn eased through the cantina, listening to the Mexican's harangue on behalf of his favorite cock. Several thousand dollars were at stake, but it was pride as much as money that goaded Refugio, a man whose pride was legend.

Suddenly, Refugio's voice dropped. Finn turned back, wondering what had happened to silence the arrogant smuggler. One of Refugio's bodyguards stood close to him, talking quietly, gesturing with a sawed-off shotgun. Refugio's eyebrows swept together in a thick frown. He turned to the Yaquis who stood impassively, death dangling from their hands. At his curt gesture they lowered the limp birds. While he spoke, the handlers reached into covered baskets, pulled out two fresh cocks and fastened on sets of razor spurs.

"A tie!" shouted Refugio, glaring at the crowd. Men groaned and cursed. Refugio shoved through them shouting, "A tie! No bets won or lost on a tie!"

The two new cocks saw each other and screamed challenges. The crowd looked away from Refugio, focusing once more on the cockpit where eager, violent birds were barely restrained by their handlers.

As Finn turned back toward the side door, his glance automatically searched the crowd. He found himself staring across the room into slanted Japanese eyes. Without seeming to, Finn memorized the man as he did all strangers, trying to judge height and age and weight, looking for distinguishing marks. There was nothing. The Japanese was dressed neither well nor badly, his posture was neither timid nor aggressive, his hair neither too short nor too long, his clothes neither too new nor too old. He appeared as unremarkable as Finn himself—except for Rubia, Refugio's premiere whore, clinging to the man's arm. And then Refugio himself appeared at the Japanese man's side, smiling expansively as he greeted the stranger.

Smoothly, Finn's glance moved on. There was nothing

to show his intense interest in the Japanese. He turned away and went out the cantina's side door, silently swearing at the necessity that pulled him away from the cockfight. In the alley Finn hurried; Refugio and the stranger had cost him forty-three seconds.

As he walked quickly toward the emergency rendezvous point, he wondered what was so hot that it could not be sent through regular channels, and so urgent that it required making contact in so public a place as the Green Parrot. Most of all, he wondered about the Japanese man who had been more important to Refugio than his pride.

Finn felt the first hot touch of adrenaline sliding into his veins. The same instincts that had saved his life so many times in Burma told him that what he had seen tonight was important. There was a new player in the deadly game whose prize was a secret known only in Los Alamos.

Juarez
106 Hours Before Trinity

Vanessa Lyons waited just outside one of the public phone booths in the Hotel Mariscal. She glanced once at her watch; two minutes remained. The tension she felt was not reflected by her appearance. Her face was as smooth as her pastel linen suit, her expression as correct as the hat that shielded her pale blond beauty from the sun.

Self-control had been taught to her by a Russian spy, a man whose intelligence was exceeded only by his cruelty. She had not found his equal until Beria had introduced her to Masarek. They had worked together very well, she and Masarek, combing the ruins of war. She and Masarek had raced American agents to Peenemunde after Germany fell, seeking scientists.

Despite the influx of German atomic physicists into Russia, it was America who had won the race to engineer an atomic bomb. America, whose land and people were untouched by the war. America, who had callously watched Russians die by the hundreds of thousands in Stalingrad, waiting for a Second Front that never seemed to come. American soldiers drank wine and screwed English whores while in Stalingrad Russians sucked on the bones of rats and died.

Eventually the Germans had been crushed, but Russia had paid an enormous price for victory. She needed time to gather her armies and secure herself against enemies new and old. Given time, the opportunities were huge. China was a vacuum waiting to be filled; Europe was chaos waiting to be ordered; and Russia was a nation whose destiny was to rule the world. All that stood between Russia and her rightful place was America—or more specifically, Los Alamos. A successful atomic bomb would shorten the war disastrously, forcing Japan to surrender before an American invasion was launched. But if America did not founder in Japan as the Germans had foundered in Stalingrad, Russia would have traded millions of lives for a few worthless Middle European countries.

Lavrenti Beria had seen the danger before anyone else. He had sent teams of Russian saboteurs to Oak Ridge and Los Alamos. The Oak Ridge team was captured. The Los Alamos team simply vanished. There was no more time to mount another assault on Los Alamos before the bomb was shipped out to Japan. The only alternative was to steal the uranium core of the bomb when it left Los Alamos.

That was proving to be no easier than sabotage had been.

Vanessa looked at her watch again. She stepped into the booth and secured the door. This time ''Jack'' had better have more for her than guesses.

The phone was warmer than her skin. She put in a coin, spoke with the operator and waited for the connection to go through to another public phone booth in Socorro, New Mexico. She suspected the American telephone operator was listening in, but was unconcerned; the few American spies who spoke Russian were in Europe, not Mexico.

"Jill?" asked a man's voice. The accent, like hers, was British.

"Hello, Jack," she said, then switched immediately to Russian.

"What have you confirmed about the Bronx shipments?"

"Speak more slowly," said the man in hesitant Russian. Vanessa repeated her question.

"The Bronx shipments arrived at Hunters Point between," he paused, translating English to Russian numerals, "18 and 2400 on the . . . 15th."

Neither Vanessa's voice nor her expression showed her triumph; now she held the lever with which she hoped to move a world. "When will the uranium leave Los Alamos?"

"Manhattan has some secrets left," he said, his voice brittle, the voice of a man under pressure. "The route is one of them."

"We must have the Bronx shipment!"

"Look, it can't be done from here! I'm not a bloody miracle worker!" shouted the man in English. Then he switched back to halting Russian. "I've confirmed from two other sources that the shipment weighs about ten kilos. There are two pieces. White metal. They aren't . . ." he searched for the correct Russian word, ". . . explosive by themselves."

"How is the uranium handled in the labs?"

"Like ten kilos of lead. It's not . . . explosive without the bomb . . ." he swore and switched to English, ". . . casing, you understand? And that's being shipped separately."

"How is it guarded? What are the passwords?"

"Few guards," he said in Russian. "No excitement. Very, very secret, you understand? No passwords yet. At Hunters Point, a Lawrence Radiation lab team will check it." He switched to English. "Do we have anyone there?"

Vanessa's answer was in Russian. "That's not your concern. Is there anything else?"

"Good luck."

"If you've done your job, I won't need luck."

Los Alamos, New Mexico
100 Hours Before Trinity

Finn dozed in a hallway on a steel chair as he waited for General Groves to see him and explain why he had called Finn out of Juarez. Neither asleep nor awake, sweating, his mind in a jungle half a world away, Finn shifted uneasily in the chair. He was caught again in the nightmare that had budded in Burma and bloomed in Okinawa, and each petal was a separate horror.

There was no mistaking the sodden heat, the feral odor of decay, the world that was every shade of green, sunlight strained through a billion leaves until everything was tints and tones of green, even the smell of death. Burma, green on green.

He was on his first patrol, leading nine men along a narrow jungle trail to a forward observation post. When he arrived at the post he was alone. He had heard no sound, not one, nothing to mark the killing of nine men one by one, his men gone as though they have never lived. But he lived, ambusher and ambushed by turns, learning each time until he was a part of the jungle, silent and quick, a deadly green shadow.

There were other times when he was the only man to survive. That was his special gift, survival. Yet each time he felt guilt as well as triumph. Most of all he felt confusion—why had God or Satan or fate left him alive and other men dead? But such questions were luxuries in a place where necessity conducted a reign of terror. Questions slowed reflexes, and reflexes were all that separated him from his dead friends and enemies, green on green.

The idea of fighting against women, of killing them, had sickened him. Then he had learned that bullets and bayonets had no sex. Men died just as finally when they were killed by a woman, or even a child. The jungle made only one distinction, that between life and death.

In Burma he learned that death, like the jungle, had neither sex nor age, only a color. He learned that whatever the question, survival was the only answer that mattered. People lived and people died. There was little to gain and too much to lose in agonizing over one death or one life, evil or good. He was no more cruel than he had to be to survive, and he did survive.

Yet it was Okinawa, not Burma, where he learned the deepest meaning of horror. Okinawa, where waves broke green and white against cliffs, drowning the screams of children hurtling down. Okinawa, where babies were thrown to the sea.

Finn woke, cold and sweating, the way he always woke when Okinawa bloomed silently in his dreams. Yet the images did not stop when he woke up. They never did.

Every aspect of Okinawa was unfaded, indelible, from General Groves' curt instructions before Finn left, to the children wheeling and turning like awkward birds down the face of the cliff.

He had been an observer in Okinawa, not a soldier. General Groves' surrogate. Groves did not trust the other generals to give Truman accurate reports of the cost of the first American invasion of a Pacific island that was home to large numbers of Japanese civilians. Groves called Okinawa a dress rehearsal for Japan. He had demanded that Finn observe it as only a former jungle fighter could.

Finn had asked why. General Groves had not answered.

Okinawa had been a disturbing experience from the beginning. Instead of fighting, as he had been trained to do, Finn waited safely until an area was secure. Then, guarded by a trio of seasoned Marines, he went in. He had quartered the battle zones despite the protests of his guards. He had seen the bodies of Americans and Japanese, and bloody meat that defied identification.

He could never remember how long he spent on Okinawa. Hours blurred into days, separate battles coalesced into a single truth; the Japanese, soldier and civilian alike, would not surrender. Women fought alongside men and children alongside their parents. But that was no more than Finn had expected, not different from Burma, a familiar shade of green.

He had talked to a boy who was thirteen and ashamed that he had not died in battle; he had not been able to keep up with the retreating Japanese force. Finn's Japanese was fluent. Under gentle questioning, the boy admitted that he was part of a large group of soldiers' families who had not been evacuated in time.

Finn followed a Marine patrol to the place where the boy said families were hidden. There the island was steep-sided, eroded by the sea. Because Finn was a VIP, he was not permitted to risk himself in what could be an ambush. He stayed behind with his three guards on one horn of a deeply curved cliff that was a quarter of a mile long. On the other horn, across the water, was a small clearing along the cliff's edge. He watched it through his binoculars, wondering if the boy's family was waiting there.

The worst of what followed was the silence. Women and children running from American soldiers until there was no place left, nothing but wind above and rocks below. It should have been the moment of surrender, when mothers gathered children in their arms, comforting them and hiding their small faces from the enemies running out of the jungle.

There was no surrender, no comfort. In silence, older children lined up and threw themselves off the cliff and onto the rocks below. Some died immediately. Younger children were hurled to their deaths by their own mothers, children's screams lost in the wind, mouths black circles in faces too young to understand. The mothers followed quickly, arrow straight, welcoming death as a place where no children screamed.

In his dreams they spun and turned and fell endlessly, and they all wore a single face, the face of a child too young to understand. The child fell, twisting until he could see his mother's face. Then he held out his arms in perfect trust that his mother-murderer would snatch him back to safety. The child fell, wrapped in trust and silence, until he smashed onto rocks and only silence was left.

Finn had lowered the binoculars because he could no longer see. The man in him raged, but the warrior in him bowed with respect. By death, if not by birth, the women and their children were samurai.

He had written about that afternoon on the cliff in one

of his many reports to Groves, knowing as he wrote that the words were useless, that nothing could convey the silence and the horror, the mangled families floating on the green tide. In the end he had said what anyone who had fought the Japanese in the jungle already knew: the defeat of Japan would require not only the death of its soldiers, but also the death of its civilians, its very culture.

In the six weeks since Finn had returned, General Groves had never mentioned the report. It was just as well. Finn was not grateful to the man who had sent him to learn the last shade of green.

He shifted his weight on the steel chair, closed his eyes and tried not to feel anything at all.

Moscow
99 Hours Before Trinity

(Cable received by Lavrenti Pavlovich Beria, head of the NKVD. Decoded.)

SHIPPING ROUTE MOST CLOSELY GUARDED SECRET LEFT AT LOS ALAMOS.

DESTINATION AND APPROXIMATE ARRIVAL TIME ARE KNOWN: HUNTERS POINT, SAN FRANCISCO, 1800-2400, 15 JULY.

HUNTERS POINT ONLY POSSIBLE PLACE TO INTERCEPT BRONX SHIPMENT.

UNLESS STOP CODE RECEIVED BY 2400, 14 JULY, OPERATION WILL PROCEED TO CONCLUSION. VANESSA

Los Alamos
98 Hours Before Trinity

Major General Leslie Groves gathered up papers, among
them Finn's Okinawa report, tapped the edge of the
packet on the desk until they were lined up and placed
them on top of another neat stack of reports. He pushed
back from the desk slowly and stretched, feeling anxiety
and sleepless nights like sand in his muscles.

The corporal who sat on a straight chair at the far end of
the office came to attention. "Sir? Do you want Captain
Finn now?"

"No. I'll get him myself," said Groves, walking heavily
across the room. "Out of the way, Corporal."

The corporal stood, picked up his 12-gauge shotgun and
pulled his chair away from the front of the safe he
guarded. Groves spun the combination lock several times
and then bent over the lock, shielding its movements with
his body. He was a big, balding man with a military
mustache and a fleshy face. He wore dress khakis that were
devoid of insignia save for his single star and the battle-
ment pins of the Army Corps of Engineers.

With precise motions, Groves stacked the papers on a
tray in the safe next to other reports, removed a box of
chocolate candy, and closed the safe's heavy door. It shut
with oiled finality. Automatically, Groves snapped home
the bolts and spun the dial several times. He straightened
slowly, walked to his desk and dropped the box of candy
on the polished surface.

Behind him, the corporal resumed his position in front
of the safe that held secrets men would kill to steal or
protect.

Groves left the door ajar as he stepped into the hallway.

The light was harsh, as barren of warmth as the gray walls. All that he could see of the Manhattan Project's top counterespionage agent was a man dozing in a chair, a western hat pulled low over his eyes. Groves was not deceived by Finn's relaxed appearance—he was as dangerous a man as the country had to offer.

"Good evening, Captain," said the General.

Finn pushed back his hat and stood in a single motion. He did not salute, but Groves no longer expected him to. The military niceties that Groves used to good effect around conference tables were not appreciated or used by fighters like Finn. It was a measure of Groves' administrative acumen that he had won Finn's wary respect.

"Good morning, General."

"Is it morning already?" Groves checked his watch. His eyebrows lifted. "By God, it is." His thick fingers probed his eyelids. The pressure of the Project's deadline tightened around him like a steel noose. "Not enough time," he muttered. "Never enough goddamned time! Who the hell do they think I am—Christ? They give orders and expect me to pass miracles and save the fucking world!" His anger was generalized, inchoate.

Groves dropped his hands and stared at Finn, daring him to comment. The sight of Finn, young and lean and tough, angered Groves. The response was irrational. He knew it, but did not particularly care. He did not have energy or time to care about anything beyond the Manhattan Project. It consumed his thoughts and his health, driving him beyond the point where men break. He had become an abrupt, tyrannical son of a bitch, but he had not broken. He had driven others over the edge of sanity, technicians and scientists, yet he always stopped himself from following. He prided himself on fighting the kind of cruel mental war no gun soldier could. And winning. He would win no matter what the cost, because the alternative was failure on a world-wide scale. That was something no gun soldier had to face.

"Gun soldiers," muttered Groves, staring at Finn without really seeing him. "God in heaven I'm sick of gun soldiers!" Then he realized that he was thinking aloud. "Follow me," he said, turning his back on Finn.

The guard watched Finn as he entered the room.

"That's all, Corporal. Out," said Groves as he went to his desk.

The guard said, "Excuse me, General, but this man is not wearing a security badge."

"Corporal, get your ass out of this office *now!*" Groves' voice was sharp and thin, full of sudden rage.

The guard straightened his shoulders, saluted stiffly, and left.

"Damn puppies are as lethal as hell in this office," said Groves as the door closed. "Too bad they can't do shit about leaks in the lab." As he sat down, he waved to the corporal's vacant chair. "Sit down, Captain. Chocolate?"

Finn shook his head.

Groves pulled the box toward himself, selected a piece of candy and put it into his mouth. He knew that sweets were softening his body as surely as lack of exercise, but he ate the chocolate anyway. It was one of the few pleasures Manhattan Project had left him. Other men escaped the Project's pressures by drinking or whoring obsessively, but Groves ate chocolate. He considered it safer than the other outlets.

"The President read your Okinawa summary," Groves began. "That part about the women and children was just what I needed to make my point about the cost of invading Japanese islands."

"I'm glad somebody benefited."

Groves looked up sharply, but Finn's face was expressionless, as always. It irritated Groves not to be able to read a man's reaction on his face. "There's going to be a lot more women and children dead before this is over," snapped Groves. "I thought a gun soldier like you would realize that."

Finn crossed his arms over his chest and waited.

"The President's gun generals sure as hell know," Groves continued. "I just read a scenario for the invasion of Japan. Operation Downfall." Groves laughed shortly. "Whose downfall, theirs or ours? Men, munitions, battleships, destroyers and airplanes and every other damn thing we can get over there before the Russians jump in and steal us blind," said Groves, reaching for another chocolate. "Operation Downfall will be in two stages called 'Olympic' and 'Coronet.' We'll start with the island of Kyushu. Don't look so uneasy, Captain. I'm not telling you anything the Japs don't already know. Our intelligence tells us that the Japs already have a copy of the invasion plans. They've set up headquarters in Hiroshima to reinforce the island defenses. As we've all heard, the Japs are rather good at defending islands." Groves shook his head. "A forewarned, entrenched enemy, fighting on his own ground. Christ! Well, Captain, would you care to guess what the casualty estimates are?"

Finn shook his head. His face was closed, angular, unreadable.

"Still don't talk much, do you?" said Groves.

"I don't learn anything when I'm talking."

"They say one million casualties. I say that's so damned conservative as to be a lie. The goddamned gun generals will suck us into an invasion and then once we've started we have no choice but to slug it out one Jap at a time. Two million is more like it. Two million dead and wounded."

The figure seemed to freeze Finn. "Okinawa. The children . . ."

"It's nice to know you're human after all," Grove said, studying Finn's face. "I was beginning to wonder what it would take to get inside your guard."

Finn's pale eyes never left Groves as the General reached for another piece of chocolate.

"When you started reporting to me, I didn't tell you what you were supposed to protect. All I gave you was a few Top Secret code names to listen for in Mexico." Groves squinted at Finn through bloodshot eyes. "But you never gave up trying to find out, did you? Well, that was part of what I wanted. You couldn't know any more than we leaked out of here. So tell me, Captain, what have you learned?"

"The Russians have spies inside Los Alamos," said Finn.

"I know that! You harp on it often enough! Isn't there anything else? Have you found out what the Manhattan Project *is*?"

"No. Unlike the Russians, I don't have any informants inside the Project. I only know what I can steal from the spies who steal from you."

"What, precisely, is that?" demanded Groves.

"You're trying to develop a new weapon. Probably a new kind of bomb. About six feet worth of bomb, maybe more."

"Christ! That's too close. Who the hell told you that?"

Finn shrugged. "Whores, GIs, drunken technicians, a scientist here and there, plus a few small spies I shook until information fell out. Then I put the pieces together. The spies in Juarez are suddenly very active. My guess is that whatever you're doing here is in the final stages."

Groves studied Finn narrowly. "I'm glad you're on our

side. Do you have any idea what kind of bomb?''

"There haven't been any big explosions around Los Alamos, and the Wendover crews haven't dropped anything big at the Salton Sea in California," said Finn, "so I'd guess that the Manhattan Project is trying to develop something special in the way of incendiaries rather than explosives. Tokyo burned pretty well, last time we tried it."

Groves smiled narrowly, pleased that the core of secret Project seemed to be intact. "You look at past battles, Captain, a common fault of gun soldiers. What we're working on here is the future—a bomb that will end the war in a single stroke."

"I doubt it," said Finn. "The Japanese look at past battles, too. They're a tough race, General. You have to fight them to appreciate just how tough."

"You sound like God Almighty MacArthur," snapped Groves. "There's more to winning this war than guts, guns and gore."

"Then it will be the first time in history that there was," retorted Finn.

"Exactly! History has seen nothing like it. If this bomb works, it will be the equivalent of dropping forty million pounds of TNT all at once!"

"That's impossible," said Finn flatly. "That's like dropping 20,000 one-ton bombs at once! Even if you could get 2,000 planes in the sky at the same time to carry the bombs, you couldn't drop them all in the same place at the same time. I've heard some wild things about the Manhattan Project, but this is outrageous."

Groves laughed. "It's also true."

Finn leaned forward, studying Groves as though he had never seen the General before. "You're serious," he said. Then, "If we have weapons like that, what in Christ's name are we doing planning an invasion? No country could stand against that much firepower, especially a country made up of densely populated islands!''

''Not bombs, Captain. Bomb.''

''Just one bomb? Just one *plane*?''

Groves smiled and leaned back. ''You continue to surprise me. First your tear-jerking report on Okinawa, and now this. You've grasped in a few seconds what I've spent months—years—trying to get across to other gun soldiers. There have been times that I believed that only the Russians understand the importance of what I'm doing here.'' Groves laughed too loudly, saw speculation leap in Finn's eyes, and stopped laughing abruptly. ''You wonder if I'm crazy, don't you? Don't you!''

''If what you said is true, the whole world is crazy.''

Groves rubbed his eyes. They were bloodshot and sore after too many nights with too little sleep. Even when he lay down, he saw a clock on the back of his eyelids, and the clock's hands would inexorably point toward the moment at the Trinity test site when he would know whether World War II would end quickly or a new Russian world would begin.

The phone rang, startling in the silence.

Imperial General HQ
Tokyo
98 Hours Before Trinity

(Radio transmission received by Japan's American Intelligence Section. Decoded.)

RUSSIANS ARE FRIENDS TO NO ONE, LEAST OF ALL JAPAN.

THEY REFUSE TO COOPERATE HERE, AS THEY REFUSED IN LISBON.

MANY RUMORS OF NEW, VERY POWERFUL AMERICAN WEAPON, IMPOSSIBLE YET TO DETERMINE NATURE OF WEAPON.

RUSSIAN SPIES WELL ESTABLISHED IN LOS ALAMOS. RUSSIAN SPY MASAREK IN JUAREZ. M PLANS TO STEAL AMERICA'S SECRET WEAPON AFTER IT IS SHIPPED TO CALIFORNIA.

I WILL FOLLOW, AND STEAL FROM HIM. KESTREL

Los Alamos
98 Hours Before Trinity

Finn sat very still, his shoulders aching with tension. He stared at the box of chocolates on Groves' desk and tried to conceive of 40 million pounds of TNT exploding all at once. The General's voice as he spoke on the phone was a meaningless rasp. All Finn really heard was the echo of his own disbelief: *One plane? One bomb?*

His mind could accept the bomb as one more stage in man's long history of weaponry, but his emotions were appalled by the deadly possibility. Only a man who had felt the sickening intimacy of his enemy's blood flooding over his hands, blood as thick and red as his own pouring out in a final bright gush of life, only men who had fought and bled, killed and died within sight of their enemies knew what death was and what it was not. Death was not glorious or brave, cowardly or sublime. Death was irrevocable, green on green.

He wondered if Groves knew that simple truth, or if it mattered what the General knew or did not know. Finn

knew. Man had gone from caves and clubs to cities and
bombs. The progression was not accidental or incidental.
It was inevitable. Today it was not enough to wage war on
men. You must also devastate the enemy's ability to
manufacture arms—his cities. The industrial revolution
had ensured that cities and the means of producing
weapons were inseparable. "Military targets" had become
a phrase without meaning. Detroit made cars in peacetime, tanks in wartime and the civilian population lived
there all the time; Detroit was a city.

Groves' voice rose, dragging Finn out of his own
thoughts. He looked at his watch and was startled to see
how much time had passed since Groves answered the
phone.

"Yes," said Groves, "I know about that traitorous
petition!"

Groves paused, then laughed harshly. "Humane war?
For the love of Christ! What do scientists know about
humanity or war? It's all a game to them, and the Army is
supplying their toys!"

The silence stretched until Groves' breathing seemed
unnaturally loud. When he spoke again, his voice was
brittle.

"Then tell those *scientists* that it is being arranged—over my protests. Tojo's engraved invitation,"
Groves glared at Finn, "will go out this morning." Groves
paused. "Guarantees? I can't even guarantee that the goddamn bomb works, much less that we'll find the Jap spy in
time for him to see it go off!" Pause. "No. It's too late to
get fancy. It's set to go in forty-eight hours. If your
scientists don't like it, Dr. Lawrence, they can sit and
wring their hands at the bottom of the tower!"

Groves put down the receiver with enough force to
jangle the bell. He looked through Finn. Then Groves

blinked and seemed to snap into focus.

"Did you hear enough?" asked Groves.

"The more I hear, the less I believe."

"Get used to it. Have you seen any new Japanese faces in Juarez?"

"I was watching one when your men found me."

"Describe him."

"Mid-thirties, silver at temples, military bearing, looks fairly impressive. I didn't get close enough to see more."

"Sounds like him." Groves smiled. "He was the Emperor's chief operator in Europe, headquartered in Lisbon. Code name, Kestrel. He specialized in technological matters, a scientist as well as a spy. I want you to lure him to the bomb test."

"You want me to give the biggest secret of the century to an enemy spy?" asked Finn, cutting across Groves' words. "That's a textbook definition of treason, General." His voice was calm but he felt adrenaline sliding into his blood and questions hammering in his mind.

"Those are your orders," said Groves, smiling.

Finn shook his head in disbelief. "I'd like those orders in writing."

"So would I, Captain. So would I. But neither of us will get them." He looked at Finn with eyes that were sane and desperately tired. "The President has been pressured into offering the Japs a preview of what hell will be like if they don't surrender."

"If the President read my Okinawa report, he knows there's nothing we can teach the Japs about hell."

Groves looked down. He fiddled with the chocolate box, lifting and replacing the lid. His expression was haunted, his hands clumsy. Finn had seen other men act like that when caught between two conflicting impera-

tives. Finn sensed that one imperative was Groves'
legendary obsession with secrecy; the other was a direct
order to forgo secrecy. Finn would have had more sympathy, had he not guessed that he was caught in the same
box.

"Christ on a crutch!" Groves snarled, staring at Finn.
"I never know what you're thinking and I've got to know
before I trust you with the whole goddamn world!"

Finn waited tensely, but Groves did not continue. "I'm
thinking," said Finn at last, "that you're a man in a box.
I'm thinking that I'm in the same box. I'm thinking that I
wish to hell I had some idea how big the goddamn box
is!"

"As big as the world. As small as an atom." Groves
laughed oddly, watching Finn. "No, I'm not crazy—no
crazier than I have to be to get the job done. You've got a
head full of questions about Los Alamos and the bomb
and Kestrel and you and me, but believe me, you don't
want to know the answers, not really, because then you'll
be as crazy as I am. You'll have to measure every blink,
every breath, every thought you have or don't have against
one awesome truth: in your hands will be the power to save
or lose a world. Not just a war, Captain. *A world.*"

The hair on Finn's arms and neck moved in an animal
reflex. He wanted to believe that Groves was insane, because no man should have the power to save or lose a
world. Yet he did not want to believe that the most secret
project in America, the project he was sworn to protect,
was in the hands of a madman.

Finn did not know which alternative was worse—Groves
sane or Groves insane. Finn was not even sure he wanted to
choose. All he was sure of was that his body was flushed
with adrenaline, poised to fight, to kill, to flee if
necessary, jungle reflexes screaming at him until he

sweated, but there was nothing to fight, nothing to flee, nothing to do but sit and listen to a man who might or might not be mad.

"Welcome to the Manhatten Project," said Groves, watching Finn. "That was just the start. You're going to hear it all, beginning to end, and then you'll know why for the next few weeks you'll be the most important man on earth." He smiled and gestured toward a hot plate on top of a filing cabinet. "Pour us some coffee, Captain."

"It should be tea," said Finn as he handed Groves a cup. Then Finn took his cup, sat down, and stared at the General. "Convince me that I'm not in Wonderland."

"And that I'm not the Mad Hatter?" Groves' smile was grim. "That shouldn't take long. The OSS reports that the Russians are gearing up to invade Japan and plan on taking China along the way."

Finn nodded. He had guessed as much. It was Stalin's style to take and control. But Finn knew the Russians; if they held that much of the world, there would be no peace until America was annihilated.

"The only way we can prevent that is to end the war before the Russians can invade China or Japan," continued Groves, "or before we're sucked into invading Japan ourselves. The only way we can do that is to use the atomic bomb to end the war." Groves looked haunted for a moment. "Assuming the damn things works," he muttered. "No, it *will* work. It *has* to!"

"What do you mean? Aren't you sure?"

A curt gesture from Groves silenced Finn.

"Later," said Groves. "For now, just listen." His voice became angry, then thickened with contempt as he spoke. "A few of our own scientists are petitioning the President not to use the bomb. They act as though it's morally superior to kill the enemy one by one with bayonets.

"And then," he continued, "there are the scientists who want to arrange a demonstration—invite the Japs over, explode the bomb, and then say, 'Now that we've frightened you, why don't you be nice boys and surrender.'" Groves grinned. *"Scientists."*

"Perhaps they have the right idea. Seeing the equivalent of 20,000 tons of TNT go up at once might make even the most fanatical soldier surrender."

Groves looked sour. "Maybe, maybe not. But between the sob sisters crying not to use the bomb, and the gun soldiers crying about their guts-and-glory invasion, Truman has his ass in a sling. Politics—God, the messes the politicians get us into." Groves glared at Finn. "So there will be a demonstration, and it by God better work!"

Groves unlocked a drawer, reached in and pulled out a thin file. "The test is scheduled for 0200 on the 16th. Two days from now. I want this Jap spy to see it, but I don't want him to know we want him to see it. I'll give you as many men as you need to track him down."

"More warning would have helped," said Finn. "If he's any good, he'll smell a setup."

"Truman didn't make up his mind until yesterday. I called you in immediately."

Finn took the folder and read it quickly. There was little hard information, a testimony to the Japanese spy's skill and elusiveness. Once the padding of speculation was stripped away, all that remained was that Kestrel had been born of an old Japanese family, had been raised in the samurai tradition, entered the Imperial Army as an officer, studied physics in the United States, spied in Lisbon and was a master of unarmed combat.

There was one picture, taken when Kestrel graduated from the University of California at Berkeley. The picture was twelve years old, but Finn recognized the man he had seen in the Green Parrot. The clean line of the chin, the tilt of the head, the alert eyes, the smile that was confident without being aggressive—all were unchanged by the years between Berkeley and Juarez.

"Is that the man you saw?" asked Groves.

"Yes. He was in the Green Parrot yesterday, talking to a Mexican whore called Rubia. She's very good at sucking information out of GIs. She gives the information to Refugio and he sells it to whoever is interested. I'll just make sure that Rubia gets the right information."

"Won't she be suspicious?"

"You haven't seen my agent. Twenty and looks fifteen. That red-headed son of a bitch is the only person I know who lies better than a whore. He's been to Rubia a lot lately. She won't be suspicious."

Groves grimaced. "I don't like depending on a prostitute."

"She's just the bait. I'll give Kestrel the hook myself, through a more reliable source. Ana Oshiga, Takagura Omi's secretary."

"That traitorous bitch," muttered Groves.

"If Kestrel is any good as a spy—and that skinny file says he's damn good—he'll have collected enough information by now to be red hot on the subject of Los Alamos. And he's a samurai as well as a spy. What I'll tell him will make the test irresistible."

"You're sure?"

"The only way I can be sure is to sack him up and bring him myself."

"No. It can't be official. Anyway, I want you at the test site. Or rather, above it." Groves smiled grimly. "You don't believe me yet, not really. After the test you will. Then you'll know how important the rest of your job is—guarding the uranium on its way to Tinian." He drummed his knuckles on the table. "Could you send one of your agents with Kestrel?"

"Why don't I just give him an engraved invitation signed by President Truman and the Joint Chiefs of Staff?" Finn closed the folder and dropped it on the desk. "Where do you want him, and when?"

"By 0100 of the 16th, Kestrel should be on the north side of Oscura Peak. That's fifty miles, north-northwest of Alamogordo. That should give him a good view of Trinity Site, where we'll detonate the bomb."

"If I'm that specific, he'll know it's official. I have to give him just enough pieces to let him discover the answer himself." Finn frowned. "How close does he have to get to be impressed?"

"Any closer to the blast than five miles and he'll be cooked."

"How about just curling his hair?" suggested Finn dryly.

"Ten miles. Twenty. Thirty. Maybe more."

"*Thirty miles!*"

"If the atomic bomb works, it'll be as obvious as sunrise."

"You keep saying 'if.' Don't you know?"

Groves slammed his hand on the desk. "There's more to this than whores and coded messages, Captain. We're dealing with a totally new kind of energy. It comes from the binding force of the most basic structure in the universe, the atom. Have I lost you?"

"No, General, I'm standing right in front of you."

"See if you can stay in front of this. We're building two kinds of atomic bombs, using two different heavy metals. One bomb uses plutonium, one uses a very rare isotope—type—of uranium called U-235. Both plutonium and

U-235 are very *very* scarce. The uranium bomb is relatively simple. The plutonium bomb is not. Getting it to go off is like setting fire to a bucket of water. Everything depends on sixty-four perfectly shaped charges set in a perfect circle around a perfect sphere of plutonium. If the charges go off simultaneously—and by God I'm talking about hundred-millionths of a second!—the plutonium will be evenly imploded, critical mass will be reached, and BANG! Still with me?''

Finn nodded, although all he was certain of was that he was getting more hard information about Manhattan in two minutes than he had in two years of digging.

"Now, we've had hell's own time getting the pluto-nium's charges to go off together. The only way to be sure we've got the engineering right is to test the bomb. The scientists want that. The sob sisters want that. The gun soldiers want that because they think it won't work and then they'll get their goddamn invasion. But I don't want the test because once that fat round bomb goes off we only have one atomic bomb left.''

"For the love of Christ—you can't win a war with one bomb, no matter how powerful it is. You *are* crazy, General!''

"Maybe,'' agreed Groves as he picked a piece of choc-olate out of the box. "We won't have enough plutonium to make a second plutonium bomb until August. So we'll wait until then to drop the uranium bomb. That way, if one atomic bomb doesn't convince the Japs, we'll have a plutonium bomb to follow up. But one bomb should do it.'' Groves looked up at Finn. "That's what you'll be guarding. The bomb that will end World War II.''

"*If* the bomb works.''

"You better pray it does, gun soldier.''

Finn looked away from the General. The smell of chocolate seemed the only real thing left in the room. The past ten minutes were as disjointed and bizarre as any he had ever survived. Two impossibly powerful bombs made of metals he had never heard of; one bomb slated for a test and one for Japan, and a third one not even built yet. Tactics that seemed foolish, if not diastrous, a demonstration that wasted half an arsenal for no better reason than politics.

"What you've told me doesn't make sense," said Finn, his voice flat.

"It doesn't have to—you're a captain, not a general. All you have to know is what to do. First: you will get that Jap spy in place no later than 2200, July 15th. Second: you will drive to Fort Bliss, get on the C-46 that will be waiting and fly over the test. Third: you will be in Hunters Point Naval Shipyard in San Francisco by 0700 of the 16th of July."

"There's only one of me, General. I can't be sure Kestrel stays in place unless I stick with him. That doesn't give me much time to get to Bliss and then to Trinity, and then fly on to San Francisco."

Groves shrugged irritably. "I didn't say you had to lead the damn Jap up the mountain. Just give him enough information that he can't stay away and follow him long enough to be sure he's going in the right direction. Then get your ass to Fort Bliss."

"And when I get to Hunters Point?"

Groves smiled. "Beginning at 0700 of the 16th, you'll stand guard over a billion dollars' worth of uranium 235, the guts of the only atomic bomb that will be left in the world. The uranium will be loaded on the battleship *Indianapolis* by 0700. The ship will weigh anchor at 0800. You will sit on that uranium until you deliver it to Colonel Paul Tibbets on a Pacific island called Tinian. Then he, not you, will become the most important man in the world. Do you understand your orders?"

"Yes. But why send me to Hunters Point? I don't know a damn thing about atomic bombs or battleships."

"You're a survivor, Captain. You should have died twenty times in Burma or Mexico, but you didn't. If the *Indianapolis* is attacked and men with their skin on fire and their guts hanging out run around screaming, you wouldn't panic. You'd get that uranium into the special raft we're shipping with you. You wouldn't stop to play Good Samaritan, you wouldn't let wounded survivors into the raft with you, you wouldn't do one fucking thing but keep that uranium afloat. There aren't many men I could say that about. But I've read the reports about you. I've watched you. You're as fast and nasty as those rattlers you grew up with. You'll get the job done no matter who you have to kill. Is that clear enough for you?"

"Yes, sir. Very clear."

"Good. Now come with me. I want you to see the material you'll be guarding. Uranium 235 has some special characteristics you should be aware of." Groves laughed as though he had made a joke, but did not explain the punchline. "Captain."

"Yes?"

"If that uranium goes to the bottom of the Pacific, I'd advise you to go with it all the way. And don't bother holding your breath."

This time General Groves did not laugh.

Moscow
97 Hours Before Trinity

(Excerpt from NKVD document sent by courier to Vanessa Lyons. Decoded.)

COMMENCE IMMEDIATELY FINAL STAGES OF BRONX INTER-
CEPT. DO NOT FAIL. STALINGRAD WILL BE AVENGED. LAV-
RENTI BERIA

Los Alamos
97 Hours Before Trinity

Silently, Finn followed General Groves through the administrative building. Once it had been a dormitory for
wealthy boys. Now it was a warren of small offices. Beyond
the windows, the Jemez Mountains lifted their rugged
faces to the sky.

There was a stretch of dusty gravel lined by rectangular
government-issue buildings. To the east, the sky grew
lighter second by second; a lemon-colored dawn was
bleaching into a white desert day. Lights in all the buildings were still on. They had been on when Finn arrived at
midnight. Los Alamos recognized neither night nor day,
only the consuming imperatives of war.

Once the plateau had been a beautiful setting for a
boarding school. The cabins remained, but were surrounded by angular buildings and signs that said,
RESTRICTED, MOST RESTRICTED, or POSITIVELY NO
ADMITTANCE. A high fence enclosed Los Alamos, giving it
the appearance of a prison camp, an appearance reinforced
by guards who patrolled the perimeter of the fence with
dogs and automatic weapons.

The faint scent of heat and dust gave way to something
more subtle, more pervasive. Finn's neck prickled. He
could almost smell the acrid sweat of tension, of sleep-
lessness, of fear. It was the odor of men living under in-
human pressure because each day brought more impossi-

ble demands, demands that must be met because the alternative was unthinkable.

"Until seven months ago," said Groves, as they walked, "we were afraid that the Germans would build an atomic bomb before we did. England couldn't have held out against that. The English Channel would have become a German bathtub. That would have made the Normandy invasion impossible. If the Germans had put the bomb together first, there would have been no V-E Day."

The General kept his voice low out of habit. Finn sensed a terrible strain in it. He tried to imagine what it was like to know that the future of many nations quite literally depended on your own success or failure. It was the kind of responsibility that could erode a man's nerve and ultimately his sanity. Then he realized that it was precisely the kind of responsibility Groves had wished on him. Suddenly Finn felt as though he was back in the jungle again, walking a narrow trail into ambush. Only this time much more was at risk than his personal survival.

"Fortunately," said Groves, "the Germans didn't get a chance to make the bomb."

"Were they close?"

Groves shrugged. "Not as close as we are. Hitler was too stupid to know the bomb was his best chance for victory. He kept meddling with his scientists. Roosevelt had more sense. He didn't care how we got it done, just so we did it. Truman is the same way, when gun soldiers and sob sisters leave him alone."

"What about the Japanese?" said Finn.

"They're working on two weapons. The first, called Project A, is an atomic bomb. They aren't as close as the Germans were to building one. Hitler didn't give the Japs any help. He didn't trust his little yellow brothers. The Japs worked long enough to understand the engineering problems of the bomb. They decided that a bomb was possible, but there was no way any country could build a workable bomb before 1950. On my worst days I agree with them." Groves grimaced. "The Japs figured the war would be over by 1950, so they put all their efforts into Project B."

"Do we know what that is?"

"A weapon that kills with light."

"What?"

"Light. Like a flashlight, only a million times more intense."

"Does it work?"

"Yes. But OSS says the weapon is too cumbersome to take into battle. It's just a matter of time, though. Like the bomb."

There was a long silence that ended in Groves' sigh. "Christ," he muttered. Then, "You've studied the Japs so long you're practically one yourself. Do you think they'll ever accept unconditional surrender? They've got to know that they're losing the war."

"Losing face is worse than death. They won't—can't— accept unconditional surrender. It would be racial suicide. But in Juarez, I've heard rumors of peace feelers from Tokyo."

"That's all they are—rumors. Stalin told the President that the Japanese overtures to Russia were too vague to act on."

"Russians have less to gain from peace than we do," said Finn.

"Cynical soul, aren't you?"

"So is Stalin."

"And Truman is a realist. After Pearl Harbor, the voters would have his nuts if he gave the Japs an easy peace." Groves knuckled his eyes. The skin around them was slack, darkened by fatigue, the same fatigue that had eroded his military posture. Yet as he straightened, he again exuded a sense of unswerving, almost fanatical purpose. "It always comes down to the bomb. So be it."

Groves walked toward a building that had a sign in front of it stating:

G Division
Omega Site
Gamma Building
POSITIVELY
NO ADMITTANCE

The sign was small, plain, unobtrusive. The building was new, almost raw. The guard saluted Groves, then looked from him to Finn.

"He's clear, soldier," said Groves. "His name is Finn."

"Yes, sir."

The guard got out two small cardboard badges and wrote a name on each. Inside each badge was a strip of undeveloped film.

"Turn this in when you leave, sir."

The guard clipped one cardboard square onto the General's collar and one onto Finn's. When they had moved beyond the hearing of the guard, Groves spoke quietly.

"I want you to appreciate just what you are guarding. Words like rare and scarce don't really describe it. Irreplacable comes close. The guts of the bomb is about eight kilos of U-235."

"Less than twenty-five pounds?" asked Finn. "Is that all that you need to make a 20,000-ton bang?"

"Yes, but we're dealing with one of the rarest elements on earth," said Groves. "To get it, you start with an ore called pitchblende. There's about an ounce of pure uranium in each tone of ore, but that's the least of the problem. There are two kinds of uranium. We only use one kind,

U-235. We have to separate it from the U-238 *atom by atom*. To get seven pounds of U-235, we have to process half a *ton* of U-238. It's an engineering nightmare.''

Finn listened while his eyes checked off doors that were closed and open. The smell of tension was stronger here, enclosed by pale green corridors and rooms. Then he realized that the smell of tension was on his own body, too.

''We're not separating uranium here,'' said Groves. ''That's done in Tennessee. Here we just assemble the bomb.''

''How does the separated uranium get from Tennessee to Los Alamos?''

''Convoy. Well-guarded but discreet. The fewer people who even suspect there's something valuable being shipped, the better I sleep. We only get a few micrograms at a time, anyway.''

''How does the uranium get from here to Hunters Point?''

''No. No one knows that yet, not even the men who will take it there. And I won't tell anybody else until they're beyond Los Alamos and whatever goddamn Russian spies we haven't caught yet.''

Groves gestured Finn into a long, narrow room that overlooked a laboratory. Between the room and the lab was a lead-lined, chest-high wall topped by a row of leaded glass windows. Every detail of the lab was outlined by cold light pouring down from ranks of fluorescent lamps.

''We can hear them,'' said Groves, gesturing to a ceiling speaker, ''but they can't hear us.''

Inside the laboratory stood a container that resembled a nickel-plated milk can. The top was off, revealing a thick lead lining.

''See that can?'' asked Groves. ''That's what the ura-

nium will be shipped in. It will be welded to a cabin floor of
the *Indianapolis*.''

Finn looked at the cylinder. It was about eighteen inches
in diameter and about two feet high. The top had a curved
metal handle like the lid of a garbage can. The container
did not look big enough to hold the future of the world.

Finn looked beyond the can. There were only three men
in the laboratory. Two of them were seated at a table
against the far wall, apparently taking notes. They had the
look of men who had been up all night. The third man
looked equally tired. He was seated on a high stool near
the center of the room. In front of him was a table. On the
table was a black metal box with dials, meters and what
looked like a long narrow microphone attached by a cord
to the box.

The table also held a glass-walled container that looked
like an ordinary aquarium turned on end. At the bottom
of the container, in about three feet of water, was a lump
of white metal. A smaller piece of the same metal was suspended above the water from a tripod that straddled the
aquarium.

"Those two pieces are all the pure uranium-235 in the
world," said Groves.

Finn looked at the metal. He could have held both
pieces in his hands at once. They did not look powerful
enough to blow up the room, much less Japan.

"How tricky is uranium to handle? Is it like nitro-
glycerin?"

"No. It won't explode if you drop it. Uranium is more
subtle. It's radioactive, which means it naturally gives off
high-energy particles. A few of those particles won't hurt
you. Too many will kill you. But so long as you keep those
two chunks of uranium apart, they're about as dangerous
as cookies and milk.

"Now," continued Groves, "the closer together the pieces, the more energy they give off, and the more dangerous they are. If you set those chunks down next to each other you'll get lots of radiation, some heat and a little light. Deadly as hell, but no explosion. But if you slammed that U-235 together quickly, with an explosive charge, the atoms would radiate their particles all at once, literally blowing themselves apart. That gives you one hell of a bang. Those eight kilos of U-235 are the explosive equivalent of forty million pounds of TNT."

Finn looked at the gleaming metal and found such power hard to believe.

The experimenter on the stool flipped a switch on the unmarked box near the aquarium. Immediately there was a distant crackling sound, like slow static. He called out a reading to the men at the far side of the room.

"Same as before," verified one of the men.

"What are they doing?" asked Finn.

"The aquarium holds salt water. If the *Indianapolis* goes down, we want to know how a dip in the ocean will affect critical mass and chain reactions."

The experimenter fiddled with the pulley that controlled the U-235 suspended over the aquarium. The pulley gears were stuck, the result of too much water dripped onto them during a night of experimentation.

"The larger piece of U-235 is at the bottom of the pond," said Groves. "It's about three times as big as the piece hanging from the pulley. The two pieces are made to fit together like a baseball in a glove."

The U-235 was attached to a pulley hook by a hastily rigged net. The experimenter unhooked the net from the pulley, set aside the uranium, and cranked on the pulley impatiently. Without the weight of the metal dragging down, the pulley worked fairly well.

Groves glanced at the experimenter and the two other men slumped on stools at the far end of the room. In spite of their obvious fatigue, there was an air of anxiety about them. The experimenter reattached the U-235 to the pulley.

"It's their last chance to work with the metal before it's shipped. No one has ever had this much U-235 before. There are lots of theories to test and damn little time to do it in."

The pulley stuck. The experimenter swore.

"Six twenty-five," said one of the men at the back of the room.

The experimenter said nothing. He applied more pressure to the pulley. The net holding the U-235 descended a few inches. The sound of static increased.

"What's that?" asked Finn. "What is he doing?"

"The box is giving out the static," said Groves. "It's a radiation counter. It tells us how many particles are being radiated. Remember, the closer the two pieces, the more particles are knocked off. The more particles, the more danger."

The man on the stool adjusted the radiation counter until the sound of static was reduced to a series of slow clicks. He turned the crank on the pulley. The net holding the U-235 descended two inches closer to its companion. Instantly the clicking sound increased. The man stopped, made a note on his pad, read the notation aloud, and then readjusted the radiation counter. He turned the crank again. It stuck. One of the men in the back of the room groaned.

"Goddamn it, not again!"

The experimenter ignored the complaint. He pressed and jiggled until the pulley gears came unstuck and the isotope descended. The counter snarled. He readjusted it, calling out numbers.

"Every time he adjusts the radiation counter," said Groves, "he decreases its sensitivity. Otherwise you wouldn't be able to measure anything beyond mild radio-activity without overloading the machine."

The scientist turned the crank. It balked, then responded. The U-235 dropped closer to the larger piece of metal at the bottom of the aquarium. Clicking sounds blurred into a low howl.

"Radiation is like a germ," Groves muttered. "You can't see it but it can hurt you."

The rapid signal of the counter reminded Finn of a rattlesnake's warning, except that the counter's sound had a mechanical perfection that no animate life could attain. The difference was subtle and pervasive; it made Finn uneasy. He understood dangerous snakes and dangerous men, but the invisible danger of radiation was alien to him.

There was an abnormal intensity to the experimenter's actions as he worked with the reluctant pulley and measured the shrinking distance between the two pieces of U-238—and between himself and a lethal unknown.

"How much radiation can a man take?" asked Finn, not looking away from the table where the two pieces of metal communicated with each other in a series of ascending clicks.

"We don't know."

"Then how do you know if you've gotten too much?"

"Skin lesions form that look like burns. Bruises form. Nausea. Vomiting. Diarrhea. Hair loss. Fever. Bad fever."

"Is too much radiation fatal?"

"Yes."

"How long does it take?"

Silence. Then, reluctantly. "There have been accidents. Only one death, thank God. It took four days."

"But it could be slower? Or faster?"

"Probably, depending on the man and the dosage. We just don't know. No guarantees, Captain. Not one."

Finn stood without moving, measuring the increasing tension as the experimenter adjusted the radiation counter again, causing the buzz to slow into separate clicks. The man gingerly moved the pulley handle, made notes, called out numbers, and eased the small piece of U-238 closer to its mate at the bottom of the aquarium.

The counter came alive again with a low buzzing sound. Tension coiled invisibly around the experimenter, but his voice was steady as he read off a series of numbers for his colleagues at the back of the lab. His words issued from the ceiling speaker grille like a disembodied counterpart to the counter's metallic buzz.

"We did it differently before," said Groves. "We used a contraption we called a guillotine to test critical mass. But we didn't have this much pure isotope then."

General Groves' words faded as the counter's voice strenghtened. The man on the stool was cranking the pulley again. It moved under the man's careful urging, then stuck. The man pressed lightly. The pulley did not budge; its mechanism was gummed by repeated exposure to salt water. The uranium bullet hung about four inches above the target. The experimenter pushed harder on the crank, to no effect.

"We're supposed to have it ready to ship by 6:30," said one of the observers in a tight voice. "It's 6:28."

"I know. I know!" The experimenter swore and pressed harder on the crank. Then he backed up the pulley and lowered it quickly. It balked again at the same spot. He backed up further and lowered again, knowing there was not enough time to dismantle the mechanism again. It must work *now*.

The scientist's concentration gave way to frustration. He

cranked the pulley all the way to the top, then reversed it with rapid, angry motions, again and again. The pulley reached the same spot and balked, again and again, until the last time when something snapped and the U-235 plunged down into the aquarium and came to rest fitted against its mate.

The radiation counter screamed.

Instinctively, the scientist tried to separate the U-235 with his bare hands. The pieces were smooth, heavy, infinitely slippery and fitted too well with each other.

"Jesus Christ!" cried the scientist. He clawed at the two pieces of metal until they finally separated and he could drag one deadly piece out of the pond, stopping the chain reaction.

The radiation counter's scream died to a whisper as the scientist set aside the smaller piece of U-235 that he had retrieved from the aquarium. He sagged against the table, breathing raggedly, like a man at the end of a long run. Less than four seconds had passed since the pulley had broken.

"Stay away from there!" said Groves as Finn leaped toward the door leading to the lab. Groves' hand clamped around Finn's wrist with surprising strength. "Listen to me!" cried Groves as Finn jerked free. "There's nothing you can do. He's poisoned, and if you get too close you could be poisoned too!"

Behind the glass, one man rushed toward a phone, the other toward the scientist who was slumped over the table, staring at his wet hands as though he had never seen them before. He groaned and let his hands drop to the table.

The radiation counter sang as his hands passed near the sensitive probe. The scientist jerked back his hands. The counter became quiet. He brought his hands close to the probe once more. The counter sang of deadly radiation.

With a strangled noise, the scientist lunged away from the counter. The other two men looked at each other, then at everything except the experimenter's deadly hands.

Finn stared at each man's face, a rictus of terror and sickness overlaid with sweat. He had seen such expressions before, Marines watching helplessly as children plummeted onto rocks far below. He knew that feeling, the worst shade of green in all of the jungle's green hells.

And he knew he looked like the men behind the glass, sweating and afraid.

"That counter goes with me," said Finn, turning his back on the lab. "I'm not going to sit on a bomb I can't hear ticking."

Los Alamos
88 Hours Before Trinity

Heat from the desert floor a mile below twisted up the plateau's rugged sides. Walking out of Omega Building was like walking onto a griddle. General Groves wiped his face, but it was more than heat that made him sweat. The laboratory accident had delayed the uranium's departure. There was still ample time to drive it to Hunter's Point —he had allowed for everything, even accidents—but that did not make him sweat any less.

If there were any more long delays, he would be forced to fly the uranium to San Francisco. That was something he was determined to avoid. There was too much country in the west. If the plane went down, the uranium could be lost forever. He had a horror of that, of the uranium falling out of the sky, disappearing into the cracks of the empty land. So long as the canister stayed on roads, he felt reasonably reassured; if something came apart, he would know where it had happened to the nearest yard. The ocean was a different proposition, more difficult to control, more dangerous. He had done what he could about that—Finn.

Behind the General, strapped to a dolly, the nickel canister burned in the sun. The soldier pushing the dolly was sweating freely. Even on wheels, the canister was unwieldy, unreasonably heavy for its size.

Behind the soldier walked a man in civilian clothes—business suit, hat and tie. He carried a Thompson submachine gun with professional ease. He watched everything but the canister itself, his dark eyes as restless as his body was calm.

The small procession stopped in Omega Building's loading area. Five cars were parked on the asphalt. None had military markings. All but the first car carried four men. The first car had three. The middle car's trunk was open, revealing a steel framework. The framework was welded to the car's body.

"Load it," said Groves.

Two men from the middle car got out and hoisted the canister off the dolly. Though both men were strong, the canister was difficult to handle. Metal rang against metal as the canister landed in its specially built cradle. One of the men swore and rubbed skinned knuckles while his partner locked the canister into place. The car settled on its heavy springs.

Groves watched the locks close and the trunk lid slam down, locking automatically. The keys to the cradle and trunk were already in Hunter's Point. Anyone who wanted to remove the canister before then would need a cutting torch and a lot of patience.

The man who had guarded the uranium on its short trip

from the lab got into the back seat of the first car. The open door revealed two more submachine guns in a rack on the floorboard. The driver looked up at Groves. The General made a curt gesture. The first car drove off.

Precisely three minutes later, the second, third and fourth cars left. The third car contained the uranium. Three minutes later, the last car left. All cars were in continuous radio contact with one another. They would check in with the General at frequent, predetermined intervals. There was no way the car or canister could be lost.

Yet Groves stared at the road a long time after the last car had disappeared. He hated knowing that the uranium was physically out of his grasp.

Juarez
75 Hours Before Trinity

The eye of god was dusty. Tiny flecks of desert grime had settled on the god's eye over the years, blurring the sharp geometric patterns woven at the center of the design. The tiny tassles at each point of the diamond-shaped framework were dirty, their bright colors made drab by time and neglect.

Kestrel stared at the single eye, admiring its symmetry and symbolism . . . and the irony of its position over one of the busiest beds in Juarez. Perhaps the Aztec god whose eye hung there found the prepaid writhings of two or more bodies amusing, but Kestrel doubted it. Even the benign gods of his own Buddhist upbringing looked upon prostitution with displeasure.

As for himself, Kestrel felt like a man condemned to a curious penance in one of hell's more grubby anterooms.

Voyeurism was foreign to his nature, but he had spent many hours crouched in a tiny, concealed alcove just off Rubia's crib. Through the imported Indian screen, Kestrel had seen a procession of straining buttocks and heard a quantity of practiced moans and lusty grunts.

Kestrel eased his cramped muscles by flexing his body subtly, using the discipline of karate that had become second nature to him. The discipline was mental as well as physical. It helped him to endure all of this in order to learn what Japan must know.

With a sigh, Kestrel looked from the dead god's eye to the intricately carved screen nine inches from his face. The figures on the screen depicted all the coital permutations that flexible, determined human bodies could attain. Kestrel wished that reality had one-tenth the elegance of the screen's stylized matings. He had learned that viewing the unvarnished sex act was more distasteful than titillating, and more tedious than either.

He had discovered military secrets from the GIs who thrashed so inelegantly on Rubia's soiled mattress. He could not trust the little Rubia to pass on all that she learned; both her English and her loyalty were erratic. Thus, he was forced to crouch behind erotic carvings and witness acts that were stupefyingly unerotic.

The soldier who had just come into the room with Rubia looked not much older than the sixteen-year-old whore. He was short and red-headed, one of the instant lieutenants that America had ground out to meet the needs of war. This was his fifth visit to Rubia. She had told Kestrel that the soldier never questioned why she spent an hour with him, yet charged no more than she did for her ten-minute tricks.

From what the soldier had said, Rubia was the only diversion in a series of boring assignments that stretched from the edge of California's Salton Sea to El Paso, Texas. For months he had observed, measured and retrieved the remnants of the empty bomb casings that were dropped one at a time onto the desert from B-29s flying so high they were invisible. For a very young second lieutenant who had expected to return to civilian life laden with medals and war stories, the assignment on the shores of a landlocked sea had been a bad joke with no punchline in sight.

As he often complained to Rubia, the whole purpose of the bombing runs seemed to be to test a proximity fuse that was supposed to explode a bomb several thousand feet above the desert. To the lieutenant, developing a proximity fuse when there already were bombs that exploded on impact made little sense. Moreover, to develop a fuse that would explode two thousand feet up was insane. No bomb was powerful enough to do much damage if it exploded that far off the ground. His commander had speculated that the fuse was for a leaflet bomb to scatter propaganda over Japan.

El Paso was even more boring; nothing to do but follow technicians around as they strung wires between concrete bunkers and a tower five miles away in the desert. Nothing about his assignments made sense to the young soldier, except the smiling whore whose fingernails made little dents in his erection.

"You are muy hombre today," Rubia said, squeezing him. "Almost I believe that you have no other woman since you come here."

"Another woman?" he said in a thick voice. "Not a chance. I've been on duty the whole goddamn time."

"Come," Rubia said, tugging on him, leading him toward the battered mattress. "Come and tell your little Rubia how it was with your time."

"Not a goddamn thing happened, as usual."

The soldier let Rubia open his shirt as she had already opened his pants. She stood against him so that every time she moved, her full breasts rubbed over his skin. He watched her hands and his own body, liking the contrast between his full pink flesh and her narrow brown fingers.

"It was bad?" said Rubia sympathetically, kissing his neck. She disliked kissing her tricks, but Kestrel was paying her to make the gringo feel very special. "Pobrecito," she murmured, licking his throat with slow, deliberate strokes.

"We sat and fried our asses on the same goddamn piece of sand whle they measured and muttered. I mean, who the fuck cares if the tower is exactly five miles from the bunkers? It's stupid!"

"Estupido," agreed Rubia, pulling him down on to the bed, guiding him until he lay on his stomach with her astride him, kneading the white, freckled flesh of his back. "Muy estupido. To sit and sweat there when you could sweat with me in my bed."

The lieutenant gasped as her hands moved between his legs. He tried to roll onto his back, but Rubia held him immobile.

"Not yet, muchacho," Rubia said, laughing at his eagerness.

The lieutenant groaned and lay facedown on the mattress again. Rubia bent over until her breasts rested on his back. Her teeth bit into his shoulder. He shuddered, but did not object. Marks from other bites covered his back.

"I do not believe," whispered Rubia, "that a man like you, so strong, does nothing more than sit in the sand all day. Do you not even play with your cock, muchacho?"

Rubia bit the soldier's ear and cheek and neck, all the while moving her hips as though he were already inside her. She sat up and turned her face toward the screen. Smiling, she put her hands over her breasts and moved her hips in silent invitation to Kestrel.

"Tú eres muy macho," Rubia said in a husky voice, staring at the screen while she stroked her own body. "I will do anything you want. Anything."

Kestrel heard the promise in the girl's voice. The lieutenant heard it also. He moved convulsively, forcing Rubia to let him roll over. When he was lying on his back, Rubia slowly moved her hips over the soldier without letting him penetrate her, teasing him, prolonging his pleasure. Rubia was very good at her work, a natural whore.

"Let me—" gasped the soldier, his hands grabbing Rubia's maddening hips.

Rubia laughed. Her laughter sounded genuine, surprising Kestrel. He had not thought her capable of emotion. Then he realized that she was amused by the man who was helpless between her experienced legs. Kestrel felt almost sorry for the young lieutenant.

"No, no, muchacho," Rubia laughed. "You have not yet promised to me that you will come back soon." She reached down and pinched him firmly. It was enough to dull his need so that she could bring him to an even sharper pitch of excitement. She lay full length on him, teasing him mercilessly. "Promise you come back only to me."

"I'll try to get back before we leave," he groaned.

"Leave?" Her teeth paused above the vein beating blue against his neck. "You come back, no?"

"I'll try. But the tests went well. Those flyboys said if we ever got to Wendover, the drinks were on them."

"Wendover?" said Rubia, fondling him with her tongue. "Is that a—how you say it—a bar?

The soldier laughed and pinched her nipples hard enough to hurt. Rubia did not pull away; she was used to rough handling.

"No, baby," said the lieutenant. "Wendover is an airbase in Utah. But don't worry. I'm not going way up there. From what I overheard yesterday, I'm going to stay in the goddamn desert with that goddamn tower and all those goddamn wires going out across the flattest, hottest desert this side of hell."

"Must you go far from here?" she pouted. 'I miss you when you're gone too long."

"Not that far," he said, grabbing her breasts. "It's north of some place called Magord or Amgordo, some Mex name. There's gonna be some big test soon and we're supposed to be Johnny on the spot."

"Test?" asked Rubia, working her fingers down his body. "It sounds of danger, no?"

"Shit," said the lieutenant in disgust. "We should be so lucky. Unless they give purple hearts for sunburn, I'm gonna finish this damned war with nothing to show for my time. Now come here!"

The soldier grabbed a handful of Rubia's tangled, dark blond hair and forced her mouth down on his.

Behind the screen, Kestrel squatted on his heels, waiting. Either conversation or sex would begin soon. If it was the latter, he could get out of this grubby peephole.

Rubia freed her lips and tried to get the soldier to talk more. After a moment, she sensed his determination and knew that she could not put him off much longer. It would be better if sex appeared to be her desire, too.

"No more talk," Rubia said in a low voice as she slid off his white body. She lay on her back and moved invitingly. "Or do you not want your little Rubia like she wants you?"

The lieutenant mounted Rubia in an ungainly rush.

Silently, Kestrel eased out of the cramped passageway through a side door, removing himself from the purview of the god's eye staring blindly over the sweating buttocks of the red-headed soldier.

Juarez
66 Hours Before Trinity

(Radio transmission received by Kestrel. Decoded.)

WE HAVE NO INDEPENDENT CONFIRMATION OF YOUR SUG-GESTION THAT A SPECIAL WEAPON IS BEING SHIPPED OUT OF LOS ALAMOS.

RUMORS OF IMPENDING TEST OF NEW, VERY POTENT AMERICAN WEAPON. IMPERATIVE YOU REMAIN IN JUAREZ TO CONFIRM OR DENY RUMORS.

REPEAT. IMPERATIVE. MAJ. GEN. SEIZO ARISUE IMPERIAL ARMY INTELLIGENCE

Juarez
61 Hours Before Trinity

Takagura Omi's house was on the edge of Colonia Chino, the Oriental ghetto surrounded by Juarez. It was a cultural rather than an economic ghetto, since Takagura was a very wealthy man. Some of his business dealings were legitimate. Most were not. In 1930, his export-import business had been financed by the Japanese Imperial Army. Today the business thrived by itself, especially the illegal portions. The profits went into financing a network of spies, thugs and politicians who made Takagura's influence felt from Mexico City across the entire northern tier of Mexico, and into the Little Tokyos of southwestern America. Takagura was still an officer in the Imperial Army, a believer in the Son of Heaven's divinity, and a fanatical militarist. His utter loyalty to Emperor Hirohito was one of the few certainties Kestrel had found in Juarez.

Kestrel set aside his cup of tea, silently wishing it had been coffee. He had acquired a taste for coffee in America, a preference that was reinforced during his years in Lisbon. Takagura's home, however, was rigidly in accord with traditional Japanese diet and manners. The few exceptions —shortwave radio, telephone, electricity—did not include such Occidental amenities as chairs, raised beds, or coffee.

The sound of footsteps came through translucent walls. Kestrel turned and stood up in a single motion that spoke of controlled power. He waited, motionless. The light from a corner lamp poured over him, making the silver strands of hair at his temples gleam. Outside the room, a silhouette flowed over the shoji screen like a black ghost. The paper screen whispered aside, revealing Ana Oshiga, Takagura's secretary. She bowed and greeted him in precise Japanese.

"I hope you are comfortable, Kestrel-san."

Kestrel looked at Ana's pale, heart-shaped face. Like electricity in Takagura's traditional Japanese home, Ana did not wholly fit her surroundings.

"Yes, Ana-san," he answered politely, although he had not slept at all and had yet to wash the whorehouse grime off his body.

Ana naturally walked with the long-legged stride of an American woman, but she was hobbled now by a narrow kimono. Her voice, too, was American, pitched for life lived behind plaster rather than paper walls. As with most Nisei and Isei, she was taller than the Japanese norm.

"The honored wife of Omi-san said that you requested my presence," Ana said.

"English, please," said Kestrel. Although he trusted his host's loyalty, Kestrel himself had bribed too many servants to trust Takagura's. "Did you finish interviewing Refugio's whores after I left with Rubia?"

Kestrel's face did not show his distaste for prostitutes and hours spent watching their work. Ana's face did, although she had done no more than question the women. He had seen Mexican sluts condescend to Ana, a woman they considered their sexual and racial inferior. He understood Ana's hatred of them. He even sympathized. He did not let sympathy get in the way of necessity, however. He needed a fluent, trustworthy translator. Ana.

"They added nothing new," answered Ana, trying to be as expressionless as Kestrel, and failing. "The number of Americans from Socorro and Los Alamos has doubled or tripled in recent weeks. They drink heavily, screw badly, pay too much, and sometimes go crazy." Ana frowned. "Several of the sluts mentioned the same man. He ran up and down the halls, drunk, naked, yelling, 'We've done it! I'll never have to see that fat asshole Groves again!'"

"Was the man a soldier?"

"I asked. The whores described him as bearded. He didn't wear dog tags or military signet rings. His clothes were civilian, including the underwear."

Kestrel looked beyond Ana, thinking about the crumbs of information he had gathered from Refugio, Rubia, and now Ana. Rubia's red-headed soldier had mentioned a test "soon," and that whatever it was had originally come from Los Alamos. Ana spoke of a bearded civilian running through a Mexican whorehouse yelling that something was done. Was it too much to assume that whatever weapon was being built in Los Alamos was going to be tested and then shipped to California, and from there overseas for use against Japan?

"You're sure that he said, 'We've done it!'?" asked Kestrel. "Was he speaking Spanish or did one of the sluts know English?"

"Yolanda—the young one with the broken nose—speaks some English. She said he yelled the same thing again and again, until someone threw him into the alley. She's sure she remembered it right. She's also the one who thought to check his clothes and jewelry."

"Good. Pay her extra."

"I did."

"You've done very well for me, Ana."

Ana smiled, pleased that she had pleased him. "Thank you," she said, bowing formally. "It is my duty and pleasure to serve the honorable representative of the Son of Heaven."

The words, gracious in Japanese, sounded awkward in English. Ana flushed slightly. Kestrel bowed like a Japanese, then smiled at her like an American and took her hand. Ana's flesh deepened, but she did not pull away. Kestrel was the first samurai she had ever known; he fascinated her. He knew it, and used it. He let go of her hand and indicated the lacquered tray holding teapot and cups with no handles. "Would you pour tea for us?"

Kestrel watched her fill the cups neatly and gracefully, a skill learned under Takagura's demanding eye. "You do many things well," he said, taking the cup she offered him. "Did Refugio have any questions when you delivered the money to him?"

"No. He must like you. He only counted it once."

Kestrel laughed. "He will count it twice more when he is alone."

"That may be a while," said Ana, sipping her green tea. "He's flying with that man Masarek to Mexicali. The Englishwoman is going along. His mistress, I suppose."

"When are they leaving?"

Ana looked up, startled by the change in Kestrel's tone. "He's probably gone by now. I'm sorry. Should I have stopped him?"

Kestrel did not answer for a moment. He felt cold, felt time draining away from him. First the hints that the weapon was done, that it would be tested soon, and suddenly the Russian was gone as though there were nothing further of value left at Los Alamos. He was too far behind the Russian. Japan was too far behind the Americans, one man and a country stumbling along picking up crumbs from an international spy feast that had just begun in Lisbon and could too easily end here, before he and Japan had more than a taste of the meal.

"I'm sorry," said Ana.

Kestrel realized that she had said it several times. He curbed his thoughts and fears with the discipline that was as much a part of him as his slanting eyes. "It's not your fault that I came here too late, knowing too little."

Ana spoke hesitantly, as if she were afraid to disturb him. "Takagura has many contacts in Mexicali. And I—my family lived in San Francisco before they were driven into concentration camps."

Kestrel listened to the bitterness in Ana's voice. Hatred was the reason she had abandoned the country of her birth. Hatred, a gift for languages and administrative skills worthy of a person twice her age had made her invaluable to Takagura Omi's espionage and import business. But hatred was a dangerous thing in a spy. He was grateful that

he did not have to use Ana beyond her capacity as translator and go-between. He had the active spy's distrust of
untrained agents.

"Takagura trusts Refugio's greed," said Kestrel. "I'm
forced to do the same."

"He said he'll call from Mexicali when he knows more
of what Masarek wants. Perhaps I should stay with you
until then."

"Why?"

"Refugio will have to speak Spanish so that Masarek
won't understand what's being said. But you don't understand Spanish."

Kestrel smiled wryly. "Again, I find you invaluable."
He touched her hand.

Ana's pleasure at the compliment and touch was as
transparent as her eagerness to stay with him. "You'll
have time to tell me about Japan. I've never been to my
country."

"First, I need to know more about America."

Ana frowned and looked away. "What do you need to
know?"

"Does Takagura have men in San Francisco?"

"It's been very hard since Pearl Harbor. They locked up
the Japanese, you know," Ana said stiffly.

"Yes, I know." He also knew that Japan had overnight
lost most of its information network on the West Coast.

"All of Takagura's contacts who are still free are
Mexicans. Refugio's cousins. In fact, Takagura arranged to
sell my father's flower shop to the Reyes brothers after my
father was sent to Manzanar. Refugio's cousins paid almost
nothing, but," she shrugged, "even that was more than
most Japanese got for their property."

"Does the name 'Magord' or 'Amgordo' mean anything to you?"

Ana frowned and repeated the words to herself several times. After a few moments she shook her head. "Are they Spanish words?"

"They are the same word, and probably Spanish. I believe it's the name of a place in New Mexico, a desert area, probably on or near a military installation. It's probably, but not necessarily, convenient to Los Alamos."

"Where is the map I brought you yesterday?"

While Ana cleared cups and teapot off a low table, Kestrel got the map. He spread it out, concealing the table's intricate mother-of-pearl inlays. Ana knelt and looked at the map. Her eyes were very dark against the pale background of her rice-powdered face. The hair framing her cheeks was black, gleaming, untouched by silver. She bent closer to the map until her breath almost touched his hand as he traced a road that followed the Rio Grande toward Los Alamos.

"Amgord . . . Magordo," muttered Kestrel. His finger moved over such place names as La Mesa and Las Cruces, Truth or Consequences and Socorro, Albuquerque and—"Algodones? No, it was *gordo* or *gord*, not *godo*."

He traced the road through Santa Fe to Los Alamos and then on north, but found nothing. He traced down along the west side of the Rio Grande, ranging out 200 miles or more and then on down to the border. The only place name he paused over was Mogollon.

"That's high country," said Ana. "Forest, not desert."

Kestrel read the map's legend and reached the same conclusion. He began searching the area east of the Rio Grande and north to the New Mexican border.

"Alamogordo." Kestrel stopped, measuring the sound of the word against what the soldier had said. The "gordo" sounded right. Magordo could correspond to "—mogordo." It was as close to a match as he had come, but he was not entirely satisfied. His glance moved on, looking for a closer correspondence.

There was no other place name that had the sound of "gord" or "gordo" in it.

Kestrel's glance came back to Alamogordo, testing the place against what the soldier had said. It was in the desert. It bordered on two large military reservations, one of which was almost exclusively used as a firing range. From the map, it looked to be a desolate stretch of land, suitable for testing dangerous new weapons.

"Is that it?" said Ana, looking at the area under Kestrel's hand. "Jornada del Muerto," she murmured. "It must be a terrible place to be called that."

Kestrel looked at the map. The northwestern area of the reservation was labled Jornado del Muerto. "What does it mean?"

"Journey of Death."

Oddly, Kestrel smiled. It was a site and a name a samurai would have chosen for using deadly weapons. But the military reservation covered almost 3,000 square miles. Where in all that emptiness would the test be held? And how elaborate would the preparations be? The soldier had mentioned bunkers and wires and a tower. The wires could be used to hook into a power supply, if the weapon was a lethal beam of light. The tower could be used either for observation or as a target. Yet, the use of bunkers suggested a concentrated blast, an explosion from a bomb rather than a death ray.

Whatever the weapon, construction had taken place recently, and that meant trucks to haul materials and people, and roads for the trucks to move on.

"Those young soldiers," Kestrel said, looking up from the map, "the ones who said they had been building a road through hell and were thirsty enough to drink the Rio

Grande dry . . . were they working out of Fort Bliss?''

"No. Socorro.''

"Odd. They were soldiers, not scientists or technicians?''

"Yes, but they probably were building roads for the Los Alamos people. Everyone is told to say Socorro, never Los Alamos.''

Kestrel looked at the map again. Socorro was north-northwest of Alamogordo. Between the two towns was a dirt road skirting the desolate military reservation. If the soldiers were actually working from Socorro, building roads to transport people and equipment for the Los Alamos test; and if Rubia's soldier had told the truth about the test location being north of Alamogordo; then the test itself would probably be held in the upper third of the military reservation.

That still left 1,000 square miles.

"Flat,'' murmured Kestrel. "He said it was the 'flattest, hottest desert this side of hell.' ''

The contours on the map were skimpy, but mountain peaks were marked on the range that ran diagonally through the reservation. Either Salinas Peak or Oscura Peak would give a good view of the remaining flatlands. Salinas Peak was more west of Alamogordo; Oscura Peak was more north. It might be the place to watch the test from.

But the question remained: How soon was "soon"?

Juarez
60 Hours Before Trinity

Finn drove through Juarez automatically, his mind still absorbing the ramifications of what he had learned in Los Alamos. Weapons were as old as man. People had been shifting and reshifting the balance of power ever since the first time a hairless ape grabbed a stone and crushed his enemy's skull. All the weapons that had come since that moment were simply refinements of the original idea of lenghtening the reach and efficiency of the human arm. Yet—

One bomb. One plane. One hell of a bang.

Finn's hands tightened on the wheel as he guided the speeding car. He recognized that bombing cities was a rational military tactic, no more or less cruel than a scorched earth strategy which left the enemy starving, civilian and soldier alike. As a means of avoiding a grueling, gruesome, inch-by-bloody-inch invasion of Japan, the atomic bomb was without parallel.

But so many dead, so quickly, lifetimes measured in milliseconds.

And would there be others, like the experimenter, who would not be lucky enough to die in the first raw white instant of power?

Finn slowed and turned on to a street leading to the oldest part of Juarez. The city was quiet, its life hidden from the afternoon sun. The second stories of most buildings overhung the sidewalk, creating tunnels of shade for the few pedestrians. The square was overhung with large, soft-green pepper trees that cast feathery shadows on the baked clay ground. Water tumbled down a stone and tile fountain.

The car's tires made no sound as Finn turned onto the sandy unpaved street that led to his house. He stopped the Ford in front of an old adobe with a faded canvas awning protecting its one large window. Finn got out and closed the door quietly.

He crossed the small patch of sand serving as a front lawn. The house belonged to his father's friend, an official in the Mexican government. Finn had furnished the adobe with a solid oak kitchen table, chairs, and a leather-sprung bed with a mattress filled with corn shucks and a few sprigs of sage. It was the kind of bed he had been raised on, the bed that he had dreamed about in the nightmare hammocks of Burma. The bed was crisp, dry, and smelled of the desert.

The only other furnishings were lamps, a telephone and a stove. On a rack in a corner of the single room, which contained the bed and the kitchen, were a 12-gauge pump shotgun, an M-1 carbine with a canvas shoulder strap, and a long-barreled Remington. Opposite the rack, three swords hung on the bare adobe wall. Two of the swords were Japanese, the short and the long sword of a samurai. The third sword was Mexican, a ceremonial saber inlaid with silver and gold.

Even in the diffuse light that entered through the small panel windows set in the thick adobe walls, the swords shone with bright, hard light. The Japanese swords combined elegance and balance with efficiency; the Mexican sword combined pride and wealth with a killing edge. It had been carried into battle against gringo invaders by a Mexican Creole general who had died at the hands of Finn's great-grandfather. The sword's handle was bound in gilt-braided cord after the manner of its time.

Pride and violence, the twin obsessions of the cultures that had forged the swords. And now a new culture, a new weapon, a weapon that was made not of steel but of an unbelievably rare element, a metal that could end a war and begin a world.

Finn stood just inside the door, letting the coolness of the house wash over him. Before he could close the door, the telephone rang imperiously and Ghost, his cat, streaked into the room. He shut the door and answered the phone with a quickness that echoed the cat's.

"Bueno," he said.

Finn recognized the voice at the other end of the line, a woman's voice, cool and precise, professionally remote. Sarah Campos was the chief operator at the phone exchange in El Paso. All calls from Juarez to the United States, and vice versa, went through her switchboard. She, like Finn, was paid by the American government.

"You will want to know about new voices?" she asked.

"Yes."

Finn waited, so focused on Sarah's call that he barely noticed the cat stropping itself on his boots.

"There were two. Yesterday. Both British. One was the man I told you about before, the one who calls from that little town close to the cottonwoods."

"Yes." Socorro was the town closest to Los Alamos. Finn had mentioned the anonymous caller to Groves, suspecting that the man might be one of the British scientists working in Los Alamos. "Did you recognize the second man?"

"It was a woman. She was calling from the Mexican side, a public phone booth."

"What did they say?"

"Not much that I could understand. They spoke English at first, then they switched to another language, very hard and deep in their throats. I think it was German. It sure wasn't Chinese or Japanese. The woman spoke the language very well. The man had problems. He used English, too. It sounded like they were planning a trip to New York.''

''Oh?''

''They kept talking about Manhattan and the Bronx, and something about not being able to ship stuff directly to the Bronx. He finally said in English, 'Look, it can't be done from here!' He was angry.''

For a moment Finn forgot to breathe. Then he drew in air silently and said, ''Anything else?''

''No. They didn't talk very long.''

''If you hear any more from them, let me know right away.''

Finn replaced the receiver very slowly, but his mind was racing and his skin was hot with more than desert heat. Russian sounded enough like German to confuse an untutored ear. Masarek was in Juarez with a woman who had a British accent. Two priceless pieces of silver-white metal were on their way to San Francisco.

General Groves had been very wise to keep the route of the Bronx shipment secret; otherwise it seemed that the Russians were set to intercept the shipment. Without the uranium, the war would not end short of a grueling invasion of Japan, an invasion that would culminate in 2 million casualties and a Russian world.

Ghost yeowed bleakly, as though she shared Finn's thoughts. Her front paw touched the toe of his boot and the tip of her tail flicked across his knee.

''Hello, Ghost.''

The cat sat on her haunches, inspecting the room as though seeking mice in its corners or lizards on its clay walls. Then her turquoise eye met Finn's and she yeowed again. She was poised, healthy and obviously a recent mother.

"Hungry?"

Ghost looked away disdainfully. She could survive without Finn, which was the only reason he had allowed her into his life. Since Burma, he had permitted no living thing to depend on him.

Finn straightened swiftly, found a small can of evaporated milk in the kitchen and punched two holes in the can with his pocket knife. He poured the viscous fluid into a saucer and stepped aside.

Ghost's nose moved and her whiskers twitched as the thick scent of milk washed over her. She walked slowly to the dish, her every movement telling Finn that she could live very well without him. The milk was like Finn, nice, but not necessary to her survival.

"That's right, cat," he said softly. "No guarantees."

Jacame
50 Hours Before Trinity

Refugio drove without lights through the dry desert night as though it were noon. Drops of sweat gathered in his enormous black eyebrows like rain in a raven's wings. That was the only outward sign of the strength and concentration required to hold the rocketing Cadillac on the narrow dirt road. Refugio dominated the car with a combination of drama and ruthlessness that was uniquely Mexican.

Vanessa Lyons braced herself in the back seat, trying not to be shaken loose by each bump, each rut, each lunge and swoop of the heavy car. She assumed that Refugio was indulging in the strutting maleness she detested in all Latin cultures. She glanced at Masarek, silent in the front seat. He balanced against the careening car with the cold self-control that was his trademark.

Vanessa started to speak, then decided not to. Her orders had been clear. All speed. Although her orders were now nothing more than ashes flushed into the sewer, their urgency remained. They had flown from Juarez to Mexicali and now were rushing toward the place where they could safely cross into the United States.

Refugio glanced in the rearview mirror, attracted by the movement of Vanessa's head. Moonlight made her gold hair shimmer as though it were burning. Her eyes were the dense blue of expensive English china.

And she was watching him.

Refugio's black eyes shifted to the passenger in the front seat, the man called Masarek. Contained, quiet, Masarek would have made a good smuggler or soldier or assassin. Refugio suspected that Masarek had been all three. Though his hairline had retreated into gray and his face showed the first inroads of age, Masarek moved with the ease of men half his years.

The car's metal joints rattled and groaned over a straight segment of road that had attained the washboard surface common to unpaved desert tracks. Gradually the car slowed until its roostertail of dust no longer leaped toward the white moon.

"Is something wrong?" asked Vanessa, using the breathy voice she affected when she wanted men to underestimate her.

"Do not worry, chica," said Refugio, smiling and turning toward her to show teeth that were hard and white. When he spoke English, his light accent gave his words a deceptively gentle edge. "I drive slow now for the same reason I drove without lights. We are close to Jacame. The American border patrol knows that Jacame is a poor place. Only smugglers have money for cars. Bueno. We do not show our lights."

Vanessa looked out the window, but saw nothing. Then

she noticed the tiny brillance of lights scattered in the distance like fallen stars.

"Is that it?" she asked.

Refugio chuckled. "No, chica. That is Jacumba, on the gringo side. The Mexicans in Jacame have no electricity. What do smugglers need with light?"

"Are you sure the Americans don't know about your route?" asked Vanessa, skepticism clear in spite of her husky voice.

Refugio shrugged. "If they knew my route, they would put me in one of their grand calabozos with hot and cold water and never let me out. They want me very much."

"Then why don't they shoot you?" asked Masarek in a colorless voice.

Refugio glanced at the other man. "That's what you would do, no?" He laughed. "That's what I would do, too. But the gringos won't shoot me because that would be against their rules." He looked at Vanessa in the rearview mirror. "It is a foolish idea they took from your country, no?"

Vanessa agreed, but did not answer, irritated to find that she agreed with Refugio about anything that smacked of politics. One of the things that had driven her first to Fabian socialism, then to Marxism and finally to radical communism, was the British male's insistence on living— and often losing—by arcane rules of chivalry.

Refugio laughed again, the full-bellied laugh of real amusement. "So the Americans have nice rules and I have nice pleasure breaking them. They will never catch me because I am a *man*, not a gentleman."

Vanessa stared out the window, ignoring Refugio. "How far are we from the border?"

"That way," said Refugio, gesturing widely to her right, "Perhaps a kilometer. But from my house, much less."

The car bounced off the dirt road onto something that was little better than a goat path. Ahead of the straining car, an amorphous black blot resolved into a cluster of small, worn houses. Whether through neglect or design, the windows of the houses were so dirty as to almost obscure the lantern light burning within.

A pack of rough-coated dogs burst from the direction of the houses. Lean, half-starved, the dogs raced toward the Cadillac as though it were their natural prey.

Refugio neither slowed nor turned aside. He aimed the car into the center of the pack. At the last second the dogs scattered to either side, snapping at tires before giving up and trotting back toward the houses.

The buildings were scattered in a random arrangement dictated by the rumpled nature of the land. What once might have been a town square was now the final refuge for a canted, three-wheeled wagon and the rusty remains of cars that had no wheels at all. Dirt and sand crept up the sides of the vehicles, engulfing them silently, blurring the boundary between artifact and desert, past and present. Just beyond, almost hidden by the wreckage, was the communal well. It was circled by a low stone wall and roofed by a ragged wooden structure. When the car bounced by, doves fled into the night, cooing their distress in liquid tones.

The car skidded to a stop in a turbulent cloud of grit that was swirled away by the pre-dawn wind. Refugio got out, stretched, and walked to meet the two men who were approaching from separate directions. Like those men, Refugio was just over medium height, black-haired, with brown skin and ebony eyes. Unlike him, the men were bent by poverty.

"Buenas noches, don Refugio," said the first man. Then like an echo, the second man said exactly the same words. "Buenas noches, don Refugio."

Both men moved toward Refugio with the subtle stiffness that came from a combination of grinding labor, indifferent health and growing age. They wore the loose white cotton pants and camisa of the Mexican peon, and greeted Refugio with the deference of vassal to lord.

"Buenas noches, Jorge. Cómo estas?" said Refugio. "Juanito," he said, recognizing the other man. "Cómo estas?"

In low, rapid Spanish, Refugio gave orders. Then he turned his shoulders against a gust of dry, dirty wind and walked back to the car. He noticed Vanessa's window had been rolled down and knew she had been listening. He wondered how much she had heard, and how much she had understood. Earlier that night he had spoken Spanish within her hearing, describing in moist detail his seduction of a young girl. Not once had Vanessa's expression revealed that she understood the language.

"Come, Señor Masarek," Refugio said. "You will see that my house is as I told you."

Even before Masarek was out of the car, Vanessa was standing in the cool, dry wind.

Refugio saw Vanessa walking toward him, her slim silk-sheathed legs silver beneath a loose blue skirt that rose with every breath of wind. Refugio started to object, then shrugged. Apparently Masarek did not mind parading his fine-boned bitch in front of hungry dogs.

Refugio led the way to Jorge's house. Without knocking, he pushed open the door and walked in. Vanessa and Masarek entered, followed closely by Jorge and Juan. The Mexicans could hardly take their eyes from the delicate curve of Vanessa's legs. In such a setting, she was like a stroke of lightning—unexpected, brilliant, dangerous.

The house smelled of kerosene and chile peppers. A

small lamp with a cracked chimney sat on a heavy wood table in the middle of the room. The lamp's wick was so short that the flame barely illuminated the dark center of the room, leaving deep shadows all around. Masarek scanned the circling darkness. Eyes stared back, watching him unblinkingly.

Refugio lifted the kerosene lamp off the table. Shadows drained like dark water from the impassive face of a fat woman and the bunched, curious faces of her children. Their eyes glittered, following the lamp in Refugio's hand. Jorge and Juan moved to opposite sides of the thick oak table, then lifted it aside with a precision that suggested long practice.

"You will see," said Refugio. "Below this floor is a shaft, then a tunnel that goes to the American side. The tunnel is not large. It is good only for moving people and small things such as opium. But you have told me that what you want moved is smaller than a man, no?"

Without waiting for an answer, Refugio made a curt motion. Jorge bent and pulled aside the rug. Beneath the rug the faint outline of a trapdoor was revealed by the dim kerosene light. Moving quickly, Juan opened the trapdoor and Jorge lowered himself into the darkness. A second lamp flared below, dispelling the absolute black of the shaft. A ladder suddenly poked up into the room.

"The señorita will wait here," said Refugio.

As though she had not heard, Vanessa walked toward the ladder, grasped its splintery sides and started down. Refugio gave Masarek a quick, probing look, but the East European seemed indifferent to Vanessa's show of independence.

Vanessa vanished, descending with quick, precise steps until she came face to face with a leering Jorge. He had stood below, watching her descent with singular attention.

"You are a swine," said Vanessa in Russian. "An eater of shit."

Jorge smiled and nodded, responding to the intimate tone rather than the incomprehensible language.

"Your betters are dying in Russia right now," continued Vanessa, "dying so that your miserably begotten children won't be slaves of class oppression. But you don't care about that, do you? Like all peasants, you only care about your gut and your balls. You belong to the decadent past. You are as stupid as you are ugly. You disgust me. Swine."

Vanessa smiled while she whispered the final word. Then she stepped aside, making room for Masarek, who was quickly followed by Refugio. The Mexican moved easily, almost carelessly, holding the lamp. The ladder and tunnel were as familiar to him as the gold rings he wore on both hands.

Masarek moved differently in the depths of the tunnel, as though his body were tightly coiled against a lurking danger. The lantern light revealed faint lines on his face, traces of an emotion Vanessa recognized but never before had associated with the assassin—fear. It was the first flaw she had found in Masarek's seamless competence.

Holding the kerosene lamp high, Refugio slowly moved his arm until every curve of the circular chamber was revealed. The walls of the tiny room were rough, composed of an aggregate that looked as unstable as the gravel it once had been, when the desert was the bottom of an ancient sea. Compressed by the passage of eons, stones and dirt had combined.

The walls of the chamber were not shored, except in one spot where a softness in the aggregate had spilled several cubic yards of material onto the floor. Walls, ceiling and

STEAL THE SUN   85

floor were a uniform sand color that turned to gold in the
lantern light.

"It is just as I told you, no?" said Refugio when he had
finished lighting every corner of the small anteroom at the
head of the tunnel. "See?"

"I see a little dirt room and what could be the opening
of a tunnel over there," said Masarek, gesturing contemptuously toward the opposite side of the chamber. "I have
only your word that the tunnel—if that is a tunnel—goes
anywhere."

"Come then, I will show you." Refugio smiled cruelly,
for he had seen Masarek's instant of fear. "The tunnel was
dug by Chinese to smuggle other Chinese. They are not a
big people, señor, as you will find out when you use their
tunnel. The walls come in very close."

Refugio laughed silently, and the sweat in his massive
eyebrows winked as though sharing the joke. As Masarek
turned toward the tunnel, he decided that when the smuggler's usefulness was done, he would teach Refugio the
meaning of terror. And then Refugio would die.

Imperial General HQ
Tokyo
50 Hours Before Trinity

(Excerpts from radio log of American Intelligence Section
of Imperial Army Intelligence. Decoded.)

AMERICANS SOON WILL TEST NEW WEAPON IN DESERT NORTH
OF ALAMOGORDO, NEW MEXICO. NATURE OF WEAPON STILL
UNKNOWN. IT IS SMALL ENOUGH TO BE CARRIED BY ONE
MAN, YET POWERFUL (OR UNPREDICTABLE) ENOUGH TO

REQUIRE A DISTANCE OF SEVERAL MILES BETWEEN OBSERVERS
AND TEST.

ANOTHER WEAPON SOON TO BE SHIPPED FROM LOS ALAMOS
TO SAN FRANCISCO. FROM THERE, IT MUST BE ASSUMED THE
WEAPON WILL BE PUT INTO USE AGAINST JAPAN.

RUSSIAN SPY PLANS TO STEAL WEAPON IN SAN FRANCISCO. I
WILL GO THERE AND STEAL WEAPON FROM HIM. KESTREL

(Reply. Decoded.)

ANY WEAPON SMALL ENOUGH FOR ONE MAN TO CARRY
CAN'T AFFECT JAPAN'S IMMEDIATE FUTURE AND THEREFORE
IS NOT TO BE FEARED. THERE MUST BE TWO DIFFERENT
WEAPONS.

REMAIN IN JUAREZ AND DETERMINE THE NATURE OF WEAPON
TO BE TESTED IN THE DESERT. MAJ. GEN. ARISUE

(Reply. Decoded.)

ANY WEAPON THAT SETS ALLIES AGAINST EACH OTHER MUST
BE ENORMOUSLY VALUABLE TO AN ENEMY. URGENTLY RE-
QUEST PERMISSION TO FOLLOW RUSSIAN TO SAN FRANCISCO.
KESTREL

(Reply. Decoded.)

REQUEST UNDER CONSIDERATION. MAJ. GEN. ARISUE

Beneath Mexican-American Border
49 Hours Before Trinity

Once, half-revealed by a swinging yellow light, they saw Buddha staring from a wall niche, his dust-covered eyes contemplating far more distant borders than the one the tunnel had been built to circumvent.

"The Chinese," said Refugio as he passed the niche, "built this tunnel with the skills they learned on gringo railroad crews, and then they used this tunnel to smuggle thousands of Chinese into the United States."

"My father's uncle," Refugio said, "married the only child of the man who owned the houses on both sides of the border, and the tunnel between. She was Chinese, but our family wanted the tunnel very badly. She died soon and he married a good Mexican girl. The tunnel is ours now, as is only just. The Chinese are very good smugglers, but they are not very good Mexicans."

The atmosphere was neither fresh nor stale. It had a peculiar, dense taste to it, as though the same air had been there since the tunnel was built.

"How deep are we?" asked Vanessa.

"Deep enough to die if the tunnel gives way," said Refugio.

The tunnel walls seemed to lean in, absorbing light and sound. Refugio's voice was clear, but it did not carry as well as it should have. The air was thick, flat, deadening, yet the lamps still burned with a muddy yellow flame. Suddenly the walls changed from aggregate to wood, a dark hallway more than 150 feet long. Sand that had seeped and trickled between the timbers lay in small drifts across the floor and grated beneath their feet.

"This is the bottom of an old river. The ground is very

soft. More than thirty Chinese were buried alive here before they finally brought in timber from the north of California. They had many Chinese, you see, but very little wood.''

In the silence it seemed that they could hear individual grains of sand sifting between cracked timbers, and the wood itself sighing under the interminable burden of heavy earth.

Beyond the shored-up section, the floor ascended steadily. Walking became more difficult. Pebbles rolled beneath their feet as they climbed back toward the surface. At the foot of a short stairway, Refugio pulled hard several times on a dirty cord that was strung along the wall.

When he turned away from the wall, the light from the lamp he was carrying washed over Vanessa. The thick yellow glow and velvet shadows mellowed her brittle beauty. Refugio stopped, caught by the unexpected softness of her body in the light. He stared at her with eyes that were as intrusive as hands. Vanessa ignored him.

After another long look, Refugio led Vanessa and Masarek up the stairs, through a short passageway and into a room that resembled a wine cellar. Instead of a trapdoor in the ceiling, the exit was a full-sized door set in the far wall. The door was heavily carved and lacked anything resembling a handle. Refugio waited several moments, then swore beneath his breath.

Shielding the door with his body, Refugio pushed against the wood in several places at once. With a click, the door swung slightly toward him. From the other side of the door, a shaft of blue-white light fell over them, dimming the lanterns into insignificant yellow puddles. Refugio opened the door all the way.

''Welcome to the United States,'' he said, smiling and gesturing toward the hard white light made by electricity rather than kerosene. "Jucumba, California."

Masarek went through the door first, relieved to be out of the tunnel. Vanessa followed, looking around carefully, suddenly conscious of the weight of the pistol lying inside her purse.

The house they entered was an odd mixture of Mexican, Oriental and American culture. The eaves curved upward, echoing the pagodas of China and Japan, an echo repeated by the elegantly painted silk screen that divided the room. The hard lights, the indifferently made furniture and the picture windows were American, as was the telephone and the varnished wood cabinet containing a radio. The curtains and rugs were distinctively Mexican, aflame with colors. The shrine holding a gilt-and-blue plaster Madonna was also Mexican.

A man appeared, moving slowly, with the awkwardness of age. When he came closer, it was clear that he was not so much aged as crippled. He walked as though his knees were as rigid as his shins. Unlike the Mexicans, his skin was more red than brown, though his hair was as black as theirs.

"Don Refugio," said the man in quick Spanish. "I was just coming to open the door for you."

Refugio grunted. "Verdad? But I could not wait all day, so I opened the door myself. You are getting too slow for even this job."

"No, no," said the man. "I am not too slow." To prove his words, he ran three shuffling steps across the room. "See, don Refugio? I am very fast."

Refugio shrugged and turned away. "Stay fast, viejo. I have no other jobs for a cripple." Refugio switched to English for the benefit of the two foreigners. "That man is Ridgewalker. He used to be an Apache and a smuggler. Now he is an old woman with no knees."

Masarek looked at Refugio, then at the Indian whom age had robbed of quickness and pride. "Send them all away," he said. "I won't discuss business in the presence of servants."

Masarek's voice was hard, his body relaxed. Being above ground had regenerated his confidence. Refugio sent his men away with three curt words in Spanish. After the men were gone, he leaned against the carved door until it clicked into place. When closed, the door blended into a wall of carved panels that depicted mountains and waterfalls and elegant trees bending beneath an invisible wind.

Vanessa walked to a heavily curtained window. She pulled the cloth aside slightly, ignoring the two men. In the distance she could see the buildings of Calexico and Mexicali, a single entity but for the geographic accident of an international border dividing their sprawl into two unequal cities.

Refugio turned to Masarek. "You have seen my houses and my tunnel. It is as I told you—a very safe way to take something across the border. Well worth the $15,000 I will charge for its rent."

"I would not pay you that much if the tunnel bypassed hell," said Masarek, his voice colorless.

"You are also buying my services—and my silence."

"Both have yet to be proved."

"Perhaps the price is too high," Refugio conceded, shrugging, "but you have not told me what it is you want done. I have shared with you the secrets of my work and you have shared nothing. So my price is high. Offended pride, you understand."

"Your price is ridiculous."

Vanessa listened to the two men argue. Refugio oozed reason, while Masarek displayed casual contempt. She listened, counting the houses between herself and the outskirts of Calexico. When she had counted them four times, the men were no closer to agreeing than when she had started.

Vanessa let the colorful curtain fall back into place. ''Refugio.''

At the single word from Vanessa, both men stopped arguing. Refugio turned and stared at the white-skinned woman whose voice was oddly different. When she spoke again, he realized that her speech had lost its intriguing breathiness.

''Our employers are willing to pay you, within reason, for your services. Fifteen thousand dollars is not within reason. Ten is. No,'' she said when she saw Refugio begin to speak. ''I'm not bargaining. Ten thousand dollars or nothing at all.''

Refugio knew inflexibility when he met it. He hesitated, then nodded a curt agreement. Ten thousand was three thousand more than he would have settled for.

''That's too much money, of course,'' said Vanessa. ''In return for it, you will cooperate completely with both Masarek and me. If I tell you to do something, you will do it without argument.''

Vanessa waited, measuring the proud Mexican with a single glance.

''Yes,'' he said at last.

''Good. As for what you will help us smuggle—and yes, steal—you don't need to know anything beyond what Masarek will tell you.'' Vanessa's smile took none of the hardness from her voice. ''Nor,'' she continued smoothly, ''do you need to know our real names or anything else about our lives. Any man you send after us will be fortunate to walk away as well as your tame Apache.''

While Vanessa spoke, she produced a packet of money from her purse. With a deft movement of her hands she fanned the money, twenty $100 bills. Refugio stared.

"If you agree to the terms," continued Vanessa, "you can have this $2,000 now. If you don't agree, you may keep $500. You may, of course, try to take the rest, and then Masarek will kill you. Do we have a bargain, Señor Refugio?"

Vanessa's long fingernail traced the fan of bills, making them rustle seductively. Refugio smiled. He took the bills with a swift movement that surprised Vanessa.

"You are una bandida," Refugio said appreciatively. "You understand how to get what you want. That is good."

The words were said softly, in the tones of a man speaking to a lover. Refugio's dark eyes looked at every inch of Vanessa. He pocketed the bills and laughed quietly.

"We'll do well together, you and I," Refugio said in a warm voice. "Bandida."

Refugio's caressing laugh and eyes repelled Vanessa. She turned aside and saw Masarek's face. To anyone who did not know him, his expression had not changed, but Vanessa knew Masarek. She smiled, hoping she would be nearby when Refugio could no longer laugh.

"Masarek," Vanessa said coolly, "will stay with you from now on. You'll leave today for Hunters Point." Her eyes narrowed. "You're sure that Ho's truck won't be searched at the gate?"

"My cousins say it is an open secret. The truck hasn't been searched for more than a year." He smiled. "The Navy probably knows about the betting slips in the truck, but it's a small thing. Soldiers gamble. If not with Ho, then with someone else."

Vanessa hesitated, then nodded curtly. The laundry truck was an unavoidable risk.

"When will I get the rest of my money?" asked
Refugio.

"In the tunnel, after you return from San Francisco."

Refugio nodded slowly. "Bueno."

"Yes," said Masarek, "it will be good." His smile was
calm, predatory. "Very good."

Juarez
40 Hours Before Trinity

"Momentito," said Ana. She covered the telephone re-
ceiver with her palm and whispered in rapid Japanese to
Kestrel. "Refugio calls. He must speak Spanish because
Masarek is there."

Kestrel set aside his rice bowl and watched Ana with an
alertness that belied his lack of sleep.

"Cuidado," warned Ana, speaking softly yet very
rapidly into the phone. "They may know more of the
language than you believe."

Refugio's harsh laugh came clearly through the phone.
Then he spoke so quickly that even a Mexican would have
had difficulty understanding him. Ana frowned, concen-
trating.

"Momentito." Ana covered the receiver and spoke to
Kestrel in soft Japanese, bending over until her face was
only inches from his ear. "They are to leave immediately
for a place called Hunters Point, San Francisco. It's some
kind of a military base. They are going to steal something.
He isn't happy about the risk, but has agreed to do it anyway—for more money, of course."

"Yes," said Kestrel impatiently. "But what is he going to steal?"

Before Ana could ask Refugio, his voice came loudly through the telephone. He was yelling in English and cursing in Spanish.

"My men are Mexican, pendejo! If I speak English to them they don't understand me when I ask for two cars with California license plates. But someone must get the cars because you won't let me leave the house. It's too bad you don't speak Spanish so you understand what I say to my men. Qué lástima, cabrón! You'll just have to trust me. Or maybe you'd rather walk to San Francisco and back?"

Refugio's voice faded. Ana held the phone to her ear, then shook her head in answer to Kestrel's silent query. Abruptly, Refugio's voice returned, speaking Spanish in a normal tone.

"What are you going to steal from Hunters Point?" asked Ana quickly. She listened, covered the receiver, and turned back to whisper to Kestrel. "He doesn't know. He'll take two of his men, plus Masarek and the woman. He needs two cars with California plates. The licenses and the cars have to be legitimate. After Hunters Point, they'll switch vehicles and drive back to the tunnel in the second car."

Kestrel frowned harshly. General Arisue had ordered him to stay in Juarez until his orders were clarified. Yet Kestrel was fascinated by a prize that was worth the insane risk Masarek was taking by invading an American naval base.

"Ana. Are you sure Refugio said Hunters Point?"

"Yes."

Kestrel's frown deepened. Hunters Point was one of America's major Pacific naval depots, debarkation point for many of the warships that harried the Imperial Navy.

"When will he be at Hunters Point?" asked Kestrel.

Ana spoke rapidly, listened, then turned to Kestrel. "The car they'll use after Hunters Point has to be in Oakland by 3 A.M. on the 16th, so he assumes that the theft will occur before then."

The 16th. Less than two days away. If he had to stay in Juarez because of the test, then someone would have to go to Oakland in his place. He could not trust Refugio to deliver the weapon unless someone was there, watching him. But the only person who could go in Kestrel's place was Ana. Takagura had been adamant in his belief that Ana was the only other person he could trust with the Emperor's highest secrets.

Yet the thought of sending Ana made Kestrel deeply uneasy. She was trained only for the safer aspects of espionage, translating periodicals and enemy documents obtained by other agents who risked their lives to steal the information.

"Can Refugio get the cars or does he need Takagura's help?" asked Kestrel.

"The cars are taken care of," said Ana after a moment. She added, "They're paying him 15,000 American dollars."

Kestrel shrugged. "Our bargain remains. Three times what they pay him, I will pay."

Ana's eyes widened, but none of her shock showed in her voice. She spoke into the phone and then listened.

"The Englishwoman will meet them in Oakland after the theft and drive back with them to the tunnel. She's more than just Masarek's whore. She is his equal, perhaps his superior."

Kestrel's eyes narrowed, emphasizing the harsh planes of his face. Ana looked away quickly; this was the Kestrel she sensed beneath the polite, polished exterior, the samurai she both admired and feared.

"Where will she meet them?" asked Kestrel.

Ana asked Refugio, waited, then translated quickly. "Oakland. I know the place he means. On the waterfront. Factories. Cars and many trucks. A few more won't be noticed."

"Tell Refugio not to kill the woman when he kills Masarek. I want to question her. Tell him if I can't meet him on the waterfront, you will. You'll pick up him, the woman, and whatever they stole and bring them to his cousin's flower shop. When I get there, I'll give him $15,000. The other $30,000 wil be paid when we're safe in Mexico. Do you understand?"

Ana nodded, understanding too much—and not enough. She buried her unease beneath a rush of Spanish. Then she paused, said "Si" and hung up.

Eyes hooded, body perfectly still, Kestrel sat a few feet away, watching her. He had not intended to involve her so deeply in his actions. She was born American, not Japanese, and was alien to the samurai tradition. He doubted that she had ever seen more than her monthly blood. He hoped she would not be there when Refugio killed Masarek. He hoped she would not have to see those agonizing minutes when sweat dulled the English woman's bright hair and the woman screamed and begged until finally answers tumbled out of her bleeding lips, words and sense and nonsense, anything to stop the pain. . . .

Kestrel sighed, regretting General Arisue's orders. But perhaps the bomb test would not be for several days. Then he would have time to go to Hunters Point and Alamogordo both. He must find out the test date soon. But first he must give Ana something more to hold on to than vague yearnings for Japan. She was too American to die for something she could not touch.

He held out his hand. His voice was gentle. "Will you sit beside me?"

Ana's fingertips brushed Kestrel's palm. Her nails were smooth quarter-moons, as gently curved as her body. When she sat down, the hem of her silk kimono settled across his thigh. She moved to gather in the cloth, but his hand stopped her.

"Beautiful," said Kestrel, stroking the rose-colored silk that glowed against the black fabric of his trousers. He looked up suddenly, holding her with his dark Asiatic eyes. "I don't want you to go to Hunters Point, Ana. I don't want you to be hurt. But I may have no choice."

Kestrel's voice was as gentle as his fingers touching Ana's robe, but the truth of his words was not gentle at all.

"Unless," his fingers moved from the silk of her kimono to the silk of her skin, "there is time for me to go to San Francisco and get back before the test. But I don't know when the test is."

"I've tried to find out," Ana said quickly.

"I know. It's not your fault. It's karma." Kestrel's smile was genuine and sad.

"I don't mind going back to San Francisco," Ana said, running the words together, hoping to cover the lie and knowing it lay in the middle of her words like a stone. "I'm just . . . frightened."

Kestrel gathered Ana into his lap as he would a child. He felt the warmth of her hands through his shirt as she held on to him fiercely, as though she could share his strength just by touching him.

"You're very brave. Yes," he repeated, sensing argument in her suddenly stiff body, "brave. You gave up everything you knew out of loyalty to a country that lives only in your mind."

Ana said nothing. In the silence came the sound of wind chimes turning in a slow stirring of air.

"When I was a child—" Ana's voice trembled, then broke.

"Yes, Ana?"

"I didn't belong anywhere." Ana spoke quickly. "My playmates were Mexican, not Nisei, because my father was a field worker. But I wasn't Mexican. When I was older we lived in San Francisco, but by then I was more Mexican than Nisei. In school they told me I was American and I believed them until—until—"

"Pearl Harbor."

"Yes!" Ana looked up at Kestrel, her eyes deep with tears and rage. "A country I'd never seen bombed a place I'd never heard of and suddenly I was a criminal! A *Jap*!"

Ana closed her eyes, shuddering with the effort of controlling herself. When she spoke again, her voice was calm. "They were right about one thing. I am Japanese."

Kestrel shook his head, knowing Ana was never more American than when she defied the American government and fled. The true Japanese were still scattered across America in prison camps, accepting their karma with the unflinching loyalty and stoicism of their Japanese heritage.

But Kestrel did not tell Ana his thoughts; he could not, for she would not understand that slanted eyes and silk kimonos did not make her Japanese. Yet she had courage, and she was a sweet warmth in his lap.

Kestrel bent his head until his lips rested on Ana's neck. She pressed more closely to his chest.

The phone rang. Ana made an involuntary sound of rebellion. Kestrel's lips brushed the curve of her ear.

"There is time," he said. "I've waited since I first saw you."

The phone rang, demanding.

Ana shifted in Kestrel's lap. Through the silk of her kimono she felt his heat and desire. Reassured, she smiled and leaned across him to pick up the phone.

"Bueno," said Ana, settling comfortably against Kestrel.

"Bueno, señorita. Como esta?"

Ana's hand tightened on the phone as she recognized the clean, unaccented Spanish of the man who always made her feel like a child. The world and the war returned to her in a cold rush. Her rebellion showed in her voice and in the tension of her body.

"Finn."

A momentary tightening went through Kestrel's body, followed by a deep relaxation that permitted him to focus only on the instant that was before him. He was wholly alert in the presence of his enemy, alive in a way Ana would never understand. He had no doubt that Finn was his enemy. When he had described the man in the Green Parrot to Ana, she had immediately identified Finn. She hated the American, but they met anyway, whenever Takagura had misleading half-truths or cunning lies to pass on to U.S. intelligence agents. Although Ana had not admitted it, Kestrel sensed she was afraid of Finn.

Kestrel listened with Ana as Finn spoke. "I thought you might like to tell me more about why Japan will win the war. Fifteen minutes? Same place?"

"Wait," said Ana. "I'll have to see if Takagura needs me."

Ana covered the phone and waited for Kestrel's response. Her expression was neutral.

Kestrel knew that it was his choice—send Ana to Finn or keep her here and make love to her as she wanted. He needed Ana's cooperation, but even more, he must have her allegiance. Yet he must also have more information about Alamogordo, quickly, and the man called Finn was reputed to know many secrets.

Kestrel lifted Ana out of his lap as if she weighed no more than the telephone she held. Although her expression did not change, Kestrel sensed first her stiffness, then her resignation.

"Yes," said Ana into the phone, her voice flat, "I'm not wanted here."

Kestrel's hand closed over the mouthpiece of the phone. "Tell him one hour." His fingers caressed the nape of her neck, then slowly withdrew.

"Momentito," Ana said, her voice light, almost breathless. "Takagura Omi's friend needs a translator. An hour, Finn. I will meet you in an hour."

Ana hung up before Finn could either agree or object. Behind her, buttons clicked lightly against wood as Kestrel laid his shirt across the table. He unrolled his sleeping mat with a single quick movement.

Juarez
38 Hours Before Trinity

The newspaper rattled as Finn folded it, glanced at his watch, and then at the street. The town square was dulled beneath the weight of heat and time, a weight that dragged on the buildings, blunting adobe corners.

A mélange of smells floated through the open café door. Sun and dust, refried beans laced with chiles, fruit ripe and rotten, an open sewer thick with grit and human excrement, roses in a concealed garden. Finn smelled none of those odors unless he made a special effort. Juarez had toughened his nose in the same way that the sun had thickened his skin. Nor did he notice the flies that skated lazily down shafts of yellow light. Flies and heat and yapping dogs, Juarez in July.

Where was Ana?

Finn stared down the gloomy alley that paralleled the café, dividing it from other businesses. The alley seemed to pause, then unravel itself into paths that twisted around the intricate societies enclosed by eight tong temples, center of Juarez's Oriental colony.

Viewed from the front, the temples were clean, blank and forbidding. They showed nothing of their interior nature. Their only identification was their oddly elegant architecture and the keystones or cornerstones that displayed each temple's name and founding date.

From the outside, Colonia Chino appeared monolithic, but inside it was a warren of factions, rival tongs and nationalities. It whispered its own intrigues, lived its own lies and truths inside the body of Juarez like a benign tumor that had been encapsulated but would never be absorbed by its host.

The self-enclosed Oriental colony had provided Japan with a secure staging area for infiltration, sabotage and spying. It also precluded Finn from entering the colonia to search for Ana. His presence would trip alarms throughout the neighborhood, spreading the word more silently but just as surely as birds in a jungle. It would have been the same if he were Mexican. Outsider.

"Uno más, por favor," said Finn, holding up his empty beer bottle.

"Sí, señor," said the waitress. "The heat, she is terrible, no? Like the burning red hell the Padre talks about."

Finn smiled and nodded and silently disagreed. He

knew that hell was every shade of green.

Where was Ana? Takagura's house was less than a hundred yards away.

She had kept him waiting before, a way of showing her contempt for all things American. He had not been bothered by her disdain. She was Takagura's secretary and confidante, and Takagura ran the Oriental population of Mexico. She was worth waiting for, even though much of what she told him was lies. To him, lies were valuable; they told him what the Japanese considered important enough to try to hide.

The beer was icy against Finn's teeth, a sizzling coldness in his throat. He savored the flavor and chill as he watched the narrow shadows in the alley where Ana would appear. And then she was there, walking toward him, her brilliant silk dress shimmering and lifting like a butterfly in a breeze.

When Ana stepped into the full sun, her face looked startlingly pale, the result of rice powder rather than natural pallor. Her eyebrows were like black arrows slanted above her dark eyes. Her lips were scarlet.

Ana's makeup was less severe, less stylized than that of a Kabuki dancer, although Finn could see that was her model. Her defiant accentuation of racial traits spoke of defensiveness rather than pride or theatrical necessity. Like the Japanese dancers she emulated, she was constrained, dissonant and humorless.

But watching Ana's easy American stride, Finn sensed the irony of her allegiance to Japan, a country where women moved with mincing steps and downcast eyes. Ana moved from dense shadow to brilliant sun with certainty, almost defiance. She was being watched, and knew it.

Finn smiled. Today he would shred that certainty. He

would begin by speaking in Japanese, a language he had never used with her.

"Welcome," Finn said, walking out through the café door. His brief bow was as graceful as his Japanese. "Follow me, please. This café cannot equal your elegance, but the tables are clean and the beer is as cold as a winter moon."

Reflexively, Ana began to return Finn's courtesy in the same language he had used. Then she realized that it was Japanese, not Spanish he had spoken. Startled by the purity and fluency of his speech, she stared at Finn, almost expecting to see Kestrel's dark eyes looking back at her. But this was Finn, not Kestrel. Finn's pale eyes, catlike in their predatory appraisal, watching her. At first she thought his eyes expressionless. Then, gradually, she realized that expression was there, very controlled, a shadow in the depths of his round Western eyes. Emotion so completely controlled was more unsettling than no emotion at all.

Finn saw Ana's discomfort. His smile did not make her feel more at ease. Off-balance, she allowed him to lead her into the café and seat her.

"What do you want?" she demanded in English.

"My words are for you, not for the Mexicans across the aisle drinking beer. Speak Japanese unless you'd prefer the privacy of my house." Finn smiled again. "Of course, no one would be surprised if we went there, just two lovers wanting to spend a little time between the sheets, talking about the softness of a bud's inmost petals."

Ana's flush showed even beneath her white powder. When she tried to stand, to leave, Finn moved so quickly she had no time to resist. His hands held her in the chair. As he bent across the table toward her, he saw that her lips were slightly swollen. There were rosy shadows on her throat. It was obvious that she had come to the café from a lover's bed. No wonder she had been late.

"Which will it be?" said Finn. "English at my house or Japanese here?"

"Here," whispered Ana.

Finn's hand moved with surprising quickness. His fingertip brushed her lips. "Tell your lover not to be so rough next time."

Ana flushed so completely that Finn felt the heat on the skin of her arms. He let go of her, thinking how ill-suited she was for her chosen role as spy. Hatred of America and fluency in five languages had made her invaluable to Taka-gura Omi. But she needed more discipline to be a good covert agent or more cunning to survive being a bad one.

"It doesn't matter," said Finn gently. "The last petal is unfolding. The game is almost over."

"I don't know what you mean about petals and games," said Ana, her voice as rigid as her body.

"It's a shame you aren't a samurai, Ana, or a sparrow hawk. Then you could fly north with me and watch the war end just after midnight tomorrow. Then America, not Japan, will be the true Land of the Rising Sun. Two dawns will come, two dawns within the space of a few hours. What samurai would not kill or die to see that? What sparrow hawk could resist flying there?"

"I don't know what—"

"—I'm talking about?" finished Finn, smiling. "Then listen very carefully, Little Blossom. Listen as though Japan's life depended on it. America has a new ally—the sun. Our sunrises will shake the earth and change the face of the world. I'll think of you when unscheduled dawns rise over Japan and cities vanish in one white instant of fire. Are you listening, Little Blossom?"

Ana was still except for the slight trembling of her lips. "Yes," she whispered, wondering why at this moment Finn should remind her of Kestrel. Then she realized it was Finn's uncanny ability to focus himself completely on the moment that reminded her of her lover. "Yes, I'm listening."

Finn smiled and switched to English. "Don't comfort yourself by thinking I'm crazy. I'm not. I'm simply a man who will watch dawn come twice to an obscure New Mexican peak." He stood in a single movement and leaned over until his lips brushed her perfumed ear. "Goodbye, Ana. You picked the losing side."

Juarez
37 Hours Before Trinity

(Radio transmission received by Kestrel. Decoded.)

REQUEST DENIED. DISREGARD SAN FRANCISCO. PURSUE TEST RUMORS TO ALAMOGORDO. MAJ. GEN. ARISUE

Juarez
37 Hours Before Trinity

Finn stared down the alley that held nothing but sunlight and shadows. The taste of Mexican beer was in his mouth and echoes of the Japanese language in his throat. It had been a long time since he had spoken Japanese.

The sun was hot, yellow-white, its light like a hammer blow. He squinted, pulled his hat lower and crossed the street to the office of the Juarez telephone exchange. In the hot, crowded lobby, he paid his pesos, gave a number in El Paso and went to a booth. The phone was hot to his touch. A woman answered.

"Sarah?"

"Yes."

"Must be at least 102° in the shade today."

"You're getting soft," Sarah said automatically, as she dialed into the trunk line his code word designated. If he had said 89° or 93° or 98° he would have been given a different line.

"May I help you?" asked a polite male voice.

"Once in a blue moon," replied Finn.

Finn heard relays closing, then one ring. The phone was answered immediately.

"Yes."

"That's what I like about you," said Finn as he heard the familiar voice. "You're agreeable."

"And you're negative."

"Affirmative," said Finn, completing the recognition code. "I've set the hook. I'll stay with the fish until I'm sure he's headed in the right direction."

"It would be nice to know exactly where the fish was going."

"I'll stay with him as long as I can. Or would the General prefer me to miss my ride?"

"No. Be on the runway by 2000."

"By 2000? That's cutting it very thin. He may just be crossing the border then. I can't be sure he'll get close enough for our purposes."

"The General is more worried about him getting *too* close."

Finn felt the sweat gather in his palm, then descend his wrist in a slow trickle. "I don't like it."

"Write a memo." Then, "Relax. The General has complete confidence in you."

"Wonder what it feels like," muttered Finn.

"What?"

"Complete confidence."

The voice at the end of the line laughed once, a sound without humor. But Finn did not expect humor from a man whose self-given code name was "Basket Case," a war casualty with neither legs nor eyes nor testicles; just one hand, a voice and a mind that knew every shade of green. Finn hung up and headed out of the telephone office, leaving the voice trapped in the hot black phone.

He drove quickly to his house. In the sandy vacant lot next door a Mexican boy was kicking pebbles with naked brown feet and great intensity. Finn watched for a moment as the child took aim, kicked, and sent a stone clicking against two others. Jorge was alone but not lonely, absorbed in a game no one else understood. His small grunt of satisfaction told Finn that the boy had just scored well.

"Jorge?" said Finn, requesting rather than demanding the boy's attention.

Jorge turned, recognizing the voice. "Hello, Finn."

Jorge carried eight years on his thin shoulders and three times that much in his clear black eyes.

"Ghost has had kittens," said Finn.

Jorge shrugged, but anticipation tugged at the corner of his mouth. "Again?"

"Again. These things happen," continued Finn, sitting on his heels so that his eyes were on a level with the boy's.

"Yes," Jorge said, rubbing a scratch on the back of his left hand. "My mother is the same way."

Finn smiled, but his voice did not change. The cat's well-being was a serious thing to the boy. His family had been too poor to buy milk for the starving gray kitten Jorge had brought home. Finn's oblique intervention had saved the cat's life and the boy's pride.

"Ghost has a hard time with kittens, for she has no husband to help her," Finn said. "But she's used to that by now."

"Yes," agreed Jorge with a sigh. "It's hard on her."

"Ghost could survive by herself," said Finn.

"Yes." The boy seemed to shrink back into himself.

"But," Finn's hand opened, revealing two silver American dollars, "a little canned milk would make it easier for her."

"Yes!" said Jorge, his eyes reflecting the silver shine of the coins.

"I must go for a while, and Ghost can't buy or open cans of milk."

Jorge nodded.

"Will you do that for her?" asked Finn, holding out the two coins.

"Oh yes! But," said Jorge, putting his hands behind his back to lessen the silver temptation of the dollars, "that is too much money. That would buy milk for every kitten in Mexico."

Finn laughed. "There is no other favor," he said, gently pulling the boy's hands to the front of his body and giving him the coins. "While you are at the store, get some milk for your brothers and sisters as well."

"My mother—" began Jorge, closing his hands without taking the coins.

"Your mother," said Finn, "is too pregnant to shop for kittens and milk."

Jorge hesitated. Finn waited.

"Yes," said the boy at last, "she is too much pregnant."

Jorge's hands closed around the coins, one dollar to each brown palm, one smile for each silver dollar. A rare thing, two smiles so close together.

Before the boy could speak, Finn stood up. "Gracia, Jorge. The cat and I thank you."

Finn turned away.

"Señor?"

"Yes?" said Finn, looking back over his shoulder, his eyes pale in the deep shadow of his hat.

"When will you be back?"

Finn smiled but did not answer. He went into the house and began packing, wondering how long it would take Ana's information to reach Kestrel, and what Kestrel would do when he heard about two dawns rising on an "obscure New Mexican peak."

The suitcase snapped shut. Finn grabbed it, locked the house and got behind the wheel of the car. As he started the Ford, he hoped Ana was clever enough to connect "obscure peak" with the mountain's Spanish name—Oscura Peak.

Juarez
23 Hours Before Trinity

The man was past middle age, his skin mottled by time and poverty. His face was lined by grime and sweat, but like many peasants who could not afford sugar, his teeth were still good. His eyes were strange, with an epicanthic fold that was neither Oriental nor quite Indio, but something in between.

Kestrel ran his dirty hands through his hair again, dulling the silver patches at his temples even more. He stared at the driver's license, then at the mirror. Deliberately, he rubbed his thumb across the picture on the license, further blurring it. He compared the mirror's image and the license, which he had insisted must belong to a real person.

The match was not exact, but it was good enough for most purposes. For the rest, if someone looked too closely, the license would be the least of Kestrel's worries.

A shoji slid on its rails with a smooth, secret sound. Kestrel's right hand went to his waist where a hidden knife waited.

"Ana?"

"Yes."

Kestrel's hands returned to the business of making himself look like an Indio peasant. "Any difficulties?"

"No." Ana's voice was lifeless, as it had been since the moment Kestrel said he must go to Alamogordo and she to San Francisco. She closed the shoji behind her. "Nisei Battalion documents are a staple of Mexicali's forgers."

"Are they good?"

"They look real to me," said Ana, but her voice lacked enthusiasm. "They're—" She looked at Kestrel for the first time, astonished by the change. "Kestrel?"

Kestrel laughed and started to touch Ana's cheek. She recoiled instinctively from the rough, dirty hand.

"It's good, neh?" he said, smiling at her.

"Very good."

"Now, tell me what the American said."

Ana told him. "But you must not go to New Mexico," she finished.

Kestrel concealed his impatience. He needed Ana too much to alienate her now. "I'm only an Indio," he said. "Who will notice me?"

"But—"

"And then I'll become a soldier, a loyal member of the Nisei Battalion. If I don't meet you in San Francisco, I'll meet you in Jacame." He looked at her for a long moment. "Japan needs you, Ana. I need you. Will you do what I ask?"

"Yes, I'll—" Her voice thinned. She hesitated, then said, "Yes."

"Good. Now tell me again what you'll do after I leave."

"I'll drive to San Francisco, to my father's old flower shop. I'll be made up to look Mexican." Ana's voice was a monotone that did not wholly conceal her fear. "Refugio's cousins will give me one of their delivery trucks. I'll drive it to Oakland and park at the transfer point by midnight of the 15th. I'll hide in the back of the truck until Refugio comes. Then I'll drive him back to the flower shop. If you aren't there by noon of the 17th, Refugio will . . . kill the woman. His cousins will bury her. I'll drive to Refugio's tunnel and cross into Mexico. If you . . . If you are still missing, I'll take the stolen weapon to Takagura. He'll have the rest of Refugio's money."

"Excellent," said Kestrel. Then, "Don't look so frightened, Ana. No one will be looking for you in America."

"It's not that. It's Finn. You don't know him," she said in a rush. "He was playing with me, smiling and so arrogant and—don't go! It's a trap!"

"Finn would not bother to lure me into America, question me, and kill me. If he wanted me, he would have come for me by now, here, in Mexico."

"But he said 'an obscure peak.' He must have wanted you to know about Oscura Peak."

"Perhaps he underestimated your cleverness at unraveling his game. Perhaps he's so confident that he has become careless."

"Finn?" Ana laughed. "It's a trap!"

"I am samurai." He turned away and washed his hands in a basin. He dried them carefully before he took the forged papers from Ana. He studied them with thoroughness that he gave to all important things. "Yes. Much better than I expeced." He looked up from the papers. "And yours?"

"I have papers under my own name, as well as the name of Ana Ortega." She pulled coupons out of her purse. "For gasoline. Take half of them."

"Your own name?" said Kestrel, taking a second book of coupons she held out.

"They just updated my old papers. No one is paying much attention anymore."

Kestrel measured the bitterness in Ana's voice and wondered if his lovemaking had given her enough to believe in after all.

"Ana, if there were any one but you to go!"

"I know. That's not it. It's not San Francisco."

"Then what?"

"Alamogordo! Finn did everything but give you a map!"

"Ana, Ana," sighed Kestrel. "Did Finn invite you to see the sun rise twice, or were those your words?"

"Finn's."

Kestrel smiled at his opponent's irony. "Then I must go. No samurai could ignore an invitation from a man who is a poet as well as a warrior."

"Finn would know that about you," said Ana bitterly.

Kestrel nodded, a gesture that acknowledged her truth

and closed the subject with one motion. "The uniform. Is it ready?"

Ana unwrapped the package she had carried into the room. "American uniforms are also a Mexicali specialty," she said. Then, whispering, "Don't go."

Kestrel did not answer. He was busy inspecting the uniform of a Nisei soldier. Everything was there—the proper shoulder patches with unit designations. He looked up and smiled.

"This is very good."

Kestrel rewrapped the uniform and packed it in a scuffed suitcase. "You must leave for San Francisco," he said. "You have less than twenty-four hours to get there."

"And you," said Ana. "Where will you go?"

Kestrel smiled. "I have an appointment with the American dawn."

Los Alamos
18 Hours 30 Minutes Before Trinity

(Excerpt of cable received by Gen. Leslie Groves. Decoded.)

AS YOU READ THIS, I AM ON MY WAY TO POTSDAM. . . .

THE GADGET MUST BE READY TOMORROW. I CAN'T DELAY THE CONFERENCE AGAIN. IF YOUR BILLION DOLLAR TOY DOESN'T WORK, WE'LL GO DOWN AS THE BIGGEST FOOLS IN HISTORY.

RUSSIAN TROOPS MASSING ON CHINESE BORDER . . . SKIRMISHES REPORTED, BUT NO "PENETRATION IN DEPTH" YET.

THAT GODDAMNED GADGET BETTER WORK. STALIN WON'T
BE IMPRESSED BY A BUSTED FLUSH—AND NEITHER WILL TOJO.
                                    HARRY S TRUMAN
                                    PRESIDENT, UNITED STATES

Berkeley, California
13 Hours Before Trinity

The phone rang. Vanessa lifted the receiver before the bell
could sound again. "Hello," she said, then nodded at
Masarek.

Refugio had started across the room but Masarek
motioned him to stop with a chopping movement of his
hand. Refugio sat down very slowly, angered at being
ordered around in his own house.

"Good," said Vanessa, too softly for anyone but
Masarek to hear. "And the location?" Vanessa waited,
listening carefully. "Guards?" Pause, then with soft disbelief, "Just one? Are you sure?" She waited, listening.
"After you're finished, don't forget to tell the guard that
another inspector from the lab will check the container
again before it's moved."

Suddenly, Vanessa's face became expressionless. "It
makes no difference *who* will return, or when. Leave the
questions to me and the obedience to you." There was a
long silence. "Don't call here again. You'll get a call at
your home sometime before midnight. Have the ID
ready."

Vanessa's voice became more gentle, but her expression
did not change. "You've done very well, comrade."

Vanessa hung up and said in Russian, "Fool."

"A useful fool, I trust?" answered Masarek in Russian.

"Very. If anyone at Hunters Point questions your credentials, the name 'Grummin' has been added to the roster of the Lawrence Radiation Laboratory as a 'health inspector.' "

"Passwords? Guards?"

Vanessa laughed. "No passwords. One guard."

"Impossible!"

"No, merely subtle. This General Groves is interesting; apparently he understands that one man guards a secret better than a batallion of men." She smiled. "Or maybe it's just that the capitalists are afraid to let their own soldiers too close to one billion dollars in a small can."

"One billion dollars!"

Vanessa smiled, pleased by Masarek's reaction. "It's worth more than that." She moved until she was so close to him that she could smell the residue of tobacco smoke on his skin. "It's the key to the world. Tonight we steal it and then we, personally, are going to present it to Stalin."

Masarek lit another cigaret, frowning around the smoke stinging his eyes. "If the comrade's information is good. . . ." He shrugged. "One guard. Can we trust the information?"

"The comrade was sure. He said, 'It's a *naval base*! What the hell do they need guards for?' "

Masarek grunted. "Just like an intellectual. He thinks because they are at war and wear uniforms they are soldiers. Fool."

Vanessa took Masarek's cigaret, drew a deep breath and returned the cigaret to him. "At least he's a well-briefed fool. Someone from the lab will inspect the Bronx shipment at midnight. The uranium will be stored in Delta warehouse on the southeastern side of the base. The shipment will be inspected again at 0700 of the 16th, after it's loaded aboard the *Indianapolis*. That gives us seven hours to steal the uranium.''

''Why are they inspecting this shipment so often if they don't want to call attention to it?'' asked Masarek.

The question surprised Vanessa. She understood that radioactive materials could be dangerous, but she had seen no need to explain that to Masarek. So long as he followed her orders, there was no need for him to worry.

''He didn't say why.'' Vanessa paused, then added, ''If it were important, he would have told us.''

Masarek cocked his head as though listening to what Vanessa had not said as well as what she had. Then he shrugged, pulled hard on the cigaret, and muttered, ''I don't like depending on intellectuals.''

''They don't allow assassins or even ordinary communists at the Radiation Laboratory,'' Vanessa remarked. ''The Americans are narrow-minded about some things.''

''And stupid about others, it seems. But they did well enough against the Germans.''

''Only after one million Russians died at Stalingrad. Only then did the pig shit Americans think it was safe to open the Second Front. Do they think that Russians died so that Americans could rule the world?'' Vanessa's laugh was humorless. ''Tokyo will be the Americans' Stalingrad. Stealing the Bronx shipment will be the same as killing one million American soldiers!''

Across the room, Refugio and two of his men began talking in Spanish. Masarek watched them for a moment before he turned back to Vanessa.

''When do you want me to kill Refugio?''

''He'll try to kill us in the tunnel,'' said Vanessa, ''or at least to hold us up for more money.''

''Of course. So when do you want him dead? I could kill him now, I suppose, since there is only one guard.''

"No. Later. After we steal the uranium."

Masarek nodded. "The transfer point would be best," he said. "I'll kill the Mexicans when we change vehicles in Oakland. Then we'll drive to the tunnel, cross back into Mexico and have the uranium on the first ship to Russia. Very simple."

"Refugio is not as simple as he looks."

Masarek dropped his cigaret onto the rug, then ground out the ember with a casual twist of his heel.

"I've killed many like him. Cunning, but they die just the same." He saw Vanessa's sideways look at Refugio. The Mexican saw it also; his smile was as insulting as a hand beneath her skirt. "You would like to kill him yourself?" suggested Masarek.

"I would like," said Vanessa, "to put a bullet through his thick black peasant hair into the base of his skull."

Masarek smiled slightly. "I give him to you."

"What about his men?"

Masarek yawned. "They'll be dead before you pull the trigger."

Vanessa smiled and put her hand on Masarek's cheek where the curve of his jaw met his hairline. "Be sure it's Refugio who opens the car door in Oakland. I'd hate to kill you by mistake."

West of Trinity
4 Hours 40 Minutes Before Trinity

Lightning raked the cloud tops and the desert below. Thunder belled so close that it overpowered the sound made by the C-46's laboring engines. Rain fell as though to make up for a thousand years of drought; the drops made a continuous drumming sound. The plane bucked and sideslipped in a pocket of treacherous air.

Finn braced himself in the fold-down seat behind the copilot. The pilot swore in a monotone and fought to keep the plane under control. Lightning burst in a sheet of incandescence that arched from horizon to horizon. In the instant before Finn's eyes reflexively closed, he saw separate drops of sweat stand out on the copilot's forehead. Thunder exploded around the plane, shaking them like dice in a cup.

"—of a bitch!" The copilot's yell emerged from the fading thunder. "You won't be able to see anything in this shit!"

The radio crackled loudly. Earlier, the copilot had turned the volume on full; it was the only way of hearing an incoming message. Each time lightning split the night, the radio went wild with a blast of sound that reminded Finn of the radiation counter stowed beneath his feet.

". . . *me? Over.*" The radio's voice was thin, as though it had been pounded flat by thunder.

The copilot switched the radio to transmit. "This is Blue One," he shouted into the mike. "Repeat last message. Repeat last message. Over."

". . . *is de . . . ceed . . . second . . . target . . . immed . . . you . . . me? . . .*"

The pilot and copilot looked at one another. The pilot shook his head. "One more time."

The copilot leaned over the mike and yelled, "Blue One to Blue Three. Repeat. Repeat. Repeat. Over."

The radio crackled explosively, echoing nearby lightning.

". . . *test is delayed. Proceed to . . . immediately . . . read me? Over.*"

The copilot yelled to Finn, "Did you get that? The test

is delayed. We're supposed to go on to California."

Finn looked at his watch. Almost one-thirty. The test had been delayed twice already; he would be lucky to make it to Hunters Point on time.

"Let's go!" yelled Finn, giving a thumb's up gesture just as lightning turned the cockpit white.

The pilot banked steeply away from the test site, climbing for the relative calm between the squall lines that had been sweeping across the desert from the Gulf. As the co-pilot yelled his understanding of the new orders into the radio, Finn checked the black radiation counter between his feet. It was intact.

Thunder rattled the plane, making his teeth ache. He settled himself in for a long, unpleasant flight.

San Francisco, California
1 Hour 12 Minutes Before Trinity

Chill and wild, the wind off San Francisco Bay gusted down streets darkened by wartime, rattling windows where shards of light glinted between blackout curtains. Some windows had not been covered at all, showing light like great blind eyes. The seamless coastal midnight of 1941 had given way to complacency as people shed the inconveniences of a war they believed they had already won.

Unnoticed by anyone, San Francisco had gradually returned to being a civilian city. Bakery trucks, laundry trucks, cabs, meat trucks, garbage trucks, buses, pimps, whores, cops and thieves competed for space on the city streets.

Among the delivery vehicles moving over streets glistening with a condensed fog was a pale laundry truck with

Chinese ideographs and a small number 7 on the door.
The truck pulled up in the alley behind a Cantonese
restaurant. The driver stretched and slowly got out to make
the last civilian stop on his route, dropping off clean linen
and picking up napkins smelling of ginger and soy sauce.

Masarek moved his head just enough to watch the back
of the restaurant. He was so close to the parked truck that
he could smell oil oozing out of a leak in the crankcase.

The driver's heels grated on the broken surface of the
alley. A rectangle of light bloomed at the back of the
restaurant.

Other than narrowing his eyes, Masarek did not move to
evade the light. He had chosen his clothes and his cover
well; light did not separate him from the surrounding
darkness.

The driver and dishwasher exchanged a few desultory
Cantonese obscenities as clean laundry was traded for
dirty. Masarek waited, poised for the moment when the
restaurant door would close and the sound of deadbolts
slamming home would be loud in the alley's silence.

The rectangle of yellow light vanished. Deadbolts
thumped into place. The driver began closing the van's
rear doors.

Masarek flowed out of hiding with no more sound than
the fog. His right hand covered the driver's mouth at the
exact instant that his stiletto slid between the man's ribs
and pierced his heart.

Death was immediate. There was no time for fear or surprise, escape or error. Masarek heaved the body on top of
tea-stained tablecloths, slammed the van's doors, and
climbed into the driver's seat. The laundryman's death
had taken less than three seconds.

Refugio was hidden where the alley met the street. At

the sound of the driver's door closing, he gathered himself for a rush at the truck, certain that Masarek had somehow missed his quarry.

The truck stopped at the head of the alley. The door on the right opened soundlessly.

"Get in!"

Masarek's hissed command galvanized Refugio and the two men waiting with him.

"In the back!"

One of Refugio's men tripped over the driver's body.

"Madre de Dios! Salvador," hissed Refugio. "You are as clumsy as a boy with his first woman!"

Salvador rolled off the body with a curse, checking his clothes for bloodstains. There were none. The man had died before his heart could pump blood out of the single wound the stiletto had made.

Refugio and Salvador helped the third Mexican, a man named Lopez, to strip the corpse of its uniform shirt. The truck swayed as it turned onto the main street, making the men's work more difficult.

"You," said Refugio, handing the shirt to Lopez, the smallest of the three men.

Lopez looked over the shirt. There was a tiny stain on the back where capillaries had oozed in the instant before the driver's blood pressure had dropped to nothing. Lopez looked from the stain to the man who had killed with such precision.

Refugio followed the glance. He knew what Lopez was thinking; but Salvador was also quick, silent and deadly. And there would be three to Masarek's one.

"Put it on," said Masarek. "You'll drive."

Lopez pulled on the shirt. It still carried the dead driver's warmth. Lopez traded places with Masarek, who went to the back of the truck and crouched, gun in hand, watching everyone.

"Go!" said Masarek. "Quickly!"

Hunters Points, California
29 Minutes Before Trinity

Evans Avenue pointed like an arrow toward the gate at Hunters Point. Inside the mammoth naval shipyard, most streetlights and buildings were properly hooded. Even so, there were occasional islands of illumination. Churned by the wind, rain made ragged patterns in the light.

At the front gate, Shore Patrol sentries hunched inside their peacoats and cursed the wind, the military and the bad luck that had given them duty on such a filthy night. They hardly interrupted their cursing to wave through routine traffic—food and fuel and laundry. The vehicles shuttled back and forth, weaving Hunters Point into the fabric of civilian San Francisco.

The cream-colored van with Chinese ideographs on the door was just one of many vehicles the sentries had seen. Laundry trucks at Hunters Point were as common as Spam in field rations.

"You sure this is the right truck?" asked Lopez as he began to slow for the gate.

"It's number seven," said Refugio in a low voice. "Now be quiet, fool!"

Lopez puffed on his cigaret and tried to ease the strain of the too-small uniform across his shoulders. His dark face was lit by the cigaret glued to his lower lip. There were premature lines at the corners of his eyes from squinting against the perpetual upward curl of smoke. His nervousness showed in the deep red glow as he sucked hard on the cigaret.

Masarek crouched in the back of the truck, watching. He did not expect to be challenged by the guards—it was the right truck, the right guards, and the right night. No enlisted man would search the truck that carried the punchboards and betting slips for all the illegal gamblers in Hunters Point. But there was always the chance of a mistake, a new guard or a greedy guard, or an officer who had decided to inspect the gate. . . .

The Shore Patrol waved through the laundry truck after a single look at the number 7. Masarek relaxed slightly as the truck picked up speed. He would have had a difficult time explaining the three men hidden in the back of the van, and the dead man who did not quite fit into a laundry bag.

Once inside the base, Lopez killed the headlights and slid unobstrusively into the random movements of trucks, staff cars and occasional Shore Patrol Jeeps. The van rolled unchallenged through the darkness, its tires sucking moistly on the wet roadways.

"Second right," said Masarek from the rear of the van.

Refugio translated quickly, not wanting Masarek to know that Lopez understood English. The three men in the back braced themselves as the van turned. Other than clipped directions and translations, no one spoke. The only sound was Salvador's fingernail slowly marking time on the stock of a sawed-off, twin-barreled escopeta that lay across his knee. The shotgun looked small in his thick hands. When he turned to look at Refugio, random light picked out the claw-shaped scar on Salvador's temple.

"Left."

Refugio's fingertips traced and retraced the lines of a silver-plated .45 caliber Army pistol that rested on his knee.

"Right."

Masarek's voice was thin, soft and precise. His head was never still.

"Left." Masarek's head turned, listening.

The van swayed, then evened out as it negotiated the hard left turn. Now the vehicle was threading its way through narrow alleys behind warehouses and armories, alleys piled high with equipment. The supply line that had been created for the invasion of Japan had been filled beyond its capacity. Hundreds of tons of clothing and food, vehicles and fuel drums spilled out of warehouses. Field artillery pieces, self-propelled howitzers and other instruments of war towered over the van. Like millions of men, the supplies waited for a Presidential decision.

"Slow down."

Refugio's translation was like a garbled echo. Lopez eased off the accelerator, guiding the van along ever more cluttered roadways.

"Park on the right."

Lopez backed into a spot behind a ten-foot-high pile of crated gasoline barrels. It was unlikely that the van would be spotted there. Lopez shut off the engine and turned to speak to Refugio.

"Silence."

Masarek's command needed no translation. No one moved or spoke while Masarek listened. He heard nothing but the random pops and pings of metal cooling in the van's engine. He turned his head several times, listening, but he heard neither the soft scuff of his private fears nor the tramp of military feet, nothing but the engine cooling.

Masarek waited. He had survived forty years of Russian

politics by being patient. He listened again, barely able to credit the information that a single guard had been assigned to the canister of 7-235. One man tonight, two men tomorrow to load the canister aboard the *Indianapolis*, and no one on base knew what was inside the unimpressive container.

No one except Masarek.

Masarek's mouth curved slightly beneath his long nose. Using just one guard was clever. Who would believe the canister was valuable, when chocolate bars were better guarded? Yet he could not help wondering if the shipment was not a trap for men such as himself.

Deftly, Masarek screwed a silencer onto his pistol and pushed the gun into the waistband of his dark pants. His American sportscoat covered the gun, and a white shirt now concealed the thin black sweater that had made him invisible in the alley's dank night. Clipped to the shirt pocket was a Lawrence Radiation Laboratory ID badge.

Masarek stood, crouching slightly to avoid the roof of the van. He did not move as quickly or as freely as he once had, but the difference was apparent only to him. He pulled off the back watch cap he wore, revealing the fleshy shine of a receding hairline. Quietly, he eased open the van door.

The narrow aisles between ranks of equipment were empty of all but the rain-wet wind. In the distance, light from an unhooded lamp made a fuzzy sphere of illumination. Masarek set himself against the wind and stepped onto the pavement. After a final, long moment of listening between gusts of wind, he walked toward a solid black rectangle squatting across the night. Several thin strips of light revealed the presence of ill-fitting doors.

As soon as Masarek stepped down, Refugio began counting.

Masarek walked away from the truck without a backward look. In his hand was a voltmeter and an empty battery pack. Both pieces of equipment were useless, but the guard would not know that until it was too late.

The front door of the warehouse swung open with a sound of tin scraping over cement. Masarek disappeared.

Refugio counted to fifty, then signaled to Salvador. He left the van in a rush and stole along the warehouse to a padlocked rear door. Heavy wirecutters gleamed like mercury in his big hands. He waited for a gust of wind to rattle the warehouse, then lifted the cutters. Steel parted with a clicking sound. Salvador held his breath and sweated.

Nothing moved but the wind.

Five seconds after Salvador vanished inside, Refugio slid through the open door of the warehouse. Lopez followed. The door shut behind him with a slight snick.

The unshielded light at the far end of the warehouse pushed long, irregular shadows out of the heaped-up machinery and cartons. Refugio and his men merged with the shadows filling one side of the warehouse. Whatever noise the men made was covered by the wind prowling outside.

At the far end of the warehouse was a small storeroom created by partitioning off a corner of the building. A sentry in green fatigues sat on a chair beside the padlocked door of the storeroom. An M-1 carbine lay across his lap. Deliberately, Masarek let his feet scrape on the concrete floor. The sentry's head snapped up.

"Filthy night, isn't it?" said Masarek above the sudden drumroll of rain on the tin roof.

"What the hell are you doing here?" said the sentry, more surprised than alarmed.

"I'm Grummin, from the lab. Didn't they tell you?" he held up the voltmeter. "I'm supposed to check the can again. You want to see some ID?''

Masarek approached the sentry with a sure, soundless stride. With one hand, he unclipped the badge on his shirt pocket. The sentry held out his hand for the ID. The badge was cool in his palm, shining with reflected light. The sentry compared Masarek's face to the picture on the badge.

At the last instant, the sentry sensed something was wrong. He started to raise his gun. There was a blur of movement as the edge of Masarek's hand slashed across the sentry's throat. The blow was deflected by the man's desperate twist, so that he was stunned rather than killed outright. He retched convulsively, trying to breathe through a crushed throat.

Masarek's gun extended from his hand like a silver finger. The report was shockingly soft, almost inaudible beneath the sound of rain. The bullet exploded in the sentry's brain, killing him before he could blink.

"Quickly!" said Masarek, his voice quiet yet urgent, signaling Refugio forward with a curt motion of the gun.

Refugio and his men stepped out of the shadows. For the next few minutes they would be wholly vulnerable, sharing a warehouse with a murdered sentry and a Top Secret shipment.

Masarek grabbed the sentry, holding him upright while he pulled the back of the dead man's peacoat over the back of the metal chair. When he let go, the sentry stayed upright, held by the rigid chair inside his jacket. With a quick jerk, Masarek pulled down the sentry's watch cap so that the tiny black circle in the center of his forehead did not show. When Masarek was finished, the sentry appeared to be staring off into the distance, wide-eyed, unblinking.

"Wirecutters."

Masarek's command was soft, yet Lopez leaped forward

as though cut by a whip. He took the wirecutters from Salvador and went to the padlocked storeroom door. His hands shook. The wirecutters turned uselessly and slipped off the padlock's case-hardened loop. Masarek took the cutters, shifted their grip to the softer metal of the hasp and dispatched the lock in one neat stroke.

A rectangle of hard light from the warehouse expanded silently across the tiny room. In the center of the light squatted a small cylinder. Only Masarek knew that its code name was Bronx and that it was the key to the world.

Refugio stepped into the room, unable to believe that there was nothing more inside it than this unimpressive little garbage can.

"Is that all?" said Refugio, gesturing contemptuously at the canister. "That's not big enough to hold two million dollars in gold."

"No," agreed Masarek, "it isn't."

"You said—"

"I said nothing about gold." Masarek's smile increased until its cruelty became unmistakable. "Fool. That ugly little can cost one billion dollars."

"Hijo," whispered Refugio, awed by an amount that transcended even his avarice. "Diamonds?"

For an instant, Masarek's contempt gleamed out of his shadowed eyes. But when he spoke, his voice was neutral. "Not diamonds. Power."

"I don't understand," said Refugio. "What—"

"You aren't being paid to understand. Take the can to the truck."

Masarek stepped back, trying to keep his elation from showing. He had already said too much, but it did not matter. Refugio and his men would be dead before they could give away any secrets.

At Refugio's signal, Salvador stepped up, gripped the

canister's handle, and was nearly pulled off of his feet. The canister contained 200 pounds of lead shielding. Masarek watched Salvador's veins thicken and pulse across his forehead until the claw-shaped scar was crimson. The canister rocked, lifted, then settled with a clang onto the cement floor.

''Get back,'' Masarek said.

Salvador stepped back, watching contemptuously as the smaller man tested the canister's weight. Masarek could barely rock the can. He stared at it, assessing the unexpected barrier it represented.

Even if they could lift the can, its awkward, unexpected bulk would slow them dangerously. Worse, once Refugio and his men were dead, Masarek and Vanessa would not be able to move the canister by themselves.

''Open it,'' said Masarek, stepping back.

Salvador worked over the heavy latches that secured the lid of the canister. They opened stiffly. With a grunt, Salvador lifted off the heavy lid. A piece of silver-white metal with the blunt-nosed shape of a bullet gleamed inside the thick-walled canister. Though the piece of metal was barely bigger than Salvador's fist, it was surprisingly heavy.

Carefully, Salvador lifted out and set aside the hunk of metal. It wobbled on the concrete floor, then settled on its blunt nose.

The next piece inside the can was a plug of slate-colored metal. Beneath the plug was a second piece of pale metal, nearly three times the size of the first piece. It was spherical and contained an indentation the size and shape of the blunt bullet.

Salvador set the larger sphere next to the smaller one. He did not notice the faint blue glow that licked over the facing surfaces of the spheres.

Masarek looked at the three pieces of metal and decided quickly to leave the cylinder. Vanessa had spoken only of the two white pieces of metal.

"Tell Lopez to get the small piece," said Masarek. "Salvador, the large one. No," he said, as Refugio bent to retrieve the dark cylinder. "We don't need that one. It will just get in the way."

The vague blue glow died as Lopez removed the smaller piece of pale metal. Salvador picked up his piece awkwardly.

"Madre," he muttered in Spanish, "it's as warm as a woman's breast."

"What did he say?" snapped Masarek.

Refugio shrugged. "Nothing. It feels to him like a woman's breast."

Masarek made a sound of disgust. "Tell them to move quickly. If someone finds us now, we're as dead as that sentry."

They hurried to the van, drove quickly between rows of weapons, then headed toward the gate. Before the rain stopped, the laundry truck with Chinese ideographs and the number 7 on its door left Hunters Point as easily as it had entered.

Alamogordo Test Range
Trinity Site Base Camp
7 Minutes Before Trinity

The desert was cold and black beneath ragged clouds. It had rained intermittently through the night, and lightning had walked along the stretch of land known as Jornada del Muerto. Journey of Death.

Nine miles from Ground Zero, General Groves waited in a small bunker. A short distance away, Dr. Robert Oppenheimer and his senior staff paced in other bunkers, trying not to show what the delays had cost their nerves.

The test should have been over, success or failure measured on a thousand instruments; but nothing was ended, nothing settled. Rare summer showers had delayed the 0200 test and then the 0300 test, stretching men's control, making them overreact to distant thunder.

General Groves waited, outwardly impassive. Earlier he had marched Oppenheimer up and down the base camp, trying to relax the brilliant, nervous scientist. Relaxation was impossible. Each flurry of cold rain, each delay, had heightened the tension until Groves decided to test the bomb at 0530, come hell or high water.

He regretted that the weather would keep one of Colonel Tibbets' men from overlying the site in a B-29, but the test itself was more important than the flight. Tibbets would just have to wait until Japan to see what kind of air turbulence was generated by an atomic bomb.

Though it was futile in the darkness, Groves found himself peering toward the 100-foot-high steel tower. Suspended inside that tower was a plutonium bomb, impervious to the fears and aspirations of men, illuminated by the random brilliance of lightning.

A man stood next to Groves, staring into the dark as the General was staring. A match flared, then seemed to divide in two as the end of the man's cigaret ignited. The man was dressed in civilian clothes, although his posture was military. Groves knew his name was Lattimer, but had never learned his first name.

"I still don't like it," said Lattimer. "We bust our asses keeping this a secret, and then you pass information to a goddamn Jap spy. I hope Finn got him in real close. Be the last thing that bastard sees this side of hell.''

Groves turned toward Lattimer, whose face was suddenly illuminated by the glow of a cigaret. ''You better hope Kestrel survives. Then the war hawks on Tojo's cabinet will have something new to think about. Or would you rather end the war one Jap at a time?''

''No. I've been there, General. Anything is better than that.'' The man's cigaret glowed as he took a long breath. His hands dropped to the heavily smoked glasses he had been issued. ''Christ! Why don't they get this show on the road!''

Alamogordo Test Range
3 Minutes Before Trinity

Kestrel sat in his parked car, a darker shade of black against the desert night. Each minute was one closer to sunrise, and the near-certainty that he would be discovered, yet he waited with unflinching patience.

Less than twenty minutes until dawn. Kestrel wondered if the test had been screened from him by ragged curtains of unseasonable rain. If so, the weapon was not what he feared and dawn would come only once today.

With narrowed eyes, Kestrel examined the surrounding land once more, seeing little but varying densities of black. Between ragged clouds, the stars in the east were changing subtly, more mecury than diamond, dulling by increments too small for the human eye to measure. Slowly, land solidified, blacker than the night. A long western wind blew, bringing scents of rain and earth and distance.

An intuition of movement brought Kestrel's eyes to the southern horizon. Nearby, dark gray against the dense pre-dawn sky, a nighthawk cruised, alert for the least sound or movement that would reveal its prey. For an instant longer the raptor flew in swift calligraphy against the sky, then the bird vanished as silently as it had come.

Kestrel opened the door of the car carefully, knowing how far sound carried across desolate land. He got out and leaned lightly against the car's cold metal fender.

Reflexively, he stretched the long muscles of his legs and then the shorter muscles at the back of his neck where tension had clamped down, impeding the flow of blood. He took a slow breath, filling his lungs with the sharp, clean air of the New Mexican desert. Then he stepped away from the car, moving with a speed and silence that recalled the nighthawk, relaxing as his body lifted and turned in stylized exercises that had been old before America was discovered or named.

Tension drained out of Kestrel's body, leaving him both alert and calm. Slowly he searched the land again, looking toward the unborn dawn where stars paled, looking toward a horizon that was still concealed by dark and distance.

A great white blister of light burst into searing incandescence along the eastern horizon. Kestrel's eyelids snapped shut even as his head turned aside, but darkness did not come to him. The explosion had burned indelibly into his retinas, creating an afterimage of shimmering purple. Pain scalded his eyes and he was afraid that he was blind, condemned to a lifetime of seeing unearthly brightness, punishment for daring to look into the searing white center of light. Long seconds hung like souls in judgement. He forced his eyes to open and learned he was not blind, and then wished he were.

The raw white light was like a thousand suns burning as one, or a single new sun burning a thousand times closer to earth.

White light thickened, turning into yellow, and a column of clouds churned frantically away from the desert floor. A blazing circle of orange formed at the top of the boiling column. Nearby clouds bloomed an eerie violet, lit from beneath by an uncanny dawn.

The silence was absolute, awesome, a world holding its breath while the future irrevocably sheered away from the past. Even as Kestrel felt a sensation of warmth like sunlight over his body, he realized that he was counting seconds, had been counting since the first searing white instant, trying to measure his distance from chaos. With each silent second he numbered, his fear increased. The explosion had been so far away that sound had not yet reached him. He had been blinded, cowed, and he had yet to hear the column's voice.

Nearly a minute later came the sound of sky compressed into a terrible rolling thunder. The violent column of cloud still rose, carrying with it a distinctive crown. Kestrel felt the heat and the light and the thunder and could not believe that he was at least ten miles away from the explosion.

A vast exhalation of wind streamed over him, lifting his hair and pressing his shirt against his sweating body while his lips soundlessly shaped incantations he had thought lost with childhood. Only when he realized that the wind was coming from the east instead of the west did he really believe what he had seen. At that same moment he also realized that his body was poised in futile fighting reflex, one foot slightly forward, hands extended, fingers rigid.

But no man could fight the sun.

Kestrel stood alone on the dirt road, transfixed by the furious column that still clawed upward, a column capped by an unearthly crown, silent again after the shock waves had expanded past him out into the desert. Gradually the greenish light faded, superseded by a distant sun's light growing calmly, silently, out of the east.

As though freed by the second dawn, Kestrel spun toward his car, unable to think coherently, knowing only that he had seen the future and it was American, not Japanese, a future without pride or ritual or tradition. Terribly new.

Moscow
5 Minutes After Trinity

(Excerpt from NKVD radio log. Decoded.)

AMERICANS EXPLODED ATOMIC BOMB. OUR AGENT WAS NOT AT TRINITY SITE. DETAILS TO FOLLOW.

Alamogordo Test Range
Trinity Site Base Camp
25 Minutes After Trinity

The atomic cloud churned upward until it was eight miles tall, a pillar of gold burnished by sunrise. Groves watched the culmination of Manhattan Project with a feeling of awe and exhilaration that had not diminished in the twenty-five minutes since the atomic bomb had blown apart itself, the night, and a square mile of desert. That huge, boiling column vindicated every argument he had made, every dollar he had spent, every man he had broken with his relentless demands. The atomic cloud was awesome, beautiful; it towered like a god over the men who gathered at its feet.

"I wonder if Moses followed something like that to the Promised Land," said one of the technicians.

There was no answer, nor did the man expect one.

Dr. Oppenheimer looked at the awesome column and its tumultuous crown and was reminded not of the Old Testament, but of the Bhagavad Gita: *I am become death, the destroyer of worlds*.

Nearby, Lattimer measured the towering signature of the bomb. "Jesus Christ on a crutch. You might as well tell me to keep the Mississippi River a secret."

General Groves shook his head. "It doesn't matter now." His voice was confident, almost exultant. "The war's over. One of those bombs and Japan will be finished."

Lattimer dragged on his cigaret and blew out smoke in a long sigh. "Maybe. But it will take at least two atomic bombs. The Japs won't believe the first one. Hell, *I* don't believe it and the goddamn thing is standing on my goddamn toes!" He sighed again and ground out his cigaret butt. "At least two bombs, General. It's just flat fucking unbelievable the first time."

Groves looked at Lattimer, the voice of the past, a gun soldier who could not read the future even when it consumed the very sky in front of him. Groves turned back to the mushroom cloud that changed as he watched, transforming itself as it had transformed the world. He nodded his head, satisfied. The general who had never been in a shooting war had accomplished something all the gun soldiers in the world had not been able to do—he had given his country a victory.

Alamogordo Test Range
Trinity Site
33 Minutes After Trinity

(Top Secret memorandum to Secretary of war Henry L. Stimson.)

At 0530, 16 July 1945, in a remote section of the Alamogordo Air Base, New Mexico, the first full-scale test was made of the implosion type atomic fission bomb. For the first time in history there was a nuclear explosion. And what an explosion!

Maj. Gen. Leslie R. Groves

Washington D.C.
47 Minutes After Trinity

(Cable sent to President Truman at Potsdam Conference. Not encoded.)

PATIENT OPERATED ON THIS MORNING. DIAGNOSIS NOT YET COMPLETE BUT RESULTS SEEM SATISFACTORY AND ALREADY EXCEED EXPECTATIONS. LOCAL PRESS RELEASE NECESSARY AS INTEREST EXTENDS GREAT DISTANCE. DR. GROVES PLEASED. HE RETURNS TOMORROW. I WILL KEEP YOU POSTED. END

(Reply. Not encoded.)

I SEND MY WARMEST CONGRATULATIONS TO THE DOCTOR AND HIS CONSULTANT. END

San Francisco
1 Hour After Trinity

Sunrise rarely came to San Francisco in the summer, except in a gradual, almost imperceptible increase of gray light diffused through fog banks couched on steep hills around the Bay. Suspended in damp swirls of earthbound clouds, the Bay Bridge's curves and thrusts of steel supported traffic that thickened with the light.

Military traffic had once been treated with deference, but now olive drab trucks and Navy blue Jeeps had to butt and shoulder with civilian vehicles, their passengers eager to leave the war behind. The sound of the struggle tumbled off the bridge and down to Oakland's dirty industrial waterfront like a harsh rain.

The cacophony scraped Vanessa's nerves. She moved restively in the back seat of her parked car, watching through mist for the pale shape of a Chinese laundry truck. She adjusted the dark blue scarf that hid her bright hair. From the outside of the car she was invisible.

The distant bob of a flashlight warned Vanessa that a night watchman from one of the nearby factories was making another indifferent round. The presence of Vanessa's car did not excite any interest. There were always private and commercial vehicles parked at random along the street and in parking lots, waiting for jobs or for gas ration coupons or money or spare parts. Vanessa had watched each of the vehicles carefully when she first arrived, but had seen no one.

Absently, Vanessa rubbed her neck where the dark navy sweater chafed her skin. She wore no makeup. Her face was a blank, an artist's canvas ready to hold whatever would be painted on.

Tonight, a plain face suited Vanessa's purposes. On other nights, a meticulously gilded face had served her well. For herself, she did not care. She had been born into the wealth of an English merchant family, but the predictable turns of such a life—marriage, children, church, bowing to male desires six days a week and to a male God on the seventh—repelled her. Beauty had given her a weapon against men, a weapon that she used with equal measures of cruelty and contempt.

When making and breaking romances no longer excited her, Vanessa had moved easily to affairs of the mind. First Fabian socialism, then Marxism, then radical communism attracted her, each one more exciting than the last, and more dangerous.

A man who called himself Melinkov had recruited Vanessa for the NKVD, using a combination of ruthless intellectual and sexual domination. She rarely thought of Melinkov now; the memory of her subjugation was uncomfortable. Yet she owed him much. He had taught her about human weakness.

Slitted headlights flashed as a vehicle turned onto the waterfront. Vanessa sat back far enough not to be picked out by the hard light. Traffic was thicker than she had expected for the hour, a fact which pleased her. The laundry van and dark coupé would not attract any notice.

Blend in. Don't stand out. That was what both Moscow and London had taught her. She never forgot it.

Another set of lights, set wider and higher, brought Vanessa fully alert. The momentary surge of adrenaline stained and then further bleached her cheeks as a pale van came toward her out of the brilliant halo of light from an unhooded streetlamp. Automatically, Vanessa ducked, her fingers wrapped around the grip of a pistol hidden beneath the blanket that both concealed and warmed her.

The van rattled by without slowing. On its side, the inelegant shapes of a plumber's helper and a Stilsen wrench crossed in unconscious parody of the U.S.S.R.'s Hammer and Sickle.

Slowly, Vanessa let out her breath and settled back into the seat. She allowed herself one brief glance at the radium-bright face of her watch.

Five thirty-five.

They were late. No, not late. No time had been set for the rendezvous except after dawn and before eight o'clock. She looked up from her watch. Her blue eyes were intent on the street, her right hand warming the metal grip of her silenced pistol, waiting for Refugio.

Oakland, California
1 Hour 19 Minutes After Trinity

Ana looked at her watch for the seventeenth time since the last car had passed her hiding place inside the flower truck that had once belonged to her father and now belonged to Refugio's cousin. Five forty-eight. Barely thirty seconds passed before she again peered at the glowing, blue-green dial. Daylight was coming on, but even more slowly than time was passing.

Her hand moved to yank aside the dark curtain separating the back of the van from the front, but she restrained herself. Her arm dropped to her side. Radium lines leered up from her wrist. The second hand seemd frozen in place.

With a small sigh halfway between fear and impatience, Ana wriggled further back between the tall wicker baskets that held thick bouquets of flowers. The rank odor of daisies and the too-sweet smell of dying roses choked her.

She beathed shallowly through her mouth, blaming the dense smells for her sweating palms; nausea coiled like a snake in her stomach.

She hated being back in America. She hated the stale wet waterfront air. She hated the flower van, its memories and its tightness and the darkness where roses overwhelmed her. Most of all she hated herself for being terrified of the moment when Refugio would kill Masarek and drag the blond woman into the truck.

How would Kestrel question the English spy?

Ana decided not to watch. She did not have to see any of it. Kestrel had told her only to bring the van to this place and then hide in the back until Refugio came. The van's open engine compartment would answer any questions—obviously the vehicle had broken down and was waiting for a tow.

She had done what Kestrel asked. Now she must wait, and she was very bad at waiting. "Just like an American," Kestrel would say if he could see her impatience. But she was *not* American. She was Japanese, and therefore patient.

Ana leaned against the cold metal side of the van. The funeral smell of roses settled over her.

Trinity Site
2 Hours After Trinity

Lattimer signaled Groves urgently. The General, who had been congratulating project technicians and enjoying his triumph, was tempted to ignore the sign, but something about Lattimer's tense posture compelled attention. Groves walked over to him.

"Well, what is it?"

"Admiral Purnell's office, sir, in San Francisco," said Lattimer, indicating the phone on the desk. When Groves picked up the receiver and began to speak, Lattimer interrupted. "General, if I were you, I would clear the whole area."

Groves studied the security man, first puzzled and then alarmed. Lattimer's anxiety was contagious.

"Sir," said Lattimer. "There's a problem with the Bronx shipment. Please let me clear the room."

Groves could feel the tension now, a tightness beneath his rib cage. With his right hand, he unconsciously touched the left side of his chest, probing for the buried knot of fear.

He waited while Lattimer herded people out of the office. As soon as the door closed, Groves turned to the phone.

"Groves speaking. What the hell is going on?"

The answer was fuzzed by the patchwork of connections between San Francisco and Trinity Site, but Admiral Purnell's words were clear.

"I was hoping you could tell me, General. You remember those mysterious packages you sent to me for immediate delivery elsewhere?"

"Yes," snapped Groves. The tension in his chest increased, making it hard for him to breathe.

"Someone apparently couldn't wait for Christmas. One of the packages was opened."

"The big one?" said Groves, thinking how easy it would be to sabotage the bomb's fifteen-foot-long casing with all its wiring, timers and fuses.

"No. The small package. The canister."

"Jesus God!" Groves swallowed, trying to suppress his fear and fury. "Anything missing?"

"How would I know?" asked the Admiral coolly. "No one told me what was in the package in the first place."

"What's left of the package?" Groves' voice was thin with the effort of staying calm.

"The can, its top and a metal cylinder that fitted inside."

"One piece? *Just one?*"

"Yes."

"What color is the piece?"

"What color!" exploded the Admiral. "Dark-god-damn-gray! General, an eighteen-year-old ensign was murdered! Now by God you are going to tell me what the hell is going on!"

Groves did not answer. He could not. His world had just imploded like the spherical charge of a plutonium bomb. His plans, his country's plans, a world given back to gun soldiers who would spend millions of lives to invade islands defended by fanatics. And Russia—Russia hovering like a vulture at a feast.

"Oh God," he groaned, seeing the morning's victory shattered. "*Oh my God.*" He tried to breathe but could not. His chest was held in a vise of pain, his mind paralyzed by the rapid swing from victory to catastrophe. "How did it happen?"

"I don't know," snapped the Admiral. "The theft and murder occurred between 0200 and 0630, Pacific War Time."

Groves glanced at his watch. The uranium had been stolen at almost the same moment the atomic bomb had been detonated. He wondered whether the irony was accidental or purposeful. The thought that his enemies were laughing at him broke his paralysis. He began to think again, to take command.

"Let me talk to Finn."

"His plane spent most of the night ducking thunderstorms," said Purnell. "I sent a man over to Alameda Air Station to pick him up. He'll call you as soon as he's on the ground."

Groves swore viciously.

"Finn takes over the investigation the instant he gets to Hunters Point," he continued. "You will give him every possible assistance. You will treat his every suggestion as coming direct from the President—which it does." Groves paused, staring blindly out of the bunker, seeing an atomic cloud spread across the sky. "Call the local FBI office. We're going to need every agent they have. Tell them what you know. I'll call Hoover myself."

"Hold it, General. My Shore Patrol and Naval Intelligence boys are pretty damn good and—"

"No. You will do nothing but what I told you."

There was a long silence. Then Purnell said, "The FBI will insist on knowing what's missing."

"They can insist until their jaws lock. Whether or not they find out is up to the President."

"I see," said Purnell. He cleared his throat. "You'll put all those orders in writing, of course."

"Of course. But not even the Joint Chiefs of Staff have the security clearance to read them."

There was another long silence. Only the hiss of static told Groves that the line was still open.

"Is there anything else, General?"

"Put the package back together and sail at 0800 as ordered," said Groves brusquely. "With one difference. Finn won't be sailing with you. He'll stay behind and find out what the hell happened."

"You're sure his security clearance is up to the job?"

Groves ignored the sarcastic question.

"Thanks for the help, Admiral. The next time I want something delivered, I'll use the Army."

General Groves broke the connection, sat down in a desk chair and immediately began to dial another number. After the third try, he gave up. His hands were shaking too much to continue. Lattimer took the phone from him.

"What number, sir?"

"Washington. Hoover. Federal Bureau of Investigation. Goddamn everything to *hell*!"

Lattimer wiped the sweat off his lips and began to dial.

Juarez
2 Hours 7 Minutes After Trinity

Takagura Omi picked up the receiver, silencing the telephone's strident ring. At the moment, the patriarch of Mexico's Oriental population was alone in his office, waiting for this call. Kestrel's voice came to him across the wire, distorted by distance and emotion. He spoke rapid Japanese.

"Just before dawn," said Kestrel, "my host staged an incredible event. I was blinded by the light, deafened by the sound and felt heat as from a rising sun. I was at least ten miles away from the event. *It was like nothing ever before seen on earth.*"

Takagura waited, but Kestrel said no more. With a sigh, Takagura spoke. "Are you sure Japan has seen nothing like it? Not even the resemblance between baby and adult?"

"Japan has nothing like what I saw. Please advise our father that a new sun rose this morning, and it rose on a new world. Old ideas of honor and ignominy must be examined in the light of the new sun. Do you understand me?''

"Are you advising our father to bow to a barbarian dawn?''

"Even samurai can't fight the sun.''

Potsdam
2 Hours 13 Minutes After Trinity

(Cable received by President Truman. Decoded.)

URANIUM STOLEN FROM HUNTERS POINT. REPEAT. URANIUM STOLEN. WILL KEEP YOU ADVISED. MAJ. GEN. LESLIE GROVES

(Reply. Decoded.)

FIND THAT URANIUM BY 0530, 18 JULY, OR I WILL BE FORCED TO MAKE GO DECISION FOR FINAL STAGES OF OPERATION DOWNFALL. ONCE I HAVE DONE THAT, THERE IS NO TURNING BACK. REPEAT. FIND URANIUM BY 0530, 18 JULY, NEW MEXICO TIME, OR MANHATTAN PROJECT WILL BE NOTHING BUT A FOOTNOTE IN THE HISTORY OF WORLD WAR II. PRESIDENT HARRY S TRUMAN

(Reply. Decoded.)

RESPECTFULLY REMIND MR. PRESIDENT THAT BOMBING IS NOT SCHEDULED FOR SEVERAL WEEKS. PLEASE GIVE US MORE TIME TO RECOVER URANIUM. MAJ. GEN. LESLIE GROVES

(Reply. Decoded.)

ONLY A HORSE'S ASS WOULD GO TO WAR WITH ONE BOMB.
DO WHATEVER YOU HAVE TO. BUT RECOVER URANIUM BY
0530 OF JULY 18. IF YOU DON'T, THE SHOW WILL GO ON WITH-
OUT YOU.

THAT IS FINAL. REPEAT. FINAL. PRESIDENT HARRY S TRUMAN

Washington, D.C.
2 Hours 26 Minutes After Trinity

"General Groves is on the line now, sir."

J. Edgar Hoover's manicured hand closed over the phone. Although he had rushed to his office after receiving the President's extraordinary call, Hoover was dressed to the same exacting standard he required of his agents.

"Good morning, General." Hoover's voice was moderate, his diction as precise as the crease in his pants. "The President told me you would give your complete cooperation in the Bureau's investigation of the incident at Hunters Point."

"You must have had a fuzzy connection, Mr. Hoover."

"What?"

"The FBI is cooperating with *me*, not the other way around."

Groves' voice was gruff and uncompromising. He was one of the few officials in Washington who did not owe J. Edgar Hoover the time of day.

"The President," said Hoover coldly, "didn't tell me what he needed the FBI to investigate. My men are the best in the world, General, but they must at least know the nature of the crime they are to solve."

"Theft of a highly secret material."

"Yes. Well . . . ?"

Groves said nothing.

"What, precisely, was stolen?"

"Until ten minutes ago, there were four men in the United States who had the security clearance to answer your question. I just gave official clearance to a fifth. His name is Finn. He's in charge of the Hunters Point investigation. He'll tell your agents what he thinks they need to know in order to help him."

"That's arrogant nonsense! I can't send my agents on a Top Secret snipe hunt when I don't even know—"

"Can't or won't?" cut in Groves. "The President told you to cooperate. Who's running this country—you or Truman?"

"The President, of course!" snapped Hoover. "Not you."

"At least we agree on who's President. Now you just hang up and get on the telephone to Potsdam and let President Truman explain what *his* FBI agents can or can't do."

Over California
2 Hours 26 Minutes After Trinity

The pitch of the C-46's engines changed slightly, waking Finn. He stretched stiffly and looked out the window. Beneath the plane's nose, night had dissolved into luminous gray. He tapped the copilot's shoulder.

"How long?"

"About twenty minutes." He looked at Finn's jeans

and boots, then at his face. "Uh, should I be calling you, 'sir'?"

"Don't bother." Finn flexed his body, trying to restore circulation to stiff muscles. "How soon?"

"Half an hour, at most. I'm already picking up commercial radio from San Franc. Uh, I want to thank you for not throwing up all over the place back there. We did the best we could, but it was a sure-enough bastard." He motioned toward a spare set of earphones hanging from a clip. "Catch up on the world. The news is just coming on."

Finn pulled on the headphones. The reception was scratchy, but the level unaccented voice of the newscaster came through clearly.

"*. . . Truman arrived yesterday in Potsdam for a summit meeting that most analysts agree will set the shape of the postwar world. His meetings with English and Soviet leaders begin later today.*"

Finn smiled to himself, imagining what Truman would tell Stalin about the atomic bomb.

"*In news closer to home, Congress begins debate today on aid for veterans. In New Mexico, a munitions dump exploded with a flash that was seen fifty miles away and a boom that was heard five times as far. No one was hurt.*"

Finn's pulse raced and the words of the newscaster faded as he lifted off the headset, staring at the earphones without seeing them. That was no ammo dump that had exploded. There was not enough ammunition in the entire state of New Mexico to account for a blast that could be heard for 250 miles. Manhattan Project had given birth today, spectacularly. He tried to calculate the explosive power involved, but gave up, accepting Groves' estimate of 20,000 tons of TNT. There was only one kind of target big enough to warrant such a bomb—a city. Manhattan's child was raw, awesome power, power intended to terrify an enemy into submission.

He hoped it would do just that. He hoped that children would never again rain down into the sea. The death of a city was a terrible price to pay for the end of the war, but was a lesser evil than an invasion that killed millions by ones and twos and drove mothers to destroy their own children.

Finn left the disembodied newsman's voice dangling from a cockpit clip. He returned to his bench and dozed against the wall, dreaming in shades of green, a familiar dream, where children struggled and screamed silently but still could not fly.

The tires shrieked as the plane touched the runway at Alameda Air Station outside of Oakland. A crisp seaman met him at the foot of the ladder.

"Captain Finn," he said, saluting. "I have a message for you from Code Name Relief."

Finn, expecting to hear of the bomb's success, yawned and said, "Give it to me."

"The message is: 'Someone opened the oyster. The pearl is gone.'"

Adrenaline flashed through Finn's body, burning away the drugged residue of a sleepless night. The world narrowed to a single instant—now. He leaned toward the sailor. "Repeat that."

"Yes, sir," said the sailor, backing away from Finn. He repeated the message with the precision of a man used to relating nonsense codes. "'Someone opened the oyster. The pearl is gone.'" He waited. When Finn made no further demands, the sailor added, "Here is a new set of orders, sir. You're supposed to call this number on the base. If you'll follow me, there's a phone right off the flight apron.''

Finn followed automatically. He did not see the buildings or hear the planes taking off. His whole being was focused on a single question: *Who had taken the uranium?* Kestrel? No, he had not had enough time to get from the test to Hunters Point. Masarek? Finn thought of the cold, competent Russian. He had the nerve, but not the resources to steal the bomb by himself. If it was Masarek, he must have had help. Refugio, certainly. But Refugio did not have the vision or the resources for such an incredible theft. What of the blond woman who had been seen with him? Was she more than his mistress? Was it she who had planned the theft?

"Sir. The phone," said the sailor, holding out the receiver. He looked nervously at Finn, then backed away so that he could not overhear what was said.

Finn took the phone. He dialed the number on the slip of paper. He identified himself and listened to random clicks as contacts closed and relays opened. He guessed who he would be talking to even before he heard Groves' voice.

"What the hell happened?" said Finn. "Do you know anything beyond what was in the message?"

"Empty canister in the Delta warehouse," said Groves. "One dead sailor on the floor beside the can."

"Just one? How many guards were there?"

"One!" exploded Groves. "Hunter's Point is a fucking *military base*! Why the hell should I assign a platoon of guards on a military base! All that would do is call attention to what should have been the biggest fucking secret since the date of the Second Coming!"

Finn understood Groves' logic—and its flaw: setting the

canister in the middle of a bunch of soldiers was not the same as having the can *guarded* by a bunch of soldiers. The average soldier could not be presumed to guard his own ass unless he was given a direct order. A gun soldier knew that. A desk soldier did not. But pointing out that fact to Groves would not put the uranium back in the can. Or end the war. Two million dead children falling.

"Any other details?" said Finn, his voice hoarse.

"That's all that goddamn Admiral Purnell could tell me."

"That's a lot."

"I don't need sarcasm from an insubordinate gun soldier!"

"Not sarcasm," said Finn. "If they got in and out and only killed one man, then it stinks of an inside job. Somebody knew where to find the can, and how to get on and off base without being noticed."

"But the Navy didn't know what was in the can!"

"Other than you and the guards who accompanied the shipment, who knew when the uranium would arrive, where it would be stored and how it was guarded?"

"No one," began Groves, then stopped. "The Lawrence Radiation Lab. They check₂d the can at midnight, but they were briefed about it earlier. *Scientists*," said Groves in a choked voice. "God save us all from sob-sister scientists!"

"I doubt that they stole the uranium."

"Why?"

"Crying about war and loving your fellow man is one thing. Murder is another. None of your scientists is naive enough to mistake treason for legitimate protest."

"Then who did it? The Japs? Did we tell Kestrel too much?"

"I'm betting on the Russians. Have your men check all

the phone calls they can from New Mexico to San Francisco in the last forty-eight hours. It may give them a lead. Rerun all the security checks in Los Alamos and at the Lawrence lab. Put somebody to work on a list of people who knew about the shipment. I hope it isn't a long one.''

"You're at the top of it. Who gets the job of checking you out?''

"General, if I stole it, you're up shit creek without a paddle.''

Groves' silence was agreement. He sighed. "I told the Navy you're in charge of the investigation, with powers second only to God and the President. I told the FBI, too. They didn't like it either. Their local agent in charge is named William Coughlan. Hoover has assured me Coughlan will cooperate.

"If Coughlan doesn't cooperate, I'll hammer him flat,'' said Finn.

"Do what you have to. The President only gave us two days.''

"*What*? But the bombs won't be dropped for weeks!''

"He doesn't have any choice. If we're going to invade, he has to set the machinery in motion. There's more to an invasion than guns and soldiers—once you've gotten the ball rolling, you can't stop it short of Japan. You have until 0530, July 18th. That's Mountain War Time.''

"Two days,'' said Finn bitterly. "Even God needed six.''

"God wasn't fighting the Japanese.''

Hunters Point, California
2 Hours 50 Minutes After Trinity

The Shore Patrol guard wore dress blues, white gaiters, and a pistol belt. He saluted the Office of Naval Intelligence license tags on Finn's Ford coupé. Finn flipped open his new credentials and handed them out the window.

"We were told to expect you," said the guard, returning the credentials with another salute.

Finn silently wished that nothing had been said about his arrival. Now, everyone would be covering his ass as fast as possible. He glanced at the other Navy ratings in the guard booth. Their pistols were clean, their faces alert, and the gate lowered to prevent anyone leaving the base. But Finn knew without asking that the guards' attentiveness was a case of spit and polish an hour after inspection.

"Good morning to be alive, right, sailor?" asked Finn.

"You bet, sir," said the sailor. The other men laughed. Their pleasure was as clear as their young smiles. Finn recognized the source of their smiles; it was the relief of survivors, of the ones who had not died on the floor of a Navy warehouse. He recognized their near-shame and sweet elation because he had felt it himself.

Finn engaged the clutch and accelerated away from the gate. He drove quickly through the base, not slowing until he turned the car down a narrow passage between two warehouses. He had to brake hard to avoid a Shore Patrol Jeep that was parked across the alleyway, blocking it completely.

"Restricted Area," said a sailor as Finn rolled down the window. "Back up and turn around on the doub—"

Finn held his new leather folder out the car window. The badge shone impressively, but it was the facing security clearance which stopped the sentry's voice. The man saluted crisply.

"Delta warehouse, sir?"

"Yes."

"Straight ahead, sir." The sailor turned and yelled over his shoulder. "Move the Jeep!". Then, to Finn, "You can't miss it, sir. Fuel barrels piled high as a battleship."

Finn squeezed past the Jeep, then picked up speed between rows of war materials stacked in static review. He was stopped twice more, the last time by a civilian who took time to inspect Finn's credentials.

After Finn parked near the warehouse, he sat quietly for a moment, staring at rectangular buildings, square stacks of stenciled crates, the angular bulk of weapons . . . a cubist painting done in shades of black and darkest gray.

That was what the thieves would have seen, but now there were people everywhere, blurring the clean lines, uniformed men with carbines at port arms and holster flaps unsnapped. They prowled and snarled, barking orders at one another as though it still mattered. Every measured stride and cold glance tried to prove that the theft had been a bizarre accident, the wildest fluke, a miracle made in hell.

The only people who did not seem defensive were the men in street clothes who wove among the bristling guards. The civilians wore relaxed confidence that bordered on smugness; they had not made the mess, but by God they were going to clean it up. Their conservative suits, white shirts, dark ties, gray snap-brim hats, wing-tip shoes and cold eyes were as distinctive as any uniform. Finn could almost see their FBI credentials inside the breast pockets of their suit coats. He could count fifteen agents without turning his head. There were more inside, and still other reinforcements at the gates.

The federal agents were good enough in their way, but they were little more than soldiers without uniforms, men trained away from originality, men who had so little leeway within their regulations that they guarded their few perquisites as jealously as a hen guarded its chicks.

He needed roosters, not hens. He needed men as quiet and smart and deadly as Masarek, who had infiltrated an enemy base and stolen 2 million lives.

Two days. My God. Just Two!

Finn felt as he had in Okinawa, the jungle behind him and the cliff in front, riding a seesaw of fury and helplessness, watching children fall.

Two days. Two million lives.

With a savage motion, he banged open the glove compartment and removed his .45 caliber automatic pistol. The gun's size was a drawback that he tolerated because it had better stopping power. The .45 had been designed as a man-killer, and had never been excelled. The smaller .38s worn by the gentlemen of the FBI did not wrinkle their suits, but Finn was not a gentleman, and their sartorial regulations were not his.

Finn checked the gun's clip and worked the slide to chamber a cartridge. He cocked the pistol and set its lever safety. The movements were quick, precise, automatic. He used his senses of touch and hearing almost as much as his eyes. Satisfied with the gun's readiness, he tucked the .45 into a belt clip at the small of his back. Then he slid out of the car, pulled his jacket down over the gun and headed for the warehouse that was the focus of all the anxiety. He walked with obvious purpose, a tall, lean man whom other men automatically gave way to.

In the warehouse, thin gray illumination seeped through a row of dirty skylights, but did little to soften the utilitarian interior. It was cold and dank and ugly.

A sudden flash of light drew Finn's pale eyes. He glanced down a short aisle between stacked crates and saw a FBI technician with a Speed Graphic camera and flash-gun lining up another shot in the doorway of a small store-room.

Noiselessly, Finn moved down the aisle and into a loose knot of a half-dozen men, FBI agents and Navy officers, all staring at the young sentry whose dead eyes stared through them into nothing at all. The sentry's cap was a dark blot five feet away, flung there by the officer who had yanked it off a dozing sailor and discovered a corpse.

One or two of the officers glanced at Finn, then re-turned their attention to the body held upright by a pea-coat pulled over the back of a chair. There was little talk.

Finn eased around the fringe of the group to get a closer look at the upright corpse. The face was young. A velvet-cheeked boy who had never seen death and so could not recognize its smiling, two-footed approach.

The sentry's carbine lay on the floor near his right hand. The fingers of that hand were open, as though in death the boy was reaching to recover his weapon. The other hand was knotted into a fist by pain or rage or surprise. Or was it something else, somethine more tangible than emotion?

Finn waited until the photographer withdrew. Then, before anyone else could step forward, he crouched on his heels beside the body. The forehead wound was small, neat, and had been inflicted at close but not point-blank range. The blood around the hole was minimal. The heart had stopped a beat or two after the bullet penetrated the skull.

The men around the body began to talk among them-selves, speculating and arguing. Finn glanced up quickly. Satisfied that no one was interested in him, he inspected the sentry's clenched left hand. There was definitely something inside the cold fingers, paper or plastic, something thin. It could be nothing more than a candy wrapper.

"You through taking pictures?" said Finn, looking up at the photographer.

"Yeah. The lab boys are next."

Finn began to pry gently at the left hand. The fingers were locked in a spasm that death had hardened into stone.

"Who the hell do you think you are?" asked a harsh voice.

"Finn," he said, without looking up. "Who the hell are you?"

"Everybody here knows me. William Coughlan, FBI. Anybody know you?"

Finn stood up slowly, abandoning for the moment the cold left hand locked around a secret. He turned to face the voice and found an FBI agent wearing a dark-gray hat and a matching gray wool suit. He was of average height and above average weight. Otherwise, his appearance was conventional. Emotion was written on his skin in shades of red. The agent had the face of an Irish drinker and bulldog jaws set to bite.

"Give me a reason I shouldn't throw you out on your smart ass," said Coughlan, eyeing Finn's clothes with disparagement.

The same cold blue Irish eyes watched as Finn reached into his back pocket and pulled out the new leather badge case. Holding it at eye level, Finn let it drop open. Coughlan's square left hand swallowed up the leather folder.

Coughlan turned away slightly, as though to look at the credentials with the indifferent aid of the skylight. The movement concealed his right hand. The hand reappeared suddenly, wrapped around a .38.

Neither Finn's face nor his body moved. Coughlan's eyes told Finn the FBI man meant business.

Coughlan measured Finn's sudden stillness with a smile. "You come marching in like you own the place and then lay credentials on me that smell like wet ink. You can understand, cowboy, how I might be a little suspicious."

"Put the gun away, Coughlan. I'm your new boss and you're wasting my time."

"My orders come from Washington."

"Call Operator 34. Ask for 778 in Washington, D.C. They'll tell you the same thing. I'm your boss." He turned back to the dead sentry.

"Hold it!" There was no compromise in Coughlan's voice.

Finn straightened and turned around like the jungle fighter he was.

"Riley!" said Coughlan, backing up. "Check him for weapons."

A young man stepped forward smartly. His gray hat and suit were almost identical to Coughlan's clothes. Only the tie was different; Riley's had a subtle pattern, while Coughlan's was plain.

Riley ran his hands quickly over Finn, impersonally exploring armpits, crotch and insides of boots. Coughlan's eyes lingered on the slim, deadly boot knife that Riley found, but neither man spoke.

Riley nearly missed the .45 beneath Finn's jacket in the small of his back. Almost as an afterthought, the FBI agent patted around Finn's belt, looking for more knives. When Riley's fingers touched the outline of a gun, his eyes showed a flicker of shock. He jerked out the gun and showed it to Coughlan.

"An elephant gun," said Coughlan. "You expecting elephants?"

"Yeah, but all I find are jackasses. Call the number."

"Cover him," said Coughlan. "Use the gun. If it goes off, it'll be a clear case of justifiable suicide. The rest of you men beat it until I come back."

Everyone left but Finn and Riley. Finn wished that it had been Coughlan who stayed. He was an overweight, overweening son of a bitch, but he knew what he was doing. Riley was an amateur by comparison, and amateurs made stupid mistakes.

"Okay," said Riley, "we'll just stand here quietly while Coughlan checks you out." Riley smiled almost in spite of himself. "I don't know whose shit hit the fan, but it sure spread far and wide. So don't push Coughlan too hard, cowboy. He's had all the crap he can take."

Finn shook his head. "It's just begun," he said. "It's just begun."

Oakland
2 Hours 58 Minutes After Trinity

Refugio drove through a steel-gray world punctuated by the bloom of taillights. Fog billowed around the van, concealing and then revealing the vehicles sharing the gloomy early morning with the laundry truck.

"This time we take the bridge, yes?" said Refugio.

Masarek studied both sideview mirrors before answering. There was nothing suspicious following them. The cars were full of yawning shopgirls and waitresses, shoe clerks and accountants. Taxis carried stockbrokers and lawyers. Police cars came and went without a single glance at the off-white van.

"All right. This time cross the bridge."

"Bueno," yawned Refugio, his tiredness only partially feigned.

Except for a single stop to add a piece of black electricians tape that changed the truck's number 7 into a 17, Masarek had kept Refugio driving throughout the dark hours, twisting and turning and doubling while Masarek watched the mirrors for headlights which appeared too often or followed too long.

As the van approached the bridge, Refugio's hands tightened imperceptibly on the wheel. The moment was coming when Masarek must die, and nothing was going as Refugio had planned. Masarek had put him behind the wheel, neutralizing him. As soon as the van had passed through the gates at Hunters Point, Masarek had taken Salvador's shotgun, as well as Lopez's and Refugio's .45s. There had been no time to protest. Masarek had moved quickly, unexpectedly, just at the moment of victory.

Even worse, Masarek had found the knives inside their sleeves. He had even found the little chrome-plated Beretta in Refugio's boot. Masarek had not, however, found Salvador's thin razor wire with the little hinged bar on each end. It looked like a belt buckle, but was really a very efficient garrot.

Masarek's eyes moved restlessly, his head tilted, listening, always listening for the scuff of death's footsteps beneath the hiss of passing traffic. He suspected nothing in particular and everything as a matter of principle. Civilian traffic streamed around them. Nowhere were there signs that the United States was a country at war, and that San Francisco was a vulnerable target.

"Children," said Masarek. "They're all children. They think that war is temporary and their lives are forever. They haven't learned that war is forever and life only a flicker. That's why they'll lose, and then they'll whine and wonder why we broke their toys.''

The Bay Bridge loomed out of the fog ahead. Cars flowed on and off freely, for traffic was not yet at its morning peak. No troops guarded the approach or the spans rising out of the mercury Bay.

Masarek measured the Bay Bridge with the eye of an engineer, looking for vulnerable spots and calculating the amount of explosives needed to bring it down. ''They make it easy for their enemies,'' he murmured.

''Maybe they're just playing with us,'' said Refugio. ''Maybe all this is like the fat worm hiding the steel hook.''

Masarek smiled. ''Their grandchildren will speak Russian.''

Refugio yawned again, then removed one hand from the wheel to rub his eyes. Masarek watched the hand, but his gun no longer moved to follow Refugio's every twitch. Once Masarek had put their weapons under his feet, he had relaxed slightly.

Both Salvador and Lopez knew that any move toward Masarek would result in Refugio's death. As Refugio was their patron, their cousin, their half-sister's brother-in-law, and their brains, they waited for his signal. When it came, they would do their best to kill Masarek before he could kill Refugio.

Until then, they sat in the back of the van on a cold floor with a dead man and two odd chunks of metal, each wrapped in separate laundry bags. The dead man stank of feces, and the metal slithered about with every movement of the swaying van.

''I'll have to change lanes soon,'' said Refugio, ''unless you want me to drive past the waterfront and then come back.''

Masarek leaned over to check Refugio's side mirror. At

first Refugio had thought that such a move would give him a chance to kill Masarek; but every time Masarek leaned, the pistol's bulbous silencer dug intimately into Refugio's groin. He was not going to risk his manhood for a chop at Masarek's neck.

Three against one with a gun. A Mexican stand-off of sorts. Refugio smiled wryly. In all such contests, the victory went to the wary.

Masarek leaned back. The motion removed the gun, but did not change its target. "Get off the bridge. Go directly to the waterfront. I'll tell you where to stop. Remember. No sudden stops or turns."

"I'll remember," said Refugio, feeling the sweat that came to his face each time the gun poked at his crotch. "But what if one of these tired little shopgirls crashes into a third little clerk and I have to stand hard on the brakes?"

"Then you're dead."

"You're an unreasonable man," said Refugio, but he said it in Spanish. Kestrel had warned him not to underestimate Masarek merely because the Russian took orders from a woman. Refugio wished he had given more thought to Kestrel's words.

Refugio waited for an opening before changing lanes slowly, cautiously. It galled him to drive like a timid girl, treating red lights and speed zones as though they were serious matters instead of markers in a game of skill and nerve. Nonetheless, he drove like an American, for Masarek's gun was never far away.

The fog was lighter in color now, more dove than steel, but still a dense exhalation concealing the morning. Cars parked a half-block away were invisible. Nearby cars were studded with moisture that gathered and ran in eccentric streaks.

"Left," said Masarek. Then, as the van completed the

turn, "Right at the next corner."

Refugio drove the van through two turns, both times a bit fast, testing Masarek. The Russian said nothing. He was intent on the side mirrors and the cars parked along the street.

"Right again."

The van bumped over rough, foggy streets which paralleled the factories, warehouses and storage yards of the waterfront.

"Almost there?" asked Refugio, stressing the word "almost." He wanted to look over his shoulder at Salvador but did not dare.

Salvador picked up the verbal cue. He grumbled about the rough ride and shifted to a kneeling position as though to ease his cramped legs. Masarek glanced back at him, but said nothing. The movement seemed natural enough.

Suddenly the van swayed as Refugio swerved around a pothole and then braked sharply. Salvador sprawled forward, swearing bitterly in Spanish. The canvas bags containing the uranium skidded toward the front of the van, touching and rebounding off one another in an invisible flowering of energy. Masarek's gun wavered, then returned to Refugio's groin with enough force to make the Mexican wince.

"Be careful!"

Salvador pulled himself upright. The long-armed Mexican was closer to the front of the truck now, kneeling rather than sitting, a killer in blue jeans whose fingers ached to feel the slim cold bars of the garrot as it sliced through flesh.

Slowly, casually, his thumb hooked into his belt buckle, ready to grab and twist, freeing the razor wire in a single ripping motion.

Wanting to look back, knowing he must not, Refugio

drove along the uneven street. The moment to consummate Kestrel's plan was drawing closer with each turn of the tires, but he did not know which car concealed Vanessa's polished blond hair. Was it the black one with the broken window or the faded red one with a crumpled fender? Or was she even here?

Refugio had to force his hands to relax on the wheel. Like a wild animal, Masarek had a sixth sense for danger, sniffing and listening, head turning, eyes probing, but most of all listening, always listening.

"Can I tell my men what we're looking for?" asked Refugio, willing his voice to be casual. "Even from back there, they could help you."

"One word of Spanish and I'll blow your balls off."

Refugio shrugged, concealing a surge of rage. He had planned for something like this while Vanessa talked on the phone to her San Francisco spy and Masarek watched and listened. Always listening, that one. A wild animal. Killing him would not be a sin, not like killing a real person.

On the left was a white van with its engine compartment open and a single red rose painted on its side. Refugio's hands gripped the wheel, his knuckles showing pale yellow. Masarek noticed neither the sudden tension nor the parked flower truck, for he had just spotted Vanessa's car.

"There!" he exclaimed.

"Como?" said Refugio with a guilty start.

"The dark green car."

There were three dark cars within view, all parked on his side of the street.

"Which one?"

"Slow down! There! Third car on the right. See the red blanket?"

Refugio slowed to a crawl, peering out the windshield. He spotted the car with a blanket shoved carelessly onto the rear-window ledge, blocking most of the window.

"Where is the woman?" asked Refugio. Kestrel would be very angry if Vanessa were not captured for questioning. He could not even set Salvador onto Masarek until Vanessa was within easy reach.

"Stop next to the car, wait for a moment and then park ahead of her. She'll wait in the car for us."

Refugio followed the instructions, turning as though to peer into the car. Out of the corner of his eye he saw Salvador, who was not quite close enough to the Russian to be certain—and Refugio wanted Masarek's death to be very certain indeed.

Refugio pulled even with the green car. Vanessa's face appeared briefly in the side window.

"Good," grunted Masarek. "Now park up ahead."

Refugio pulled forward, jerking the van when he let out the clutch. His clumsiness covered Salvador's forward creep. Only a few inches, but it was all Salvador could safely manage.

As Refugio angled the van toward the curb, he knew the time to attack had come. He wished to every saint he had ever known that a gun were not pointed between his legs. But it must be now, while Masarek's mind was divided between Vanessa and the men in the van.

"Masarek."

It was the first time Refugio had spoken Masarek's name since they had left Hunters Point. It was meant to be the last.

Salvador's garrot sang free of his belt as he lunged for Masarek. The Russian turned at the unexpected sound even as his hand started to squeeze the trigger. Refugio's fist lashed out, trying to knock away the gun, but it was like trying to bend stone.

Only the garrot saved Refugio, the razor wire tightening with a jerk that yanked Masarek off-balance a fraction. Not much, hardly a finger's width, merely the difference between a bullet through his thigh and a bullet through his balls.

Refugio bellowed like a gored bull, but he held on to Masarek's hand and gun. He bellowed again, straining against the Russian's strength. They were locked together, clawing for control of the silenced gun.

The first snap of Salvador's wrists failed to kill Masarek. In the split instant before the garrot closed, Masarek had jammed his left hand between the razor wire and the vulnerable flesh of his neck.

The garrot bit deeply into Masarek's hand, drawing blood from a cut so fine that for an instant the Russian did not even feel it. When wire met bone, Salvador's momentum was broken. Masarek tried to turn the gun back on Salvador, but Refugio held on despite his wound, preventing Masarek from shooting the man whose cruel hands were sawing on the wire.

Lopez leaped into the fight, grabbing for the bulbous silencer. The gun was forced upward just as it coughed once, then again, clearing its throat of two deadly bits of metal. One penetrated the sheet metal ceiling; the other struck a strut and rebounded, tearing through Lopez's face. He screamed and staggered, one eye gone. He dropped to his knees, clawing at his face. He was dead before his forehead bounced off the van's floor.

The gun hawked twice more, sending bullets screaming off metal surfaces. Salvador yanked on the thin wire, struggling to pull the garrot through the bone in Masarek's thumb and then through the flesh on his neck.

The muzzle of the pistol wove erratically, a blind black eye. Sweat ran down Salvador's face and his heavy arms bulged as he pulled against the stubborn bone. The razor wire jerked, found new purchase on the thumb joint, and sliced through to Masarek's neck. Gagging helplessly, he jerked the trigger again and again. Bullets grazed Salvador's hand, but the pressure on Masarek's neck did not lessen.

Refugio felt his own strength give way to pain, but he clung to the Russian's arm, spoiling the assassin's aim. Desperately, Masarek tried to throw himself up and over the back of the seat, bringing himself closer to Salvador and thereby easing the bite of the wire. But his movement gave Refugio the leverage he needed. He forced the pistol back on its owner. Masarek's twisting struggle could not evade the bullet that tore through his throat, killing him.

Breathing rapidly, Salvador wiped sweat and blood from his face. His arms hung like bags of sand and his fingers were numb. Never had it taken so long to kill a man. Never had one of his victims died so hard.

"Are you all right, Refugio?" asked Salvador, looking away from Masarek, remembering where the first bullet had been aimed. "*Refugio?*"

"The woman!" gasped Refugio. "We must get the woman!"

Hunters Point
3 Hours 10 Minutes After Trinity

Coughlan's footsteps had stopped short of the corpse. He flipped Finn's credentials at him without meeting Finn's eyes. The FBI agent's lips were puckered as though he were chewing on quinine. He faced Riley.

"Give him his gun," said Coughlan. "He's your new boss."

"*What?*"

"He's in charge of this investigation," said Coughlan, distaste in every syllable, "and you are hereby assigned to be his fetch-and-carry. So give him the goddamn elephant gun before he breaks your arm."

"For the love of God," said Riley. He holstered his own gun and returned Finn's .45.

Finn stuck the .45 in the back of his belt. "Amen, Riley. Let's give the partnership a pass."

Coughlan smiled thinly. "Nice try, but Groves—whoever the hell *he* is—said you work with us. If Riley is too much for you to handle, I'll find someone with fewer teeth. Either way, it's you and us."

Finn looked from Coughlan to Riley. "It can be easy," he said, measuring Riley with pale eyes, "or it can be hard." He pointed to the dead sentry. "Hold on to him."

Without waiting to see if Riley understood, Finn turned and squatted on his heels by the dead boy.

Riley hesitated, then grabbed the corpse, holding it against Finn's pull. It was clearly the first time Riley had touched a corpse, but he was determined not to show his revulsion.

Finn liked the feel of dead flesh no better than Riley. Willing hmself not to notice smell or temperature or texture, Finn wrestled against the cold strength of the sentry's clenched fingers. Once he almost pulled over the body. He looked up at Riley, who flushed and grasped the corpse more tightly.

Finally, Finn dragged the thick paper out of the dead boy's grasp.

Coughlan could restrain himself no longer. "You keep dicking with the evidence and the crime boys will be all over you like a cat covering shit."

"I don't give a damn about evidence. All I want is information."

Coughlan shut up.

Finn smoothed out the paper. It was an indentification card from the Lawrence Radiation Laboratory, issued to a health inspector named Mr. Stan Grummin. But the face belonged to Masarek. Finn turned to one of the Navy officers who had drifted back in Coughlan's wake.

"Did the Lawrence Radiation Lab send someone over to check the shipment?"

"Yes, Captain."

"Who?"

The ONI man consulted a notebook. "Dr. Kenneth Cooper logged in at the gate last night at 2400. He logged out at 0100. However, this sentry," his glance flicked over the corpse, "came on duty at 0130. Somebody checked, saw him alive at 0200. Dr. Cooper couldn't have been involved."

Finn's glance turned back to the card in his hand. He smoothed the card and turned it slowly so that light played over the small photograph. In spite of its recently wrinkled face, the card was new, its edges crisp and unsmudged by handling.

"You can let go," said Finn to Riley without looking up.

"My pleasure," muttered Riley. He stepped back from the corpse with no attempt to hide his relief.

"Coughlan," Finn said, "how long will it take to find out if this card really came from the Lawrence lab?"

Coughlan approached and took the card from Finn. He smoothed it out and studied the picture and the printing carefully. "Paper and printing are right, but it couldn't have come from the lab. We never did one on this guy Grummin."

"His name is Masarek. He's an NKVD agent."

Everyone in the room came to attention at the mention of the Russian secret service.

"NKVD?" said Coughlan. "I should have figured it

was the commies." He turned to Riley. "Get the guys from the Red Squad down here. I want every known commie agent, sympathizer or plain fool in San Francisco and Berkeley under surveillance by noon."

"*Hold it*." Finn's voice was like a pistol shot. "You can put a watch on known agents and idiots—it will at least keep your men out of the way. But it won't answer my question about where the card came from."

"It's a fake. It has to be," said Coughlan. "We never approved a security clearance for a goddamn Russian spy called Grummin or Masarek or whatever the hell his name is."

"Someone in that lab told Grummin-Masarek when the shipment arrived and where it was stored. That same person could have stolen a blank Lawrence lab ID card and given it to Masarek."

Coughlan scowled, but nodded finally.

"Run another check on everybody at the lab," said Finn. "Bear down on anyone who knew about the shipment. And be a prick with the men who came here at midnight."

Coughlan's scowl deepened, but he nodded again.

"And before you do anything else," continued Finn, "get a bulletin on Masarek out to the local police."

"An APB," muttered Coughlan. "San Francisco or the whole damn Bay Area?"

"Statewide," said Finn, trying to keep the bleak edge of hopelessness out of his voice. "Christ, he could be half-way to Russia by now."

With the discipline that had made him a survivor, Finn put away his feeling of futility. As long as there was time, he would keep on trying . . . otherwise the sentry would be just the first of a million casualties, death piled on death.

Finn stood and walked swiftly through the half-open

storeroom door that was just beyond the sentry's body.
Riley hesitated, then followed his new partner.

The first thing Finn saw was the open canister. His
breath hissed out between his teeth as the enormity of the
thieves' ignorance struck him for the first time.

"Sweet Jesus. The bastards don't know what they
stole!" Finn remembered the dying technician in Los
Alamos, the horror of his invisible, lethal injury. He
turned toward the men waiting outside the storeroom.
"How many people have been in here?"

Coughlan came up behind Finn and looked over his
shoulder. "No one but me. Why?"

"Did you touch anything?"

"Uh, no," said Coughlan uneasily. "We were told that
the storeroom was off limits until someone from Groves
cleared it."

Finn looked at Coughlan, sure that he was lying. It was
an investigator's nature to poke and pry, and Coughlan
was an investigator before he was anything else.

"Riley," said Finn.

The young agent took Coughlan's place behind Finn,
looking over his shoulder into the forbidden storeroom.
Finn pulled a metal keyring from his pocket and flipped it
to Riley.

"In the trunk of the black Ford coupé parked out front.
A metal box. Bring it."

In less than a minute, Riley returned with the radiation
counter. Finn took the instrument, snapped it on and
adjusted the dial. He was rewarded with a slow, steady
click, like a metronome. Finn extended the probe in front
of him like a snake stick and began quartering the storeroom.

As he approached the canister, the radiation counter
began clicking faster. When he was eight feet from the

empty canister the pulses quickened even more, sounding double time in a ghostly march. At six feet, the sound slid into a blur.

Finn stopped and recalibrated. Although the radiation was still within the range of safety, Finn felt as though the temperature of the room were increasing with each click. Sweat started on his forehead. He remembered again the laboratory and the innocent looking, deadly pieces of metal.

"What are you doing?" demanded Coughlan.

Finn ignored him. Four feet away from the cannister, Finn had to recalibrate again. He was approaching the upper level of what he had been told was the safety range. The skin on his arms prickled and contracted. He advanced another cautious step, feeling as though he were in the jungle again, and the clicks of the counter a cloud of frightened birds crying frantic warnings.

Off to the side of the lid, on a patch of concrete that looked no different from any other, the probe sensed ambush and screamed. Finn reset the counter twice, then retreated, still unable to slow the scream into separate clicks. He would leave the rest of the investigating to radiation experts. He knew enough for his own purposes. He knew that the U-235 was unshielded, and that the two pieces had been brought together as they were stolen, irradiating the concrete floor and probably at least one of the thieves.

The mental vision of shadowy men limned in the blue light of atomic radiation possessed Finn's mind for a moment, and then, like an echo, the face of the experimenter who had found the front lines of war in a New Mexico lab. If the thief—or more likely, thieves—were badly injured by radiation, they might crawl away and die like poisoned rats in some hidden hole. How would he find them if they went to ground? How could anyone find them?

Less than two days.

Sweat gathered on Finn's ribs in spite of the cool morning. The canister yawned vacantly at him, its black cavity big enough to swallow a world.

As Finn backed away from the canister, the counter's buzz diminished rapidly. He clicked downward through the scale, watching the needle drop. With a feeling of relief, he reached for the cutoff switch. But the counter buzzed suddenly and the needle slapped against its peg.

Finn stood absolutely still. Just when he thought he understood the capabilities of radiation, it ambushed him with no warning at all. Silence, then screams.

Sweating, Finn reset the counter. Coughlan, standing behind Finn near the door, walked toward the shrill-voiced box. The counter screamed as Coughlan approached the probe.

"What the hell?"

Coughlan's question was cut short by the counter's scream as he neared the probe. Finn quickly shifted the dial, diminishing the counter's sensitivity until the clicks were crisp and separate again. He looked speculatively at Coughlan, then pointed the probe toward him.

The clicks sped up.

"Hey!" said Coughlan. "What the hell do you think you're doing?"

"Stand still."

Coughlan responded to the authority in Finn's voice. The probe clicked faster as it approached Coughlan, then slowed as Finn pulled it back.

"How are you making it do that? What are those clicks?"

"I'm not making it do anything," said Finn. "You are." Finn moved the probe again, advancing and retreating from Coughlan. The clicks rose and fell in a ripple of sound.

"Whaddya mean?" said Coughlan. "Get that damn thing away from me!"

"You handled the canister," said Finn. Before Coughlan could deny it, Finn pointed the probe at the agent's right hand. "You picked up the cover, most likely."

Color drained from Coughlan's face as the counter screamed the answer to Finn's accusation. Red splotches along the line of the agent's jaw stood out against the paleness of fear.

"The thieves," said Finn, pointing the probe as though it were a flashlight illuminating a dark room, "opened the can, pulled out the first piece and set it down near the lid. Then they pulled out that," the wand pointed at the dark, solid damper that had separated the two pieces of U-235, "and—" He stopped talking abruptly. He knew the thieves had taken out the second piece of uranium and set it down next to the first, causing a storm of radiation. But he could not say that to men who were not even cleared to know that they were looking for uranium.

He turned off the radiation counter. "Riley, I saw a hose out front. Drag it in here. Coughlan, start peeling. When you get to your skin, wish you could zip out of it, too. But you can't, so Riley will wash you down."

"You're kidding," said Coughlan, but he could see that Finn was not. "For Chrissake, why?" said Coughlan, loosening his tie and belt even as he protested.

"I can't tell you."

Coughlan's hands hovered over his fly. "So help me, Finn, if you're jerking me off—"

"Peel," said Finn.

Coughlan peeled.

Oakland
3 Hours 16 Minutes After Trinity

Refugio wallowed in a sea of pain until the tide ebbed, stranding him in a dry reality. He was facedown on the front seat of the laundry van. Then he remembered the instant that the world had exploded as Masarek shot him. He sat and looked down at himself. Blood. A lapful of it. Afraid of what he would find, he explored his lap with his left hand.

The relief of finding himself intact was so great that Refugio nearly fainted again. Then came fiery pain as he brushed his hand across his left thigh.

"Refugio?" asked Salvador anxiously.

"It's all right," said Refugio, his eyes closed. "The cabrón shot me in the leg, nothing more. How long was I out?"

"Only a moment."

Refugio opened his eyes and wiped the sweat away, leaving bloody streaks everywhere his hand had been. He looked into the back of the truck. Neither Masarek nor Lopez was recognizable, but it was obvious that both men were dead.

"The blonde," said Refugio, his voice hoarse. "You'll have to get her."

"How?"

"Go to the car in back of the van. The car with a red serape in the back window. The woman who came with Masarek is hiding there. But be careful. Don't trust her."

"A rattlesnake's mate is no less poisonous for being female," said Salvador, leaning over the seat and scooping up his knife and shotgun.

"Take her—" Refugio bit off a sound of pain. With great care, he straightened slowly, so that the waves of pain did not make him dizzy. He pressed his face against the cold glass on the driver's side, then rolled down the window and peered out. The cream-colored flower truck was across the street, nearly a block to the rear. Between the flower truck and the laundry truck was a car with a red blanket in the rear window.

"The green car. Take her from it. Go to the white van with the red rose on the side. See it?"

Salvador leaned over the seat and looked. "Yes."

"A Japanese is in the truck. A friend. Knock out the blonde, tie her and drive the van up here. Just knock her out, don't kill her. Understand?"

"Yes."

Salvador turned and picked his way past the bodies to the rear of the truck. His foot hit a canvas bag containing the smaller piece of uranium and sent it skating aside until it thumped up against the bag with the larger piece of U-235. Radiation bloomed in a soundless, subtle rush of blue, so faint he did not see it.

Salvador opened the rear door and got out. After a quick look around, he walked toward the dark green car. Mist swirled capriciously, but the red blanket was like a beacon. Even so, he hesitated before he opened the car door. The car looked empty and cold, its windows unfogged as though nothing warm breathed inside. Then he saw that the windows were rolled down just enough to let out any telltale warmth. He peered inside, but saw only a back seat heaped with more rumpled blankets. Knife in hand, he opened the back door.

"Señorita?" whispered Salvador.

Beneath the blankets, Vanessa smiled, thinking it was Refugio's voice whispering to her, Refugio delivered to her by Masarek, as promised. The muffling blankets were no impediment to her silenced .38. She aimed as she had

practiced, at the exact center of the open door, regretting
only that she could not see Refugio's leer dissolve into
horror as he felt death tearing at his body.

Vanessa pulled the trigger again and again. Only the
twitching blankets marked the silent passage of bullets.
Salvador reeled backward, fell, and felt the cold surface of
the street engulf him. He reached toward the blankets as
though to warm himself. Then he felt nothing at all.

Vanessa waited beneath the blankets, holding her
breath and counting silently. Nothing moved in or outside
the car. When she reached thirty, she threw aside the
blankets and gulped air untainted by cordite and smoldering wool. All she could see of the man who had whispered
to her was a broad, blunt hand clenched around a trailing
edge of blanket.

She yanked off her dark scarf with her left hand and
snapped the cloth across the fingers clinging to the
blanket. There was no flicker of response. Deliberately,
she raised her gun and fired a shot through the hand. It
twitched from the bullet's impact, but did not bleed.
Dead. She kicked aside the hand and squirmed out of the
back seat.

The man slumped against the pavement was too big,
too broad, too thick. Refugio was smaller. She turned over
the corpse with her foot and looked into dead eyes that
were not Refugio's. Then she looked up the street at the
pale van parked neatly along the curb.

Had something gone wrong? Had Masarek been forced
to kill Refugio himself? Or was it Masarek who was dead
and Refugio alive?

Vanessa shook herself impatiently. Masarek was no child
to be killed by Mexican smugglers. Nonetheless, she would
take care to keep a car between herself and the van as she
approached it.

Refugio swore softly as the woman's gold-white hair slipped from cover to cover like a ghost. He had been watching in the sideview mirror when Salvador fell backward out of the car. Refugio could not tell precisely what had gone wrong, but he could see that Salvador was certainly hurt and probably dead. Refugio also knew that Kestrel wanted the woman alive.

Silently, Refugio rolled down the window on the passenger side of the car. The barrel of his .45 scraped on metal as he aimed back along the body of the truck. Kestrel wanted the blonde alive, yes; but he wanted the metal even more. Refugio knew he was too weak to take a live prisoner who had dispatched Salvador as coolly as a campesina grinding corn. He would have to kill Vanessa.

Vanessa darted along the curb to the cover of another car. Sweating, Refugio took aim carefully, knowing that if he waited any longer, she would be behind his van in a blind spot. His finger, slippery with sweat and blood, took slack out of the trigger. He exhaled until there was no air left in his lungs, then held very still, waiting for Vanessa's blond head to appear over the trunk of the car behind the van.

The sound of Refugo's unsilenced .45 shattered the early-morning calm. Glass exploded and bullets screamed off metal. Ana woke up in a rush of adrenaline, disoriented by the heavy smell of roses, thinking she was a child again, awakened by firecrackers thrown by her brothers to frighten her. Then she remembered where she was, and why.

Three more shots came, sounds so loud that Ana suppressed a scream only by biting her knuckles. She desperately hoped that the shots were not related to Refugio or Kestrel and hence to her, but she knew hope was false and fear was true. Kestrel was far away and she was here, afraid.

She eased aside the curtain and stared out the windshield. At first she saw only gray light and fog dripping onto the pavement, shining in the middle of the street. Then she realized that it was glass, not moisture glistening on concrete. Halfway up the block stood a car, its door open, something black huddled against the side. Farther up the street was a car with darkness where windows should be, and something black huddled against the back of the car.

Shots came like sharp blows.

Vanessa was flattened on the pavement; shards of glass winked in her hair. She tasted blood and fear and anger all at once. Her silenced gun spat several times before it was empty. She had used too many bullets on the man who should have been Refugio.

She knew if she stayed she would die. She knew she would die if she tried to get the uranium. She knew Masarek was dead as certainly as if she had killed him herself. She also knew how far it was to the border. Many things could happen, many people could die. Refugio would be one of them—if she could get out of this rancid gutter.

Vanessa squirmed backward until she was beneath a parked car. She did not notice the macadam tearing her hands or the rivulets of blood on her face from the first explosion of glass. She had only one thought in her mind: The man who had killed Masarek was trying to kill her.

With an eel-like motion, she squirmed from beneath the car, feinted toward the sidewalk, then spun on one foot as a shot exploded off the curb. Instantly she crouched over, weaving toward the green car.

Refugio swore and tried again, but as Vanessa crossed to the street side of the parked cars, she put the back of the van across Refugio's sights. He dragged himself over to the driver's side of the van. Vanessa was already inside her car. He heard an engine rev; tires shrieked on moist pavement. She turned the car around and was accelerating away from him. He pulled the trigger but no sound came. The gun was empty. He reloaded, but it was too late. She was gone.

Ana ducked reflexively as Vanessa's car careened by, then looked up the street toward the van. A shout rang out as clear as a shot. Ana looked in the sideview mirror. Behind her, far down the block, an old, fat man in a gray watchman's uniform was waving his arm to someone behind him. The watchman must have realized what a fine target he made on the suddenly empty street. He ducked back into the cover of the brick building he was guarding.

Ana wanted to follow his example, to retreat like a snail behind a protective coil of shell. She did not want to climb into the driver's seat, start the van and drive past shattered glass up to the laundry truck. She did not want to do anything except hide. But she started the van and drove up to the laundry truck anyway. Kestrel had taught her that there was more to life than fear.

She leaned across the seat, rolled down the window on the far side, and called out softly: "Refugio?"

If Ana's hair had been any color except black, she would have died in Refugio's first startled reflex. As it was, Refugio hesitated, then spoke in rapid Spanish.

"Ana? Is it you, Ana?"

"Yes. How are you?"

It was not an idle greeting. Ana was concerned by the thready sound of Refugio's voice.

"Fine," Refugio said, lying.

Refugio heaved himself over the seat into the back of the van, swearing volubly. Sweating, dizzy, he bent over the two canvas bags containing the uranium. He wanted Ana's help now, but she was only a woman; if she saw the bloody mess inside the van, she might run away. He needed her. She must drive for him, because he knew that the pain he felt now was nothing to what he would feel when the first shock of being wounded wore off.

"Refugio?" said Ana. She could not see him, could only hear him. "Do you need help?"

Refugio tried to pick up both sacks at once, but could not. The pieces of metal thumped together in their sacks, bounced, then rested against each other, separated only by two layers of canvas. The cloth blushed with a vague blue light. The heavier sack slipped out of his grasp. The blue light faded.

"Refugio?" asked Ana again.

"Yes," he said wearily. "Come to the back of the van."

Refugio opened the back door just enough to hand out the sack containing the smaller piece of uranium.

"Put it in your truck."

Ana reached for the bag before she realized that the hand holding it was smeared with blood.

"You're hurt."

"The bag!" said Refugio savagely. "Take it!"

Ana snatched the bag, flung it into the flower truck and ran back just as Refugio was trying to climb out the rear of the laundry truck. Her horrified glance went from his leg to the corpses in the van. She closed her eyes and did not open them until she turned her back on the bloody van.

"Can you walk?" she asked.

"Take the bag."

The second laundry sack was heavier than the first had been, and liberally smeared with blood. Ana flung the bag into the flower truck, slammed the door shut and rushed back to help Refugio.

The second bag thumped to a rest against a wicker flower stand in the rear of the truck. The first bag lay partway under the passenger seat. Only gray light relieved the gloomy interior of the van.

In the distance sirens keened. Ana remembered the night watchman. She had no doubt that the sirens were coming to the waterfront; they were drawn by death as unerringly as vultures spiraling down hot desert air.

With a strength that surprised Refugio, she boosted him into the passenger seat of the flower truck, slammed shut the engine compartment and leaped into the driver's seat.

The van turned around and raced along the waterfront. Ana did not notice the car parked along the street leading to the bridge, nor the driver blotting up blood that dripped into her eyes, making driving more dangerous than hiding.

When the cream-colored van loomed out of the fog, Vanessa thought that Refugio had followed her to finish her off. She grabbed her reloaded pistol and aimed toward the driver's side of the oncoming van. Refugio would have to slow down to get off a telling shot. When he slowed, she would fire.

The van swept by without pausing, but not before Vanessa recognized the man slumped against the window—Refugio. Automatically she memorized the truck's license plate. When the van turned the corner, she followed, trying to keep the van in sight without revealing her own presence. Mist and morning traffic defeated her. Before she reached the Bay Bridge, the van had disappeared into fog that would not burn off until noon.

Vanessa turned the car toward the waterfront, wondering where Masarek was and whether he was still alive. How had Refugio escaped him? Where had the second truck come from, and who had driven Refugio away? But most of all—*where was the uranium?*

Sirens ululated through the mist, converging on the waterfront. A police car ran a stop sign at right angles to Vanessa's car and roared down the street leading to the Good Luck laundry van. A second squad car quickly followed. She eased out into the intersection until she could see the van. Both squad cars jerked to a stop near it. Policemen leaped out, guns drawn. They yanked open the van's doors. No shots were fired. No one came out of it.

Vanessa drove by the entrance to the waterfront. If Masarek were in the van there was nothing she could do for him. If the uranium were there— Resolutely, she examined the possibilities of the situation. Either Masarek was alive and had escaped with the uranium, in which case he would call the prearranged number to re-establish contact with her, or he was dead and the uranium was in the van. If the latter were true, the uranium was lost to her and to Russia, and she would soon be as dead as Masarek. Beria did not tolerate failures.

There was, however, a third possibility. Refugio might have managed to escape with the uranium. He had proved to be a more formidable man that either she or Masarek expected. But now she was warned; she would find Refugio, kill him and take back the uranium.

Vanessa nodded, choosing to act on the third possibility. She must find Refugio quickly, before he realized that what he had stolen could be sold back to the Americans for more money than his greedy peasant mind could imagine. The truck was her only lead. Somehow she must trace the truck.

Jornada del Muerto, New Mexico
3 Hours 14 Minutes After Trinity

Kestrel drove the narrow desert with fierce concentration. Heat made his Indio makeup blur and run, but there was no one close enough to notice. Even so, he would have to pull off and change his clothes. A flimsy disguise was dangerous, and the need for this one was gone.

He sped toward El Paso and a public telephone that he could use to call Takagura again. The telephone call would be risky but necessary. He must have a reply to the message he had sent. If new orders had been issued he must have those, too.

Perhaps Ana had called Takagura, reporting the success or failure of Refugio.

Kestrel noticed his speed and slowed down, watching for side roads. In his haste he had already become lost once in the maze of dirt tracks threading through the Jornada del Muerto. He had bumped around for a long time before he had found a road leading back to the main highway. Now he needed somewhere to hide long enough to shed the Indio disguise.

He spotted a windmill and a dirt road, and swerved off the highway. The dirt track dipped into an arroyo deep enough to conceal his car. On the lip of the arroyo, the windmill turned lazily, filling a stock tank with water one deliberate revolution at a time. Scattered cows chewed on mesquite bushes, undisturbed by the dusty car that had coasted to a stop near the water tank.

Kestrel slid out of the car and watched the dirt track behind him. Nothing moved but thin spirals of dust rising into the sun. He stripped and scrubbed himself in the tank until no trace remained of his Indio disguise. The water was clear and surprisingly cold. The listless wind dried him as he walked back to the car. Kestrel watched the dust puff beneath his feet and the horizon endlessly falling away beneath a hard blue sky. He marveled at the land's immensity and austerity, its only inhabitants silver mirages twisting above the sand.

Kestrel stood unmoving in the pouring light, letting heat draw tension out of his body. After a few moments, he rolled the clothes he had worn and buried them in the arroyo. The cattle stared at him with languid eyes, then turned away, more interested in mesquite beans than in the enigmatic motions of man.

Dust from Kestrel's long drive across the desert had filtered into the car's trunk, but the clothes inside the metal-bound suitcase were still clean and neatly creased. Beginning with cotton GI underwear, Kestrel quickly pulled on the uniform of an American captain. He tied the narrow black tie in a knot that matched the one in his ID picture, tucked his shirttail in his tan pants, adjusted his belt, and unwrapped the shiny black shoes. They were too wide. He tied their laces so tightly the leather overlapped. He shined the toes on his sleeve in an American gesture he had acquired from his college roommate.

Smiling, Kestrel buffed the toes one last time, reassured by the ease with which American mannerisms returned to him. He knew that passing for an American was a matter of body language as much as English language. He had lived eight years in America. Its patterns were embedded in him, ready to be used.

Today his life would depend upon using them.

Kestrel unzipped the worn leather shaving kit and pulled out the papers which established that he was Captain Yokohama, decorated member of America's Nisei Battalion, on emergency leave to be at his father's death-bed. Kestrel studied the print on his papers beneath the merciless desert light. Considering the haste involved, the papers were quite good.

He folded the papers carefully into a worn GI wallet, hoping they would fool the Army Air Corps at El Paso. He got back into the car, feeling its heat engulf him. He wondered if Refugio had killed Masarek yet, and if Vanessa were tied and frightened on the hard floor of a flower truck, and how Ana was accommodating herself to sudden violence. He wondered what had been stolen, and if it would turn out to be worth even an assassin's life.

With a roar that scattered the cattle, Kestrel's car raced out of the arroyo.

Hunters Point
3 Hours 35 Minutes After Trinity

Finn left the guards at the front gate and drove back toward the mess hall where last night's guards were eating. The guards at the gate had been less concerned with checking his credentials than with proving that they were not responsible for the breach in security. Beneath their government-issue starch was relief. A sentry was dead, but they were alive. Some new weapon may be missing, but so what? The war was as good as over. It was only a matter of time.

Time, 2 million casualties and a new Russian world.

Finn felt his anger outstrip his control. He reminded himself that the guards did not know what had been lost, but that did not calm him. A clock in the back of his head hammered relentlessly, counting the minutes until 0530, July 18th. He parked the car and stalked into the linoleum and formica ugliness of a military mess hall. The four guards he wanted were not hard to spot. They were the only men in the room except for a sailor trailing a worn broom between rows of tables.

The men did not immediately notice Finn. They were in a corner of the long room, heads tilted over cups of coffee, cigarets pressed between their knuckles.

Finn waited, sizing up the men as he had once sized up jungle trails. By now the guards had told and retold their stories, assuring themselves they were not at fault for the dead sailor and stolen equipment. He would have to shock them out of that assurance.

Three of the men were young, barely out of training. The fourth was several years older, a chief petty officer with the look of a man who knew where the action was. Every base had a few men like CPO Diver. Their major battles were fought against fellow soldiers.

Finn's eyes lingered on Diver. He looked smart; he would never take a bet he could not lay off, just as he never would trade punches with the local leg breaker. All that remained for Finn was to convince Diver that all bets were off, and Finn was the local leg breaker. He walked up to the table, put on a genial smile, stopped behind the CPO's chair.

"Morning. I was told you were on duty at the gate last night. The front gate."

"So what?" said Diver, without looking up.

"So I want some information," said Finn, still smiling despite the anger building in him. "What moved on and then off base between midnight and 0600 that you didn't inspect?"

"Nothing," said Diver, before any of the other men could speak. He crushed out his cigaret and lit another before he half-turned to Finn. "Not a damn thing."

Finn's smile widened. "Bitch of a night, wasn't it? Rain and wind and all. Nights like that, a guardhouse gets to looking homey. Hate to leave it just to look at a few—"

"We inspected all thirty-seven vehicles," Diver said.

"Neither rain nor sleet, right?"

"Yeah," said Diver indifferently. "We're regular mailmen."

Diver turned back to the table, dismissing Finn. Finn's arm hooked around Diver's throat. In a single motion Finn heaved Diver out of his chair and laid him out on the table like a side of beef. Diver lunged forward, gagged and lay back again. Before the three other guards could collect themselves, Finn flipped his credentials between the coffee cups and ashtrays. "Read those and shut up."

Finn's right forearm lay against Diver's slamming pulse and his resilient, elusive windpipe. Finn leaned down until blackness filled Diver's world.

"Let's try it again, minus the horseshit. How many vehicles did you inspect?"

"About . . . half."

"Which ones *didn't* you inspect?" Finn's rage showed in his voice and his eyes, but most of all in his arm choking the man whose greed could cost millions of lives.

"Stop!" gasped Diver.

Finn lifted his arm a few inches, then slammed Diver back onto the table. "You're shit, Diver. If you'd done your job, that kid wouldn't be dead." That kid and all the other children; a world lost. "*Which vehicles didn't you inspect?*"

"The staff cars," said Diver. As he swallowed, his Adam's apple strained against Finn's forearm. "If we knew the officers, we didn't look in the trunk. Chrissake, no one expects us to! It's a dumb—"

"What else?"

"Nothing. We—"

Diver gagged.

"You're wasting my time," snarled Finn. "What about the civilian stuff?"

Diver's face was deep red. Finn lifted the pressure very slightly.

"Nothing," gasped Diver.

"What does *that* mean?"

Diver swallowed convulsively. "I can't—talk."

"Sure you can," Finn said. "You just have to try a little harder."

"A liquor truck—for Officers' Club," gasped Diver. "Never inspect that. Sealed."

Finn waited, poised for the least flicker of evasion in Diver's blue eyes.

"Mail truck," continued Diver. "Load of steel rods. Lumber. Hardware. That's all. No place for men to hide."

"That's shit, Diver."

"No! No! That's all, honest!"

Finn's fingers closed down. Diver's face went from red to purple.

"When you remember something 'honest,' " said Finn, "wiggle your ears."

After a few moments, Diver's frantic efforts to speak were rewarded with a quarter inch of breathing space.

"Laundry—truck! Officers'—laundry!"

Finn thought quickly but could not remember seeing a laundry truck on the list ONI had given to him.

"Did you log in the truck?"

"No."

"Why not? Whores? Drugs? Betting slips?"

"Betting," gasped Diver. "Goddamn you—betting!"

"Describe the truck," Finn said, easing the pressure on Diver's neck.

"White. Chicken tracks—on the door. A Chink job."

"License plate number."

"How the hell—aggh."

Finn leaned down. "Then how did you know it was the right truck?"

"Number 7—on the door!"

Finn released Diver so suddenly that the CPO did not realize he was free. Betting slips. For the sake of a few gamblers, 2 million people might die.

"The Chink has a legit business," said Diver. "Ho's Good Luck Laundry. Does dress whites better than anyone in Frisco."

"Did he leave out anything?" Finn demanded of the other three guards.

One of them, a Mexican-American with a burr haircut that emphasized his broad Indio features, met Finn's eyes.

"Dunno. He never told us a damn thing about laundry trucks. And since he kept the log . . ." The man shrugged.

Finn's glance shifted back to Diver. "What did the bookies pay you to let that truck onto the base?"

Diver licked his lips with a thick tongue. "Not much."

"And you kept it all, didn't you? None of that share-and-share-alike crap, right?"

Diver glanced nervously at his three colleagues.

"How much?" repeated Finn. His hand went to Diver's throat so quickly that the CPO had no time to flinch.

"A hundred bucks!"

One hundred dollars. Two million people. A penny for every 200 dead or maimed.

Finn reached for Diver's throat, wanting to kill the man who had sold his country so cheaply. At the last instant, he stepped back, his hands shaking. He stared at Diver. Behind the men, the mess door opened.

"Coughlan's drying off," said Riley as he approached Finn. Then, seeing Diver stretched out upon the table. "Still a war, cowboy?"

Finn looked at the agent for a long moment. Then he turned away and spoke to the three apprehensive guards.

"You three are supposed to be MPs. Take this cheap son of a bitch to the brig and lose him."

The three men hustled Diver out of the room.

"Was that all necessary?" asked Riley abruptly, gesturing toward the table.

"Anything new on the vehicles?"

"All present and accounted for. We're running the list again, of course." Then, "Was it necessary?"

Finn sighed. "I told you hard or easy and you told me whatever works. Remember?"

"Yes, but—"

Finn picked up his credentials from the table.

Riley looked at his feet, then back at Finn. "Did it work?"

"You've got coffee stains on your shirt," said Finn, taking Riley's arm and pulling him toward the door. "I know a helluva good Chinese laundry."

Riley tried to pull free, but Finn's grip was too hard, "Don't worry," Finn said, opening the door without letting go. "CPO Diver assured me that Ho's Good Luck Laundry is so popular around Hunters Point that no one even bothers to log the laundry truck in or out."

"Are you nuts?" Then, "Oh . . ."

"Yeah. Oh." Finn let go.

"Are you sure?"

"Nothing's sure. Tell the cops to put out an APB on Ho's Good Luck Laundry truck number 7. If they find it, call us and *stay the hell away from the truck*. Then notify all police departments from San Diego to Seattle to watch for male corpses that have no visible marks of violence. Special attention to men between sixteen and forty.''

Riley looked up in silent query.

"After thirty, the reflexes begin to go. By forty a man either gets out or gets killed.''

"Sixteen to forty. No marks. Anything else?''

Finn hesitated, then shrugged. If people started getting sick mysteriously, questions would be asked anyway. "If anyone goes to a hospital for burns, I want a Fed to investigate. If the person's story isn't good, or if the doctor thinks there is anything unusual about the burns, I want to know immediately.''

"If I asked why, would you tell me?''

"I wouldn't even tell myself without running a security check.''

In silence, Riley followed Finn to the car.

San Francisco
4 Hours 11 Minutes After Trinity

Vanessa stood on the street before the newspaper building and looked around carefully. She had circled the block once already, inspecting each of the parked cars, looking for agents who were looking for her. She did not find any, nor did she expect to. There had not been enough time for the local police to identify Masarek, much less put a watch on anyone in the Bay Area who might be associated with him.

As she passed the newspaper office once more, she glanced past the gold-leaf lettering to the open room beyond. Young men and middle-aged women sat typing or talking on telephones. None of the people impressed her. She did not want to count on anyone in that room, but had little choice. Masarek had not used the emergency message drop. She must assume that he was dead or captured. She could not go to any of the professional agents she knew in San Francisco; if they were not already under surveillance, they would be shortly. The whole city would be shut down while the Americans searched for the uranium. She needed an inactive agent, someone who had never really overtly worked for Russia and thus would not be under surveillance.

In the reflection of the window, Vanessa once more checked her makeup. The scratches were nearly invisible now, and her expression was calm, remote. Satisfied, she entered the office. A teenager approached her. She dazzled him with a smile.

"I'm looking for a reporter named Peter Hecht," she said.

The teenager stared for a moment before she turned and shouted Hecht's name across the office. A reporter who was hunched over a phone waved without looking up. He wore dark pants, a badly fitted sportcoat and a dirty shirt. He scribbled notes as he spoke on the phone.

Vanessa waited, letting the rest of the people resume their normal activities. Then she stepped uninvited past the wooden railing and walked across the room to Hecht's desk. He glanced up, showing alert eyes in an impatient face. Vanessa smiled. He waved at a chair beside his desk and continued talking into the phone.

"What's that address again?" said Hecht. "Yeah, yeah. Got it. You sure there were four bodies? God, that Oakland waterfront gets worse every day." He glanced toward the wall clock. "Shit, I just blew a deadline. Oh well, that gives me ninety minutes to get this story together. Okay. That's one I owe you." He hung up and turned toward Vanessa. "Did you want to see me?"

"Are you Peter Hecht?" said Vanessa, smiling warmly again despite the shock his words had given her. Four bodies on the Oakland waterfront. Refugio had escaped, but Masarek had not.

"Yeah, I'm Hecht, but I'm in the middle of a big story."

"Then I won't waste time. *I'm a student of history.*"

For a moment it was clear that Hecht did not recognize the signal. "Well, that's very . . ." His voice faded and his complexion paled as he stared at the beautiful woman who was smiling at him. "Jesus," he whispered. "I never thought I'd be called."

Vanessa leaned toward him, still smiling. "Comrade Hecht," she murmured, "the response."

Hecht took a deep breath and said, "I, too, am fascinated by historical processes . . ." He looked around, afraid one of his colleagues would overhear.

"Listen carefully," said Vanessa, "and smile. We're just old friends talking together."

He nodded and smiled unconvincingly.

"That's better. The Party has need of your services."

"Now? I just got a tip on a big story. That was the police dispatcher. Pretty soon every newspaper in town is going to know about it."

"You have police contacts?"

"Shit yes. A reporter can't live without them."

"Can you trace a license plate for me?" demanded Vanessa. "I need it quickly."

"Is that all?" said Hecht, relief obvious in his voice. "Easy. I know an Irishman on the auto theft squad."

"He doesn't know about your ties to the Party?"

"No! No one does. And it has to stay that way. My city editor hates communists."

Vanessa took a piece of paper from his desk and wrote quickly. "This is the number. I need to know the name and address of the owner, and whether the truck is listed as stolen. I'll call you in an hour."

She stood up. Hecht came awkwardly to his feet, favoring his right leg. He took the paper and glanced at it. He paused before putting the paper into his pocket.

"This isn't going to get me into any trouble, is it? I mean, I want to help the Party, but I have to maintain my cover, too. I have to get that story first."

Vanessa studied him for a long moment. "One of the four bodies in Oakland belongs to a comrade. So hurry there. Ask questions. Be sure to ask if anything is missing from the truck. But be very discreet or the police will be asking you questions."

San Francisco
4 Hours 16 Minutes After Trinity

Ana backed the flower truck into a small, ramshackle structure that served both as garage and warehouse to the Fragrant Petal flower shop. As always, she winced at the crude translation of the shop's name. English conveyed none of the subtle and complex resonances of transience, death and rebirth that were implicit in the ideograph it purported to represent.

But then, perhaps the translation was more truthful because of its limitations. Death no longer seemed either subtle or complex, merely brutal and revolting.

Ana hurried from the truck to the garage doors. The alley had been empty when she entered it. It was still empty when she dragged shut the canted wooden doors of the garage. The gloom inside was both tangible and oddly reassuring. Darkness would blur the reality in the back of the van, making easier what she must do.

Ana opened the back of the van. "Refugio?"

The answer was more groan than word. Ana hesitated, trembling suddenly. The strength that fear had given her was gone, but Refugio was still there, wounded. With a shaking hand, she switched on the garage's interior light.

She saw Refugio lying in the back of the truck, his body bisected by a wedge of light. The pure crimson covering his leg would have been beautiful had it been anything but blood. Beyond the light was his face, invisible.

Ana swayed, her knuckles white against her lips.

"Easy, chica," said Refugio. "It is much better than it looks." He tried to smile and nearly succeeded. "It is not my first wound, or my worst." His abrupt laugh startled her. "Or my last, please God."

Painfully, Refugio eased himself around until he was in a sitting position with his legs dangling over the truck. "Okay, chica. Help me inside."

He held himself erect, breathing rapidly, his face pale with nausea, more nausea than he had anticipated. For an instant he wondered if Masarek had used poison on his bullets.

Ana waited, color slowly returning to her face. She knew she must help Refugio. If he died, leaving her alone in the fragrant shambles of her childhood, all this would be for nothing.

"Wait."

Ana ran to the shop door that led from the garage to the living quarters in back of the store. The smell of bruised petals and crushed stems was everywhere, heightened by the damp air. Ana shuddered, hating the odor and the childhood it recalled.

The door was unlocked and painted a bright pink that clashed with her memories. Her father would never have permitted such a garish color to intrude upon the serenity of his household. But her father was in a prison camp called Manzanar, and the shop had been sold to Refugio's cousins for a fraction of its worth.

There were other changes inside. Colors that offended her, floors that were crusted with the sediment of a different culture, startling pictures of improbable bulls and glittering bullfighters painted on black velvet. There were religious paintings of an impaled Christ and a smiling Madonna.

One bed remained. It was used as an informal couch, covered by a rainbow serape. Ana yanked off the blanket and threw it on the floor.

She turned and ran back to the truck. Refugio was standing, holding on to one of the van doors and swearing with a fervency that most men reserved for prayer. Ana pulled his arm over her shoulder, substituting her support for that of the door.

After a few awkward attempts, Ana and Refugio learned to gauge the other's weakness and strength. A moment later, Refugio was stretched out on the bed, groaning with relief. He felt feverish, which he expected. The intensity of his nausea, however, worried him. Sweating suddenly, he fought the urge to vomit.

Ana saw Refugio's convulsive swallowing and guessed its cause. She grabbed an empty flower pail and shoved it under his nose. When he was finished, she went to the bathroom, emptied the pail, then set it by the bed.

"Thanks," said Refugio, wiping his face on the wet cloth she had given him. "It is only a little wound. The pain is not so bad, now."

"Good," said Ana, her jaw set, "because we have to clean your leg."

"Yes," sighed Refugio, letting his head drop back onto the thin mattress. He took his knife out of its belt sheath. "Can you do it or do you want me to?"

Secretly, Ana had been hoping that he would refuse her help. Without a word, she took the knife from Refugio's cold fingers, sliced through his pant leg, and peeled away the bloody cloth.

The wound was a scarlet furrow gouged across the meaty top of Refugio's thigh. Though bloody and undoubtedly painful, the wound was obviously not a serious one.

Refugio saw the relief in Ana's face. "It's as I told you. A small thing, not to be worried about."

Ana's smile was so brief that Refugio missed it. He closed his eyes and lay passively beneath her hands. She was surprisingly deft. Within a very few minutes, Refugio's leg was clean and the wound gently bathed.

Even so, the pain made Refugio sweat.

"All I could find to disinfect the wound is alcohol," said Ana.

"Good," Refugio said, clenching his teeth. "Do it."

When the alcohol washed over raw flesh, Refugio convulsed with pain. Ana forced herself to finish, then went into the bathroom and vomited until she had nothing left in her but a numb desire to wake from the nightmare of the last hour.

There was no awakening. When she went back to the room, Refugio was still there, throwing up into the tin pail. When he was finished, she bound his leg in strips of the only clean sheet she could find. Then she went back to the bathroom. She was gone a long time.

Refugio did not open his eyes when Ana returned.

"The worst is over, chica. The wound will scab and the leg will be stiff, and I will limp around for a few days like Ridgewalker."

"When will your cousin be here to open the shop?"

"Before noon."

Refugio squinted up at Ana, realizing that there was something different about her. Then he saw that now she wore her hair ratted and tousled around her face. She had put on dark makeup instead of her customary rice powder. Wedges of black at the outer corners of each eye disguised their Oriental slant, and a stripe of blue subdued their epicanthic fold. Bright lipstick thickened the line of her lips. The total effect was more Mexican than Japanese, although a close inspection revealed the delicate bones of her face.

"Good," said Refugio approvingly. "Even your own father would have to look again to be sure that he saw you." His eyes traveled over her again. "Very pretty. Why do you not do this in Mexico?"

Ana thought she looked like a two-peso whore, but did not say so. At least she would not be recognized by any of her former San Francisco neighbors. She looked at her watch. Not yet nine o'clock.

She knew she should call Takagura Omi, but could not face it yet. She was afraid that he would tell her Kestrel could not come. Then she would have to drive the length of California alone—a fugitive Japanese girl with a wounded Mexican murderer and two canvas sacks whose contents had already cost several lives.

Ana looked again at her watch, knowing she must call soon.

"What will you do if he does not come?" said Refugio, his dark eyes shrewd in spite of his pain. He knew Kestrel did not trust him. He did not resent it. He respected the Japanese spy's pragmatism. "Did he leave the money with you?"

"No."

Refugio smiled. "Don't feel bad. He didn't trust me,

either. But that doesn't answer my first question. What do we do if he doesn't come?''

''We get back in the truck and drive to the tunnel,'' said Ana. ''Kestrel left sealed instructions with Takagura Omi. Don't worry—you'll get paid.''

Ana emphasized Takagura's name, reminding Refugio that should he cross Kestrel, Takagura could make Refugio's life a preview of hell. Takagura's wealth and power extended far beyond Barrio Chino.

''It's you who should not worry,'' said Refugio, smiling invitingly. ''If Kestrel does not come, I will take care of you.''

''He'll come,'' said Ana fiercely.

San Francisco
4 Hours 31 Minutes After Trinity

Finn and Riley were parked on a hill overlooking San Francisco. The view was interrupted by streamers of fog stirred by a fitful wind. Toward Oakland the fog was dense, white and opaque. On the Berkeley hilltops it was as fine as gossamer, brilliantly backlighted by the hidden sun.

Although Finn had driven to the hilltop for the radio reception rather than the view, he appreciated the elegance of the white city swathed in mist, and at the same time could not help wondering where in all those teeming streets was Good Luck laundry truck number 7. The two men listened to reports emanating from across the city, including, finally, a report from Coughlan. His voice was harsh with static and exasperation.

''*Trucks 1, 3, 4, 8 and 9 accounted for. They smell like*

dirty shorts and they don't register on this voodoo box. Nothing in the building. Trucks 2, 5 and 6 are picking up laundry. The cops have searched them. Nothing.

"*Satisfied, Finn? Or do you want me to go over anything again?*"

Finn punched the transmit button. "Negative." He replaced the microphone and resumed staring out at the city.

"You didn't expect to find anything in those other trucks, did you?" said Riley.

"Whoever pulled off this job is a pro. He has no connection with the laundry. Probably bought the driver, or killed him and took the truck." Finn flexed his shoulders, releasing the tension of inactivity. "He'll dump the truck, switch to another vehicle and either go to ground or run."

"Then why the fuss over the damned trucks?"

"You have a better idea of a good place to start?"

"Since I don't know damn all about what was stolen, I wouldn't know whether to start shaking the local fences or to drag the local waters for stiffs in cement overcoats."

"It wasn't local talent," said Finn. "Odds are it wasn't even American talent."

Riley digested the implications of what Finn said. "That rather widens the search area."

Finn said nothing, just stared through the windshield at the city, watching the fog and waiting because there was nothing else he could do. He had discovered and described the quarry's spoor, and he had sent his beaters out through the foggy jungle. Now he could only wait for the quarry to be flushed.

And try not to count the seconds clicking by. Try not to wonder if laundry truck number 7 was here or there or anywhere at all.

Suddenly both men sat up and lunged for the volume control.

"*—in the 600 block along the waterfront. Repeat. Oak-land police responded to a disturbance involving Ho's laundry truck number 17.*"

Finn started the Ford and surged into traffic while Riley wrote in his notebook. When the voice said "17," Riley swore. He glanced at the speedometer. "What's the rush? We're looking for number 7, not 17."

"Ho only has nine trucks."

Finn slid into a bicycle-sized opening between two trucks, then braked hard for a right turn.

"Ask when the truck was found," he said. "And tell Coughlan to keep the locals the hell away from it. There's always some hero who can't leave well enough alone."

Riley spoke rapidly, his words lost to Finn beneath the sound of the Ford whining up to peak acceleration.

"They found it an hour ago."

"For the love of Christ," snarled Finn, weaving around a startled motorist, "why weren't we notified!"

Riley braced himself on the dashboard. "The APB was for truck number 7."

"*Shit!*" said Finn, his voice furious, "nobody's *that* dumb!"

"The locals hate our guts," said Riley. "The only reason they let us in on anything is because they're forced to. If you go out there screaming like Coughlan, Oak-land's finest will do everything they can to hamstring your investigation."

Finn answered by throwing the car into a controlled skid. He straightened the wheel and aimed for the Bay Bridge rising out of the gloom. The radio mumbled again.

"*Three bodies were aboard and a fourth down in the street. Coroner has them now.*"

"Tell everyone to stay away from the truck," said Finn. He thought about those eager, half-bright Oakland cops, all of them wondering what had the FBI so stirred up, crawling over the truck and soaking up radiation.

The car raced onto the Bay Bridge as Riley replaced the microphone.

"Where's the 600 block?" asked Finn.

"Bear to the right coming off the bridge, then make a hard right at the first cross street. It's on the waterfront."

"What about the Lawrence Radiation men?"

"They cleared Coughlan. They're finishing up at Hunters Point. Should be here in about forty-five minutes."

Using first brake, then accelerator, Finn slid through a right turn and onto a rough waterfront street. A roadblock of police cars appeared a few blocks away. The cop on the roadblock was big and hard-bellied. He let them pass grudgingly.

Finn parked the car, grabbed the radiation counter and walked quickly to the knot of men around the laundry truck. He adjusted dials as he went. Riley followed at a trot, the only way he could match Finn's long-legged stride.

A dozen men stood by the truck, six in police uniform, four in suits and two in the uniforms of factory security guards. Finn ignored all of them. He swept the counter's wand back and forth.

Conversation stopped; everyone stared at Finn. He moved the wand, testing the outside of the vehicle. In the silence, the click of the counter was clear. Finn moved the dial up again before opening the truck's front door and sticking the probe inside.

The clicking increased. Finn reset the dial. The clicking slowed. He checked the front seat, looking carefully at every place where the uranium might have been hidden. The seat was intact, the glove compartment empty, the wall panels untouched.

Finn turned his attention to the back of the truck. As he moved toward the rear doors, the counter shrieked. Finn retreated; there was no reason to stay. The spots that set off the counter were patently bare patches of floor. The isotope that had irradiated the floor was gone.

Slamming the door, Finn examined the number of the truck. The electricians tape that had made 7 into 17 was half-peeled off, curling back on itself like a dying leaf.

The chief of detectives wandered over to Finn. "Just discovered that little bit of tape a few minutes ago. If we'd seen it sooner," he smiled insincerely, "we'd have called you Feds right away, just like our orders said to do."

The man waited, but Finn had nothing to say.

"But don't worry," continued the detective. "Our Crime boys took care of everything. You should have the report sometime next week."

"There were two chunks of metal, one fist sized, one about three times as large. Where are they?"

The cop shrugged. "I tagged the evidence myself. Only thing we took out of that truck was bodies, laundry and weapons."

"For your sake, I hope that's true. What's your security clearance?"

"I'm Abel Jones, chief of detectives," snapped the gray-haired cop. "That's all the clearance I need."

"This truck, this block and everything that happened is classified. Top Secret. Therefore you and your men are in violation of wartime security regulations. You're under arrest."

"What? Now you listen here, you smart-mouthed son-ofabitch—"

"Can it."

Finn's voice was not loud, but it easily cut across the cop's words. "I'm not the kind of Fed you're used to." He smiled. "I'm a lot nicer."

Riley looked uneasily at Finn, but said nothing.

"If you cooperate," continued Finn, "you'll get a star on our fitness report the next time around. If you don't cooperate, you won't be around long enough to get another report. You'll be Private Abel Jones. Don't take my word for it. Please don't. Uncle Sam needs all the cannon fodder he can get."

Finn waited. Chief of Detectives Abel Jones said nothing. He turned to Riley, recognizing him. "Does this guy have more than a mouth?"

"Yes."

"Where's Coughlan?"

"On his way to boot camp."

"He's too goddamn old to be drafted."

"So are you," said Riley, "but you'll get used to it if you live long enough."

Jones looked from Riley to Finn, then back to Riley. Abruptly, he laughed. "I almost hope you're telling the truth. Be worth it to see that loudmouth sonofabitch Coughlan sweat out a forced march." He turned to Finn. "You'll get the reports as soon as I do. Anything else you want?"

"There will be men out to go over what you removed from the truck. Don't get in their way. Cordon off this block. Call back everyone who was at the scene, but keep them out of my way until I want them."

"Everyone's still here but the coroner and his men."

"Get them back here."

"You want the four bodies, too?" asked the chief of detectives sarcastically.

"That's up to the lab. But the live ones have to be checked for . . . poison."

Jones turned and walked toward the men who had been waiting beyond the truck. One of those men ignored the detective and walked toward Riley and Finn. The man moved with a hesitation that was just short of a limp. Riley took one look and swore under his breath.

"We got trouble," said Riley. "That guy is Hecht, a reporter. This is what he's been dreaming of—war and hell and all the things he'd love to write about. He won't cooperate. Count on it."

Finn studied the approaching reporter. He was Riley's age or younger. As though the reporter sensed the scrutiny, his limp became more pronounced, a visible explanation of why he was carrying a notebook rather than an Army rifle.

"Leave him to me," said Finn. "Take the counter and go stand by that fence."

Riley casually walked away, then turned and leaned on the sheetmetal fence that separated piles of rusting auto bodies from the cracked sidewalk. He strained to hear what was being said, but all he could hear was a dog sniffing on the opposite side of the fence.

The dog sensed Riley's presence, but made no noise. Nor did the animal walk away. It stood silently, poised, waiting for Riley to go over the fence or down the street. Somehow, Riley was reminded of Finn.

Riley looked up as the reporter turned suddenly and limped away, as though he wanted to put as much distance as possible between himself and the man called Finn. Riley waited for a moment longer, then walked back to the truck.

Behind the metal fence, the dog snarled.

Moscow
4 Hours 41 Minutes After Trinity

Lavrenti Beria's dark, narrow eyes neither blinked nor shifted from the speaker's nervous face.

"Read it again," said Beria, flicking his fingernail against the edge of his desk. "Slowly, this time."

The assistant risked a quick throat-clearing before he began to read from the cable in his hands. To be Comrade Beria's most confidential assistant was both an honor and a trial. Beria's scrutiny could be dangerous. The head of the Commissariat of Internal Affairs was known for abrupt and irrevocable decisions.

"Proceed," said Beria.

"Yes, comrade. 'To the Commissariat of Soviet Fisheries: Encountered stormy weather while transferring cargo at sea. First mate swept overboard, almost certainly dead. Hired crew gone. Cargo lost. Am pursuing promising methods of salvage, but require an experienced, trustworthy crew. Repeat. Trustworthy.' " The assistant cleared his throat again. "It's signed 'V,' comrade."

Beria stared at the floor for several minutes, as though he could see halfway around the world. His fingernail tapped in counterpoint to his thoughts. At least Vanessa had followed orders and avoided contacting any Russian agents in San Francisco. This was a secret operation. Only Beria himself knew the extent and necessity of that secrecy.

Cargo lost.

The fingernail hesitated, then resumed its rhythmic tapping. If only he could be sure that the U-235 would stay lost . . . but that was impossible. As long as the uranium was within American reach, the future of Soviet Russia was written on an atomic cloud.

If Russia had the uranium, however, it was America whose future was written in radioactivity. America would foolishly commit more and more of her men and wealth to Japan's conquest. When the fighting was at its height and all of America's strength was locked in final battle with the Emperor's foolish pawns, a Russian plane would fly over Japan. Or London, Or Washington, D.C.

Then a second sun would rise. A Russian sun.

Russia had every drawing of importance, every schematic, every design made at Los Alamos. Even so, the plutonium bomb, with its intricate spherical wrapper of sixty-four lens-shaped explosive charges and millionth-second timers, was beyond Russia's engineering capabilities.

But the uranium bomb was not. Russia would not even have to worry about such sophisticated items as proximity fuses. All that was required was a simple casing and a suicide crew to detonate the bomb a few hundred feet above the ground.

The possibilities were limited only by the detail of the missing uranium—and Stalin's refusal to recognize the atomic bomb as the most revolutionary political tool since the musket.

"Direct V to the nearest secure radio," said Beria calmly. "Tell V not to trust anyone in that cell. Those agents are fit only to count ships passing. I'll send one good man, usual recognition signals."

Beria hesitated. He wanted to send more for Vanessa, much more, but could not do so secretly. Even as much as he had done so far would cost him his life if Stalin found out. The Great Leader had given no orders to steal uranium. He did not even know it had been attempted. Only Beria was the right combination of visionary and opportunist and strategist to appreciate the awesome political

potential of the atomic bomb. Stalin's usually acute grasp
of global politics had been blunted by the parochial
necessities of governing a Russia at war.

Once the bomb had been presented to Russia as a fait
accompli, Stalin would accept and reward his loyal comrade, Lavrenti Beria. Until then, Beria's actions invited
misunderstanding.

Beria's nail tapped the desk four times in rapid suc-
cession. He still wished he could send Vanessa every
Russian agent in the United States, but he would be dead
or in exile before she could put them to use.

The fingernail descended to the polished desk a final
time.

"Notify me immediately of any further communica-
tions from V," said Beria, dismissing his assistant with a
motion of his finger.

Oakland
4 Hours 46 Minutes After Trinity

Finn turned off the radiation counter and walked back up
the street from the spot where the fourth body had been
found. If the dead man had carried the uranium, it was
gone now. The counter had picked up residual radiation
where the body had been, but nothing more.

"Okay, Detective," said Finn, coming up to Jones.
"Let's go over it again."

Jones arranged weapons and labeled bags on the hood of
a squad car as he spoke. "When I got here, there was a DB
down the road. Male Mexican, about thirty, powerful
arms. This knife," Jones indicated a short-bladed sheath
knife, "was near him. This bag has the contents of his

pockets. No wallet. No ID, just matches, cigarets and money.''

''Mexican or American?''

''Mexican all the way. He smoked Dominos. His dead pal in the van smoked some other greaser brand.''

Finn sorted the contents of the bag on the car's hood. The matches were from the Green Parrot. He thought immediately of Refugio, but dismissed it. Refugio's eyebrows, not his arms, were his most outstanding characteristic.

''How did he die?''

''Bullet wounds in the face and chest.''

''How about the van?''

Jones shifted a narrow cigar from one side of his mouth to the other. ''Well, the dead Chink was in the back, stuffed in a laundry bag.''

Riley looked up at Finn, remembering what he had said earlier about the driver either being bought or killed.''

''Funny thing about the Chink,'' Jones continued. ''If his shirt hadn't been off, we'd still be looking for what killed him. The wound wasn't as wide as my finger. Not a drop of blood. Whoever did it was a pro.''

Finn looked in the bag holding the Chinese driver's possessions. He riffled through the wallet, finding the paper residue of a life spent obeying white law in public and tong law in private. Nothing for Finn to use. It was the same for the bag holding more Mexican cigarets and Green Parrot matchbooks.

''Shot through the eye,'' said Jones before Finn could ask about the second Mexican. ''Fell just in back of the front seat.''

Finn nodded. He had seen the puddle of blood. He had also seen blood sprayed across the inside of the windshield, the passenger side and down both sides of the seat. As one cop had pointed out, they had had their own little war in the van.

"You said four bodies," Finn said, looking for another bag of personal effects.

"Nothing in the fourth guy's pockets but lint—and not much of that. Not even labels."

"Describe him," demanded Finn quickly. It would be like Masarek to leave no trace of his identity, not even labels in his clothes.

Detective Jones shrugged. "Male, over thirty."

"That's not much help," said Riley.

Jones took out his cigar and blew on its smoldering tip. "Ever seen a razor wire, son?"

"Huh?" said Riley.

"Well, this wire job was bungled," said Jones. "Victim got a hand under the wire before it closed. Between the blood and the usual eye-popping, his own mother wouldn't know him."

Riley made an odd sound as he swallowed.

"Hair color?" Finn asked calmly.

"Dark. Might have been gray at the temples. Kinda hard to tell, what with all the mess." Jones shot a quick glance at Riley. "You know, when you put the kind of pressure on a man's artery, not only does the face turn purple and the eyes bug out, but—"

"I'll bet," said Riley loudly, cutting across the details of death, "that you get a boot out of putting razor blades in trick-or-treat apples."

Detective Jones laughed, not at all offended. "Kid, the first thing you learn as a homicide dick is that corpses stink, blood washes off and lunchtime comes at noon."

" 'Dead is pretty much dead,' " quoted Finn. "Right, Riley?"

"Yeah. Right."

Finn turned away and walked back to the van, with both men following.

The air inside still smelled of cordite. That told him nothing new; the cordite was American-made and blood was the same the world over.

Only the uranium was unique, and it was gone.

"The way I figure it," said Jones, leaning into the front seat of the van next to Finn, "is that the guy with the wire and his pal stood behind the front seat, dropped the wire around the passenger, and—" Jones made a juicy, descriptive sound.

"The passenger stays kicking long enough to do for the pal—bang bang—but can't get to the guy pulling on the wire."

Finn's glance raked over the truck, re-creating the scene in his mind. "The driver was shot by the passenger before the wire dropped," said Finn. He pointed to a veneer of blood on the driver's side that clearly showed the imprint of a seated man. There was a bright streak where a bullet had stripped paint off the driver's door. "Went through the thigh, probably."

"Nope. None of the DBs had leg wounds. Every other damn thing but that. I checked."

"Then the driver limped away," said Finn reasonably.

"Doubt it. None of the guards saw him. And guys were looking, believe me." Jones jerked his thumb over his shoulder at the two gray-haired factory guards who were still talking to the uniformed officers. "This was the most exciting thing they'd ever seen."

Finn stared at Jones in disbelief. "Between them, those two guys are about one hundred and thirty. On a foggy night, I could steal their goddamn factory piece by piece and they wouldn't see a thing. Put out an APB for a male with a leg wound."

As Jones walked off, Finn opened a large bag and began sorting through the weapons. There were knives, hand-guns and beneath them a sawed-off shotgun with silver inlays in the stock. Finn pulled it out of the bag.

"Salvador," murdered Finn. "Refugio."

"Gesundheit," said Riley.

Finn looked up, almost smiled. "Salvador Leon is a Mexicali thug with a reputation for murder. He carries an escopeta like this and works for a crook called Refugio."

"Can't be too many like it." said Riley, looking at the gaudy gun. "Looks like whore's Christmas."

This time Finn smiled. "It kills just as dead as the plain models." Finn sniffed the barrel. "Hasn't been fired today."

Riley peered into the bag and removed a pistol with a silencer attached. "That explains it."

Finn looked up. "Explains what?"

"The guards only heard a few shots, but from what the cops said, a lot of lead must have been flying."

"Of course," said Finn matter-of-factly. "That's why no one at Hunters Point heard the sentry die."

Riley put down the gun and went toward the back doors of the van. As he reached for the handles, Finn spoke.

"Don't."

Finn's voice was flat, yet somehow urgent. Responding to the tone as much as to the command itself, Riley let go of the handles and stepped back quickly.

"What's wrong?" complained Riley. "You said there's nothing in there but blood."

"Stay away from the back end of the truck," Finn said. "Do your sightseeing from the front, and don't be too long about it."

With a motion that was becoming second nature, Finn turned on the radiation counter and walked around to the

back of the truck. The clicks increased in volume and fre-
quency as he approached the point where Riley stood.
Hastily, Riley stepped aside. The clicks did not diminish
with his absence. By the time Finn was at the back doors,
he had had to recalibrate twice. The radiation was still
within safety limits, but Finn knew when he opened the
door the counter would scream.

He moved the counter slowly across the back of the van.
The radiation was highest at the center of the bumper,
where blood had dripped from the van floor onto the
chrome, as though the surviving thief had set down the
two pieces of metal, slid out of the truck, and then pulled
the uranium after him.

Finn was accustomed to the counter now. He found it
helpful, so long as he remembered to rely on it and not the
eyes to trace the invisible patterns of radiation that he
knew were present. He concentrated, building a mental
picture of what had happened on the foggy street where
men had fought and died over a stolen sun.

Sitting on his heels, Finn swept the probe just above the
surface of the street. He was rewarded by a crackle of
sound, as though the uranium had been set on the ground
for an instant. The radiation was not as potent as that in
the truck.

The probe quartered the street alongside the van, but
no matter how sensitive the setting, there was no response
until Finn came to the place where Salvador's body had
rested. That response was relatively weak.

Finn walked slowly, avoiding the shards of glass,
windows shot out of parked cars. The counter barely
clicked, registering less than normal radiation. The sandy
sediment that lined the gutters and filled the potholes did
not set off the counter.

Suddenly, Finn bent over and fished in the gutter between a parked car and the curb.

"Find something?" said Riley.

Finn tossed a shell casing to Riley, who caught it with a quick movement of his hand.

"Check the gun with the silencer."

In a moment, Riley called out. "Nope. It's a 9 millimeter. Must be a .38 somewhere."

"Yeah. Pretty big gun for a woman, though."

"What woman?" demanded Riley.

"None of the dead men was small enough to make that print," said Finn pointing at the muddy street, "except the Chinese driver, and he was already dead. Masarek was traveling with a woman. An Englishwoman called Vanessa Lyons."

Riley looked, and then bent down and looked again. There in the gritty mud was a small footprint.

"Are you really an Indian scout?" said Riley, halfway between sarcasm and awe.

"She probably crouched half in and half out of the gutter," said Finn, "laid the .38 across the hood, and fired." He stood in the empty parking space and squinted along an imaginary line leading to the van. "Not a bad shot. She nailed the van's side mirror. Probably covered her escape."

Riley looked at the empty parking place and shrugged. "Whatever you say."

"Only one problem with my theory," Finn continued, walking up the street. "The tread patterns don't match."

Riley looked first at the tread impressions in the gutter, then at the potholes in the street next to the van. The damp soil in the potholes had taken clear impressions of the tires that last rolled over the holes. The tread pattern next to the curb did not match that in the potholes.

"Footprints don't match, either," said Finn.

Superimposed on a pothole treadmark were two footprints, side by side. The footprint on the left was half the size of the footprint on the right. The pattern on the soles was also different.

"Either a woman or a small man on the left," said Finn, "and a man on the right." He measured the distance from the van. "I'll bet the man was injured. The woman parked next to the van, helped him into her truck and drove off."

"Truck? I thought she was driving a car," said Riley, waving his hand toward the empty curb. "And why was she shooting at him earlier?"

"There were two women. The one doing the shooting drove a car. That," said Finn, pointing to the clear tread in the pothole, "was left by a truck—wide tire, diamond tread—driven by the second woman. See how deep her shoe went? As deep as his, so he was leaning on her pretty hard. She loaded him into her truck and got the hell out of here before those blind guards saw anything but their cataracts."

Riley shrugged again. "Yeah. Right."

"You don't follow it," said Finn. "Fine. Take my word for it." He stared at the footprints, wondering aloud if it had been Refugio who was shot.

Riley held up both hands, surrendering. "Who am I to question Geronimo's grandson?" he said.

"How'd you know about my granddaddy?"

Riley stood, watching Finn and wondering if he was joking.

Finn moved off, checking distances, treads, footprints and angles, trying to decipher the pattern that was there. Three people. One man, probably hurt, and two different women—one shooting and one helping the man. Was it a case of thieves stealing from each other? If so, who were the betrayers and who were the betrayed?

Refugio could have double-crossed Masarek or vice versa. Masarek's blonde was probably one of the women, but where did the other woman come from? The only woman who worked for Refugio were whores, and it was doubtful that Refugio would use a whore for anything more demanding than sex.

And Kestrel—was he involved, despite being a thousand miles away, watching the sun rise twice over a place called Trinity?

Questions and facts circled in Finn's mind. Four dead men—two Mexicans, one Chinese and one Caucasian had died on the waterfront this morning. Until he identified the bodies, he would not know which players were alive and which were out of the deadly game of hide-and-seek that had begun at Hunters Point. Until he used the radiation counter on the bodies, he would not know who had warmed himself in the forbidden fires of an earthbound sun.

"Riley."

Riley, crouched over the footprints and treadmarks, looked up almost guiltily. "Yes?"

"Let's go. I have an idea."

El Paso, Texas
5 Hours 35 Minutes After Trinity

The subtle echo of distance told Kestrel that his telephone call had gone through. He wiped away the sweat that gathered at his hairline and looked around the greasy little café again. Only an old wino was close enough to hear what he was saying. There was a click, a subdued crackle of static, then Takagura Omi's precise Japanese inflections came over the line. Though both Kestrel and Takagura spoke Japanese, they still spoke circumspectly.

"I have two letters from home for you," began Takagura the moment he recognized Kestrel's voice. "Your honored father regretfully informs you that he cannot accept your suggestion. What you described is impossible at the time and place you described it. Even the most hopeful estimates agree that the event you described could not take place for at least three years. Your father suggests that as it is 1945 rather than 1948, you may have been only a mile away from what you saw, rather than ten."

Takagura paused, giving Kestrel time to digest the unpalatable message. The Emperor—or his militarist advisors—did not believe that America had made an atomic bomb in less than three years. Because the bomb was an impossibility, therefore, Japan had no need to surrender unconditionally.

It was insane.

"Were you quite sure of the reception and translation of the message?"

"Yes," said Takagura. "I am most scrupulous in these matters."

Kestrel held the receiver and wondered desperately how he could convince the militant leaders of his country that Japan had lost the war just before dawn on a desolate stretch of New Mexican desert. A feeling of despair unfolded inside him like a black flower. He knew that if he had not seen the explosion himself, he would not believe it had ever occurred. He had read the same scientific estimates that they had, the confident statements that the uranium isotope was so difficult to collect that it would be 1948 before the Americans gathered enough for even a small bomb.

Obviously his superiors had rejected the reality of

America's atomic capability. Unfortunately, what Japan believed or did not believe did not lessen the force of the atomic bomb by a single erg.

Suddenly he felt deeply tired. "The second letter?" he asked indifferently. "What did it say?"

"I'll read it, although I want you to know I don't approve of its source," Takagura said.

Kestrel knew then that the second message came from Minowara, his patron in the Japanese war cabinet and the leader of the moderate faction that was despised by militants like Takagura.

"Your honored brother agrees with your description of the events," said Takagura. "Our comrades from the enormous mainland confirmed your description in every detail." Takagura's voice was dry, precise. "Even so, your brother does not agree with your conclusion that your . . . family . . . must lose all face in an unnecessary abasement that will last as long as there are Japanese to feel shame."

Kestrel pressed the phone against his ear as though by hearing better he could change the meaning of what he heard. His "brother" Minowara believed that Kestrel had indeed seen the atomic bomb exploded, because the Russians had confirmed it. Despite that, Minowara still maintained that unconditional surrender was "unnecessary." That was even more irrational a position than the militants' refusal to believe an atomic bomb existed.

"Does he say why abasement is unnecessary?" asked Kestrel, his voice raw with the effort of concealing his anger and exhaustion.

"The event you described can't be repeated for several months."

"Why?"

"Our . . . comrades . . . have removed the motive power."

"*What?*"

"If you remember, a necessary component of the . . . event . . . is exceedingly rare. Gathering it takes much time."

Kestrel rubbed sweat out of his eyes as he tried to make sense of Takagura's elliptical communication. Somehow the Russians had defused the American bombs. But how?

"I don't understand," he said.

"There were only two events extant," said Takagura slowly. "One you saw. The other was awaiting shipment to Japan when our comrades removed the *elemental* motive power."

Kestrel heard the emphasis on the world "elemental" and realized that Takagura was referring to an element called uranium. Apparently the Americans had had only enough uranium for two atomic bombs. They had tested one this morning—and the Russians had stolen the other!

An incredible suspicion grew in Kestrel's mind. Tiredness fell away from him as he examined the idea. Japan's "comrades"—Russian—had stolen the uranium heart of the atomic bomb. It was almost certain that the Hunters Point theft and the uranium theft were one and the same. If that was true, then it was also true that at this moment Japan, not Russia, controlled the core of the world's only atomic bomb—unless Refugio had failed or betrayed Takagura.

"Is there any message from my 'sister'?" asked Kestrel. "Is she well?"

"Yes, but her husband and her brothers aren't. Apparently overseeing the delivery of her baby was too much for them. Her husband's brothers left abruptly. Her husband is still with her, but he is . . . ill.''

Ana was well, but Refugio and his men were not. Something had gone wrong. "The baby?" demanded Kestrel. "Is the baby well?"

"Quite well. The mother wishes to know if you will see her there or will you wait until she returns?"

Relief swept through Kestrel. The uranium was safe, with Ana. "I'll go to her immediately."

"Good." Dry curiosity crept into Takagura's tone. "The birth of your first nephew seems to have pleased you enormously . . . ?"

"This isn't my first nephew," corrected Kestrel, "but my second. The first one was born this morning just before dawn."

Kestrel hung up before Takagura could reply.

The cafe's screen door banged loosely as he left. Although it was not yet noon, the sun was a white-hot hammer. Yet Kestrel did not notice the heat in his exhilaration at the news of what Refugio had stolen.

The physicist in him was impatient to see the U-235. He wanted to inspect it, feel it, to determine whether it was brittle or malleable, bright or rough, white or dark—and whether it required special handling.

The strategist in Kestrel ignored the physicist's excited speculation. The physical properties of an exotic isotope were far less important than the isotope's value as a political weapon.

With the U-235 America could force Japan to accept unconditional surrender. Without the uranium, there was no choice for America but the invasion of Japan.

With the U-235 stolen from America, the Russians could watch their hated American allies and their putative Japanese friends engage in bloody combat while Russia consolidated her power over newly conquered European territories.

And the Japanese . . . what could Japan do with a critical mass of U-235? At the very least, Japan could ready itself for the protracted invasion that American generals called Operation Downfall, an invasion the Japanese generals saw as a way to force America into negotiated surrender.

Japan's possession of the uranium would convince Japanese militarists that the atomic bomb was a reality, that a new world had been born, and that new solutions were therefore possible. The Americans could be approached now, not for surrender, but for a conference of equals. Japan could offer the uranium in exchange for an honorable end to the war.

With a U-235, it might be possible for Japan to dictate the terms of her own "surrender." Japan's self-respect could survive defeat intact, ensuring her future as a nation.

A slow cattle truck forced Kestrel's attention back to Texas. He passed the truck, and in doing so nearly missed the turnoff to the Army Air Corps base. He parked the car in a dry, almost deserted neighborhood, grabbed his suitcase and walked the quarter mile to the front gate.

The MP on duty saluted the captain's bars on Kestrel's shoulders, and at the same time inspected him more closely. Orientals were not unheard of on the base, but they warranted a second look.

"Can I help you, sir?" asked the MP, his voice clipped and correct.

Kestrel returned the salute crisply. "I left a troop train because a soldier told me I might catch a faster ride here. I'm going home."

The MP inspected Kestrel again. "Where's home?" he

asked.

"California. A place called Manzanar." Dryly. "Maybe you've heard of it."

The MP's face shifted slightly. "A Jap, huh?" he said, but there was no hostility in his voice. "Thought all of you were still in Italy."

"I was, until the Red Cross told me my father was dying. I've been on the road ever since. It's all here in the compassionate leave papers."

Kestrel removed a sheaf of travel orders from his uniform coat. The MP waved away the papers.

"That's not necessary," said the MP. "Remember, you're in Texas now. You guys from the 454th are real heroes here since you pulled the 36th out of that hole in Italy. Most of the guys in the 36th were Texans." He waved his hand toward a quonset hut a hundred feet inside the gate. "Show your papers to the officer of the day. His office is right over there. Good luck, sir. I hope you're in time to see your father."

Kestrel saluted. "Thank you, Corporal. I hope so too."

Inside the quonset hut, a large fan circulated hot air with enough force to slam shut the plywood door behind Kestrel. A bareheaded private in a rumpled uniform glanced up from a newspaper. He looked at the captain's bars on Kestrel's uniform, then at his face, then at his bars again. The private half-rose, half-saluted and called over his shoulder.

"Lieutenant! Company!"

A crew-cut head appeared over a partition. The lieutenant was scowling. His expression changed when he saw Kestrel standing at ease, his officer's insignia shining in the dim light of the hut. There was the sound of a chair scuffing across the floor and hurried footsteps.

The officer of the day was a young, very short first lieutenant whose uniform was correct in every detail.

"Lieutenant Green, sir," he said, stepping forward. "What can I do for you?"

Kestrel returned the salute and then shook hands, remembering to add enough pressure to satisfy American standards of manhood. "I was hoping to catch a ride home on one of your planes," he said, handing over the forged papers.

Lieutenant Green scanned Kestrel's orders, clicking his tongue sympathetically when he came to the reasons for the compassionate leave.

"Captain, it's never been my pleasure before to serve an Oriental member of my country's Army, but I can assure you it will be my pleasure now." He moved to one side so that he could see the Torch of Freedom shoulder patches on Kestrel's uniform: "454th, isn't it?" he asked.

"Yes."

"Then, sir, it is indeed a pleasure to serve you. Your unit is one of the most famous in the entire Army, white or Oriental. Your men taught the world what courage is. You proved you weren't yellow."

Kestrel was amused in spite of himself by the earnest young officer. "But we are, Lieutenant."

The lieutenant's eyes widened. "What do you—oh! Uh, that's not what I meant at all, sir!"

"I know exactly what you meant, Lieutenant. All men are the same color in a foxhole."

"Exactly, sir."

"About that plane ride . . . ?"

The lieutenant turned to the private. "Call the flight line. See if that C-47 has left yet. And move it, Private!"

The private obeyed with a lack of enthusiasm that was

just short of insolence. The lieutenant appeared not to notice.

"Flight's taxiing out now, sir," drawled the private finally.

"Hold the plane!" snapped Lieutenant Green. "Tell them we have a top-priority officer—a gallant member of our Nisei Battalion."

The private and the first lieutenant exchanged a long look. Then, in a disgusted voice, the private spoke into the phone. "Hold on, Sarge. We've got a Jap bumming a ride."

Oakland
6 Hours 37 Minutes After Trinity

The morgue was like every other government building Finn had ever been in. Ugly. Battleship-gray walls, dull linoleum floors, dirty ceilings hung with rows of cold lights, and air that smelled used up. He hurried down a long stretch of corridor. The cold room at the end of the hall was empty. A sign on the desk said, OUT TO LUNCH.

"Now what?" said Riley, looking with distaste at rank upon rank of drawers the size of shallow coffins. "Just grab handles and start pulling out stiffs?"

Finn put the radiation counter on the desk and began fiddling with the adjustments. Like the .45 in the small of his back, the counter had become a part of him.

"Try the files," said Finn. "Look under Ching Han Lo. That's the name on the dead driver's license. The others are John Does and could be filed anywhere."

Finn turned on the radiation counter. He moved the probe in long seeping lines, up one bank of drawers and down another. He had covered one wall when Riley looked up.

"It's not under Ching."

Finn moved over to the long wall and continued his search pattern. Even with the counter on its most sensitive setting, he could not be sure that the bodies would register. They might not have absorbed enough radiation to be picked up through the steel drawers.

"Not under Han."

Finn grunted and continued his search. As the number of drawers diminished, Finn began to steel himself for an extended rummage through drawers full of death.

"Not under Lo."

Riley slammed the file drawer in digust.

A sudden soft clicking came from the radiation counter. Then the clicks became harder, faster, like a toy train careening around a track. Riley went over to Finn.

The probe moved over four drawers, hesitating at each one, then returning.

"Twenty-four through 27," said Finn.

Riley reached for the handle of drawer 24. The drawer slid out with a squeal of steel discs on steel tracks. The counter's clicks ran together in a rush of sound. Finn took one look at the corpse's glazed, slanting eyes and shut the drawer. For Finn's purposes, the driver was the least interesting of the four bodies, victim rather than criminal.

"Was that the driver?" asked Riley.

"Yeah. That was the easy one."

Number 25 was a one-eyed Mexican. Finn swept the probe over his body. The counter clicks ran together into an angry buzz.

"This one was lucky," said Finn, looking at the corpse, then at the reading on the counter.

"Lucky?" said Riley tightly, trying not to see too much

of what had once been a man's left eye. "Just how do you figure that?"

"Bullets are quick." Finn squinted at the face. Something about the man was familiar. "Cover his eye with the sheet."

"It doesn't bother me."

"Not for you, Red. For me."

Riley jerked up the sheet. Finn rearranged it until the right half of the head was revealed. Without the gaping wound, the face looked normal except for the random smears of dried blood.

"Know him?" said Riley, understanding finally why Finn had wanted the eye socket covered.

"Maybe. There are a lot like him along the border."

Finn rolled shut the drawer and opened number 26. Beneath the sheet was a blunt-faced, broad-shouldered man with powerful arms. His eyes and hair were not much darker than Finn's, and his hands made the radiation counter sing.

Finn pulled up the sheet, covering the bullet wounds on the torso and the vaguely surprised expression on the face. "Adiós, Salvador," he said.

"Salvador?"

"Salvador Leon—smuggler, bodyguard, murderer and all-around sweetheart. He works for a Mexican crook called Refugio Reyes y Rincon." The pattern was becoming more clear now. The bodies were like tracks—physical facts devoid of emotion and politics and the exigence of war. They were something he could depend on.

"What the hell are these Mexicans doing all the way up here?"

"The usual. Theft, murder, smuggling."

"What about that other guy—Masarek—whose ID was in the sentry's hand?"

"He hired Refugio, most likely."

"But why? The job was in San Francisco, not Mexico."

Finn looked at Riley's pale, earnest face. "You're from the Midwest, right?"

'Chicago."

Finn nodded. "Ever been to the border?"

"No."

"Well, it's not some God-given black line stretching across the continent. Mexicans have been ignoring that border for centuries, and up until a few years ago, so did we. Take Refugio. His family has been working from San Francisco to Culiacán for at least a hundred years. I know, because my father's family has been chasing them for at least that long."

Finn smiled. "They've caught a few, too. But the point is that Refugio, like most Mexicans, has cousins and in-laws and uncles who are American citizens living every-where from El Paso to San Francisco. He even has some Chinese and Japanese thrown in along the line. He's one of the few Mexicans who can get in and out of Barrio Chino without an uproar.

"Now," continued Finn, "if you wanted to come into America without a passport, steal something and then smuggle it back to Mexico, and from there across the Gulf to the Atlantic, and from there to Russia—"

"I'd hire a man who knows his way around," finished Riley.

"Refugio, or someone like him," agreed Finn. "No-body knows his way around like Refugio."

"Is that how he ended up here?" said Riley, tapping drawer number 27.

"I'm not sure he did."

The drawer came out smoothly. There was some radiation, but not nearly as much as Salvador and the other man had shown.

Finn shut off the counter, set it down and pulled aside the sheet. The corpse's eyes and tongue protruded grotesquely. The razor wire was still embedded in the purple flesh of the neck, swinging with the forward motion of the drawer. Just below the right ear was an old scar left by crude surgery to relieve mastoiditis.

Finn had seen all he needed. With a quick motion of his wrist, he covered the obscene remains of the Russian spy.

Riley had his back turned and was breathing through clenched teeth. When he heard the drawer close, he turned around again. His skin was very white, almost transparent, and covered with a cold mist of sweat.

"Masarek," said Finn, indicating the closed drawer.

"Christ," said Riley between his teeth. "How could you tell?"

"Scar," said Finn, pointing to his own neck. "He must have had a lot of earaches as a kid. Too bad the doctor's knife didn't slip."

Riley said nothing. He swallowed hard. Without a word, Finn grabbed Riley and hustled him down the hall.

"Get it over with," commanded Finn, kicking open the restroom door and shoving Riley through.

Finn went back to the cold room, retrieved the radiation counter and walked down the hall again. Riley came out of the restroom, wiping his face with a wet paper towel.

"Sorry."

"You've still got your socks on," said Finn. "That's better than I did the first time around."

Finn turned and began retracing his steps to the lobby. Riley followed him down the hall and up a flight of stairs in companionable silence.

"What next?" said Riley, looking around the lobby.

"An APB on Refugio Reyes y Rincon."

"What if he's in Mexico?"

"I'd be damn grateful," Finn said. "Mexicans aren't as genteel about questioning people as we are. Saves all kinds of time."

"I'll bet," said Riley. "And after the APB?"

"I don't know."

Finn walked the rest of the hall in silence, arranging the few immutable facts he possessed in their most likely configuration. Masarek, Refugio and his Mexican hirelings had penetrated Hunters Point and stolen the two deadly chunks of metal. Then there had been a falling out. Masarek had been killed, but not before he killed two of Refugio's men. Someone had been waiting for the truck on the waterfront—the blond woman, probably. Someone else had also been waiting, another woman, the one who had helped Refugio escape: he would assume that it was Refugio who was injured. As for the uranium . . . it was either in the second truck with Refugio or in the car with the blond.

Finn ran through the facts again in his mind. The pattern fit, but he was not satisfied. Something was missing from it. Refugio was a smuggler and a pimp, not a thief. The plan for the theft must have been Russian, which meant that Refugio probably had little or no idea of what he was stealing. Yet he had risked his life to steal the uranium from a man like Masarek. If the uranium had been gold, it would make sense; Refugio knew the worth of gold to the last peso. Even if it was assumed that Refugio knew what uranium was, what could he do with it once he had stolen it from Masarek—sell it back to the U.S.? Possibly, but it was not quite Refugio's style. His political sympathies in the war lay with his pocketbook—and Takagura Omi. Japan.

"Kestrel," Finn said aloud. "*Kestrel.*"

"What?" said Riley.

Finn did not hear. He was remembering the moment he had seen Kestrel in the Green Parrot. Kestrel, alert and deadly, watching him across the body of a dead fighting cock. Kestrel's eyes had been as predatory as the hawk whose name he had taken.

Yes. Kestrel.

Los Alamos
7 Hours 7 Minutes After Trinity

"Your call is on the line, General."

Groves rubbed chocolate from his fingers with a handkerchief and took the phone. "How close are you to a solution?"

"I don't know."

"Old Give-'Em-Hell-Harry was on the horn living up to his name. I don't need to tell you what he said."

"Forty hours and fifty-one minutes," Finn said succinctly.

"What?"

"The time left until 0530, July 18th, Mountain War Time, when either we give Truman the uranium or he gives us an invasion."

"Yes, that's roughly what the President told me. Well?"

"All Hunters Point personnel vehicles are checked out and cleared. No radioactivity, except for the storeroom where the canister was opened. After questioning the gate guards, I found out that the vehicle the thieves used to enter and leave the Point was a truck from Ho's Good Luck Laundry."

STEAL THE SUN   233

"ONI was quite impressed by your method of questioning the guards," said Groves.

"It got answers."

"I'm not criticizing, Captain. If I'd wanted a bridge party, I'd have sent the officers' wives."

"The laundry truck was found by the Oakland police. They waited an hour to call us."

Groves heard the residual fury in Finn's voice.

"When I finally got to the waterfront," continued Finn, "the bodies were gone. The truck was hot, and I don't mean just stolen. The men who grabbed the isotope were either suicidal or flunkies who didn't know what they had. As far as I could tell, the uranium was still unshielded when it was transferred to another truck."

"And the men?"

"Dead. Two of them made the counter sing, but they didn't die of radiation."

"What next?" said the General bluntly.

"I have an APB out for the Mexican national whose men were in the morgue. The police and hospitals are on the alert for unusual deaths or burn cases. The FBI is checking out every eyelash and piece of lint from those bodies and the truck, and questioning everyone on the Oakland waterfront . . . ."

"Yes?" prompted General Groves.

"It's something for them to do," said Finn sardonically.

"You don't think it will help?"

"If it can be done by the book, the FBI will do it. But the book was revised at dawn this morning."

There was a silence followed by a muttered oath. "Captain, I've shut down the ports and borders. And I mean *shut down*. No ships leaving. No planes flying over. Nothing. You couldn't move a fart without my men smelling it. But that won't do any good if the thieves just sit on that uranium for the next forty-one hours."

"They'd better wrap it in lead before they roost, or they'll—" Finn stopped speaking suddenly. "Excuse me, General. Are there any other questions?"

"You just thought of something. What?"

"Lead, sir. Whoever organized this theft must have known what he was stealing. His flunkies bounced the pieces together enough that the uranium must be fairly hot by now. Whoever takes delivery is going to need some lead to cool off the pieces. Since lead is on the restricted list of war materials, all sales are recorded."

"Good idea, Finn. Get on it and call me when—"

Groves realized he was talking into an empty line.

San Francisco
8 Hours 42 Minutes After Trinity

Vanessa made a right turn and entered Chinatown, looking for addresses or signs written in a language she could understand. As she searched she tried not to think about the dangerous lie she had sent to Beria. She had no "promising" salvage prospects. She had nothing but her wits, her determination and a license plate number.

The streets seemed more narrow than those in the rest of the city, but were not. They simply teemed. People spilled out in to the streets. Voices raised in dispute were nearly drowned out by the honks of drivers who had crept around one obstruction only to be balked by another.

In the end, Vanessa found Ho's laundry more because of the identically modest, unmarked cars in front of it than because of its small English sign. The cars, as much as the curious crowd, told Vanessa that Ho's Good Luck Laundry had become a focus of police attention.

She had not really expected the FBI, although it was that possibility which had lured her into Chinatown. If the Americans knew about the laundry truck, did that mean that they had recovered the uranium? She had to know. To find out, she needed Hecht, the reporter.

Vanessa parked her own car down the block, well away from casual observation. After a moment's hesitation, she removed the pistol from her purse, tucked it well under the front seat, locked the car and hurried to the laundry.

Ho's laundry was closed. There were several men outside, trying to break up the crowd. Vanessa stood across the street, growing more uneasy. The men in front of the laundry were FBI agents, not local police. Only the FBI had men so carefully dressed.

Here in Chinatown, these well-trained agents stood out like popcorn in a bowl of peanuts.

And so did she.

She slipped into a crowded market and watched the laundry through a window that was all but covered with ideographs. She spotted Hecht easily; his limp was pronounced as he brushed past the cordon in front of the laundry. Immediately, he was challenged by an agent at the front door. Hecht gestured angrily, then produced identification from his wallet. The papers were not sufficient to gain him entry into the laundry. Arguing, gesturing and waving his ID, Hecht was escorted back behind the cordon.

He turned and began looking around, clearly trying to spot Vanessa in the crowd. She had no desire to be seen while the FBI was around.

Hecht looked for a minute longer, then limped back

down the street toward his car. Vanessa watched him
approach, waited, then left the store to intercept him a
block from the laundry.

"Did you get the license plate traced?" she demanded.

Hecht dug in his pocket and produced a slip of paper
with an address on it. He handed the paper to her.

"Detective Mullen got it for me, no problem," he said.
"Told me it's out in what used to be Little Tokyo. The
license was issued to a truck owned by Julio Rincon. It's a
commercial vehicle used for something called the Fragrant
Petal. Sounds like some kind of Oriental flower shop, or
maybe a teahouse."

"Did the police want to know why you needed the
information?"

"No. Mullen was doing me a favor just like I'd do for
him." He smiled. "He'd have been hot if he knew the
license was somehow connected with the four murders.
There's a whole lot of cops mad about being cut out of the
action."

"What do you mean?"

"Take a look." Hecht gestured back toward the
laundry. "Those are FBI agents, not local cops. They don't
have jurisdiction in local crimes. That means the murders
aren't what they were said to be—gang war over a few
betting slips.

"Then there was that cold-eyed son of a bitch out at the
crime scene this morning," continued Hecht. "He said
he'd hamstring my other leg and dump me on a Japanese
island if I printed anything without clearing it first with
the FBI."

"Was he an FBI agent?"

"Huh-uh! He wore jeans and boots. Besides, he was too
damned mean to be a G-man. Hoover keeps those boys on
their party manners in public."

"Did you find out his name?"

"Oakland cops said it was Finn."

"Finn—" Vanessa realized she had almost expected to hear that name. Everytime something went wrong with Russian plans to penetrate the Manhattan Project, Finn's name cropped up. She had been briefed about him, although she had never seen him in Juarez. He was reputed to be smart, ruthless and very dangerous. Even Masarek had respected him.

"Stay away from the laundry," she said. "Stay away from your newspaper. Don't go to your home. If Finn is organizing the search, he'll learn you turned up here after he warned you off in Oakland.

Hecht started to protest, but Vanessa kept on talking.

"What's the name of a respectable hotel?" she asked.

"Uh—the Mayfair. It's off Union Square."

"Good. Go there. Get a room in the name of John Brent. Stay there and do nothing until I call you."

"But what about my newspaper story?"

"What about the country that trained you in return for your help in a crisis like this?"

Hecht shifted uncomfortably. Vanessa knew that he had not expected to be called so soon, nor to have to give up so much.

"Finn would only cripple you," she said. "If you don't obey me, I will kill you. But," lied Vanessa, "if you obey me, you will be a rich man and a hero of Russia. Which will it be, Hecht? Finn or me?"

"I'll be in the Mayfair."

San Francisco
10 Hours After Trinity

The Fragrant Petal was in a section of San Francisco that
had been called Little Tokyo until 1941. Since Pearl Harbor, Mexicans, Koreans, Chinese and a few whites had
moved in, buying homes and businesses from relocated
Japanese at a price barely higher than outright confis-
cation.

Even so, the area was less crowded than other parts of
the city. Many businesses were boarded up, and many
signs offered rooms for rent, cheap. There were more
Mexicans on the street than Orientals, and enough fair
skins so that Vanessa would not draw too much attention.

She drove slowly past the Fragrant Petal. It was a flower
shop rather than teahouse, and in great need of paint.
Though the sign said CLOSED, she thought she saw
someone moving behind the grimy window.

Another pass by the shop did not reveal any further
movement. Vanessa drove on slowly, weighing and re-
jecting options.

Masarek was dead.

Refugio was hiding.

The FBI was searching Ho's laundry, which meant that
the uranium had not been in the van. She must assume
that the U-235 was with Refugio; she hoped that he was
inside the Fragrant Petal.

Slowly, Vanessa drove by the flower shop. The door was
closed. No one moved behind the windows. The shop
looked as deserted as the Reyes Funeral Home that was
next door. She drove down the block, watching the shop in
the rearview mirror. No one appeared in the window.

She wished that Masarek were alive. Together they could
have turned the shop and its occupants inside out. To-

gether they could have—but Masarek was dead and she dared not contact any other Russian agents in the Bay Area for fear that they were under surveillance. She must protect herself. She was Russia's only lead to the uranium. She must be bold, yes, but also careful.

A sign, ROOM FOR RENT, FURNISHED, caught her eye. The room was on the second floor of a Victorian building across and down the street from the Fragrant Petal. The window looked like it would give a clear view of the shop.

The landlord was an old Mexican with a heavy accent, a light handshake and a pimp's smile. The room was dirty, furnished with once-elegant Oriental pieces, and looked as though it had been decorated by a blind man. But the room's view of the street was even better than Vanessa expected.

"I'll take it," Vanessa said.

"When do you want to move in?"

"I'll pay beginning today," she said, "although I'll only need the room occasionally."

"Five dollars more for every man you bring to your room."

Vanessa nearly laughed. "That's far too much. One dollar."

"Four."

"Two."

"Three-fifty," said the old man, settling in for an enjoyable bargaining session.

"One-fifty."

Startled by the unexpected turn of bargaining, the Mexican said in disbelief, "But that's less than your second offer!"

"Yes," agreed Vanessa. She fanned two months' rent in her hand. "And if you don't take one-fifty, my next offer will be even less."

The landlord reached for the bills, but Vanessa hung on to them. "One-fifty?" she said, her blue eyes wide and innocent.

"Yes," grumbled the man, counting the money. He pulled two keys from his pocket and slammed them on a table. "The telephone is downstairs."

He shut the door behind him with the vigor of a man half his age. Vanessa slipped the deadbolt and went to the bay window. It was covered by curtains that allowed her to look down at the street without being seen. She dragged a chair over and began watching the front door of the Fragrant Petal.

San Francisco
11 Hours 2 Minutes After Trinity

A green Plymouth cab pulled up a block away from the Fragrant Petal.

"You sure you got it right this time, buddy?" asked the cabbie.

"Yes."

Kestrel had made the cabbie drive around the block several times, pretending not to be sure of the location. When he was convinced that the Fragrant Petal was not a trap, he told the cabbie to pull over.

"It was hard," said Kestrel. "So many changes since I went to war."

"Yeah. Sure thing."

Kestrel pulled out his suitcase, waited for the cab to disappear around the corner, then crossed the street and walked briskly toward the peeling storefront called the Fragrant Petal. Like Ana, he deplored the shallow translation. Unlike her, he did not denigrate the English language. It was a fine language for scientific inquiry.

Inside the shop, Ana was standing at her father's former worktable, fashioning sprays and wreaths. Arranging flowers was the one part of her childhood that she remembered with pleasure, the brilliant colors and petal textures shifting beneath her hands. The pungence of stems and greenery had not changed, nor had the sweet essence of petals. Her fingers, however, had. They were slow where they once had been quick, awkward where they once had been skilled.

"Damn!" she muttered, stabbing an errant spray of scarlet gladiolus into the pottery frog at the bottom of the vase.

The thick stem bent; the flower canted out at an awkward angle.

"Damned useless thing!" said Ana beneath her breath, pulling out stems until the frog was bare once more. "The flower stems are limp and there aren't even any lead frogs. How can anyone make anything?"

"It would require patience," suggested Kestrel softly.

"Oh!" The pottery frog crashed to the floor. "Kestrel!" she cried. "I didn't hear—how did you—are you all right?"

Kestrel smiled swiftly and touched Ana's cheek with his fingertips. She was so American, impatient and transparent. "My name is Captain Ikedo. I'm your cousin and I'm fine," said Kestrel, speaking rapid Japanese. "But you call me Kestrel because as a boy I was obsessed with sparrow hawks."

His dark glance flicked around the back room of the shop. There was no one else nearby. Kestrel removed his overseas cap and loosened the knot of his black uniform tie as if these were things he did every day. He walked over and stood beside Ana, selected a new pottery frog and began to rebuild the flower arrangement.

"Tell me what happened," he said, his voice both calm and commanding.

Ana watched his fingers—deft, gentle, skilled—and remembered when he had touched her as he now touched flowers. His hands paused. He was watching her.

"I don't know all of it," she said quickly. "I waited behind the curtain as you told me to do. I couldn't see the street. For a long time nothing happened. Then, after dawn, there were shots. I looked out just as a car turned around and raced by me on the street. There was another shot, maybe more, from the van."

Ana took a long breath to ease the fear that rose in her when she remembered the silence and fog, shots and fear and a van full of blood.

"I—I waited, but no one got out of the van." She touched Kestrel's arm in a silent bid for understanding. "I know you told me to wait for Refugia, but I was afraid he was—dead."

"You did well," murmured Kestrel.

Some of Ana's rigidity left her. She drew a ragged breath and began to speak more slowly. "The van—inside the van there was so much blood." She swallowed. "Dead men and blood everywhere."

Ana stared at the glowing red of the petals she had unconsciously crushed in her fist.

"Is Refugio dead?" asked Kestrel.

"No." Ana turned her hand upside down, letting crushed petals fall to the floor. "His leg, here," she said, touching the top of Kestrel's thigh. "Like a furrow plowed in raw meat."

"Can he walk?"

"With help, yes. He says it's nothing." Ana smiled. "A long scab and a limp. Except it hasn't stopped bleeding yet and he's been very sick, throwing up and—" She handed Kestrel a frond of pale green fern. "He's been better in the last few hours, I think."

Kestrel frowned. It did not sound like a superficial leg wound. "Is the bullet still in his leg?"

"No. It's a furrow," repeated Ana. She reached for the modeling clay used in complex flower arrangements. With her thumbnail she gouged a shallow trough across the clay. "Like this."

"Where is he?"

"I moved him next door, to his cousin's funeral parlor. There wasn't enough privacy here. Too many people in and out. And you told us to keep the businesses open, to act normally."

Kestrel's fingers paused, then he selected a flawless white rose and anchored it in the frog, completing his work. He had duplicated her flower arrangement, except that he substituted the single white rose for her stalk of blood-colored gladiolus. The result, like Kestrel himself, was strong and poised.

Ana led Kestrel to the interior door that connected the flower shop with the Reyes Funeral Home. As he put his hand on the door, he turned toward her.

"Memories can be as cruel as knives," Kestrel said. "Do not cut yourself more than you must, Ana. It was karma that brought you here. When it is time, karma will take you away again."

He was gone before Ana could find her voice to answer.

Kestrel was in a room without windows, without air. In one corner was a shapeless, eerie blue glow. Kestrel had never seen a blue so pure, no tint of purple, no tone of green, nothing but a flawless blue blush emanating from . . . what?

His hand fumbled for the wall switch. Blue disappeared in a soundless explosion of white light splintering off a porcelain table. In the center of the table were two white, oddly shaped chunks of metal, one of which was three times larger than the other. The two pieces were less than a hand's width apart.

Swiftly, Kestrel's fingers snapped off the light. Blue suffused the area where the white metal pieces had been. Kestrel felt an instant of incredible elation. He stood motionless, his hand on the light switch, transfixed by the eerie blue light. The binding power of the universe lay before him, radiating energy as though alive. And it *was* alive, the embryo of a deadly cloud eight miles tall. With that metal, he controlled the future of his country as surely as he controlled the light switch on the wall.

But then a secondary realization drenched him like icy rain, making his skin contract in a reaction as old as man. He was looking at the radioactive heart of an atomic bomb, and that heart was deadly to human flesh.

"Pretty, yes?" said a low voice. "As blue as the eyes of God."

Kestrel's hand hit the switch again. Light flooded the room, revealing what he had overlooked the first time—Refugio, lying motionless on a gurney a few feet beyond the radioactive glow.

It took every bit of Kestrel's discipline not to scream at Refugio's lethal stupidity. The Japanese was a physicist before he was a spy; he knew that unshielded radioactive material could be as deadly as curare.

"Yes," he said, his voice ragged in spite of his control. "They're very pretty. Where is their box?"

"Box?"

"What they were packed in."

"Oh," Refugio's voice was casual. "That was too heavy. Masarek told us to leave it."

"Too heavy," repeated Kestrel. "Was it big?"

Refugio was lying on his back, his hands on his abdomen as though to hold back cramps. The bandage on his thigh was crimson. His face was the color of old ivory.

"Not very." Refugio pulled himself upright with a motion that sent the gurney wheeling closer to the embalming table. "About like this," he said, sketching the canister with hands that shook.

"Lead? Was it lead that made it so heavy?"

Refugio shrugged. "Who knows? It was very heavy, Señor Kestrel. Madonna! Even Salvador could not lift it."

At the mention of Salvador's name, Refugio's expression changed. "Salvador is dead. So is Lopez." He sighed. "Masarek, too. He was hard to kill, that one."

"The woman," said Kestrel. "Is she dead, too?"

"She killed Salvador. I don't know if he hurt her first. I shot at her but it was foggy and my leg . . ." Refugio shrugged again. "I think the whore is alive."

Kestrel drew a breath, feeling elation slide away. Masarek was dead, but the blonde was still free. She would be gathering other agents to her, planning a means of stealing back the uranium. The Russian spy network had the regenerative power of a gifted, mythic snake: so long as the head remained intact, new bodies could be grown.

All he had was Ana and Refugio.

"You've been sick," said Kestrel.

"It's the water," said Refugio, laughing feebly at his joke.

"It's more than water. Can you walk?"

"Of course."

"Prove it. Take the smaller piece of metal and put it over there."

Refugio looked from the uranium to the table Kestrel had indicated on the far side of the room. "But why?"

"*Do it.*"

Refugio eased himself off the gurney. Using the wheeled table as a rolling crutch, he approached the embalming table.

Kestrel watched, knowing the Mexican was absorbing an enormous amount of radiation. But Kestrel suspected that it mattered no more than shooting bullets into a corpse.

The uranium rang, bell-like, when Refugio dropped it on the metal table at the far end of the room. Kestrel turned out the lights and stared intently.

"The pretty blue light," said Refugio, "is gone."

Kestrel stared silently, intently. Both spheres had been heavily irradiated. He could not guess at the consequences. After a few minutes, he still could not be sure whether it was radioactivity or his imagination that imbued the separate metal chunks with a vague flicker of blue life. He blinked, then his hand swept up, bringing light back into the room. "I'll need containers."

"There are the sacks we brought them in."

"What?"

"The canvas laundry bags."

Kestrel made a dismissing motion with his hand. "I need something heavy, something that will absorb atomic particles."

"What?"

"Iron or steel," said Kestrel. "Lead would be best."

"Why not gold as well?" said Refugio sarcastically. "It's heavy and it's not so much more difficult to get than lead." The Mexican stared at Kestrel. "Or had the señor forgotten that Los Estados Unidos is at war with Japan and such things as lead are so hard to get that my cousin wanted me to smuggle it here from Mexico?"

"Did you?"

"Too heavy," sighed Refugio. "Besides, my cousin soon discovered that not many Mexicans here can afford a lead-lined coffin. My cousin Raul even sold his flower holders for scrap when the price went high enough."

Kestrel swore silently. "I must have lead!"

Refugio licked his dry lips. "I have other cousins, señor. For a price, they will get you your lead."

"How? Where?"

"That's their problem, señor. Yours is to pay for it."

Kestrel almost laughed. Money was the least of his problems. "Arrange it," he said.

Sonoma County, California
19 Hours 15 Minutes After Trinity

It was dark, with only a thin moon-smile to aid the men creeping through the vineyard into the Salerno Brothers winery.

"Chingón!" muttered Griego Rincon as he stumbled over a two-by-four abandoned in the weeds in back of their winery.

"Shut up!" hissed Franco in Spanish. "Pick up your feet, cabrón! The house is not so far away that you can curse at the moon!"

Griego looked at the house on a knoll more than a hundred meters away. There were several lights still on in the second story of the old mansion. He walked with more care. His cousin Refugio would not bail incompetent thieves out of jail.

Franco Rincon stood very quietly, listening to the night. Other than a dog's distant barking, there was no sound. Apparently no one at the house had heard Griego stumble and swear.

"Come on," breathed Franco, jerking Griego's sleeve in silent command.

The two men slipped into the dense moon-shadow of an old fieldstone winery. They knew the way; in daylight they worked at the winery. Franco pulled a tire iron from his belt. He put the flattened end between the steel hasp and the heavy wooden door and yanked down hard. The hasp gave way with a squeal.

Again, Franco waited with his head up, nostrils flared like a wolf trying to scent enemies. At the house, a dog barked until there was a shout from the bedroom. Silence returned like another shade of black. The heavy door opened soundlessly. Griego had oiled it earlier in the day when he was sweeping out the winery. Inside, the sharp-sweet smell of fermentation settled around the men. The building was windowless, the darkness complete.

Franco pulled out a flashlight that he had taped until only a pencil of light shone out. He swept the light around, but there was no one and nothing he had not expected to see.

"Over there," whispered Griego, pulling on Franco's hand.

The flashlight wobbled, then fixed on an old wine-bottling machine. Empty bottles, metal pincers and bottle holders gleamed dully in the light. A roll of scarlet foil and a roll of bright red labels dangled overhead. A half-filled case of burgundy sat at the end of the conveyor belt.

Franco went quickly to the conveyor belt. With a muttered curse, he grabbed Griego by the arm.

"Where's the rest of it?" he snarled.

Griego cringed away from the fingers. He gestured at the cartons of burgundy that had been filled in the last few days. "There! On the bottles!"

Griego's gestures knocked the half-filled carton of wine off the conveyor belt. With a sound like the end of the world, bottles exploded against the floor. The reek of green wine rose from curved shards of glass.

On the hill, the dog barked again, urgently.

Franco grabbed what he had come for and headed out of the bottling room. Griego hesitated, picked up a full case of burgundy and followed Franco's flashlight.

The two men hurried awkwardly out of the winery, across the dirt farm-road and into the concealment of chest-high rows of vines. At a clumsy trot, Franco crossed the sandy vineyard to another dirt road where his car was parked beneath a tree.

The dog's bark continued sporadically, then faded into a silence disturbed only by the faint sound of a car receding into the distance, leaving a thin wake of dust beneath the moon.

San Francisco
25 Hours 31 Minutes After Trinity

The restaurant on Market Street catered to the all-night crowd from the Tenderloin district. Riley toyed with the limp strands of pasta coated with tomato sauce and olive oil. He took a tentative bite. Finn ate hungrily. Riley put down his fork.

"How the hell did I let you talk me into this?" said Riley.

"There was nothing else left to do. The FBI is watching

every known or suspected communist agent; one of them has been approached by a blond woman with a British accent. We put out grab notices on Refugio and a Jap spy, and what did we get?''

"Eight Mexicans, three Chinese and a Korean. Drunks.''

"We put four bodies through a FBI sieve. What did we find out?''

"We found out they're dead," said Riley.

"The weapons and the laundry van and the laundry and—''

"Nothing!''

"As for the lead," said Finn, "we now know that in the Bay Area, no new orders for lead have been processed in the last twenty-four hours. Nobody has bought a pile of toy soldiers, religious statues, frogs—''

"Frogs?'' yelped Riley. "What the hell do *frogs* have to do with this?''

"Flower holders," explained Finn, then continued with his list. "Old batteries, scrap, new batteries—I forgot something.''

"Coffins," said Riley after a moment.

"Yeah. Coffins. All the lead-lined luxury models sold recently are wrapped around dead customers." Finn stopped abruptly. "In short, we seem to be fishing in the dark with a broken hook." He returned his attention to his food.

"The problem with fishing in the dark," said Riley, "is that the damned hooks have a way of ending up in the wrong places. A man could hurt himself fishing in the dark.''

Frowning, Finn picked up the empty wine bottle. He turned it around in his hands, staring at it as though the answer to his problem were concealed in the green glass curves. He liked Riley. Even worse, he felt responsible for the young agent. Finn did not want to be responsible for any life except his own. But there Riley sat, too young, too kind. Green on green, like the glass turning between his hands. Abruptly, Finn's fingers closed around the neck of the bottle. "You ever take any physics in college?"

Riley's face showed his surprise. He nodded his head and waited.

"You know about radioactivity?"

"Some."

"What we're looking for is two pieces of white, radioactive metal. Alone, each piece is hot, but not dangerously so. If you get the pieces too close, they can get hot enough to kill."

Riley stared at the empty green bottle that was again rolling between Finn's lean hands. "What exactly does *that* mean?"

"It means that the thieves really fucked up when they left behind the lead shipping canister. They're playing with fire. Problem is, they can't see the flames or feel the heat. And neither can we."

Riley sighed. "At least I understand now why you have a hundred agents scouring the Bay Area for lead. You figure the thieves will have to use it as a shield or wrapper to absorb the radiation from the stolen stuff—whatever that is."

"Uranium," said Finn. "Pure uranium-235."

"How many micrograms were stolen?"

"Try kilograms. Close to ten."

Riley's mouth opened and closed soundlessly. He licked his lips and tried again. "I didn't know there was that much U-235 on the whole planet. How did we ever get that much all in one place?"

"I don't know. It cost around one billion bucks, if that gives you a clue."

Riley sat without moving, chewing on the information

like under-cooked sphagetti. "Well," he said at last, "thank God all the lead in northern California is accounted for."

"Wrong," said Finn flatly. "All the lead in all the places we've thought to look is accounted for."

Finn paused, staring at the wine bottle rolling between his palms. Then he put down the bottle and fingered the thick metal foil that covered the neck. The foil peeled off easily. He rolled a long strip of it between his fingers. It made a hard, heavy ball the size of a pea.

"Lead," breathed Riley. "By God, lead!"

"How many wineries are there in northern California?"

"Can't be more than fifty," said Riley. Then, hastily, "Pray to God no more than fifty."

"That's twenty-five apiece," said Finn, standing up and throwing money on the table. "Any more than that and they're all yours, Riley."

San Francisco
26 Hours 38 Minutes After Trinity

Vanessa twitched aside the white curtain, a gesture that had become almost automatic. The long night had given her too much time to think, and her thoughts had been as gloomy as San Francisco's fog.

Failure was a death sentence for her. At some unknown, but not far distant moment, Beria would decide that the chance that Vanessa would recover the uranium was smaller than the chance that Stalin would discover her secret assignment. At that moment, an NKVD assassin would be given Vanessa's name.

She looked through the glass as she had all night. No

lights had shown in the Fragrant Petal, no cars had parked nearby, no one had gone into the shop since the Japanese soldier yesterday afternoon. She had not seen him come out.

The appearance of a Nisei officer at a flower shop owned by the cousin of the man who had betrayed her and killed Masarek was too remarkable to be taken for mere coincidence. She had immediately tried to find reinforcements but the two numbers she had called were answered by people who gave her coded warnings instead of recognition signals. A third call, to a safe house in Los Angeles, had been properly answered. She was told that the FBI was openly watching every known or suspected agent in the Bay Area.

One of the Los Angeles agents was on his way to San Francisco to help her, but until he arrived, Hecht was all she had. The thought both angered and depressed her.

A light knock on the door brought her out of the chair. With her silenced pistol in one hand, she opened the door a crack, then admitted Hecht.

"Are you armed?" said Vanessa before he could speak.

"Armed?" asked Hecht, his voice rising. "You mean a gun?" He looked confused and tired, as though he had not slept well.

"This is an armed struggle, comrade," said Vanessa. "Surely even you understand that much. You're a communist, aren't you?"

"Of course," replied Hecht. "I've read all of Marx and Lenin and Stalin." The litany of names seemed to comfort him. His voice became more calm. "It's just that we're not used to the armed struggle here in the United States. We're not as advanced morally as our Soviet comrades." There was no derision in his voice; only self-pity.

"Pistols don't recognize advancement in revolution or

morality. Are you armed?"

Hecht shook his head. "I don't even know how to use a gun."

For an instant, Vanessa pitied Hecht almost as much as she despised him. There were many American communists like him, naive idealists playing at revolution. They hated, but only weakly. Few of them had the toughness of mind or body to bring down a government.

But Hecht was all she had to work with right now. She would use him until a real agent arrived, and then she would kill him.

"What the Party requires of you is simple," she said. "You will go buy a wreath for your father's funeral."

Sonoma County
26 Hours 59 Minutes After Trinity

The Sonoma County sheriff's office was nearly as old as the middle-aged deputy who was typing up a burglary report. The typewriter he used stuck with monotonous regularity, impeding a process already slowed by the deputy's lack of skill and interest.

"Damn," sighed Deputy Anthony Branscomb, reaching yet again to untangle keys.

The telephone rang. Branscomb grabbed it, relieved to set aside the report.

"Sheriff's office. Branscomb," he answered.

"Riley. FBI," said a hoarse voice. "You had any wineries robbed in the last twenty-four hours?"

"FBI? How the hell did you find out so fast? I haven't even typed up the report yet!"

"How much lead foil was taken?"

"How did you know—" Branscomb realized he was repeating himself. "Hey, is this some kind of gag?"

"*How much lead is missing?*"

"Less than twenty pounds. They'd been bottling a vat of red and—"

"Give me directions to the winery from San Francisco."

"What's so damned important about a few pounds of foil?"

"We're at war, remember?"

Branscomb sighed and gave directions with a county sheriff's intimate knowledge of short cuts.

"Right," said Riley. "Meet us there in an hour."

"Weren't you listening?" said Branscomb. "That's at least eighty miles—eight zero—and it's rush hour down where you are."

"One hour, deputy. And tell the local speed traps to stay clear of a black Ford coupé driven by a wild man in a cowboy hat."

San Francisco
27 Hours 4 Minutes After Trinity

Hecht stood irresolutely in front of the Fragrant Petal. The card in the window said OPEN, but no one was working at the counter where flowers were piled, waiting to be made into bouquets. He took a fast drag on his cigaret, threw it into the gutter and pushed tentatively on the shop door.

The door opened without the sound of the customary shopkeeper's bell. Hecht looked around nervously, expecting someone to challenge his presence. No one did.

With increasing confidence, Hecht walked past the counter and into the rear of the shop. There were more flowers bunched in tin pails, mounds of greenery under wet towels, pottery frogs of all sizes, florist's shears, tape, pins, soft clay, everything but the human hands needed to transform chaos into an aesthetic whole.

Hecht hesitated, knowing he would be questioned carefully by the woman whose name he did not even know. His footsteps sounded loud as he walked toward the door leading into the garage. He had been told to be particularly interested in the garage. He reached for the door, then froze. He could hear voices, a man and a woman speaking a language he did not recognize.

Slowly, Hecht retreated. As he did, he saw another door, this one appearing to lead from the back room of the flower shop to the funeral home next door. The connection between the two businesses was not apparent from the street. He tiptoed toward the door.

The embalming room was harshly lit. It smelled of formaldehyde and death. At either end of the room was a porcelain table with an inset drain to carry off body fluids. Near the table next to the door was a sheet-covered corpse on a gurney. On the porcelain table was a gray-white mass that Hecht immediately assumed was a human brain.

He closed his eyes, afraid if he saw any more he would be sick. Then the corpse stirred and tried to sit up, but could not. There was a large red stain on the sheet. Hecht froze, paralyzed.

"Ana?" asked Refugio, seeing only Hecht's dark shape in the doorway.

Hecht forced himself to walk a few steps into the room.

"Ana?" asked Refugio again, as much a groan as a name. "Water . . ."

Hecht looked at the man's slack face, closed eyes, thick sweep of eyebrows. The corpse was alive. He glanced around, wondering what else was not as it seemed. The gray-white mass: it was not a brain.

Voices came from the flower shop.

"What are you doing in here?"

Hecht turned toward the voice and was confronted by a Japanese wearing the uniform of an American Army officer.

"*What do you want?*"

"I'm—uh—flowers," said Hecht, finally remembering the lie he was supposed to tell if he was caught. "It's—uh—it's my mother's birthday."

"Julio!"

Julio Rincon came in from the flower shop.

"Sell this man some yellow roses," the Japanese said. "It's his mother's birthday, *so make sure he doesn't get lost.*" He looked back at Hecht. "Go with Julio."

Hecht followed Julio, paid for the roses and then nearly forgot them in his rush to get out of the shop. He did not look back, so he did not see Julio step out of the store and follow him.

Vanessa saw the man following Hecht. She watched from her window, but the Mexican kept walking down the street when Hecht turned into the apartment building. Frowning, still suspicious, Vanessa released the curtain. She opened the door before Hecht could knock.

"Well?" she said, shutting the door.

Hecht dumped the yellow roses on a chest.

"There wasn't anyone in the front of the shop," he said. "The door was open. I walked toward the back. The garage, like you told me." He talked very fast. He wanted to complete his mission, to be free of this preposterous experience and of the blond woman whose eyes reminded him of crushed blue marbles. "Before I got to the back door, I heard voices. A man and a woman. I couldn't hear words. I backed up and saw another door. It led into the funeral home."

Hecht paused, trying to decide how to go on without appearing a total fool.

"It was the embalming room. There was a corpse under a sheet and a brain on the table, at least that's what I thought until he—"

"*He?*" interrupted Vanessa sharply.

"The corpse. Only he wasn't. He said something—"

"What?"

"A name. Ann or Ana or something like that, and then he asked for water."

"Describe the man."

"Uh, he was sick. Real sick."

"Hair color? Eyes? Skin? Height?" snapped Vanessa, her voice like a lash.

"Dark," said Hecht, trying to recall things he had not really noticed at the time. "Black hair and big thick eyebrows. Yellow skin, but that's because he was sick, I think. He looked Mexican."

Vanessa felt the first stirrings of victory, a sensual excitement.

"Sick?" Vanessa asked, thinking of Refugio's furry eyebrows. Had she managed to shoot the Mexican after all? "How sick?"

"Bad," said Hecht, trying not to stare at Vanessa's moist smile. "There was blood on the sheet and he looked feverish."

"Good."

Hecht moved nervously, like an animal on a leash.

"Did you see anything that looked like a milk can?" asked Vanessa. "Metal, about two feet high?"

"Uh, no. Just flower pails."

"Anything unusual? Anything metallic?"

"The brain," blurted Hecht. "That is, the gray-white stuff that I thought was a brain. It was on the embalming table and it was kind of shaped like a brain."

"Go on."

"It wasn't a brain."

"What was it?"

"I don't know. A gray-white chunk of something or other. Metal. Smooth."

Vanessa smiled, then laughed aloud. "*It's there!*" Her voice, like her laugh, was elated. The incredible power of the atomic bomb was within her grasp. "Did you see anything else?" she demanded. "How many people were there?" She waited, daring to hope that it would be possible for her alone to recover the uranium.

"Two men stopped me before I could look around anymore. And I heard at least two other people talking. One of the men who stopped me was Oriental, but he was wearing an American uniform. He seemed to be in charge. The Mexican took orders from him."

"Oriental? Be more precise. Half the world is Oriental." Vanessa's voice was flat again; from what he had told her, there were too many men in the shop for her to go in alone.

"Uh, I think the guy was Nisei. You know, a first-generation Japanese-American. His English was as good as mine. No accent."

"Mexican and Japanese," Vanessa said. "So that's how the bastard did it!" In Mexico, Refugio had an Oriental partner. Apparently he had sold the uranium to Japan. The Nisei must be here to pick it up. But he would have the same problem she did—how to move the radioactive metal without being poisoned by it. She smiled, hoping that the Japanese knew as little about radioactivity as Masarek had. If the Jap was ignorant, it would be easy to take the uranium from his dead hands.

"You'll have to be armed," Vanessa said.

"What?"

"Guns, comrade. Do you understand me?"

Hecht looked away from her hard blue eyes.

"Two .38 caliber pistols—revolvers—and one hundred rounds of ammunition," continued Vanessa, her voice as relentless as her eyes. "Have the clerk show you how to use them. You'll need to know."

San Francisco
27 Hours 11 Minutes After Trinity

Refugio dreamed that he was sinking in hot black sand. The dream was so alarming that he awoke, moaning. After a moment of disorientation, he remembered he was on a gurney in an embalming room.

He was thirsty, all but smothered by fever and the odor of death. He must get out of here, breathe clean air again. No wonder he felt weak, lying on a wheeled table surrounded by the tools of death.

Was it only yesterday he had stolen something unknown and been shot? A shallow wound, but potent. He felt as though he had spent the last day falling down a deep dry well. Above him was diffuse blue light. Below him was seamless dry midnight.

Suddenly his body knotted with pain. His stomach, long since emptied of all but nausea, attempted to throw off even that. He hung his head over the pan beside him. His whole body convulsed. Nothing came up but a vile taste.

Fever reclaimed him. His mind slid on toward the dark bottom of the well. He was faintly surprised to find water there, delicious and cool.

Gradually Refugio realized that someone was washing his face and arms. Darkness receded. He opened his eyes and saw a pair of sure, gentle hands ministering to him with white rags dipped in cool water.

"Ana . . ." Refugio blinked and focused on the nearby face with an effort. "Kestrel?"

"How do you feel?" asked Kestrel. His face did not show his horror at the bruises that mottled Refugio's red skin, signs of massive internal bleeding brought on by radiation poisoning. Gently, Kestrel placed another wet cloth on Refugio's forehead.

"Thirsty," Refugio sighed.

Kestrel's hands hesitated. Water would make Refugio vomit again, weakening him even more; Kestrel needed him for one additional task.

"First," he said, "you must try to sit up."

Kestrel braced the gurney against the embalming table while he helped Refugio to sit up. Refugio retched and trembled. Bruises formed on his skin where Kestrel's hands held him upright. After a moment, he was able to sit up without Kestrel's help.

"Very good," Kestrel said. "Now you can help me. I won't take long."

He eased the gurney closer to the embalming table. He had already laid swaths of thick foil down the length of the table, stopping just short of the misshapen sphere of uranium. Where the edges of the foil were crinkled, the vivid red of the foil's reverse side showed like flames.

Refugio stared without comprehension as Kestrel locked the gurney's wheels.

"Listen to me," Kestrel said. Refugio was weak, but his help in wrapping the uranium would reduce Kestrel's risk of radiation poisoning. "Take the metal ball and wrap it in the foil. Try to put equal amounts of foil on all sides of the metal ball. Do you understand?"

Refugio looked at the uranium and then at the foil edge with a hint of fire. "Wrap . . . this"—he touched the ball—"in . . . this." He waved at the foil.

"Yes."

Refugio tried to pick up the uranium and place it on the foil. The ball was too heavy for him.

"Roll it," suggested Kestrel. "But be careful!"

The uranium teetered at the raised edge of the embalming table before rolling unevenly onto the overlapping foil strips. Clumsily, Refugio pulled the foil up and over the uranium. The wrapping was erratic, bunched up here and nearly splitting from tightness there, but it would have to do.

Refugio sat panting, his hands trembling.

"You did that very well," said Kestrel, unlocking the gurney's wheels. "Now, hold on to me."

Kestrel pushed the table across the room to the other embalming table. The smaller piece of uranium was there, along with another swath of lead foil. Refugio wove unsteadily as the gurney bumped into the table's porcelain rim. "Let me . . . lie down."

"We're almost done," Kestrel answered. "Quickly, now!"

Refugio leaned toward the table, confused by the presence of another piece of uranium and more foil. Had he not just done this? His hand slid off the gray-white lump. He overbalanced, tried weakly to save himself, and would have fallen face down on the embalming table if Kestrel had not caught him.

"Try again," Kestrel urged.

With a great effort, Refugio herded the lopsided sphere

onto the two-colored foil. The foil tore beneath his clumsy fingers. Uranium showed through the tear like a gray-white tooth. Refugio tried to cover it with more foil, but his hands would not respond. Retching convulsed him. He was relieved when the black well leaped up, surrounding him once more.

Gently, Kestrel straightened Refugio's unconscious body on the gurney. As he did, he sensed someone coming through the doorway to help him. Ana. She reached for the half-covered metal sphere, then cried out when Kestrel slapped away her hands.

"I told you to stay out of here!"

Tears grew in Ana's eyes. "But you needed help," she said, her voice breaking between reason and emotion. "I saw Refugio—"

"Go back to the flower shop. Stay there. I'll be through in a few minutes."

Tears gathered in her lashes and slid down her cheeks.

"Please," said Kestrel, kissing her eyelids. "It is best this way." Reassured by Kestrel's gentleness. Ana left. She stopped just beyond the doorway. Kestrel did not notice. He had already turned back to the embalming table. Beneath his strong hands, uranium and foil grew into an ungainly scarlet jewel.

San Francisco
27 Hours 15 Minutes After Trinity

A knock sounded on the door.

"Who is it?" called Vanessa, reaching for the pistol concealed in her purse.

"A student of history," answered a deep voice.

"I, too, am a student of history. Come in."

The man was so thick and muscular that he almost had to turn sideways to enter the room. He was young, nearly six feet tall. His head seemed to be joined directly to his huge shoulders. He wore a merchant seaman's rough clothing and a single small gold loop in his left ear.

He walked by Vanessa without speaking. She closed the door but did not look away from him. He saw her pistol, but acted as though it were no more unusual than a wedding ring.

"Good morning, comrade," he said, smiling.

His voice was surprisingly gentle and unaccented, despite his olive skin and Mediterranean appearance.

Vanessa returned the smile in spite of herself. After Hecht's easily shocked innocence, this man with the earring was reassuring. Certainly the sight of a gun did not make him blanch. A young Masarek, perhaps. She lowered her gun.

"Welcome, comrade. What shall we call you today?"

"Slaven?" said the big man. He laughed and swept the watch cap off his shaved head. "Yes, Slaven—a poor working man who helps the cause any way he can."

Slaven's formality had a mocking quality, but it was himself he laughed at, not her.

"Tell me, Slaven," murmured Vanessa, "can you shoot?"

"Yes."

"Good. What work do you do?"

"I'm a longshoreman," he said. "Sometimes."

"A trade unionist?"

"Sometimes."

"And what do you do now?"

A sound came from the hallway, footsteps approaching. As Slaven moved toward the door, a gun appeared in his huge fist. The footsteps passed without pausing. Slaven waited until they could be heard no more. Then, before he replaced his gun, he flicked open its cylinder, inspected the cartridges and then the barrel. He handled the pistol the way a cook would handle a skillet—with utter familiarity. "Sometimes I'm a metal worker."

"Metal? Steel and lead, no doubt."

Slaven's only answer was another smile.

San Francisco
27 Hours 21 Minutes After Trinity

"I followed the gringo down the street, to an apartment above Velasquez's grocery store," said Julio Rincon.

"Were you able to learn anything more?" asked Kestrel. His eyes were patient, impenetrable.

Marco smiled. "I talked to Velasquez. He told me that he rented the apartment just yesterday afternoon to a blond woman with a foreign accent."

Kestrel glanced at Ana, who stood watching, concern growing on her face.

"Masarek's woman," said Ana. "It must be."

Kestrel nodded absently, his mind examining the dimensions of the problem. The flower shop had become a trap. He must escape it before the woman could recruit enough help to take back the uranium. Refugio was no help to him now. He was dying. Once dead, the Rincon brothers would want to strike a new deal with Kestrel; and the Rincon brothers were more American than Mexican. He could not trust them.

"Where is the woman now?" asked Kestrel.

"Velasquez thinks she is still in the apartment. I have one of the children watching to see who comes and goes."

"Children? This isn't a game for children!"

Julio shrugged. "He's only watching. I told him to stay out of sight."

"Did he see anything? Is she alone?"

"The man who bought the flowers stayed there. Another man came, too. He is very big, very strong. A mean one, señor."

Kestrel dismissed Julio with a quick nod and turned away. The mourning room in which he stood was small, draped ceiling to floor with dark velvet. The heavy folds of cloth absorbed sound and light, leaving nothing. On one wall was a massively framed portrait of a languid Cristo, a pale effeminate face on a black velvet background.

Kestrel looked away from the picture, repelled by its shallowness. Even the dusty god's eye in the Mexicali whorehouse was more meaningful than this icon. He would be glad to be free of a culture that pickled their dead in the name of a bland, androgynous god.

Frowning, Kestrel looked around the room, measuring choices he no longer had.

Refugio was dying; his useful family network would die with him.

Ana was nervous, frightened, fragile.

The Russian spy with the British accent had somehow traced the uranium to this place.

It was doubtful that he could convince Refugio's cousins to kill the Englishwoman and her friends. It was even more doubtful that the deaths would be kept secret. Attention would be drawn to the neighborhood and to him—official attention, the one thing he could not tolerate. He had a chance to secure Japan's future so long as he and his trail were invisible. But one misstep, one clear footprint revealing his presence, and his pursuers would fall upon him and tear him apart.

"I must hide," murmured Kestrel. "But where?"

Ana was watching him, sorrow in her eyes. He had never seen her so vulnerable.

"You're going." Ana's voice was as empty as her eyes.

"*We're* going," corrected Kestrel.

"You're going," continued Ana as though he had not spoken. "You're going and I am not."

Kestrel was momentarily disoriented, as though they were speaking separate languages based on separate assumptions. Then he understood what she did not want to put into words: he must flee or die. Either way, she would be left alone in a hostile land. Even if he took her with him, he would return eventually to Japan; then she would be alone.

"I won't leave you, Ana," Kestrel said, lying as he spoke, knowing he lied, and why. "How could I? I don't even know where to go. The submarine won't be off the coast for five days."

"Then we'll go back to Mexicali and wait. Refugio and Takagura will protect us."

Kestrel hesitated, deciding how much of the truth Ana could bear. "Refugio is dying. When his men realize that, we will be at their mercy. We must have a place to go where we'll be safe until Takagura can make new arrangements to smuggle us south. And we must go very soon."

"Dying? Refugio?" whispered Ana. Her eyes searched his face, and then she asked no more questions. "A place where Japanese are safe in America!" Her lips hardened into a bitter smile. "The prison camps are the only place in America where Japanese aren't noticed."

Kestrel was startled by Ana's insight, and appalled. "What about the guards?"

"They are nothing. The fences keep them out rather than keeping us in. At least, my father said it's like that at

Manzanar. And Masataka Oshiga is there. He is my father's uncle and Takagura's friend.''

''Is he a loyal Japanese?''

Ana hesitated. ''He believes in the Japanese people, no matter what country they live in. He helped me when I refused to go to Manzanar; but he also helped my brother go to war in Italy. He's very powerful because he hasn't taken sides.''

''Does he know Takagura is America's enemy?''

''Yes. But Takagura still trusts him.''

Kestrel frowned. ''Do you know how to get to Manzanar?''

Ana began to laugh, but the sound disturbed her so much she stopped. ''Yes. It's so easy. The camp is on the dry side of the Sierras. A desert where only the wind is free.''

Kestrel waited for a moment, weighing all that she had said and implied. He was as still as a stone at the bottom of a midnight pond. Then, ''Bring Julio to me. I have orders for him from Refugio.''

''You said Refugio was dying.''

''Yes, but his cousins won't obey me. Whatever I say must seem to come from Refugio.''

Ana returned almost immediately with Julio Rincon. The Mexican walked into the room, then stopped. Kestrel was standing beneath the Cristo with a handful of American money.

''Refugio is resting,'' said Kestrel. ''He asked me to give you the details.''

''Details?''

''Of his plan,'' said Kestrel, as though Julio must surely know what plan was meant.

''What plan?''

"Didn't Refugio tell you? He thought he had. The fever makes his dreams very real."

Julio moved impatiently. As Kestrel had hoped, Julio's attention was more on Kestrel's money than his words.

"How many cars and trucks do you have?" asked Kestrel, "including the ones owned by the flower shop, the funeral home and all of your family?"

Julio squinted, thinking. "We have two hearses, four black cars for the chief mourners, three flower trucks and seven or eight family cars." He shrugged. "They don't all run all of the time."

"So many?"

"We're a large family. I myself have four brothers and three sisters, and our wives also have brothers and sisters, and they, too, are married."

Kestrel smiled. "Refugio is a more generous man than I thought."

Julio looked skeptical.

"He wanted to give you all a present," said Kestrel. "A vacation. He has even picked out the cities. Everywhere from here to Mexicali."

"But our work—!"

Kestrel looked from the money in his hand to Julio. "He gave me $10,000. Surely that's enough for even such a large family as yours for three days."

Julio opened and closed his mouth. Then, "Just what is it that my cousin wants done?"

"A vacation. Leave now. Take every vehicle but one car. And, if for some reason you attract the attention of any police, a few days of silence will give Refugio a chance to get well before he goes back to Mexico."

"That's all? Take every car but one, be gone for three days and say nothing?"

"That's all."
"Good. It is done."

San Francisco
27 Hours 31 Minutes After Trinity

The door to the embalming room closed softly behind
Kestrel. Even so, Refugio was startled. His fever magnified
and distorted sounds. He wanted desperately to sleep, but
the conflicting agonies in his guts and thigh made sleep
impossible.

"Refugio."

Kestrel's voice was close, calm, cool, like water.

"Yes."

Kestrel wrung out a rag and placed it on Refugio's forehead. "The pain is very bad for you?"

Refugio did not answer for a moment, then sighed. "If
it were not a sin to wish for death, I would."

"To me," said Kestrel, "death is an interruption between lives, not a sin."

Refugio would have smiled had the pain not been so
cruel. "If I had to feel like this again, I would spit on
another life."

His hot hand closed around Kestrel's wrist as the
Japanese moved the damp cloth from forehead to basin
and back again.

"But what is worse than the pain is the time when I'm
falling and there's nothing but hot black sand around me,
filling my mouth and nose, going down my throat and I'm
choking, dying—"

Slowly, the Mexican's fingers loosened. His head fell
slackly onto the pillow. Kestrel dipped the rag in water

again, wrung it out and wiped Refugio's face. Clumps of hair fell away as Kestrel worked. Refugio began retching helplessly, too weak even to move his head. Blood gathered on his lips and he choked. Kestrel turned Refugio quickly, holding his head so that he would not gag on his own blood.

"Madre de Dios," moaned Refugio, twisting in agony. "That pigfucker poisoned his bullets. I will die."

"Yes," Kestrel said, "you will die."

Kestrel moved the rag again over Refugio's face, blurring the distinction between sweat and tears, then he lifted Refugio upright so that he could breathe without choking.

"How—long?" gasped Refugio.

"Two days. A week. Or now, Refugio. Would you prefer to die now?"

Refugio tried not to moan. Then, realizing what Kestrel had said, he stared into the slanted black eyes so close to his own.

"Suicide is a mortal sin," said Refugio, his voice shallow and hoarse.

"I'm not a Catholic," said Kestrel, "and I'm not speaking of suicide."

In the silence, Kestrel could hear Refugio's fast, shallow breathing.

"Please understand me," said Refugio, his tongue thick with pain. "I'm Catholic. I can't ask for death. Please— you must—understand. I can't—ask."

Kestrel nodded. As he lowered Refugio back onto the gurney, his head lolled back over Kestrel's arm. Kestrel's right hand moved in a blur of speed and power. With a single clean *crack*, its calloused edge broke Refugio's neck.

There was silence, then came Ana's thin, strangled cry.

Kestrel spun toward the door that opened into the flower shop. He saw Ana's startlingly pale face, her wide black eyes ringed by the hated blue makeup, her white teeth bruising her lower lip.

"Ana, Ana," murmured Kestrel. "When will you learn not to open doors?"

Ana looked at him wildly. She started to speak, but could not. She wanted to be comforted, but the only man who could comfort her was the very man who had frightened her.

"Murderer."

"You're very American, Ana Oshiga, American and Christian. You would have left Refugio in agony and called it the will of God." Kestrel went to a long counter and began opening drawers. He moved quickly, collecting the items he needed. "Bring my uniform," he said without turning around. "Quickly. And get two pails from the flower shop."

Ana watched Kestrel, carrying a handful of makeup, approach the corpse.

She fled back into the flower shop.

When she returned with the two buckets and uniform, Refugio's corpse was naked on the embalming table.

"Bolt the door."

Ana turned and fumbled with the bolt.

"They're leaving," she said hesitantly. "The Rincons. They've taken the flower trucks and the hearses and all but one car."

"Good."

Kestrel dressed the corpse. The uniform was too small. He opened up the back of the clothes with a scalpel. When he tucked the split cloth beneath the body, the rents in the back were invisible.

The corpse now wore the clothes of a Nisei and the face of an Indio. Kestrel sewed shut the mouth and powdered and rouged the dead skin. He had a certain skill with cosmetics, but the eyes defeated him. Short of surgery, Kestrel knew of no way to fake an epicanthic fold.

"Like this," said Ana.

She took the dark pencil with hands that trembled. A few deft strokes increased the slant of each eye and suggested a fold on each eyelid. Like the uniform, the eyes would now pass a cursory inspection.

"Good," said Kestrel. Then, hearing the harshness of his own voice he added, "Thank you."

Ana looked at Kestrel's eyes, then looked away quickly. "I was wrong," she whispered. "I'm a coward. I'm glad he's dead and I don't have to hear him moan and see him—but I wouldn't have killed—I couldn't—I—" She began sobbing.

"Hush. It's almost over."

Kestrel touched the tears at the corner of her eyes, then turned back to what must be done. He went to the coffin room, selected the lightest coffin he could find and dragged it into the embalming room.

He pulled the coffin onto a gurney, then heaved Refugio's corpse into it, arranged the body, and wheeled the coffin back into the storage room. He nailed the lid down.

"Bring some makeup for me," Kestrel called over his shoulder. He put one piece of foil-wrapped U-235 in each bucket. "I'll have to be an Indio until we get to Manzanar."

The garage was dark and damp, as though the sun never penetrated the interior. In the midst of the gloom was a black Chevrolet sedan. Kestrel opened its trunk and placed a bucket along one side.

He brought the second pail and wedged it as far away from the first as the trunk allowed. He waited, squinting into the dark hole of the truck. No blue haze shimmered into life. It was a crude gauge of safety, but it was the only one he had.

The heavy trunk lid slammed shut with a thick, final sound. Kestrel went to the door that opened into the alley and peered out. No one was in sight. If there were any watchers, they had been drawn off by the Rincon exodus.

As Kestrel opened the garage's big double doors, Ana ran in from the front of the funeral home, carrying two suitcases. She sat on the right side of the car, waiting for Kestrel. He slid into the driver's side and started the engine.

In the sunlight flooding through the open garage door, Ana looked pale, thin-lipped, distraught.

"Cry now, Ana. It will help."

Ana gave Kestrel a look that he could not read.

"And you, Kestrel. When will you cry?"

Kestrel drove the car out of the garage without answering. Ana did not ask the question again. Nor did she cry.

San Francisco
27 Hours 58 Minutes After Trinity

Vanessa paced the room, her body tense, her eyes brilliant with suppressed emotion. Hecht sat very quietly, his hands clenched around the cold weight of the gun and ammunition he had purchased. He watched Vanessa's luminous beauty with more fear than admiration.

"Comrade," said Hecht hesitantly, again holding out the brown paper bag, "the gun."

Vanessa gave Hecht a single, savage glance. She had

watched flower trucks and funeral cars leave their respective shops. She had watched, and been helpless. She needed fifteen men. All she had was Slaven and a nitwit with pretensions to international communism.

At the moment, Slaven was chasing one of four dusty black funeral cars. The flower store and funeral home might or might not be a trap, might or might not be baited with something significant. She must know, and she must depend on Hecht to find out.

Vanessa made a sound of disgust.

"Have I done something wrong?" asked Hecht, looking away from Vanessa's fierce blue eyes.

"You were born," said Vanessa, but she said it in Russian because she still had a use for Hecht.

She took the paper bag from him and examined its contents. At least he had managed to buy the right size ammunition. The gun itself was used, dirty, and still had a pawnshop number dangling from its trigger guard. She checked the weapon skillfully, then shrugged. It might fire a few more rounds before it fell apart.

Vanessa loaded the gun, put the hammer in the safe position and returned the weapon to Hecht. He handled it awkwardly.

"Get used to it," she said.

Hecht looked up, startled. "I thought it was for you!"

"I have one."

She returned to the window, hoping to see Slaven with an unwilling Mexican in tow. There was one thing she had to know, a question only a Rincon would answer: which vehicle contained Refugio and two lumps of U-235? She would pay well for that information.

Abruptly, she turned back to Hecht. "Go see if the stores are locked. Try the front first, then the back. If the funeral home is open, come back here immediately."

"What about this?" asked Hecht, holding up the pawnshop pistol.

"Shoot yourself," suggested Vanessa in Russian.

Sonoma County
28 Hours 2 Minutes After Trinity

The black Ford flashed between rows of grapevines falling away from both sides of the country road. Riley dozed in the front seat.

"Heads up," warned Finn. He turned off onto a dirt farm-road.

The Salerno Brothers winery was a mile off the highway. There were scattered outbuildings and two large old barns with steep roofs supported by thick fieldstone walls.

Seven Mexican field hands, braceros, stood in the front yard, shaded by a large sycamore. Finn glanced their way as he got out of the car. A restlessness in their manner caught his eye. One of the men said something in Spanish. The others laughed.

Deputy Branscomb met Finn and Riley in the doorway of the winery. A large pocket watch gleamed in his rough-knuckled hand.

"Fifty-nine minutes and a few odd seconds. Not bad at all, for amateurs." Branscomb slipped the watch back into the slash pocket of his worn green uniform pants. "Back here," he said, leading them into the cool interior of the winery.

The sweet-sharp smell of green wine filled the building. Twenty-foot-high redwood holding tanks lined the aisle, their round sides girdled by steel hoops and wooden pipes black with age and moisture.

Three men waited at the rear of the building. Two were obviously brothers, perhaps twins. Their khaki work clothes, graying hair, tanned faces and hipshot stance were alike. The third man was the sheriff, tall and just beginning to go to fat. He looked like a shrewd, hard, country politician.

"They're yours, Riley," said Finn, his voice too low for anyone else to hear. "Give them your best Boy Scout two-step while I look around."

"Nuts to you," whispered Riley. He smiled and held out his credentials for the waiting men. Finn slid off without a word.

"Can't quite understand what interests the FBI about a two-cent breaking-and-entering clear out here in the boondocks," drawled Branscomb. "All that's missing is a case of wine and some lead foil, bright red. The wine was raw and the lead wasn't worth much."

Sheriff Brown chuckled. "Must have been Mexicans. They're the only ones dumb enough to steal green wine."

Riley grinned companionably. "Well, Sheriff Brown, I'd like to tell you all I know, I really would, but," he paused and lowered his voice, "it's related to national security."

"That a fact?" said Sheriff Brown, lighting a cigaret.

Finn walked aimlessly until no one was looking in his direction, then headed for a small room lit by two naked bulbs hanging from frayed black wires. A short conveyor belt dominated the room. At one end of the line were empty, long-necked bottles. Pipes ran from a vat to the bottling machinery. Corks waited in metal claws.

The smell of raw wine was overpowering. At the other end of the conveyor belt several bottles had been smashed on the floor. Glass glittered up from pools of wine darker than blood. Broken glass crackled beneath Finn's boots.

In the deep shadows behind the conveyor belt, Finn sat on his heels, examining the bottling machine and the floor. He could just make out the shape of a footprint where someone had stepped in a puddle of wine and then onto the dry concrete floor. He struck a match and examined the stain. The print was striated, as though cut from the tread of a worn tire. Probably a left shoe, for the outside of the heel was worn down the left side.

It was a familiar print in Calexico's dusty streets; huaraches, poor man's sandals with soles cut from old tires, cheap and nearly indestructible.

Finn dropped the match. It fell into the puddle of wine, hissed briefly and died. Shadows returned to hide the thief's footprint. Finn went back to the main room. He saw that Riley had his notebook out and was writing quickly.

"Mr. Salerno," said Finn.

Both brothers looked up.

"Do you use braceros?"

"Yes," said one brother.

"All our men are Mexican nationals," said the other. "Except for Franco Rincon, the foreman. He was born in California."

Finn recognized the name Rincon, and felt the first surge of victory heat his blood. "Get your braceros in here. Start with that bunch under the tree out front."

"You'll want the foreman, too," said one brother as the other left to round up the braceros. "He translates for us. None of the field workers speaks English."

"You want to question them?" Riley asked Finn.

"You get the first round. Play it nice and easy and dumb. If they step in it, I'll take over."

Salerno returned with eight Mexicans in tow. Their easy

flippancy was gone. The winery was dim after the bright morning outside. Squinting, the men tried to see why they had been dragged back to the scene of the previous night's crime.

Riley flipped through his notebook as though looking for the right questions to ask. "Do any of you speak English?"

A man shrugged. "I do."

Finn looked at the man narrowly. He was compact, muscular, and had a lazy yet aggressive air about him. He was wearing boots.

"Your name?" said Riley.

"Rincon. Franco Rincon."

"Translate for me, please." Despite Riley's smile, it was more of a demand than a request.

Franco shrugged again. "Sí. I will talk for you."

"Ask them if they saw or heard anything last night. Tell them that it is a matter of great importance."

As Franco spoke, Finn watched carefully, studying the Mexicans. Franco was at ease in his position of command. He was accustomed to leading men rather than working in fields. The men were lined up in a loose, informal row, like guerrilla soldiers. Four of them wore huaraches. None of them seemed particularly interested in what Franco was saying. He turned back to Riley. "They know nothing."

"Tell them there's a reward," said Riley. "A hundred—no, a thousand dollars."

Franco translated.

The men made sounds of both greed and awe. One man in particular was impressed.

"That's five times what we were paid!" he said in Spanish.

"Shut your hole, Griego!" warned Franco in the same language.

Finn stepped up to Franco and began speaking in rapid, hard Spanish.

"Why should he keep a closed mouth?" Finn demanded. "What was he paid so little for? He looks tired. Maybe he was up all night, no? Maybe he is hung over from drinking the green wine he stole here."

Franco looked at Finn's eyes, then looked away. Finn moved quickly to intersect Franco's gaze, but he did not touch the Mexican. Not yet.

"You, Franco. I'm speaking to you," said Finn. "Tell me what that little man is keeping inside his closed hole."

"Nothing," said Franco, trying not to give way before the man with the soft Spanish words and hard gringo eyes.

"Are you a little boy that you can't speak for yourself?" Finn demanded of Griego.

Griego looked into Finn's unforgiving eyes, then glanced nervously at Franco.

"Don't look to him," said Finn. "Franco says close your hole, but it is not Franco who will feel my fists and boots break his balls. It is you who will feel that, unless you talk to me."

"Shut up, Griego!" Franco shouted. "His threats are only air. This isn't Mexico. He's not permitted to hurt you."

Smiling, Finn said in English, "I was hoping you'd bring that up, pendejo."

As Finn turned, his hand swept down to his boot and came back up holding a knife.

"There's this little clock in my head," he said casually. "Tick tick tick tick." The knife moved back and forth like the arm of a metronome. "Seconds going by. Tick. Tick. Nothing's quite as dead as yesterday, amigo. Would you like to talk about last night or be sent back to yesterday?"

"Now just a minute, mister," said one of the Salerno

brothers. "Franco's a good foreman. You can't threaten him like this."

"Freddy," said Sheriff Brown, taking the brother by the arm, "you and Bob have been promising me a taste of the thirty-nine crop. Now is as good a time as any, and better than most."

Sheriff Brown took the Salerno brothers and led them out of the barn.

Branscomb looked at Finn, who ignored him. The deputy turned to Riley, who hitched his shoulders in a don't-look-at-me shrug. Finn watched Franco. Franco watched the knife blade flicking from side to side, marking off seconds. Riley realized that he himself was silently counting, had been counting since Finn's knife had appeared.

Twenty-five. Twenty-six. Twenty-seven.

"Time's up, pendejo."

Even with that warning, the foreman was not prepared for the speed of Finn's attack. Before Franco could blink, Finn had seized Franco's middle finger and bent it flat along his palm in an agonizing grip.

Franco paled. Other than that, he gave no sign that he felt pain.

"That's what I thought," sighed Finn. "One of the tough ones."

Finn started to lead Franco away.

Deputy Branscomb stepped halfway in front of Finn. "Now I'm the last one to question God's will," said Branscomb easily, "but I'd sure like to know why you're going to do whatever you're going to do with Salerno's Mexican."

Finn decided it would be quicker to explain than to push back.

"You know what machismo means?" asked Finn.

"Balls. Manhood. Something like that," said Branscomb.

"Close enough. Franco here is muy macho, so whatever I get from him will be the hard way." Finn shrugged. "His choice. But I don't have time to beat the truth out of him, so I'll have to use this."

The knife glittered as Finn moved it abruptly. He spoke in Spanish. The field workers gasped and stepped back. A few crossed themselves. Franco did not move because he could not, but sweat slid from his forehead to his dark cheeks.

"What did you say to them?" asked Branscomb.

"I told them that Franco will either talk to me or he won't have any manhood to protect."

Finn brushed past the deputy. Franco moved in unwilling lockstep, prisoner to Finn's excruciating grip. In the silence, the remaining men could clearly hear boots crunching over broken glass. The two men disappeared behind a vat of raw wine.

Finn's voice cut through the silence. "Talk to me, pendejo."

The waiting men heard no answer. Then came the sound of a man spitting. Something heavy slammed against the vat. There was a grunt, then the snarl of ripping cloth. Franco shrieked, high and terrible, a sound of primal terror. The sound climbed unendurably, then stopped as abruptly as it had begun.

Finn appeared suddenly out of the vat's odorous shadows.

"Tú!" said Finn, pointing to Griego. "Ven acá! Pronto!"

Riley stared. For the first time he confronted the fact that this might be more than a brutal bluff. Finn's voice was as frightening as the bloody knife in his hand.

Griego looked around hurriedly, but there was no escape. He began speaking so quickly that his words sounded alike. Finn listened. Gradually his face lost its savagery. He asked a few clipped questions. Griego answered eagerly. Finn spoke again, gesturing to the vat behind which Franco lay. Griego nodded.

Finn put his knife back in his boot.

Riley started breathing again until Finn grabbed Griego's left foot, looked at the sole of the huarache, then released the foot so quickly that Griego staggered.

"Bueno," said Finn. "Andale!" He turned toward Riley. "Go up to the house and call Coughlan. Tell him to surround the Fragrant Petal flower shop in Little Tokyo. Surround it, seal it off, but don't go in. Understand? I don't want anyone leaving that place, and I don't want anyone going inside until I get there."

"Right," said Riley. He hesitated. "Look, you didn't really hurt that guy, did you?"

"Make the call," said Finn, turning back to the braceros. "I'll clean up here."

San Francisco
28 Hours 39 Minutes After Trinity

The curtain fell into place. Vanessa turned and moved across the room, passing Hecht without looking at him.

"The mortuary was closed," he began, closing the door behind him. "I couldn't hear anyone moving around there or next door. The garage was open." He watched Vanessa warily. "There weren't any vehicles inside, not even a hearse. I tried the inside door and—are you listening?"

Vanessa opened her purse, screwed the silencer onto her

pistol and went to the door. "The shops were locked, one garage was open, there was nothing inside," she summarized. "Anything else?"

"The door inside the garage was locked, too."

"That's all?"

"Uh—yeah."

"Then shut up."

Vanessa stood with one hand on the doorknob. In her other hand, the silencer made the barrel of the gun look unbalanced. She listened intently. Suddenly she opened the door, keeping it as a shield between herself and the hallway.

Slaven hurried into the room, dragging a Mexican teenager with him. The boy stared around the room, his eyes large and dark. "Where's Uncle Refugio?"

Vanessa looked at Slaven, who had not let go of the boy's arm.

"His name is Jaime Reyes. He stopped for gas," said Slaven tersely. "He works in his father's mortuary."

Jaime looked at the people in the room, confused. Then he focused on Slaven, the man who had known so much about his uncle. "You said Refugio needed me."

"Yes," said Vanessa smoothly. "He wanted you to tell us about the Japanese man in the Army uniform."

Jaime looked at each face, white skin and light eyes—strangers. He looked away. "All the Japanese left a long time ago. They went to prison camps."

"This one came back."

Jaime shrugged. "Then you know more than I do, señorita."

Slaven raised his hand. Jaime did not see the motion, but Hecht and Vanessa did. She shook her head slightly. Slaven's hand returned to his side.

"The Japanese man met Refugio at the Fragrant Petal

yesterday," Vanessa said coolly. "Refugio was sick. Now the Japanese is gone. Where did he go? Did he take Refugio with him?"

"Quien sabe?" said Jaime indifferently.

Vanessa's eyes narrowed. "I'll pay you one hundred dollars if you answer my questions."

Jaime looked at her with contempt. "Only a gringo would sell his family for one hundred dollars."

"I see," said Vanessa. "How much do Mexicans charge? Two hundred? Three?"

Jaime spat on the floor and turned to leave. Slaven's open-handed blow sent the slightly built boy reeling into Hecht's lap. Jaime's eyes were wide and dark with shock. Blood lined his lips where flesh had split against teeth.

Slaven advanced on the boy.

"He can't be more than fourteen!" protested Hecht, struggling up to block Slaven's advance. "Communists don't make war on children!"

Slaven turned to Vanessa. "Do we really need this bourgeois shit?"

Vanessa looked at Hecht. He glared back, showing more resolution in defending the enemy than he had in aiding her.

If Jaime were killed, Hecht would rebel; and it was clear that Jaime would have to be killed. Her silenced gun coughed twice. Hecht crumpled, his eyes wide with disbelief. Vanessa prodded him in the groin with her foot. When he did not move, she faced Jaime again.

"Tell me about Refugio and this Japanese."

Jaime stood mute, staring at Hecht and shaking his head in silent negation. Vanessa hissed a Russian epithet. The impact of Slaven's fist sent Jaime spinning. Feet tangled with Hecht's legs. He fell, unconscious, before Slaven could hit him again.

"Not like that, you ox!" Vanessa snarled. "He's no good to us with a broken neck!"

Vanessa slapped Jaime awake with quick, measured blows. His eyes focused. Fear and pride fought for control of him. Pride won. He would not show weakness in front of a woman. He spat in her face.

The spittle slid down Vanessa's cheek, but she seemed not to notice. She seized Jaime's hand and bent his index finger backward until it broke. Jaime's scream was cut off by Slaven's big hand, but the boy's writhings continued as Vanessa ground bone against broken bone.

Suddenly, Jaime was talking, words tumbling out, saying whatever would stop the pain.

"The Japanese man—told us to go for three days. He stayed—with Refugio." Jaime's breath shuddered, but his voice did not break. "The Japanese man stayed. Refugio is—very sick."

"Are they still in the funeral home? Tell me quickly!"

Jaime cringed. "I don't know! I was one of the first to leave!"

But Jaime's eyes had shifted away from hers, undermining the plea in his voice. Vanessa's hand closed over his. Jaime screamed again.

"They were afraid of you! Velasquez told my uncle about you. The Japanese decided to leave. They talked about prison camps. I think—I think they will take Refugio there until he is better."

"Where?"

"Where all the Japanese went. Over the mountains. Manzanar."

Vanessa crouched over Jaime, her eyes hooded, weighing what the boy had said. It made sense except for the part about Refugio going to Manzanar. From Hecht's description, he was too weak to make the trip. He was probably dead, laid out on a table in the Rincon mortuary. If not, he soon would be. She would see to it.

"The Japanese man," said Vanessa suddenly. "Who is he?"

"They called him Kestrel," said Jaime weakly, faint with pain.

Vanessa tweaked Jaime's broken finger.

"Please," he said, crying hopelessly, "That's all I know about him. Japanese—Kestrel. Refugio knew him in Mexico. That's all, I swear on my mother's honor."

Before Vanessa could touch the boy again, Slaven called her name. She looked up. He was at the window, watching the flower shop. His body was tense, poised, a fighter waiting for the bell to sound.

"What is it?" said Vanessa.

"Cars. Four, five, six. Four men to a car. More in the alley, I'll bet."

"Police?"

"No uniforms," said Slaven, "but they're police. You can smell it."

"Are they coming here?"

"No, they're surrounding the Fragrant Petal. They've got guns out. They kicked in the door of the shop."

Vanessa swore savagely. If Refugio were still alive, he was now out of her reach. So, perhaps, was the uranium.

"What now?" said Slaven.

Vanessa glanced from Hecht's body to Jaime, pale, sweating, cradling his maimed hand. He could tell her nothing more, but he could tell the Americans everything. She knew he was too young to read the death in her eyes. He would suspect nothing until the instant he felt the cold mouth of the silencer against his ear.

The soft sound of the shot drew Slaven's attention away from the street for an instant. Vanessa stood, letting

Jaime's body slide to the floor. She went to the window, careful not to show herself. A half-block away, the street was filling with men in dark suits.

"Put them in a closet," said Vanessa.

"And then run?"

"No. We'll wait and see what the Americans find."

San Francisco
29 Hours After Trinity

Finn woke up quietly, completely, like an animal sensing the approach of its prey. He sat up in the seat. San Francisco sped by him on either side, a kaleidoscope of buildings and people. Riley glanced at Finn, then turned his attention back to the city streets. He gunned through a traffic signal just as it changed to red. Finn said nothing. He had not spoken since leaving the winery. He had simply tossed Riley the car keys, wedged himself into the front seat of the car and fallen asleep.

"Don't worry," Riley said curtly. "I won't include your stunt in my report. Mr. Hoover wouldn't understand. He doesn't believe in intimidating crooks—just agents. His motto is don't hit or threaten the bad guys, just convict them."

Riley looked quickly at his passenger. Finn's expression was bleak, but not as forbidding as it had been when he had walked out of the winery.

"No," continued Riley, "Mr. Hoover doesn't appreciate scare tactics at all." He drew a deep breath. "That was a scare tactic, wasn't it? I mean, you didn't really castrate that poor sonofabitch."

Finn looked through Riley. He had dreamed of children and Okinawa again.

"Did you?" Riley repeated.

"What would you have done?"

"I'm not you!"

"That's right. You're not me."

Riley looked away from Finn's pale, measuring eyes. Neither man spoke again until Riley stopped the car in front of the Fragrant Petal. Finn took one look at the flower shop's splintered door and began swearing in soft, vicious Spanish.

"I told Coughlan to wait for us," said Riley.

Finn grabbed the radiation counter, slammed the car door and stalked toward Coughlan, who was standing with a group of agents on the sidewalk in front of the shop.

"—and the old lady two doors down said that they all left about an hour ago," continued an agent, looking at his notes. "I'm not sure about that last bit. You know these people. If you're not one of—"

"Coughlan," snarled Finn, "you were told to stay the hell out of this place."

Coughlan lit a cigaret, blew smoke over Finn's shoulder. "That so? The word I got was to surround and take the Fragrant Petal." He looked over Finn's shoulder to Riley. "Right, kid?"

Riley studied Coughlan for a moment, then said, "Wrong."

Coughlan covered his surprise with a shrug. "That's the problem with verbal orders—no records."

"Hijo de la gran puta!"

"What's that mean?" demanded Coughlan, turning back toward Finn.

"It means you're a lying bastard whose mother sold her cunt for a living." He felt rage stretch over him like a tight, hot skin. "Get out of my way."

Coughlan flushed. His hands became fists. Finn waited, smiling, his eyes pale and intent. After a long moment,

Coughlan stepped aside. Finn walked past him to the shop's splintered door.

"Your information was crap," Coughlan yelled after him. "There's nothing in there but flowers!"

Without answering, Finn switched on the radiation counter and began sweeping the shop. The odd, clicking box drew curious glances from the agents who were tearing the flower shop apart.

"What are you looking for?" asked one of them.

"Same thing you are."

"Shit," said the man in disgust, throwing aside a dripping bouquet of flowers and peering into the bottom of the vase. "You don't know any more than we do. How in God's name can you look for something without knowing what the hell it is!"

"It's smaller than a bread box."

"Fuck you," said the agent, reaching for another soggy bouquet.

The counter clicked slowly, indicating normal radiation. Finn moved quickly to the rear of the shop, sweeping the probe in front of him as though searching for land mines beneath the floor. When the probe passed near the narrow bed, the counter's clicks blurred into a buzz.

The agent who was dismantling the bathroom stuck his head out to locate the source of the noise. He walked over to the bed.

"Out," said Finn, jerking his head toward the front of the shop. "Poison."

The agent left hastily. Finn moved the probe, delineating the area of increased radiation. He felt himself tense in the presence of his invisible enemy. The residue was well below danger level, even at its most intense in the center of the torn-up bed.

The garage showed slightly elevated readings, but

nothing definitive. Impatiently, Finn returned to the
narrow bed in the rear of the flower shop. He set down the
counter and shook out the sheets, looking for blood.

"Waste of time," said Coughlan. "We already did
that. Clean sheets, dirty mattress."

Finn began on the mattress. It was thin, lumpy, soiled.
He flipped it over. New, dark brown stains were superimposed over older stains. Coffee, wine, menstrual blood—
the stains could have been caused by utterly normal
things.

Finn switched on the counter. Its clicks slurred together
excitedly when the probe neared the fresh stains. Finn
rubbed his fingers over the stained area. Dry. Refugio
might have bled there, but not within the last few hours.
Too late again. Too little time. *Shit*. He threw aside the
mattress and stood up.

There was the sound of glass breaking, followed by a
hoarse "Goddamn it!" The door connecting the flower
shop to the funeral home opened. An agent came through
nursing a cut hand. He kicked shut the door and headed
for the bathroom.

Finn stared at Coughlan.

"Next door," said Coughlan. "A mortuary. The Rincon brothers own it, so we're searching it for good measure."

"For chrissake!" exploded Riley. "You could have told
us!"

Coughlan ground out his cigaret butt on the cement
floor. "Thought you knew, kid, working for God like you
do."

Finn shoved past Coughlan and into the embalming
room. As he entered, the counter's clicks became a buzz.

"Line up," snapped Finn to the surprised agents in the
room.

The agents looked beyond Finn to Coughlan. He nodded. Finn moved the probe over each man. The two agents who had been searching the right side of the embalming room set the counter screaming.

Finn turned on Coughlan. "Keep pushing, pendejo. You'll get some dead heros to decorate your dreams."

Coughlan looked away uncomfortably.

"Get those two men hosed off," Finn ordered. "The rest of you clear out."

There was a rush for the door. Only Riley remained.

"You, too," Finn told him.

"I know what to look for."

Finn looked at Riley's smiling, stubborn face. "Stay put until I say otherwise." He advanced on the left side of the room, methodically swinging the probe in quick arcs. Except for a spot at the head of the porcelain embalming table, there was little sign of radiation. He was both relieved and disappointed.

"Rummage all you want along that side, but stay away from the table," said Finn.

Riley crossed the room and began opening drawers and cupboards. Finn went to the opposite end of the room, adjusting the counter as he walked. Two feet from the second embalming table, the counter's muttering became a sustained scream. His hands tightened on the probe. Sweat started on his skin. He circled the table, wary as a wolf. When he shifted the probe to the sinks or floors or walls, the howl became a whisper. Only the table raised the counter's full cry, yet the surface was bare.

"But there's nothing there," said Riley.

"There was. The damn fools must have had the pieces right on top of each other."

Finn retreated until the counter quieted. He cursed the invisible power that was as much his enemy as time was.

"Get the lab people down here. Seal off the room. Don't take any crap about it. This place is hot!"

Finn hustled Riley out of the embalming room and slammed the door. Riley posted a guard, then followed Finn out to the street and in the front door of the funeral home. Without a word, Finn turned on the counter and went over the open casket displays with the probe. The counter remained quiet. Sweat cooled on his skin, but the wariness did not leave his stance. He was a man expecting to be ambushed.

The storage room was next. Finn hefted each coffin before he used the probe on it.

"What are you doing?" Riley asked.

"Seeing if they're lead-lined."

"Oh."

Riley went down the other side of the room, jostling coffins. None felt heavy enough to be lead-lined. He reached the pale pine coffin resting on a wheeled table, as though waiting to be rolled out to a hearse. Its lid was nailed in place. He tried to lift the corner of the coffin. It was heavy.

"Finn, I think—"

Finn was already there. The counter crackled like a radio in a lightning storm. "Out. *Get out!*"

"If it's lead-lined and you're still getting a reading," said Riley, "then it's too damned hot for anyone, including you!"

Finn knew Riley was right, but it did not change what must be done. He shoved Riley through the door, set down the counter and picked up the claw hammer that had been used to nail the coffin shut. For an instant fear held him; then his arm descended. The hammer smashed through the lid. He shoved the probe into the hole.

The counter howled.

For an instant Finn thought he had found the uranium. Sweating, he jumped the setting on the counter twice. The howl became a murmur. The coffin was hot, but not as hot as the table had been. The uranium was not here.

Finn let out his breath, shut down the counter and wiped off sweat with hands that shook slightly in the aftermath of an adrenaline storm. When Riley returned, Finn did not object. The two of them wrenched off the coffin lid.

"A Jap," said Riley, peering into the deeply shadowed interior of the coffin.

Finn pushed the table out of the darkness. Light slanted across the corpse's face, revealing huge, bushy eyebrows.

"Refugio," said Finn flatly.

"But—"

"Made up to look Japanese." Finn fingered the uniform. "Nisei Battalion. So that's how he moved around the country without being noticed."

"Refugio?"

"No. Kestrel. The Emperor's best spy."

Finn studied the corpse for a few moments longer, then heaved the lid into place. "Is Coughlan tracking down the people who own this place?"

"Yeah. Bulletins are out on the Rincon brothers and on all vehicles owned by the two families."

"At least Coughlan is good for something. I wonder how good he is with a shovel."

"Huh?"

"This one was ready for the cemetery," said Finn, tapping the pine box with his knuckle. "They had plenty of time to bury the uranium, and plenty of excuses. They're undertakers, after all."

Riley glanced at his white, uncalloused hands. "I'll round up some men and meet you at the car."

San Francisco
29 Hours 29 Minutes After Trinity

Unhappily, Vanessa stared out the window at the men milling around near the Fragrant Petal. When she spotted Finn, she called Slaven over. The big longshoreman stood so that he could look over Vanessa's shoulder without exposing himself to the street.

"The tall man in the white shirt—see him?" Vanessa said.

"Yes."

"Remember him. When he leaves, follow him. When you can, kill him."

She turned away from the window, took a map from her purse, and began tracing possible routes to Manzanar.

Northern California
29 Hours 45 Minutes After Trinity

The gas station attendant watched Ana count ration coupons and dollars into his hand. He gave her change, a perfunctory leer, and moved on to his next customer.

Ana started the car and drove around to the back where the restrooms were. Kestrel was not in sight. She turned on the car radio and waited, half-dozing, the radio a commentary on her hidden fears.

". . . ports and borders of the state are still closed. The War Office, when asked, had no comment other than the original statement that the closure has to do with matters of utmost national security. So for you folks planning a drive to Mexico, our advice is—don't. Only emergency vehicles are allowed across, and only then after a careful search.

"The Longshoremen's Union says it will enter a formal protest unless port and shipping activities are returned to normal by midnight, July 19th.

"In other Bay Area news, the San Francisco police say that they have no new leads on the spectacular quadruple murder on the Oakland waterfront yesterday morning. The—"

Ana snapped off the radio. she had enough pictures in her head of the murders; she had no need of the radio announcer's speculations.

Kestrel opened the driver's door. Ana slid over to make room for him. Without speaking, Kestrel got in, started the car and headed east, toward the tall mountains that were still so far they were only a blue shadow on the horizon.

Covertly, Ana studied Kestrel. Disguised as an Indio, he was a blunt-faced, coarse-seeming stranger. Beneath his disguise, he was fine-boned, almost elegant, but still a stranger. And a murderer; and her lover.

Ana leaned against her locked door, closed her eyes and tried not to think. In time, she began whimpering uneasily as her mind reshaped the last two days into frightening red dreams. Kestrel spoke to her softly, his voice sliding between the spaces of her fears, calming her. When his fingers lightly caressed her cheek, she sighed and slipped deeper into sleep.

San Francisco
30 Hours 33 Minutes After Trinity

Damp, sinuous hills curved away in every direction, brilliant green on green that emphasized the white of grave markers. Soft blurs of color glowed where people had left bouquets to die among the white stone forest.

The cemetery reflected the pretensions of San Francisco's wealthy and the aspirations of its poorest immigrants. Huge alabaster angels hovered over marble crypts. Simple granite headstones told of families born on the eastern fringe of America and buried along its western margin. Crosses engraved with ideographs spoke succinctly of Oriental Christians dying in an alien land. Baroque Spanish crosses depicted Christ crucified, writhing in eternal agony over the graves of Mexican immigrants.

Finn and Riley stood near the top of one hill, watching unhappy FBI agents dig in damp clay. The turf had been peeled back and stacked to one side, revealing freshly packed graves. The work had gone quickly; the graves were less than two days old.

The radiation counter next to Finn was smudged with dirt. He and Riley had dug up their assigned grave, opened the coffin and found a dead, nonradioactive old woman, her hands stiffly crossed. The other two graves were being opened by less dedicated workers than Finn and Riley.

Looking at his blistered hands, Riley swore. "I hope to Christ we get more to show for this than raw meat."

"Is that Coughlan?" asked Finn, pointing down the rise to one of the thin gravel roads that wound through the hilly cemetery.

Riley squinted against the morning sun. Two men were

walking away from one of the nondescript cars favored by the FBI.

"Yeah. That's Coughlan."

"Who's with him?"

Riley shrugged. "He's not FBI. No hat."

"You're not wearing a hat either," Finn pointed out.

"I'm the Son of God," said Riley. "Remember?"

"Not a job I'd want."

They walked down the hill to intercept Coughlan, meeting near the gravesite where two agents stood chest deep in the earth, wielding shovels. The man with Coughlan was a Mexican, past middle age, heavyset and sullen. Coughlan ignored him.

"We're chasing Rincons all over the place. We came up with a hearse and a flower truck so far," Coughlan told Finn. "Nothing in either of them but Mexicans."

"Did they say anything?"

"Just that they were taking their families on a trip."

"How was their English?"

"Lousy. But I got the point across."

"I'll bet. Speak slowly, and if that doesn't work, shout."

Coughlan flushed. "I got answers. They were going to Monterey on a vacation. They hadn't seen Refugio recently, and they'd never even heard of a Jap called Kestrel or a woman called Ana."

"They're lying. Refugio is in there in a coffin." Finn knew the Mexicans were Japanese pawns, sent out to lay false trails that would cover the only trail that mattered—Kestrel's. Each trail had to be explored, costing time, costing lives, and the uranium got further and further out of reach. "Sweat them," he said. "They probably don't know much, but whatever it is, we need it." He looked at the Mexican who was standing behind Coughlan. "Who's this?"

Coughlan almost smiled. "You said you wanted to personally interview anyone who'd seen any new faces on the block recently." Coughlan jerked his thumb over his shoulder. "This is Velasquez. He rented an apartment yesterday to a whore he'd never seen before."

"What about her?"

Coughlan snickered. "She turned three tricks the first day. I think it was there, anyway. He held up three fingers. Jesus, you'd think they'd learn English if they're gonna live here. Took me half an hour to get through to him."

"Just three?" asked Finn.

"Yeah." Coughlan shook his head. "Just three! She must be as ugly as my mother-in-law."

Suddenly Riley grabbed Velasquez, tearing his shirt. "He understands as much English as I do. He smiled at that crack about your mother-in-law." Riley's fingers dug into flesh. "What else are you keeping back?"

"Riley!" Coughlan's voice was shocked. "Let him go!"

The Mexican protested first in Spanish, then in desperate English.

"Back up, Coughlan," Finn ordered. "Riley's done better in thirty seconds than you did in thirty minutes. Listen to him."

Finn turned to Velasquez. The Mexican looked up hopefully. Finn spoke in hard border Spanish. "The whore. What did she look like?"

"Blond," said Velasquez, switching to Spanish with relief. "Very pretty. She was not of the Southwest, though. She did not sound like you or me."

"British?"

"Who knows?"

Riley, sensing that the answer displeased Finn, gave Velasquez a hard shake.

"Please, señor," said Velasquez. "I do not know. It was not a soft accent. She spoke no Spanish. Does that help you?"

Finn shrugged. The woman's accent could have been Canadian or British or even Bostonian; it proved nothing.

"The men who went to her room," said Finn. "Were they from the barrio?"

"Only one." Velasquez snickered. "Rincon's nephew, Jaime. Only fourteen, that one, but already an eye for the women."

"What about the other men?"

Velasquez turned his hands upward. "Who knows? One had twenty-five years, more or less. The other was older. I think that man was her pimp. A bad one. He brought Jaime to the whore's room."

Finn turned back to Coughlan. "Did you pick up the whore?"

"No one home. She's probably out drumming up trade."

"Search her room. If she's there, bring her to me." Finn turned to Velasquez. "Anything else about her?"

"She paid for two months," said Velasquez. "Cash. She had much money. That's all, señor. I swear it on my mother's grave!"

Finn looked impassively at Velasquez. "Let him go."

Riley released Velasquez so quickly that the Mexican staggered. Coughlan started to berate Riley, who turned his back on everyone and watched the two nearby agents shoveling out a day-old grave. Their suitcoats had been put aside, folded neatly inside out to prevent grass stains. Shoulder holsters were coiled on top of the coats like sleeping reptiles.

As Coughlan led Velasquez away, Finn stood quietly in the late morning sunlight, alternately rubbing and stretching the muscles in his shoulder. From the open grave came the sound of a shovel rasping along a coffin lid. With a sigh, Finn bent over and picked up his radiation counter.

"Back to work, Riley."

As Riley turned toward the grave, a movement up the hill caught his eye. A man was walking over the crest of the hill carrying a bouquet of flowers. He threaded among the crowded headstones without looking up, apparently unaware of the activity just down the hill. To all appearances, he was simply a mourner who had come to lay flowers on a grave.

Riley looked away, then back suddenly. Something was wrong. The flowers in the man's left hand were old, petals falling like pastel rain, revealing a bright shine of metal in the right hand hidden behind the bouquet.

"*Finn!*" yelled Riley.

Finn's reflexes responded instantly. He threw himself to one side, rolling and drawing his gun. Two closely spaced shots exploded through the graveyard silence. A bullet plowed up dirt where Finn had been an instant before. Finn's return fire blazed uphill, seeking a target in the thicket of granite headstones. Lead screamed from stone to stone.

As he fired, Finn rolled into the shelter of the open grave. One agent flung himself out of the grave, clawing for his gun. A shot picked up the agent and slammed him onto the grass a few feet away, dead. The second agent crouched at the far end of the grave, out of Finn's way.

Riley was down in front of the grave, clutching his left leg, his hand bright with blood. Thirty yards above him, faded flowers lay in a fan, dropped by the man as he dove for cover from Finn's return fire. As Riley brought up his gun, the attacker took aim over a baroque angel.

"Stay down, Riley!" yelled Finn, firing as he spoke.

Granite chips scored the man's cheek. He ducked back behind the thick stone marker.

Finn watched the marker over the sights of his pistol, waiting for any flicker of movement. Whoever the attacker was, he was no amateur. He had the advantages of surprise, uphill position and cover. It was the kind of assassination Masarek would have planned, but he was dead. The killer was probably his replacement, trained by the NKVD.

Out of the corner of Finn's eye, he saw that Riley was down. Blood welled from his thigh in rhythmic spurts. He was behind the thin cover of a knee-high cross. He had his pistol in one hand and was trying unsuccessfully to stop the flow of blood with the other. If he did not get help fast, he would bleed to death.

Finn fired once, taking another notch out of the grave marker that concealed the attacker. Immediately, the man fired from the other side of the marker, a shot that kicked dirt into the grave. Finn ducked and heard another shot, followed by a sharp cry from Riley.

"Six," said Finn, tearing off his jacket. "Come *on*, Coughlan! Where the hell are you!" He flung his jacket over the edge of the grave. When no bullets came, he leaped out, firing a shot to keep the attacker off-balance.

As Finn dragged Riley to cover, the other agent swarmed out of the grave, snatched his gun and dove back in. Bullets screamed around the grave again. The attacker had reloaded quickly.

Finn threw himself across Riley and fired two quick shots that sent the man scrambling back for cover. By touch alone, Finn snatched a fresh clip from his belt and slapped it into his .45. His eyes scanned the close ranks of granite monuments, looking for a hint of movement.

From fifty yards to Finn's right came three shots, Coughlan firing as he ran uphill. To be protected from the new angle of attack, or to counter it, the man had to change position. Finn raised his gun, waiting, his hand steady. The attacker gathered himself, took two long steps, and dove for the cover of a blank-eyed, eight-foot-tall angel.

Finn's three shots echoed as one, a continuous roll of sound. The man twisted in midair, arms flung out and legs limp, as bullets shattered his spine. His body slammed against the eroded granite angel and slid down to the damp green grass.

From the grave, the agent poured bullets into the body. Ricochets whined among the headstones. Finn did not even look up; he knew that the man was dead.

In a single movement, Finn rolled off Riley, pulled a knife out of his boot, and opened up Riley's bloodstained pantleg with a sweep of the blade.

Arterial blood leaped and ebbed, marking each quick beat of Riley's heart. Finn's thumb sank into Riley's thigh just below his crotch, squeezing down on the ruptured artery. The leap of blood dwindled to a slow seep of scarlet a few inches below Finn's hand.

Riley groaned and tried to sit up.

"Don't move, hero," said Finn. "A bullet nicked your artery."

Riley looked at the bright patches of blood smeared across his legs and Finn's hands. He stared at Finn, then at the open grave.

"At least you won't have to carry me far," Riley said, trying to smile.

"Shut up," said Finn, but his voice was gentle. "And if you ever again yell a warning *before* you hit the dirt, I'll shoot you myself."

Riley's face twisted with pain. He closed his eyes and his breath sighed out.

Coughlan ran up, panting. He looked at the blood covering Riley and spilling over onto Finn. "How bad is it?"

"The agent over there is dead. As long as I keep Riley under my thumb, he has a chance."

Coughlan looked at Riley's white face and the blood welling slowly beneath Finn's hand. "So you're a goddamn doctor, too."

"Use your mouth to get an ambulance. My hand is getting tired."

Coughlan hesitated, reluctant to leave Riley. Finally he ran toward his car. The agent left in the grave slowly climbed out and walked up the hill toward the man sprawled at the foot of the blind gray angel.

Riley's head moved as his eyes fluttered open.

"Finn . . ."

"Don't talk."

"Gotta know," whispered Riley.

"You're going to be fine."

"Not that," Riley said, his voice weak, his eyes trying to focus on Finn. "That Mexican . . . in the winery. You didn't really . . . cut off his . . ."

Riley went limp. Only the slow, bright welling of blood from the wound in his thigh told Finn that the agent was still alive.

In the distance came the first thin wailings of sirens closing in on the graveyard's green hills.

Northern California
31 Hours 3 Minutes After Trinity

Even in mid-July, Tioga Pass was a frigid spectacle of ice fields and granite peaks. The road was a narrow gravel ribbon twisting across steep rocky ridges. Where avalanches or rockslides had occurred, the road diminished to a rutted trail gouged out by road crews. The road had been all but destroyed by winter. Potholes big enough to snap an axle were common.

Kestrel drove with singular concentration, sparing only a glance at the slate-gray turbulence of clouds building around the nearby peaks. July blizzards were not unknown in the high Sierras; the wind was tipped with ice.

The black Chevrolet lunged from curve to curve, laboring under the demands of the road and the altitude. Sudden lightning stalked the heights and thunder belled deafeningly. Hail came in a brutal fall that drowned out even the thunder.

Ana stared at the unforgiving landscape as it turned pale beneath the onslaught of ice. The car slid sickeningly, scraped along a cliff wall and lurched back to the center of the narrow road. A rear wheel thumped into a pothole.

The car bounced wildly, slamming Ana first toward the windshield and then against the door. Only Kestrel's grip on the steering wheel kept him in his seat. The undercarriage banged and squealed against rocks concealed by hail.

In the trunk, uranium danced.

Tuolumne Meadow was all but hidden by clouds and falling ice. Only the flattening of the road told Kestrel that he had reached the upper limits of the pass. He peered out at the alpine meadow. His shoulders and the long flat muscles of his upper back were knotted from wrestling with the wheel. He had chosen this mountain road to avoid the possibility of a roadblock on the heavily traveled Donner Pass. His greatest danger was being discovered before he could slide into the anonymity of the Japanese faces in Manzanar. He would stay there until the first frantic rush of American security slackened into acceptance that the uranium was gone. Only then would he risk crossing into Mexico; and even then, he would avoid Refugio's tunnel. If the Americans did not discover it and set a trap there, Masarek's woman would.

The hail stopped abruptly. Tuolumne Meadow was behind them. Before them, the road dropped thousands of feet to the desert floor in a series of violent corkscrews. Trees vanished, replaced by rocks in tones of gray and ocher and rust. The land was dry and unyielding.

Neither Ana nor Kestrel spoke as he drove the road, cliffs on one side and a void on the other. The road was so narrow that a minor miscalculation would send the car end over end to smash on the land a mile below.

Finally the mountains yielded to the high desert. With a feeling of relief, Kestrel headed for the two-lane blacktop road that undulated along the dry side of the Sierras. Half a mile short of the new road, he pulled over and shut off the engine.

"What's wrong?" asked Ana.

"I want to check the trunk."

Kestrel got out and stretched. Above him the sun was high and hot, the hailstorm no more than an improbable memory. The air here reminded him of New Mexico, clear and pungent and dry. He walked back to the trunk. In the instant that the dusty lid popped up, he saw that the two pieces of uranium were touching.

Reflexively, Kestrel slammed shut the trunk, then realized that did little good. The car's steel body could not shield flesh against a critical mass of U-235. The only protection was to separate the lumps of uranium.

Even knowing that, it took all of his discipline to open the trunk again. The uranium was at the back of the trunk, jammed into a corner. A pale wash of blue showed even in the full outpouring of desert noon.

Except for the suitcases, the pails and the uranium, the trunk was empty, not even a jack or a tire iron to knock apart the nestled pieces. And while he hesitated, radiation grew. He would have to separate the uranium as Refugio had, flesh against isotope, almost certain death.

But death was always certain, the sole door to new life.

"What's the odd light?" asked Ana. She had come around the trunk to stand near Kestrel.

Kestrel did not answer. He leaned into the trunk and grabbed the smaller ruby parcel. It was warm. In the instant he held it, he sensed, or perhaps only imagined, a subliminal current of energy pouring through his hand. Immediately he tossed the uranium into a pail. The pail wobbled, then was still. He put it along the right side of the trunk.

The pale blue glow flickered and died as silently as it had been born.

Kestrel dumped the larger piece into the second pail, moved it away from the first, and wedged both pails as securely as he could. As he worked, he noticed that the rough ride had abraded and torn the foil on both pieces of uranium, revealing the shine of naked metal beneath.

Nausea coiled inside Kestrel. He controlled it swiftly, knowing it originated in his mind rather than his body. Refugio, with far greater exposure, had not become incapacitated until several hours after he was exposed.

For an instant Kestrel considered trying to flee to Mexico while he was well enough to travel. Then he put aside the temptation. The tunnel was known to Vanessa; more ordinary routes across the border were controlled by the Americans.

If Japan were to use stolen uranium to bargain for an honorable peace, it would have to do so from an enemy prison camp called Manzanar.

San Francisco
36 Hours After Trinity

Exhaustion gnawed at Finn. The clock that had ticked in his mind since Hunters Point seemed to accelerate as it approached Truman's deadline. Twelve hours from now, just before dawn, time would run out for him and for 2 million men. He wondered whether Groves at his desk in New Mexico was feeling the first cold touch of despair. No time. Not enough time. But always plenty of blood staining the green land.

Finn shook his head, banishing his bleak thoughts. He climbed the stairs two at a time, going to the apartment above Velasquez's grocery store. He had exhausted the leads and false trails from the funeral home and flower shop. Now there was only the trail left by a blond woman with a British accent.

The door to the apartment was guarded by a young FBI agent who reminded Finn of Riley, whose blood had dried beneath Finn's fingernails; Riley, who was still unconscious after surgery to repair his femoral artery.

"Has anybody been inside?" asked Finn.

"No. We were told to wait for you."

Finn shifted the radiation counter to his left hand and tried the door. Locked. He lifted his foot and kicked the latch out of the jamb with one powerful blow.

The sitting room was empty, but the air had the coppery scent of blood. There were dark pools of blood dried on the carpet. Finn looked around quickly and turned on the counter.

"Stay behind me," he said.

He went into the small bedroom. It was empty. The counter remained quiet. He opened the small bedroom closet. The body of a man and a child tumbled slowly into the room. He bent over the man's body, recognizing Hecht. He had died of two bullet wounds, one in the heart. The child was Mexican, with thick eyebrows that reminded him of Refugio. The boy had been executed by a single shot behind his ear. His right index finger had been broken before he died. The finger was bruised and swollen. Torture, then execution. He wondered what the blond woman had found out by torturing a child. For an instant he thought about the boy who fed his cat, and the thirteen-year-old Japanese in Okinawa. Children should not die that way.

Coughlan walked into the room with another man who had the wary eyes of a street cop.

"Finn, this is Detective Mullen from the San Francisco Police Department." Then, to Mullen, "Tell him."

Mullen looked ill at ease as he shook hands with Finn. "I don't really—Jesus! What happened?" he said, noticing the bodies sprawled behind Finn. "Hecht! My God! I ran a truck registration for him yesterday," he said, pointing to Hecht's body. "I didn't think too much about it until today, when the FBI got interested in the place the truck was registered to—the flower shop down the street."

"Yesterday?" said Finn. Yesterday! That meant that the woman had a long lead on him, and he had little time left to overtake her. He turned to Coughlan. "Does your Red Squad have anything on Hecht?"

Coughlan looked surprised, then thoughtful. "Doesn't

ring any bells, but I'll check the name anyway."

"Doubt if you find anything," said Mullen. "I've been swapping favors with Hecht for three years, and he's never said anything radical in my hearing."

Finn's mind raced ahead of the conversation. He had been following two sets of tracks—Russian and Japanese—and finally they were beginning to converge. But he did not have enough time to wait for the trails to touch and become one. He had to guess, and guess accurately, where the trails would meet. He looked around the room, certain that he was close to the answer.

His glance was held by pale roses lying on a chest whose black lacquer surface reminded him of Kestrel's impenetrable eyes; and Refugio, dead, wearing the uniform of a Nisei captain. Hecht dead, and the Mexican boy. All of them connected somehow. All had more in common than violent death. He must find the connection, quickly, before all the time in the world was only a handful of seconds.

Hecht. Hecht had asked Mullen to run a license plate. Hecht was dead, probably murdered by the same woman who had asked him to trace the license.

"That license plate—did it lead back to the Rincon brothers?" asked Finn.

"No," said Mullen. He pulled a piece of paper out of his pocket. "It's a commercial vehicle owned by the Fragrant Petal. The purchaser is listed as Takeo Oshiga. The Rincons just rented it."

Finn's exhaustion gave way to adrenaline. Takeo Oshiga, father of Ana Oshiga. Ana, secretary and confidante to Takagura Omi. Takagura, who was Refugio's partner.

Suddenly the tracks Finn had seen along the Oakland waterfront made sense. A man and two women—Refugio, helped by Ana and pursued by Masarek's blonde. Refugio, hired by the Russians to steal or smuggle the uranium out of the United States. Refugio, selling the Russians and the uranium to Japan. To Kestrel.

But something must have gone wrong on the water-front. Instead of killing the Russians and fleeing to Mexico with the uranium, Refugio had lost two men, been wounded himself and allowed Masarek's woman to escape. He had kept the uranium, though, with Ana Oshiga's help. Ana, whose father had owned a flower shop in San Francisco before Pearl Harbor, a flower shop now owned by Refugio's cousins.

Then there was Kestrel, shrewd enough to steal the prize. He had come into America wearing the uniform of a Nisei captain—how he must have savored wearing the battalion patch whose motto was "Remember Pearl Harbor."

But even Kestrel had not foreseen hot uranium and a dead Refugio. Ketrel must be getting desperate. With Refugio dead, there were no more Mexican contacts in America to abet the Japanese. Kestrel and Ana were isolated now, two Japanese adrift on a sea of Western faces.

Nor could they find others of their race to hide behind while they made new plans to smuggle the uranium out of America. From Seattle to San Diego, the Little Tokyos of America had been closed down, boarded up, sold and abandoned. By the hundreds and the thousands, the Japanese had been transported to "relocation camps" well away from the Pacific Coast.

The camps! That was where Kestrel would hide. It was not only a sea of like faces, it was safe—who but a Japanese would think of hiding in his enemy's jail? But there were many camps. Which one would Kestrel choose? He would need some assurance that he would be welcome or at least tolerated.

"Mullen. Where is Takeo Oshiga now?" asked Finn.

"The registration forms were forwarded to Manzanar. You know the place? A relocation camp on the other side of the Sierras."

Finn did not know the place, but he soon would. "Coughlan, call the people at Manzanar. Tell them to open the inbound gates. Anybody wants in, let him in.

"And then tell them that I'll personally execute the guard who lets anyone out."

Manzanar, California
36 Hours 28 Minutes After Trinity

From the road, the car was invisible, concealed in a dry ravine. A wind moaned over the desert, leaving enigmatic patterns in the sand. The car was quiet but for the rustle of newspaper when Kestrel turned a page. Beside him on the front seat was a pile of unread periodicals.

Kestrel folded up the section he had read and put it on the floor. The noise startled Ana, who had been dozing in the back seat. She sat up.

"Is it time?"

"It's only five o'clock," said Kestrel, glancing at his watch. "It won't be dark for several hours. Go back to sleep."

"I can't. I keep thinking about Manzanar."

"Don't worry about getting into the camp," said Kestrel. "Manzanar won't be well guarded. Why should it be? Where would an escaping Japanese go?" He waved a hand at the desolation surrounding them. "Only the gate has soldiers, and we won't use the gate."

Ana looked at the stack of newspapers and magazines on the front seat. Kestrel had bought one or two in each little hamlet he had driven through on the way down the east side of the Sierras.

"There's nothing in those but propaganda," said Ana. "Lies and more lies about what a generous victor America is. All lies!"

Kestrel shook out the July 17th edition of the San Francisco *Chronicle*. "American newspapers are naive, malicious and often trivial, but they aren't echoes of their government. They tell more about the war than my own government does, and tell it more accurately."

"For example?"

"Your newspapers tell me Russia is more America's enemy than her ally. That would be useful to Japan, if Russia weren't also our enemy." Kestrel turned the page. "Russia is a sword with every edge honed and no handle—whoever uses it risks cutting himself more deeply than his opponent."

"Where does the *Chronicle* say that?" Ana asked.

"Where are the pictures of smiling Russian soldiers playing poker with American GIs in Berlin?" countered Kestrel, pointing to a feature story.

"Those are British soldiers," said Ana, reading over his shoulder.

"Exactly. Not a single Russian smiling for the camera."

A wave of nausea rippled through him. He breathed slowly, deeply, until it passed. Sweat suddenly covered his skin. Another surge of nausea gripped him. Deliberately, he folded the newspaper and put it back on the pile beside him.

"Where are you going?" Ana asked as Kestrel opened the car door.

Her only answer was the sound of the wind scouring the land. The car door closed, leaving her alone with the taste of dust on her tongue.

Manzanar
38 Hours 37 Minutes After Trinity

The wind blew unhindered across the desert, sweeping up dust and grit, shaping and reshaping the land with careless power. Inside the squat, fieldstone guardhouse, the wind's restless howl was reduced to a low cry of anomie.

The private turned over another card, yawned, and stuck the card back into the deck. He rejected the next three cards, cheating at solitaire with bored indifference. Occasionally he looked at the utilitarian clock on the wall or leaned forward to get a better view of the dirt road leading up to Manzanar.

The sound of the car's approach was masked by the wind. When the guard saw the dark green sedan slide to a stop and glimpsed the blond woman at the wheel, he hurriedly gathered up the cards and straightened his uniform.

"Vanessa Lyons, BBC," said the woman, coming up to him and holding out her credentials in a slim white hand.

The guard took the credentials, gave them a cursory inspection and returned them to Vanessa.

"I'll call Captain Anderson. He'll give you a tour of the facilities and answer whatever questions you have." The private spoke carefully, like someone reciting from memory. "It will be the captain's pleasure to entertain you at dinner at 1900."

"I really wouldn't want to put you to that much trouble," began Vanessa earnestly.

"Our pleasure, ma'am," said the private in fervent tones. "It's a welcome break in the routine."

Vanessa looked at the empty land, the cramped stone guardhouse, and the windblown sand. Ugly rows of barracks sat back from a wire fence clotted with tumbleweeds and miscellaneous debris. She could well imagine the boredom of the men assigned to guard a well-behaved group of Japanese in the middle of desolation.

"It's necessary for my research that I go without an escort," Vanessa said.

"Of course, ma'am. After dinner, you'll be on your own. The Japs here are very polite. You shouldn't have any trouble after the captain introduces you around."

Vanessa agreed to the inevitable. She smiled warmly. "Would you be so kind as to call Captain Anderson right away, then. I'm very anxious to look around."

"Yes, ma'am!"

The private turned away too quickly to see Vanessa's beguiling smile condense into a hard line.

Outside of Manzanar
39 Hours 21 Minutes After Trinity

Darkness gathered like a tide, pooling in nameless ravines, spilling out across sand and sagebrush, lapping at the awesome Sierras. Kestrel watched the exquisite transformations of light with a poet's eyes, knowing that each day's end was a beauty never before revealed.

"Wait here," he told Ana, "until I come back for you."

Ana watched him walk around to the back of the car. The raised trunk lid cut off her view. She heard the rattle of the rusty tin pails. There were two distinct thumps as the heavy metal balls hit the bottom of the pails. The trunk lid closed, revealing Kestrel again.

Although color had been drained from the land, some light remained. Ana saw Kestrel turn away from the car, carrying one pail in his right hand. He scrambled out of the ravine which hid the car. For a moment he was silhouetted against the blue-black sky, then he vanished.

Ana hesitated for only an instant before she got out of the car as silently as she could and followed Kestrel. She was worried by the change that had come over him since he had first opened the trunk in the high Sierra pass. Since that moment he had seemed to recede from her like a dream, becoming more distant as the afternoon light had thickened into sunset.

Ana knew he was ill. She wanted to help him, but did not know how. He could be so remote, folded in upon himself like the immaculate curves of a lotus bud, aware only of his own silent center.

Yet when he had sensed her growing fear, he had gathered her into his arms, held her within his silence like a precious memory. She could not sit now and watch him walk alone into the night.

Sand and rocks turned beneath Ana's feet. Brittle brush caught the folds of the dress that was bright red by day, black in the twilight. Cautiously, she peered up over the edge of the ravine.

Thirty feet away, Kestrel waited, his face a distinct paleness against the dusk. He was looking toward her. She realized that he had heard her follow him. She shrank back, not wanting to face his anger. His footsteps approached, then stopped at the edge of the arroyo.

"I just wanted to help . . ." Ana's voice thinned into silence.

Wordlessly, Kestrel set down the heavy pail.

"You've been so far away," said Ana. "I was afraid you would't come back."

Just as the silence became unbearable to Ana, Kestrel reached out to her, pulled her against him. His skin was cool, chilled by night closing swiftly around him.

Ana held on to him with surprising strength, understanding only that at this moment he needed her warmth. He kissed her very gently, and just as gently released her.

"If you must follow me," he said, "you can bring the other bucket."

"I'm sorry. I'll go back. I'll wait for you."

"No, it's better this way. Bring the bucket."

She turned away.

"Wait," said Kestrel. "In this you must obey me. When you carry that bucket, do not come close to the other bucket. The buckets must not touch."

"Yes."

She scrambled back to the car, snatched up the handle of the pail and returned. Kestrel had climbed out of the ravine. He pulled her up its crumbling side with an ease that belied sickness. Thirty feet away from him, the other tin pail glowed faintly in the twilight.

"Wait here," said Kestrel. "When I pick up my pail, follow me. When I walk, you walk. When I stop, you stop. Don't talk. Sound carries far in this land."

Ana followed Kestrel across a subtle rise in the desert floor. The land looked flat, but was not. It was like an enormous rumpled sheet draped across the foot of the Sierras.

With each step the desert and the night closed more fully around her. Her eyes continued to adjust, finding illumination where she thought there was none. Kestrel set down his pail and walked back to Ana.

"Manzanar is just ahead," he murmured. "I'm going to bury the buckets before we go in. When we get through the fence, I'll hide until you find your family."

Kestrel dug in the sandy soil near the base of a clump of sagebrush, using one of the pails as a shovel. Each time the metal lip of the pail scraped over hidden rocks, Ana held her breath. The sounds seemed loud in the desert's vast silence, as vivid as lightning at midnight. Kestrel, knowing that some noise was unavoidable, kept on digging.

He lowered the larger piece of uranium into the hole he had made. Quickly, he shoved in a layer of loose soil, tipped the bucket on its side in the hole, and filled both bucket and hole until only a half-inch of metal pail poked above the sand to mark the burial place. Thirty feet away, he repeated the process with the smaller piece of uranium.

When Kestrel was finished, he selected three small branches from the litter at the base of the sagebrush clump. He used the branches as guides pointing from one piece of uranium to the other. The third branch he jammed into the lip of the rise. Then he stood motionless, memorizing landmarks that stood out of the increasing gloom.

The lights of Manzanar glowed more brightly with each moment, so close Ana thought she could touch them. It was an illusion fostered by clear air and her own anxiety; Manzanar's outer fence was a hundred yards away, the barracks several hundred yards beyond that.

"Come."

Ana started at Kestrel's voice so close to her ear. Silently she followed him. When they reached the fence, Kestrel took a small pair of wire cutters from his pocket. The cutters were suited more for florists wire than Army fencing, but Kestrel was both strong and patient. The wires parted.

Kestrel guided Ana through, then pulled a tumbleweed over to conceal the break in the fence. Ana waited, her heart beating so loudly that she could hear nothing else.

"This way," breathed Kestrel.

He led her closer to the barracks lights. As they approached the buildings, they heard voices raised, people calling back and forth across the barracks rows. The smell of a compost pile replaced the astringent odor of sage. A garden's orderly rows marched toward the first building a few hundred feet away.

Kestrel stopped. Ana moved until she was so close that his breath warmed her lips.

"I'll wait for you here," said Kestrel. His hands framed her face. "If you aren't alone, I must assume you are a prisoner. I will kill whoever is with you, Ana. Come alone if you can."

Ana remembered Refugio's swift death, but the memory had no impact. She realized suddenly that she did not care who Kestrel had killed, or that he might kill again. She buried her face against his neck.

"Just be here when I come back," she whispered fiercely. "Nothing else matters."

Kestrel smiled against the silky coolness of her hair. "You're becoming more Japanese," he whispered. "Now if you could only learn obedience. . . ."

Ana laughed softly. Her lips brushed his, then she slipped from his arms into the impersonal embrace of night.

Manzanar
40 Hours After Trinity

Ana walked between rows of plywood and tarpaper barracks, looking for "apartment" number 39A. All around her, people hurried through the night, pushed by the wind that was as much a part of Manzanar as the blowing sand. Several times she was frightened by the sight of uniforms, only to realize that they were worn by Nisei soldiers on leave, visiting their families in Manzanar.

At first Ana kept her head down, avoiding direct glances. Then she realized that the camp was too big for a strange Japanese to be noticed. What was one more among Manzanar's thousands?

She found apartment 39A at the end of a long barracks row, facing the Sierras. The public washrooms were nearby, and the fence was only a short distance.

Reluctantly, Ana faced the barracks where her father and mother lived. She hoped that her brother was still in Italy. She did not want to argue about loyalty tonight. Nor did she want to confront her sad, worn father. For a moment she considered going directly to Masataka Oshiga, her father's uncle. It was Masataka who had given her money and a letter of introduction to Takagura Omi in Juarez. But it was also Masataka who had helped her brother enlist in the American Army. Masataka was like a weaver, knotting up the disparate threads of the American Japanese communities, carrying messages between families torn apart by war. Japanese loyalists and Americans alike claimed Masataka as their own.

Ana did not know where the truth of Masataka's loyalty was. All she knew was that he had helped her, and Takagura trusted him in many things. But Masataka was traditional; he would expect her to go to her father first. If she did not, Masataka would simply ignore her.

Cold wind rocked Ana, deciding her. She took the three stairs in a rush, opened the door and stepped inside before she could change her mind. The wind snatched the door out of her fingers and slammed it shut behind her.

Startled, an old man looked up from his chair. For a long moment he and Ana stared at each other.

"Ana! Where did you come from? What are you doing here?"

He spoke the inelegant Japanese she still heard in her dreams. She looked at him with a familiar mixture of anger and love. He was small, worn away to bones, hands knotted by a lifetime of labor.

"Ana?" said her mother, rising from a floor cushion. "I was just writing to you! What—?"

"Listen. Both of you. No one knows I'm here. I've brought a—friend. He's sick. He needs a place to stay for a few days."

"The hospital will—" began her mother.

"No! No one must know he's here. It will just be for a few days, until he's better." And, added Ana silently, until Takagura can arrange a safe passage south for Kestrel and the odd, heavy metal he guarded so carefully. She looked at her father. "He's weak. Surely you can give shelter to a weak friend?"

"Is he Takagura Omi's friend?"

Ana hesitated, then decided on the truth. "Yes. He is a samurai. A true Japanese!"

Her father's expression became closed. She watched, wanting to scream at him as she had done years ago, when the relocation orders had been signed and he had obeyed without even arguing.

"Then he is America's enemy," said her father.

"He's too sick to be anyone's enemy." Ana turned toward her mother, but she looked away, waiting for her husband's decision. "Just a few days," Ana said. "No one will know. Please! He's outside and it's cold. He needs help!"

"All right." Her father's voice was rough. "Bring him in out of the wind. But no promises, daughter. We have much to talk about."

Manzanar
40 Hours 20 Minutes After Trinity

The black desert night was crisscrossed by golden
rectangles of light from barracks windows. After 9:00 A.M.,
most of the inhabitants of Manzanur stayed inside.

Vanessa buttoned her dark jacket against the wind and
set off between two rows of barracks. Conversations among
the people still outside gusted with the wind, words in
Japanese and English, but nothing that had any meaning
to her. By the time conversation reached her, it had been
shredded by the wind. Each time she tracked the sounds to
a group of people, the conversation died.

"Good evening," said Vanessa, coming up to a group
of two men and a woman. "I'm Vanessa Lyons, from the
British Broadcasting Company. I believe Colonel Mahan
made an announcement to the camp about me earlier this
evening."

The three people bowed politely. There was a murmur
of low-voiced greetings.

"Have you been in Manzanar since it was built?"

No one answered. The three people bowed again, but
said nothing. If they understood English, they did not
reveal it.

"Where did you live before?"

The Japanese bowed to Vanessa and silently walked
away.

The next group she approached did not speak English
either. They listened to her, bowed politely and melted
into the darkness with more bows and apologies. Vanessa
tried several other groups with no better luck. The
Japanese had built their own society in Manzanar, closed
and circumspect, all but impenetrable. It would take time
and luck to find an inmate who would help her.

Impatience and anxiety tightened the lines of her mouth. If anyone should decide to do more than a cursory check on her BBC credentials, she would have a lot of explanations to make. She had to find the Oshiga apartment before that happened.

Finally she tried a group of four boys, all in their early teens, all with the casual mannerisms of Americans.

"Good evening," said Vanessa, smiling brilliantly. "I'm Miss Lyons of the British Broadcasting Company. I'm supposed to interview the Oshiga family, but I've lost my way."

"Which Oshiga family?" asked one of the boys.

"The one from San Francisco. He owned a flower shop called the Fragrant Petal."

The boy smiled apologetically.

"Sorry, Miss Lyons. Perhaps Mrs. Tamamura can help you. She's from San Francisco. She went down to the washhouse just a while ago. Perhaps she is still there."

The boy pointed down the row of barracks. Vanessa saw a well-lit building. When she turned back, the last boy was closing the barracks door behind him.

Vanessa strode down the dirt path to the washhouse. There were five women inside, all past middle age. They looked up from their laundry, bowed and waited for her to speak.

"Good evening," Vanessa said. "Is one of you Mrs. Tamamura?"

The women looked at Vanessa for a moment, then bowed gain.

"Ta-ma-mu-ra," said Vanessa slowly.

There was no response.

"Oshiga?" said Vanessa. "Ana O-shi-ga?"

The women blinked, folded their hands, and bowed politely.

"No Eng-lish," said one of the women with soft finality.

Vanessa's smile was brittle. She turned on her heel and left without another word.

After the human warmth of the washroom, the night seemed even colder, filled with wind that tasted of sand. She started up another row, toward the USO barracks on the far side of camp. Lights and music streamed out of the building. BBC credentials in hand, she entered the barracks and began asking about a family called Oshiga that had once lived in San Francisco.

Above the Sierras, California
41 Hours 47 Minutes After Trinity

The Piper Super Cub bounced and sideslipped, caught by the edge of a storm massed over the high Sierras. Finn braced himself and stared down at the land below, straining to catch a glimpse of Manzanar's distant lights between filaments of cloud. But except for an occasional explosion of lightning, he could see nothing.

He wedged himself against the window and closed his eyes, fighting the tension that was making his nerves leap. He breathed slowly, deeply, letting tension drain out of his body until he was poised without being tight, alert without being jumpy. It required all of his discipline to remain that way. An hour into the flight, Coughlan had radioed that a blond woman with a British accent and BBC credentials had entered Manzanar. She had come alone. She was using the name Vanessa Lyons. She said she was working on a story about Japanese-Americans in relocation camps.

Finn remembered the dead Mexican boy with the maimed hand. She must have tortured the name Manzanar out of the boy. She was almost certainly responsible for the assassination attempt at the cemetery. She was ruthless, intelligent and had the nerves of a tightrope walker. The only good news Coughlan had passed on was that Riley was off the critical list.

Lightning burned across the night, followed by enormous thunder. Finn did not open his eyes.

"Not much bothers you, does it?" said the pilot.

Finn looked at the middle-aged Army major who had volunteered to fly a stranger over the Sierras on a stormy night. "I'm glad it doesn't show."

The pilot laughed, then cursed as an updraft hurled the little Piper toward the stars. "At least you're not puking all over the place."

Finn stretched as much as he could in the small cockpit and wished for coffee. Suddenly he leaned to the right, staring out his window between the last streamers of storm. "Lights at three o'clock!"

The pilot checked his gauges. "Manzanar. Where do we land?"

"On the highway. There are roadblocks five miles on either side of the camp. Pick one and set me down as close to it as you can."

The pilot gave Finn a speculative look, but asked no questions.

The roadblocks were lit by flares and headlights shining along the black surface of the highway. The pilot brought the plane in low, tracing the road with his landing light. In the beam, smoke from the flares bent across the highway in a diagonal line. The plane jerked and shuddered in the grip of the wind.

"Hang on," said the pilot. "This could be a bitch."

The pilot was good; the plane bounced only once. Even on the ground, the wind jerked at the Piper as it taxied toward the Army Jeeps parked in the traffic lanes, blocking and at the same time illuminating the highway. The plane stopped six feet from the Jeeps.

Finn looked over at the pilot and nodded appreciatively. "Nice work."

The pilot sighed. "I'm damn glad I don't have to do it again."

With no wasted motions, Finn unbuckled himself, grabbed the radiation counter, and climbed out of the plane. The night shuddered with wind.

The guardhouse showed as a black blot in the middle of the road. The private stopped the Jeep next to the field-stone building. As Finn climbed out, the guardhouse door opened, illuminating him with a wash of light. The Jeep turned and gunned back toward the highway, leaving Finn alone with the man who was emerging from the small stone house.

"Captain Anderson?"

"Yes." The captain looked oddly at Finn. "I was told to expect you—and to stay out of your way."

"Any trouble?" Finn asked, following Anderson back into the guardhouse.

"Not yet. The Englishwoman was trying to interview people, but she didn't have much luck. The Japanese are very polite, but they don't say much."

"They lived in paper houses for centuries," said Finn. "They've raised civility to an art—and turned it into armor."

Anderson smiled sardonically. "Last I heard, she was in the USO canteen. Not many people are out at this hour. A few gamblers going back to angry wives, or some kids sneaking off to be alone. She'll probably give up and go to bed soon.''

Finn disagreed, but said only, "Is there any rumor of new Japanese in the camp?"

Captain Anderson paused as though listening to the wind. "Agent Coughlan asked the same thing. I've done what I could to find out, but—have you ever been around a prison?" Without waiting for an answer, the captain continued. "The inmates run them. Any prison—every prison. But especially this one. We don't know any more about these people than we did the day they arrived. Less, really. We thought they were enemies, then. Now—who knows?"

Anderson poured coffee out of a vacuum flask into two cups as he talked. He handed one cup to Finn. Finn drank steaming coffee and studied the schematic of Manzanar on the guardhouse wall. The camp was a warren of barracks laid out in military rows, functional living quarters for several thousand men, women and children. Almost one-fifth of the inmates were U.S. citizens. The rest were Japanese nationals. All had reason to resent the government he represented.

Even if Manzanar's population remained neutral, the camp gave Kestrel thousands of Japanese faces to lose himself among. Finn glanced at the clock on the guardhouse wall. Less than six hours left. Six hours, thousands of Japanese and two lumps of uranium that could be buried anywhere.

Finn turned back to the captain. "Every prison has informants.''

"There's just no point, here. The Japanese aren't going to riot. It's not their way. The ones who felt differently never came to Manzanar in the first place."

"Would they tell you if one of Hirohito's spies dropped in for a visit?"

"It would depend on what the spy wanted from them. They solve their own problems in there, and they don't make any waves while they do it. Oh, every once in a while Mr. Oshiga will ask the colonel's advice, but it's just a polite gesture. They are very polite."

"Oshiga? Takeo Oshiga?" asked Finn.

"No. Masataka. He's Takeo's uncle, I believe. Or grandfather. The Japanese in Manzanar may bow to us, but they *obey* Masataka Oshiga."

Finn turned back to the wall map for a moment, as though willing it to reveal the location of a Japanese spy, the daughter of a San Francisco flower seller, and the uranium whose value was measured in lives as well as dollars. Somewhere inside Manzanar a second sun waited to rise, a sun that would kill thousands and thereby save hundreds of thousands from dying in an invasion of Japan.

"Look," said Captain Anderson, "why don't I call out the troops and search the place one apartment at a time?"

"No." Finn's tone was smooth, final, leaving no possibility of question. He faced the captain. "All I need is one of your men for a few minutes. I'll meet him by the front fence. Which barracks does Takeo's family live in?"

"Thirty-nine, apartment A. Back by the rear fence, first row, near the washhouse."

"Does Masataka live there too?"

"No."

"Good. What's the name of Masataka's wife?"

"Kiku."

Finn reached back under his jacket, snaked out his .45 and checked it. Anderson stared at the gun.

"Jesus. You aren't going to shoot her, are you?"

Finn returned the gun to its holster in the small of his back and picked up the radiation counter again. "If you don't hear from me in an hour, call General Groves. He'll tell you what to do."

He opened the guardhouse door and stood for a moment as though testing the wind. The door closed behind him. He was alone in the desert night. As he faced the lights of Manzanar, he felt the skin of his neck tighten and move; hidden among those lights was the power to change the world.

He walked toward the camp with long strides.

Manzanar
42 Hours 19 Minutes After Trinity

The USO barracks was the only one fully lit. The wind blew through cracks, stirring the American flags that were draped everywhere. Vanessa sat at a table just inside the front door, smiling and talking with a young, slightly drunk lieutenant, an Isei, second-generation American. He lacked the personal and cultural reserve of many who lived in Manzanar. She had led the conversation to the subject of life in San Francisco before Pearl Harbor.

"Did you know the Oshigas?" she asked. "They had a flower shop in Little Tokyo. I heard he was sent to Manzanar."

"You bet," said the lieutenant, finishing off his beer. "His son was with me when I got this." He thumped on the cast covering his right leg. "Hell of a fight. We were lucky to come out alive."

Vanessa smiled, concealing the leap of her nerves. Finally, a Japanese who was not afraid to talk. "Is the whole Oshiga family here?"

The lieutenant frowned. "Ana—his sister—went to Mexico. It nearly killed her father."

A feral alertness swept over Vanessa. "Mexico?"

"Juarez, I think." He shrugged. "It's not a popular subject with the Oshigas."

"I understand," she murmured. "They are loyal Americans." Fools. "Do they still live in apartment 28B?"

"No, it's 39A," said the lieutenant, signaling for another beer.

Vanessa controlled the impulse to leap to her feet and run out of there. She must stay for a few minutes more. The lieutenant must not suspect that she was going to the Oshigas' apartment. She smiled and pretended interest in what the lieutenant was saying about the Italian campaign.

Manzanar
42 Hours 29 Minutes After Trinity

"He must stay here!" said Ana fiercely, her voice hoarse from the long argument that had followed her appearance with Kestrel in her father's apartment. "You can see he's ill! What harm can one weak stranger do to any of you?"

"Tonight, the man you call Kestrel will stay," said Takeo. "I wouldn't dishonor our house by refusing shelter to a sick man."

Unconsciously, Ana looked around her father's "house"—a 20' by 25' segment of barracks—with a combination of contempt and sadness. Her father noticed her expression, but he said nothing about her lack of respect.

"Tomorrow," Takeo said, "we go to Masataka-san and ask the honor of his wisdom. He will hear you, and the man Kestrel, and then Masataka-san will decide what to do."

"But—" began Ana.

"Enough, daughter!" whispered Takeo. "Masataka-san is wise. He will tell us what is best for the Japanese in Manzanar."

"There *are* no Japanese in Manzanar," hissed Ana, "just 2,000 faceless Americans!"

Ana turned and stalked past her mother to the apartment door. As she opened it and stepped out, wind snatched the door out of her grasp. It slammed behind her, shaking the plywood and tarpaper building.

"Ana! *Ana!*"

She pretended not to hear her father's angry cry. Hunched against the wind, she walked to the women's latrine. It was crowded with women preparing for bed. She turned away and walked around the building, waiting for it to empty of people.

Vanessa heard Ana's name called above the wind, and saw her stalk out of 39A. Vanessa hesitated, then followed, believing that Ana Oshiga, lately of Juarez, would lead her to the Japanese man who had so shrewdly stolen the uranium.

Manzanar
42 Hours 41 Minutes After Trinity

The knock on the outer door was hurried, light, barely perceptible over the wind. Takeo reached to answer it, then remembered the uninvited guest in the sleeping cubicle.

"Who is knocking?" called Takeo softly in Japanese.

"Kiku sent me, Takeo," answered a man's voice in the

same language. "Come quickly, please. Masataka is very ill. Kiku asks that you and your wife come now."

"Yes," said Takeo quickly.

He turned to tell his wife, but she had heard. She gathered up jackets for both of them and hurried to the door. As Takeo pulled the door shut behind him, a tall man stepped out of the shadows. Behind him waited another man, a soldier.

"Go with the soldier," Finn said in Japanese. "You won't be hurt, but you must be quiet. Do you understand?"

Wind blew, nearly drowning Takeo's soft "Yes."

"Is Ana inside?"

Takeo hesitated, then made a gesture of sadness or despair. "No."

"Where is she?"

"We argued," said Takeo, his face expressionless. "She left."

"When?"

"A few minutes ago."

Finn looked at the soldier and nodded. The soldier led Takeo and his wife away. When they were gone, Finn turned and quietly opened the door. The wind gusted suddenly. The door thumped shut despite Finn's attempt to prevent it.

The sound penetrated Kestrel's sleep. He stumbled to the surface of his fever dream, carrying a tiny mountain in a silver pail. As he staggered, the mountain grew, a silent expansion that consumed his strength. The pain crinkled, turned scarlet and peeled away, revealing the white shine of the growing mountain. Too heavy for his arms, he had to carry the mountain on his shoulders, his body bent and twisted and the mountain swelling as silently, as irrevocably, as the dawn.

He was outside himself, watching himself struggle, straining to balance a mountain as big as Japan on his back. The mountain continued to grow, snow-topped, conical, an immense volcano wrapped in its own perfection, waiting for the annihilating instant of release. His body and the mountain trembled. The world exploded into a column of brilliant white silence.

He screamed, and the column answered in a burst of rolling thunder that was also white, the flawless white of death.

Kestrel awoke, feeling the last of his dream in the sweat that gathered on his flesh. He was very thirsty. He rolled onto his side and looked around the tiny, bare corner divided from the rest of the apartment by two sheets. A small window with four panes of glass looked out onto the blank wall of another barracks. The curtain had been washed so many times it was nearly transparent.

An origami bird and two pictures clipped out of a magazine were all that decorated the plywood walls. Dust sifted through the ill-fitted window, coating a floor bleached by repeated scrubbings. Near the bed, a pitcher of water and a glass made intersecting rings on the floor.

Kestrel lifted himself on one elbow and poured a glass of water. He drank slowly, despite his hot thirst. His stomach and bowels accepted the water without rebellion. Feeling stronger, he lay back and tried to sleep, but something kept intruding into his awareness.

Quiet. It was too quiet. He had gone to sleep with the murmur of Ana's family in his ears, but now there was nothing. Even if everyone was asleep, there should be a multitude of small noises, breathing and the rustle of sheets, the random sounds of people in the grip of dreams.

But there was only the wind.

Beyond the sheet dividers, footsteps suddenly sounded, crossing the floor, coming closer. One sheet was pulled aside. A man stepped into Kestrel's small room. In one hand the man carried a black box set with dials. In the other was a gun.

Kestrel recognized Finn immediately, not from his height or race, but from the way he moved—like a hunting cat, utterly controlled.

Finn tore down the sheet dividers with two hard jerks. He cataloged the area in a glance, from the thin curtains and the fresh water-rings on the floor, to the calm, powerful man lying on the bed, watching him with the opaque black eyes he had last seen across a cockfighting pit in Juarez.

"Kestrel."

Finn's statement was barely louder than the wind. Kestrel knew he could deny the name, and knew that denial would be futile. There had been no doubt in Finn's tone.

Cautiously Finn approached the bed. He stopped just beyond arm's reach. The Japanese smiled and opened his hands on top of the Army blanket.

"You have nothing to fear from me," said Kestrel in Japanese. "I am ill, a scabbard without a sword, harmless."

"You are samurai," answered Finn in the same language. "Like fire, you are always armed, always dangerous."

"Ana was right to fear you," murmured Kestrel. With subtle movements, he gathered himself for the fight that must come.

Finn glanced quickly around the room, missing nothing. If the uranium was here, it was hidden beneath the floor. With his left hand he set down the radiation counter and switched it on. The counter clicked excitedly. He pointed the probe toward Kestrel. A sound like cloth ripping filled the room.

"Get out of bed, slowly."

Finn spoke in English, but Kestrel responded immediately. He sat up in stages, feigning more weakness than he felt. Fever had dulled his reflexes; until he knew the extent of his weakness, he would not attack. Nor would he acknowledge despair. That would drain his strength as surely as fever.

"Lie down on your stomach," said Finn, pointing toward the opposite corner of the room. "Turn your face to the wall and put your hands behind your head."

Kestrel looked at the perfect, circular eye of the gun that followed each of his movements. He stretched out on the cold floor as Finn had ordered.

"Lie very still."

With quick, wary glances back at Kestrel, Finn shook out the bedclothes. When he was sure there were no hidden weapons, he swept the probe over the bed Kestrel had occupied. There was radiation, but not as much. Kestrel, not hidden uranium, was the source of the counter's excitement. Finn controlled his disappointment with an effort. To be so close and not to find it—

"Where is the uranium?"

Kestrel did not answer.

He measured Kestrel with pale eyes. The Japanese was ill, but hardly incapacitated. Kestrel would be more difficult to break than the Mexican at the winery. Finn did not have enough hours to try Kestrel's threshold of pain, and then to separate lies from half-truths and misleading truths.

"Where is Ana?"

Kestrel said nothing, merely watched Finn and waited for an instant of carelessness. Finn swept the probe over Kestrel as he lay on the floor. The counter shrieked. He stepped back, set down the counter, and turned it off. In the drafty corner, Kestrel shivered and tried to suppress the metallic taste of defeat.

"You can get back in bed."

Kestrel went to the bed. He pulled the thin Army blanket around his shoulders and sat, watching his enemy, waiting for the chance to win or die.

"How much do you know about what you stole?" asked Finn.

"I'm a physicist."

"I see." Finn's voice was almost gentle; Kestrel must know he had absorbed too much radiation.

Finn's eyes measured the Japanese spy, wondering what was the quickest way to break him. How do you threaten a man who might already be dying? Kestrel stared back, measuring Finn in turn. With a quickness that was not lost on Kestrel, Finn holstered his .45 and faced the Japanese with empty hands.

"You could trade the uranium for a hospital bed or safe-passage home."

"No."

Finn accepted it. He had expected no less.

"What do you think you can do with the uranium? Japan doesn't have the ability to turn it into a bomb."

For a long moment Kestrel said nothing. Then, "The uranium will be returned to America when Japan is offered something less degrading than unconditional surrender."

"That won't happen."

Kestrel became very still, his expression as opaque as his eyes.

"I'm not taunting you," said Finn, switching to Japanese. "I'm merely weighing time against the fall of cherry blossoms. The world has moved much faster since you saw two dawns rise over Jornada del Muerto. The bomb may be more merciful than any other choice your nation has."

Wind hissed through the silence.

"Listen to me." Finn spoke in English now, his words as plain as the rings of water next to Kestrel's bed. "If the uranium is not in my possession before dawn, America will be committed to invading Japan."

Finn paused, but Kestrel neither moved nor spoke.

"Japan will fight to the last child, hoping to drive the cost of unconditional surrender so high that America will accept a lesser peace, one with room for Japanese pride. But that won't happen." He paused momentarily, remembering Okinawa, green jungle and sea and dying children. "Russia will conquer China on the way to declaring war on Japan. When Japan is crushed—and that is inevitable—Russia will demand part or all of Japan in payment. At best, Japan will be like Germany, divided. At worst, Japan will belong to Russia, a subject race with neither pride nor future."

Finn waited. Kestrel still did not speak. Wind keened, filling the silence.

"Do you believe Russia is your ally?" asked Finn. "Do you know that Russia has refused to approach America to sue for peace on Japan's behalf? Russia doesn't want the war to end yet. Russia *wants* America to invade Japan. If the war continues long enough, Russia will rule the world."

"But I've seen what the atomic bomb can do!" said Kestrel. He leaned forward, and his voice was resonant with suppressed emotion. "Japan will be bombed into unconditional surrender. How is that different from being subjugated by the Russians?"

"If there is an invasion, Japan will surrender to a conquering army. If there is an atomic bomb, Japan will surrender to the sun—there can be no loss of face in that."

It was the same thing Kestrel had told his superiors in

Japan; but it was a bitter thing to hear on an enemy's lips. *No man can fight the sun.*

"America would occupy Japan," said Kestrel, feeling anger fight with fever for control of his body.

"But America won't insist on destroying Japan. Even now, we're rebuilding our former enemies in Europe. What is Russia doing?"

"Perhaps Russia is wiser. What she exterminates now, she won't have to face in the future."

Finn smiled narrowly. "I agree. But which country would you rather see defeat Japan? That's all that is left to you, Kestrel—a choice of conquerors."

"Japan signed a Neutrality Pact with the Russians."

Finn's laughter was hard, humorless. "You're not stupid or naive. Don't pretend to be." Finn looked at his watch. "You have three minutes to choose your conqueror."

"You don't know what you ask! Have you seen what that bomb can do?"

"I've seen Japanese mothers murder their own children rather than surrender. Is the atomic bomb worse than that?"

Kestrel closed his eyes, fighting to control himself. How could he, one man, choose his country's future? What Finn asked of him was impossible. His anger drained into an anguish worse than any pain he had known before. Yet when he spoke, his voice was calm.

"If I choose Russia as Japan's conqueror, I suppose you'll torture me to find out where the uranium is." Kestrel contempt was plain in his smile.

"I don't have time to break you," said Finn in a matter-of-fact tone. "I'll have to kill you."

"But then you would lose the uranium forever."

"So would Russia."

For the first time, Kestrel looked surprised. "Russia?"

"You should have killed Masarek's woman. She's here, in Manzanar. And, unlike Japan, Russia can take that uranium and turn it into a bomb." Finn's smile was grim. "You're not the only one making choices tonight."

"A choice of evils," Kestrel hesitated. Pain seeped into his voice. "That's not much choice at all."

"It's the only kind men get." Finn glanced at his watch. "Two minutes."

Takeo's Apartment, Manzanar
42 Hours 47 Minutes After Trinity

Ana hesitated in front of the barracks door, torn between the cold wind and her father's anger. She pulled open the door.

Vanessa lunged, grabbing Ana's hair. The silenced gun was like a cold finger laid along Ana's neck, seeking a target in the room beyond. Her eyes moved quickly, seeing everything.

At the first sound, Finn had thrown himself aside and reached for his gun. He never heard the bullet that hit him. A searing, paralyzing pain went through his left shoulder. From the corner of his eye he saw the gun turn on him. He felt the sinking agony not of fear, but of helplessness. He gathered himself for a futile lunge.

"Run, Ana!" yelled Kestrel in Japanese as he heaved the water pitcher across the barracks, ruining Vanessa's aim.

But Ana could not escape Vanessa's grip. The Russian's gun centered on Kestrel rather than on Finn. "Don't move!" she commanded.

Ana stared at Finn, then at Kestrel. "I'm sorry. I didn't know she was behind me."

"Speak only Japanese to me. That way at least one of our enemies will not understand."

"What's he saying?" demanded Vanessa harshly. "Tell him to shut up!"

Finn's eyes flicked from Kestrel to Vanessa as his hand moved by increments toward the gun in the small of his back. Vanessa's blue eyes shifted. The gun muzzle twitched toward him.

"No one leaves Manzanar unless I personally give the OK," said Finn calmly.

The gun muzzled hesitated.

"There are patrols out on the camp's perimeter, and the highway is blocked in both directions," he added. "Without me, you're dead."

The satisfaction he took from his words was clear in his voice. He was not bluffing, and Vanessa knew it. Her expression became as smooth as a graveyard angel's. She looked away from Finn, toward Kestrel.

"Ask him where he hid the uranium," Vanessa said coldly to Ana. When Ana did not speak immediately, Vanessa's fingers dug deeply into Ana's hair and twisted. "Ask him!"

"What are we going to do?" said Ana in Japanese.

"Say nothing," answered Kestrel.

"Well?" demanded Vanessa.

"He won't tell me," gasped Ana, her face distorted by pain.

"I'll kill you unless he talks," said Vanessa. "But once I have the uranium, you're both free. And I'll make sure no one follows you."

Ana pretended to translate, her voice thin with fear.

Kestrel waited until Ana was silent. His face was expressionless.

"She'll kill us as soon as she has the uranium." The flatness of his voice needed no translation.

"Tell him," said Vanessa, "that I've changed my mind. I'll kill him first, then you."

Kestrel listened to Ana's pleas and shook his head. "No, Ana. Not for my life. Not for yours." Then fear raced in his blood as he realized that his vulnerability lay in Ana, not in himself.

Vanessa read Kestrel's answer in Ana's tears. With a final, cruel twist, she forced Ana to her knees. She laid the gun muzzle along Ana's temple and took aim at Kestrel.

"No!" screamed Ana. "I know where it is! Don't shoot him!"

"Ana!" shouted Kestrel, "No!"

"Where is it?" Vanessa whispered.

"In the desert," Ana cried out. "We buried it in the desert." She did not look at Kestrel. "I'll take you there. Don't shoot him! I'll take you!"

Slowly, Vanessa lifted the gun. "Tell him to get up," she said. "He's coming with us."

"He's sick," said Ana. "He can't—"

Vanessa's open-handed slap silenced her. "Tell him!" Vanessa gave Finn a cold glance. "You too. Get up."

Finn stood, testing the extent of his injury. Beneath the pain, bone and muscles were intact. The wound was not much worse than a crease. He used the tentative motions of an old man, inviting Vanessa to underestimate him, trying to get within reach of her white neck.

Wind rattled against the windows, making hollow fluttering sounds, like a bird beating against a glass cage. Ana stayed on her hands and knees, her eyes fixed on the floor.

Finn leaned against the wall, measuring the distance to Vanessa and her soft-voiced pistol. Too far. She was good at what she did. He looked at Kestrel, wondering if he had made his choice yet; and if so, which conqueror he had chosen.

"Turn around," said Vanessa to Finn. "Put your hands on the wall. Quickly!"

Finn turned, but not quickly. Vanessa had only the single, black-and-white choice—kill Finn or let him live. He had all the thousand gray choices in between.

The silencer rested at the base of Finn's skull. He stood very still while Vanessa's free hand probed and patted him in a travesty of intimacy. The position was as awkward for her as it was for him, and almost as dangerous. She had to work very quickly. She found his .45 and his knife and kicked them across the floor to the far corner of the apartment.

Finn watched the weapons slide away beyond reach. He put them out of his mind. They were simply tools. Useful, but not necessary. He could kill without them.

Ana and Kestrel were also searched. Ana was not armed. Kestrel's knife went sliding across the room. Vanessa stepped back, pulled off her silk scarf and threw it to Ana.

"Tie them together, knee to knee. If the scarf comes off, I'll kill both of them."

Ana fumbled with the long, narrow scarf, joining Kestrel's right knee to Finn's left. As she tied the last slippery knot, she rested her cheek for an instant against Kestrel's leg. "I'm sorry," she whispered.

Kestrel's hand brushed Ana's cheek. When she stood, there were tears on her face and his fingertips. Without meeting Kestrel's eyes, she went and opened the outside door.

Manzanar
42 Hours 57 Minutes After Trinity

Finn and Kestrel moved with surprising agility, adjusting to the odd, three-legged gait enforced by the scarf. Ana led the way to the fence, skirting gardens and chicken coops. Vanessa walked in the rear, close enough to control them, far enough to be beyond their reach.

Beyond the fence, darkness and silence were complete. No voices called across the barracks row, no windows radiated squares of light. The wind moaned, powerful and restless, redolent of sage and desolation.

They were alone in the night, ill at ease in the desert—except for Finn. Like the thousand choices between life and death, the desert belonged to him.

"Where are the patrols?" Vanessa asked him.

"I don't know." Finn smiled. "The purpose of patrols is to be hard to find."

"If they take us, you'll be the first to die."

Finn swung his bound leg forward in time with Kestrel's movements. They adjusted to their mutual bond quickly. Beyond the fence, progress was more difficult. Sagebrush and cactus grew closer together, loose sand clung to their feet, and the moon's half-smile gave only the illusion of light.

Suddenly Ana dropped behind a clump of salt cedar. At the same instant, Finn sensed the movement of a patrolling sentry. He crouched and froze in midstride, afraid that Vanessa would kill all of them, leaving the uranium buried in the desert where no one could find it. The outline of Finn and Kestrel became indistinguishable from the brush. The soldier passed twenty yards away, never knowing how close he came to death.

Finn waited, sweating, holding Kestrel immobile, until the sentry's footsteps thinned into silence and wind. He let out his breath and bent over Kestrel, who was working over the knots binding him to Finn.

"How much further?" asked Finn under his breath as he pulled Kestrel upright. The Japanese did not answer. The scarf felt looser, but not enough to slip free of. Finn swore silently and vowed to feel Vanessa's neck beneath his hands.

Silver-white against the sky, a dead branch stuck up from the opposite edge of a shallow ravine. Ana hesitated, then descended, sinking ankle deep into small windrows of sand. Kestrel and Finn slithered after her, staying upright only by the trained reflexes they shared.

Tension crept over Finn's body, stiffening him, making him clumsy. He forced himself to breathe deeply, relaxing clenched muscles until he moved freely once more. Beside him in the backness, Kestrel's breathing slowed and deepened, as though he were gathering himself for a great effort.

The climb out of the ravine was accomplished in a three-legged rush. Just over the top, Kestrel tripped and dragged Finn down. Instinctively, Finn tried to roll clear, but was held by the scarf. Pain exploded in his shoulder. Grimly, he pushed himself to his hands and knees, grabbing a fistful of sand as he rose.

"Get up!" hissed Vanessa.

"In thirty steps she'll kill us," murmured Kestrel as he struggled to his feet. His tone betrayed nothing of his thoughts, and the choice he must make very soon.

"Up!"

Finn looked out of the corner of his eye, hoping Vanessa would be within reach. She was not. Sand ground into his raw shoulder. The would bled, thick and hot. He ignored it. He helped Kestrel stagger to his feet, steadying both of them with his strength. As they hobbled forward, Finn counted steps beneath his breath.

"Fifteen. Make up your mind before she does it for you."

Kestrel heard, but said nothing. Finn smothered his fury; if they spent their energy trying to kill each other, Vanessa would surely win, "*Choose, damn you!*" hissed Finn.

Kestrel's answer was lost in the night wind.

"What's he saying?" whispered Vanessa.

"His prayers, for all I know," said Finn, anger in his voice. He yanked Kestrel upright. "He's out of his head with fever." He stopped, hoping Vanessa would come too close. Beside him, Kestrel waited, poised. Finn did not hear his words to know Kestrel had decided to kill Vanessa before he tried to kill Finn.

"Hurry up!" Vanessa commanded.

"If you want speed, untie us."

Vanessa laughed.

Ana walked on very slowly, looking for the dark shapes of branches against the pale blur of the desert floor. She cast about until she found the other branches Kestrel had used as markers. The first branch pointed to the base of a huge sagebrush clump a few feet away. Wind gusted coldly.

Ana looked at the base of the sagebrush, but could see no pale curve of metal rim. She knelt, searching the ground with growing agitation, sand running cold between her frantic fingers until she raised her hands in despair.

"It's gone!"

Ana's cry was too pitiful to be doubted. Vanessa trotted forward, making a wide arc around the men.

"It's gone," said Ana over and over. "Gone gone gone—"

A vicious slap rocked her head back.

"Don't lie to me, you little bitch! Dig!"

Ana began digging at random, not even trying to avoid Vanessa's continuing blows.

Finn felt Kestrel stiffen. "Is this the right place?" he whispered, holding Kestrel back. "The world looks different at night."

"That branch. The big sage. The number of steps. Yes."

"The wind," Finn whispered.

Ana's fingernails scraped across the metal rim of the bucket. She dug frantically, throwing sand and rocks into the wind. Finally she yanked the bucket free and dumped out its contents. The smaller piece of uranium thumped to the ground. The scarlet foil looked black in the wan light.

"Is that all of it?" asked Vanessa, sighting down the bulbous silencer to the base of Ana's skull.

Pleasure rippled in Vanessa's voice. The delight she took in the kill was the first weakness Finn had seen in her. He gathered himself to leap forward the instant Vanessa's pleasure distracted her.

Silk tightened around his knee, reminding him that he could not move without Kestrel's cooperation. The gun settled lower, almost caressing the nape of Ana's neck. His fist clenched around a handful of sand, Finn inched forward. When Vanessa pulled the trigger, he wanted to be close enough to crush her neck with the edge of his hand. At the very least, he had to be close enough to hurl sand into her eyes.

"There's another piece of uranium," said Kestrel. "Tell her, Ana!"

"There's another bucket over there," Ana told Vanessa, oblivious to death poised behind her.

The gun retreated. "Get it."

Ana hurried to the next clump of sagebrush.

Kestrel had listened to Vanessa, and watched. He knew she would begin killing the instant the second piece of uranium was uncovered. He shifted his stance, preparing for a desperate leap at Vanessa, knowing she was too far away to reach.

"Do you have it?" Vanessa called to Ana.

"No."

"Dig faster!"

Finn eased forward while Vanessa's attention was on Ana. Kestrel seemed to anticipate the movement, and cooperate. Finn wondered if Kestrel's plan was the same as his own: kill Vanessa and then kill the enemy tied to him.

"I've found it!"

Finn started to launch himself at Vanessa, but she turned too quickly.

"Stand still or die right now," Vanessa ordered. The pistol pointed directly at Finn's heart. He and Kestrel stood very quietly, closer to Vanessa than they had been, but not close enough. "Bring it here," Vanessa said without looking away from the men.

Ana yanked the bucket out of its shallow hole. Sand, pebbles and the foil-wrapped uranium spilled out as she upended the bucket at Vanessa's feet. She looked down, not trusting Ana. The instant Vanessa's attention moved, the men crept forward a few more inches. They were less than eight feet from the women.

Finn felt the sudden tension in Kestrel's body as the large piece of uranium thumped down close to its deadly mate. He remembered the accident at the Los Alamos lab, and sweat covered his body despite the cold wind. Kestrel stared, looking for a faint blush of blue light.

Vanessa glanced at the two foil-wrapped parcels, irregular and lumpy. She smiled and brought the muzzle to bear on the back of Ana's neck as Ana bent over the uranium.

"Don't be so eager," said Finn. "Or do you plan on handling the uranium by yourself?" His voice was directed to Vanessa; his free hand was clamped on Kestrel's wrist to hold him back.

"What are you talking about?" said Vanessa. She switched her pistol to her left hand and pointed it at the men.

Finn took a half-step forward and laughed. "You don't know much about uranium, do you?"

"No closer!"

Finn stood still. The muzzle of the pistol was trained on his heart. For a moment there was no sound but the wind. Vanessa watched him unblinkingly. She knew that uranium could be deadly, but she had no idea of its threshold of danger. Nor could she trust Finn to tell the truth. All she could do was watch his reactions as Ana handled the metal.

"Unwrap it," she ordered, prodding Ana with her foot.

"No," whispered Kestrel.

Vanessa did not hear. Nor did Ana. Finn did. He felt Kestrel tense and knew that something was going to happen with the uranium—what was it General Groves had said? Light, some heat and a lot of radiation if the two pieces were brought together. Was that what Kestrel was waiting for, a flash of light that would startle Vanessa? He felt Kestrel's sweat where their legs were bound together.

"I hope you know what you're doing," he said, as though talking to Vanessa.

"Shut up!"

Ana took the smaller parcel and began to unwrap it. The soft foil, battered by rough handling, fell away in pieces beneath her fingers. The uranium she uncovered had a nacreous shine in the moonlight. She reached for the second piece.

Finn and Kestrel stood as one man, poised, waiting for an opening. They watched each layer fall away from the larger piece of uranium. As Ana worked off the last layer, the heavy rounded metal slipped from her hands. It fell on top of its mate with a metallic clang. It did not roll away.

Blue light leaped from the union, a primal flash of energy that was as deadly as it was unexpected.

"What—?" Instinctively Vanessa raised her hand to shield herself from the uncanny blue light.

Finn and Kestrel leaped for her. Finn's handful of sand scoured across Vanessa's face, ruining her aim as she brought her gun up. The shot passed over their heads. Before she could fire again, the two men were on her.

Finn grabbed her right wrist as she went down beneath them. He forced her pistol up and away from his face, trying to break her wrist at the same time. Her free hand dug at his shoulder wound; agony weakened his grip. Kestrel's thumbs hooked upward, seeking her eyes. She threw back her head and his thumbnails gouged across her cheekbones.

Off-balance, the three of them sprawled on the sand. The pistol fired again, a vicious spitting sound. They rolled and kicked, each clawing for leverage, an opening, the single instant needed to deliver a killing blow.

Kestrel's weight yanked Finn aside. The knot binding them slipped, allowing the scarf to drop below their knees. The edge of Kestrel's hand chopped at Vanessa's throat. She twisted aside, taking the blow on her shoulder and throwing Kestrel off-balance. He fell, knocking Finn's hand off Vanessa's wrist, freeing the pistol. Finn clawed at the ground, seeing another handful of sand to blind her with.

His fingers closed around something hard and heavy and warm. Even as he picked it up, arm straight and swinging like a club, he knew he was holding the smaller piece of uranium. The pistol spat in the same second that Vanessa's skull fragmented beneath the smashing force of the uranium in Finn's hand.

Kestrel jerked once and groaned. Vanessa did not move at all. Finn rolled away immediately, going after Kestrel, his hands seeking Kestrel's throat. The Japanese did not respond. Finn's fingers met slick warm blood. He tore free of the scarf that bound him to Kestrel and came to his feet, the uranium still in his hand. It had been less than thirty seconds since the uranium had leaped with blue light.

The uranium in his hand showed a black rime in the moonlight—Vanessa's blood. She lay on her back, her eyes open and empty as the wind. The first primitive exhilaration of survival swept through Finn. The battle to control the world had been fought here, in the desert, using fists and fingernails—and he had won.

Ana moaned, a sound neither male nor female, fear and pain rending the silence. She crawled to Kestrel's side, unaware of the blood welling from her scalp where a fragment of bullet had split flesh to the bone.

Finn took Vanessa's gun from her slack fingers and walked over to Ana. She did not look up, simply held Kestrel and cried, blood mingling with tears on her face. Finn knelt and pressed his fingers against Kestrel's neck, seeking a pulse. He thought he found one, but could not be certain; his own heart was beating so violently.

Slowly, Finn got to his feet, still holding the small piece of uranium. He put it in one pail, then picked up the larger piece and put it in the second pail. For a moment he stood motionless, wrapped in wind, listening to Ana weep. The intoxication of victory began to ebb, leaving room for pain. His wounded shoulder burned and his body ached from blows he did not remember receiving. He bent over and took the weight of the buckets. They were heavier than he had expected, unreasonably heavy. The metal handles cut into his flesh.

"I'll come back," he said.

Ana neither looked up nor answered.

Finn turned away and walked toward Manzanar, carrying thousands of deaths and 2 million lives in his hands.